ASYLUM

SUSY SMITH

BALKAN PRESS

ACKNOWLEDGMENTS

Thank you, Judy Stohr, for the time you selflessly sacrificed to edit the many, many, drafts of this book. Your honest insight shed light when mine went dark. This book would not be in print were it not for you. To my beta readers, Bailey Pappan and Kallie Van Buren, bless your sweet hearts for taking time to read the final draft. That means more to me than you'll ever know. To my four kids and husband who encouraged me to keep going when I wanted to quit, wíblaha^n, wéwihna^n. And, to my editor, Lara Bernhardt, you are a blessing to an introvert like me.

For Nanny
Ikó, zhóma^{n}yale sho^{n}sho^{n}we

I

HELL

Hell is an asylum masquerading as a safe haven.

1

State Capitol, Austin, Texas

When U.S. Senator Thomas Monroe foresaw America's downfall and began to declare a national economic crisis, he had no idea he'd be sitting at the helm of a revolution.

On a stifling July day, two months after the "Big Crash," Thomas sat brooding at his desk. A strong, healthy man in his late fifties with more grey hair than black, he considered himself worthy of the task. He'd serve the Federal Reserve chairwoman, who labeled him Dr. Doom-n-Gloom, a big piece of crow pie the next time they crossed paths. She negated his warnings with one demeaning Forbes Magazine interview.

He shook his head, exasperated. "As if anyone could definitively say there wouldn't be another financial crisis in our lifetime," he muttered. "Look where we are now."

He unbuttoned his shirt's top button, loosened his black Armani tie. Because the Wolves of Wall Street ignored the blinding, red warning signs, the economy had spiraled into a bottomless pit. As a result, panic swept the country in waves of riots, looting, and arson.

He sunk back in his chair. Uneasiness crept up his spine like a spider. He disagreed with the president's martial law declaration and new economic reform policy through forced labor camps.

Unsure whether to follow the president's new law, the Texas governor looked to him for leadership. At Thomas' urging, the State of Texas signed a secession agreement. Once again its own Republic, the Lone Star State set a precedent and California followed its lead. His involvement with the insurrection put a bull's eye on his back. With the stroke of a pen, he made an enemy of the president.

He leaned forward, shuffled through some papers and picked up a surveillance photo of his family farm in Oklahoma, taken two days before. The picture captured his niece leading a huge sorrel horse to pasture. He studied her image with grave intent. Wind whipped her jet-black hair creating a veil that hid her pixie-like features. To say he felt no apprehension when he found it was his nineteen-year-old niece, Lacy, had agreed to stay would be a lie.

Guilt wormed its way into his gut. "She's no bigger than a half-pint of ale," he murmured. "What in God's name were you thinking, Emmett?"

He hadn't spoken to his brother, Emmett, in years. Their mother had been the wedge between them, her passing the farm to him on her deathbed hammered the final nail into the coffin of their relationship. When he called Emmett asking for help, he hoped they'd patch things up, start fresh, but Emmet refused to bury the past. Instead, he left his young daughter behind to be the necessary beneficiary he needed to occupy the farm. The image of a sacrificial lamb popped into his head.

Irritated, he dropped the photo on the file marked "Land

Trust." His family farm now sat securely in the independent State of Texas' hands. Oklahoma no longer had jurisdiction over those forty acres.

A short staccato rap jolted his heart.

"Excuse me, senator?" His assistant poked his head around the door, his blonde bangs hung like macramé fringe covering his eyes. "I have a new report."

Thomas flicked two fingers in the air, motioning the young man inside. "From where?"

"Oklahoma, sir." He shuffled inside. "We just got a message from one of our operatives at the Texas-Oklahoma border." He hesitated.

"Go on," he ordered.

"Sir, they've organized the National Guard and are moving across the state. They are gathering all citizens they can find and hauling them by train to Fort Sill."

Deep lines formed over his brow. He rubbed at the mounting pressure. "If we want control over Oklahoma, we'll have to move fast."

The nervous assistant ran sweaty hands over his khaki pants. "We don't have much time."

Thomas reached in his shirt pocket for his Marlboros, flipped out a cigarette and lit the tip. The sulfuric smell, the rag paper between his fingers, settled his nerves.

"Do we have any news on Jake Cooper? He was supposed to get a man inside the National Guard we can trust. I hoped that would be his youngest son, Jace."

"No, sir. Not a word." The young man edged to the door, his feet shuffling across the shiny tile floor.

"Well, keep trying Jake's cell and land line. Oh, and check the telegraph machine." He pulled an ashtray from his desk drawer and stubbed his cigarette. "That's all, William."

The young man left with a hasty "Yes, sir," thrown over his shoulder.

Thomas frowned. He needed a man on the inside who could control the actions of the National Guard in Osage County. His plan hinged on it. It would be a tough move. Strings would have to be pulled. Carefully. He tapped his fingers on his desk. Where in the blue blazes was Jake Cooper?

2

Monroe Farm, Shidler Oklahoma

Breathe.

"Come out, come out, wherever you are." The man's rasped, menacing tone spiked electric shocks through her system.

Just breathe, she commanded herself. Adrenaline slammed into her heart, locked it vise-grip tight. She lifted a shaky hand, placed it on her pounding chest and forced herself to concentrate. She had to find an escape. A way out. But her brain disintegrated into nothing, her thoughts too hazy to grasp.

The moon shone through the living room window casting eerie shadows along the wall. Her stalker's boots moved in a slow, methodical, click, click, click across the hard wood floor. He hunted her with steady, unerring patience. Her eyes darted to the family pictures on the wall. Would they be the last thing she saw before she died?

"I'm going to find you, Lacy," the man taunted. "Where are you?"

Her stunned brain scrambled for a face to match the familiar voice. She sucked in a sharp breath. She knew him. But why was he here?

Fists clenched, she willed him to go away. The tiny hiding space between the couch and the wall constricted her breath. Musty old leather and dust tickled her nose and tiny beads of sweat dripped into her eyes, blurring her vision. She reached for the Bowie knife strapped to her belt, a family heirloom her grandfather had given her because she'd been his favorite. It slipped through her slick palms. The sharp clank echoed off the thin walls as it skittered under the couch, lost. Her heart skidded as she heard him move closer. Hesitate. Then stop. Her chest tightened, strangling her breath.

What did he want with her? A shudder rippled through her. She held her breath as unbearable silence stretched the seconds into what seemed like years.

Then his hand reached behind the couch, grabbing a handful of hair. With a ruthless yank, he hauled her up.

"No!" she screamed. "Stop!"

Her neck stretched and popped as he pulled her over the couch's cracked leather back. She reached up, latched onto his arms, sunk her nails into his flesh, and ripped downward.

"Got some fight in you," he sneered. "But it won't be enough."

Her feet scrambled for purchase on the slick wood floor as he flung her body around to face him. She twisted and writhed against the muscular arms holding her prisoner.

She spat in his face. "I got more fight than you think."

He laughed as spittle dribbled down his cheek. "Don't struggle," he rasped then rammed her body against the wall.

Her great-grandmother's picture fell and shattered. Her mind refused to work, refused to acknowledge the situation.

Think. Damn it, Lacy, think!

"Checkmate," he breathed in her ear. "I've got you now. Nowhere for you to run. Nowhere for you to hide."

She bucked against his solid frame. "Let go of me!"

His rock-hard arms held her like a strait jacket. She grunted and rammed her foot into his shin, but her tennis shoe bounced back. Rubber on concrete. He was a brick wall. Immovable.

"Little kitty trying to escape?" His eyes locked on hers. "It's useless to fight it. You're mine."

"Let me go. Please," she begged.

"Hmm." His lewd eyes raked over her making her skin crawl under his base appraisal. "I don't think so."

With brute force, he crushed his mouth on hers. She gagged as his tongue forced its way inside. Slimy tobacco chew filled her mouth and she bit down hard. Blood flooded her senses. He jerked back, shocked. She kneed his groin, but it didn't loosen his death grip around her arms.

"Bitch," he grunted, sucking in air.

He shoved her down. The seams of her soft organdy blouse ripped as she fell. When her body hit the floor, she bounced up and threw a reckless left hook. Her small fist connected with his nose and the sickening crunch of cartilage vibrated up her arm.

He stumbled back, shook his head, and wiped blood on his sleeve. She turned and ran for the door, but he grabbed the back of her jeans, and she fell face first, smacking her right cheek on the wood floor. He snagged her ankle, jerked her back, then flipped her over and shoved his knee into her chest.

"Get off me!"

Hate etched lines around his eyes. He leaned in and whispered, "No one's here to save you, little kitty. Don't waste your breath screaming."

His work-roughened hands scraped the sides of her bare arms, all the way down to her hips. Bile rose and stung her throat. This is happening. He's going to rape me.

"Why are you doing this?" she whispered. Hot tears slid down and pooled in her ears.

He grabbed her throat and squeezed. "I've got a score to settle. Now shut up."

Spots blurred her vision as oxygen left her lungs. Slowly, he released his grip and she dragged in a painful breath. "I can't do this, I can't do this," she gasped.

"Don't you dare pass out," he warned.

He grabbed her face between his hands, crushing her skull between his rough palms. "Do you hear me? I want you awake. Want you to see my face. *My* face. And when I'm finished, I want you to pack up and move to California. You can't stay here."

His grip around her face tightened as he lifted her head off the floor. "Do you understand me, Lacy? I'll kill you if you do."

She looked into his cold blue eyes and believed every word. Her bruised hands, flush with the floor, felt the wood's smooth grain and she began counting the tiny grooves.

One, two, three, four...

The clock ticked.

Time slowed.

She forced herself to continue counting.

Five, six, seven, eight...

"Don't stay here," he warned when he finished. "Your uncle will pay for his actions. You tell him that."

She raised her head, her long hair tangled and matted to her sweaty face. "Fuck you," she choked on a sob.

He swung his leg back and gave her ribs a jarring kick.

Just count.

Nine, ten, eleven, twelve...

She counted until darkness consumed her, didn't wake until the setting sun flooded the western window. Its rays unabated by the paper-thin, gingham curtains heated her battered face, rousing her from the mercy of a forgetful sleep.

Wincing, she raised up and fingered her swollen eye and cheek, noted the tiny groove pattern indenting her skin. Shaky hands ran over her ribcage where he'd kicked her. God, it was hard to breathe.

She lifted herself to a standing position with an urgent need to wash away the filth. His filth.

"I have to get clean," she whispered. Would she ever feel clean again? She cringed as memories of calloused hands and chewing tobacco assaulted her.

She gritted her teeth and shoved them away but stopped short at her tattered shirt lying on the floor. Her head swam as the vicious flood of memories broke over her. They arced like a flash-burn, searing away her youth and innocence. Tears leaked from her eyes and she drew in a shuddering breath. That girl was gone. Razed. Annihilated. And she had no idea how to rebuild herself.

3

Cooper Ranch, Shidler Oklahoma

J ace Cooper stared at his brother in utter amazement. How could you live with someone for twenty-two years and end up strangers?

Zach rested his hands on their father's work-worn desk, his staunch gaze never faltering.

"You're freezing me out?" Jace stood. The sudden movement knocked his chair against the wall with a loud bang. "Why, Zach?"

The chain tapping against the ceiling fan kept time with his pounding brain. He rubbed his hand against his forehead and wondered when his head had ever hurt so badly. He cast a look around his father's study and his heart broke. He'd never get used to his father's absence or the fact he would have to spend the rest of his days without him.

"Until we find out who murdered our parents, yes I am," Zach stated.

His pounding head ratcheted up a few notches and

continued like the relentless, crashing-cymbals of the Energizer Bunny. "You think *I* killed Mom and Dad? This is nuts."

He ran an unsteady hand through his dark-brown hair. He needed an aspirin. Or a lobotomy.

"Well, you were the one who found them. You were the one covered in their blood."

He stiffened. The barbed statement hit its mark. Zach was right in a skewed sense. He had found their parents, dead, in the master bedroom.

His mind blocked the brutal images trying to surface. "You can't believe that."

Zach continued, his tone frigid. "I'm not sure about anything at this point. Our allegiance belongs with the governor of Oklahoma and the president. Anyone planning to overthrow our government will be arrested. You seem confused about that."

He let out a long sigh. "What in God's name are you talking about?"

"I found papers in Dad's desk drawer about you taking a military job as a mole for Senator Monroe."

And there it is, he thought.

"I told Dad I didn't want the job. He was supposed to tell Thomas Monroe no. I'm not working for the senator. You know that."

His thoughts flashed to the chaos the day the president ordered martial law and Senator Monroe's phone call asking for his father's help to stop the president's actions.

A landowner and rancher, Jake Cooper's influence in Oklahoma's political hierarchy reached far and wide. He knew Monroe and his father were buddies in high school and Monroe always stayed in touch. If he'd taken the job, would his parents still be alive? The thought plagued him.

"But," Zach emphasized, "you're still planning on moving out to the Monroe farm, aren't you?"

He gaped at his brother. "That's personal. You know how I feel about Lacy."

Zach's lips pressed in a fine line. "You can't separate the two. Thomas Monroe is planning a coup. So, choose now. Stay here on the ranch with me and we'll forget this incident."

The muscle in his jaw ticked. "What incident?"

Zach cocked an eyebrow. "Our parents' murder. Did you murder our mom and dad because you disagreed with them about helping Senator Monroe?" He leaned forward. "Did you argue over it?"

"*What*?" he exploded. "You've got to be kidding. There is no evidence I killed Mom and Dad. Jesus, Zach."

"I'm warning you, Jace. Stay on the ranch. If you don't, I'll not only have the National Guard down your throat, but Lacy's too."

He balled his right hand into a tight fist. "Don't threaten her. And stop acting like you can order me around."

Zach's eyes darted from his clenched fist to his face. "Or what?" he smirked. "Mama's boy gonna threaten me? I don't think so."

"Better watch yourself," he warned.

"I take it you're going to go to the Monroe farm? And to your little — "

Before Zach could finish, he struck. His fist connected with a loud pop to his brother's jaw and knocked him out of his chair in one swift blow.

He shook the sting out of his hand. "Sonofabitch," he muttered. He let some of the rage die before he spoke again. "I love her. Don't disrespect her again."

Zach sat up and put a hand over the instant knot. "You love her? You haven't even dated. She's your best friend's little sister for God's sake."

"Where is this coming from?" He shook his head. "I don't understand. We're brothers."

Zach stood and spit blood at his feet. "Our parents are

dead. And so are we. As far as I'm concerned, you killed our parents. If you move to the Monroe farm, you'll become a traitor to our country."

He studied his brother. When had they become strangers? Their stature was the same, but the family resemblance ended there. Zach's blonde hair and pale blue eyes matched their father's. He'd inherited his mother's unusual sapphire eyes and rich dark-brown hair. His older brother always accused him of being a mama's boy.

"I'm sorry you feel that way but there's no way in hell I'm gonna let you pin our parents' murder on me." He took a step closer. "And I suggest you think twice before threatening Lacy again because I will never let you get anywhere near her."

"I don't need your permission. As head of this family now, I'll do whatever I damn well please."

Jace flexed his hands. "We'll see about that."

4

T wo days. Lacy drifted in and out of restless sleep, consumed with visions of her family as they crossed the Nevada border into California's safe haven. Her brother beckoned her to follow. He seemed so close, so real. She reached out to grab his outstretched hand, but as her fingertips touched his, they faded into nothing.

She called to him, "Don't leave me, AJ. Save me. Please save me."

Then a black hole, void of everything but pain, swallowed her whole.

The sun rose, then set again, and the nightmares continued. After what seemed an eternity, she rose from her grandmother's bed, from the ashes of her funeral pyre. Her legs felt stiff and wooden as she strained to reach the tiny bathroom.

She forced herself into the old claw-foot tub.

"I have to get clean," she chanted over and over.

After soaping and scrubbing and rinsing her bruised body until it screamed for her to stop, she leaned her head against the cool porcelain and let her mind drift. She listened to the water gush until the hot ran cold. And cried until her tears were spent.

She gathered herself up, wrapped a towel around her battered body and stepped onto the cracked linoleum floor. She would survive this. She had to. She made a promise to stay but had no idea what to expect.

She walked into her bedroom, sat on the bed, and ran a hand over her face. Her suitcase stood in the corner, unpacked. Resigned, she rolled it next to her great-grandmother's empty antique dresser. It had been elegant and charming when her grandparents bought it. Now the tired oak drawers squeaked as she opened each one, putting away socks, underwear, T-shirts, and jeans. She left out white denim shorts and her favorite navy-blue tank with white script, "Legends are born in February."

After dressing, she walked outside to the propane tank and gave it a sound knock. Its hollow echo confirmed her suspicion. She opened the lid and checked the gauge. Empty.

"Stupid farmhouse. Now what?"

The wind whipped her jet-black hair as she looked across her family's farm. Pasture grass lay bent and browning in the scorching heat. Wispy cirrus clouds drifted over the barn roof, thinning as they floated higher and higher. She lifted her face to the hot summer breeze, sweetened by honeysuckle bushes growing wild along the outer fence-line, and wished for home.

She hobbled back to her grandmother's house, a scowl marring her face. She had no patience for her bruised thigh that throbbed with every step. Her eye had turned a nasty greenish-purple and thumped in tandem with her heart. Her body needed hot water to heal which left her one option. Boiling water on the ancient electric stove. Great.

She opened the back screen door and moved into the kitchen. Hunger pains ripped through her, reminding her she hadn't eaten in two days. She found a can of pork and beans in the pantry then rummaged through the silverware drawer for a can opener. Not bothering to heat them, she pulled out a spoon and ate from the can.

Feeling better afterward, she wandered outside to the garden where the chickweed and clover grew in stubborn defiance. She sat down on the dry ground and wondered how she'd survive living here after what happened.

"Damn it," she muttered, throwing a dirt clod at a row of crows perched on the fence. Those damn crows hung around all day yesterday, watching her with their black, beady eyes. The dirt clod rattled the fence, and the dislodged birds flew overhead, cawing and complaining. Her uneven pulse pounded as they circled overhead. A murder of crows, she thought. I should've known.

LACY WATCHED the circular fan blow cobwebs into a lively caper. Her grandmother's room, now hers, needed a good cleaning, but the ninety-degree weather made any physical exertion difficult. The old up-start farmhouse didn't have an air conditioner and any motivation to clean melted in the stifling heat. She rolled over in bed, pulled her T-shirt's sweat-soaked fabric from her back, and stared at the outdated calendar hanging on the faded, pastel green wall. What day was it? How long had it been since that night?

"Get up," she chided herself.

Her unfocused eyes gazed at the bedroom walls closing around her. She needed to get up and do something, fight against the depression hovering over her head.

She sunk underneath waves of homesickness. "I can't do this. I need to go home."

Her father left precious little gas. He'd taken two rusted gas cans and siphoned gas from abandoned cars then left them in the steel shop her grandfather built in the early seventies.

"Use it sparingly," he'd said. "Ride your motorcycle if you need to go anywhere but try to stay put until your uncle comes. He said he'd be here by the end of the month."

She shook off her father's admonition and the worried expression set deep in his eyes. She dragged herself out of bed thinking a slug moved faster. She slipped her feet into her navy-blue Converse tennis shoes and went to look for her motorcycle.

She walked several yards to the giant steel structure dubbed 'the shop.' Rust ate through the roof and the back door refused to open. She slipped a key from her shorts and unlocked the padlock to the front sliding doors. They groaned and creaked in protest as she struggled to shove them open.

She took a step inside and ground her teeth together. "Jesus H."

Plastic containers littered the floor. Black trash bags, filled with God knew what, lined the walls. Old, rusted bicycles hung from the ceiling and mice droppings turned the grey concrete black.

She searched the rubble for her motorcycle, kicking rusted Libby's green bean cans and faded Dr. Pepper bottles out of her path. She eyed her grandfather's Chevy Nova underneath a moth-eaten tarp. He never let anyone touch it and now it sat under pile after pile of newspapers and old National Geographic magazines. What a waste.

After a wide search around the perimeter, she found the black 250 Honda Rebel under another mountain of old newspapers. She gave them a hard shove and they scattered across the floor in a dusty cloud. Coughing through the haze, she pushed the bike outside.

"Please start," she coaxed, patting the grimy handlebars.

She located the gas cans and poured fuel into the tank, turning her head away from the vapors that fumed from the hot can. Her dad had left the key in the ignition lock cylinder. She turned it into the on position and pressed the button.

The engine coughed and sputtered. She adjusted the choke valve, tried again, and the bike roared to life.

"Thank God for small favors and Honda motors," she muttered.

She swung her right leg over the dusty seat, biting her lip on the pain radiating down it, and backed the bike onto the gravel drive. She revved the engine. Excitement tingled her spine as she remembered the rush that came every time she rode. She released the clutch, spun the back tire, and tore down Highway 11.

The speed exhilarated her and for a blessed moment she felt free, but every bump jarred her aching body. A painful reminder of *that* night. The hot July wind blasted her unprotected face and bare legs. The switchgrass, Indian grass, and big bluestem normally cropped down by cattle and county brush hogs, grew wild and uninhibited. The sun withered it, leaving it bent and broken.

After ten miles of dogged determination, she turned down her familiar tree-lined street. Fifty-year-old maple and cypress trees bowed inward creating a rich, green canopy above her head.

Her ribs screamed and her leg felt disjointed by the time she pulled in the drive and cut the engine. The unkempt yard and empty flower beds crushed her heart. The lawn had been her mother's baby. Her prized lavender hedge roses bloomed against the house in beautiful defiance to its desolate surroundings. She continued around the house and let herself in the back door.

Inside she wandered, soaking in the familiar sights. The pictures on the living room wall beckoned her and she studied them, transfixed. Why had no one taken them? Her family stared at her like living ghosts. She removed the most recent family portrait and studied her brother, AJ. Older by three years, AJ was her hero, her protector. Her guide through life's tricky twists and turns. She re-hung the picture and turned away, fought against useless tears.

She drifted room by room, taking inventory. Her parents

hadn't left much because there hadn't been much. Stores were depleted of toilet paper, water, and other necessities within the first week after the country's economic meltdown, labeled "the big crash." Some said it made the Great Depression's black Tuesday look like a day at the beach.

She inspected her parent's medicine cabinet. Nothing remained to ease her pain, not even a bottle of aspirin. Walking into their bedroom, she opened her father's closet, drew out an old plaid work shirt and shrugged it on. Laundry soap and musky cologne still lingered on the soft flannel fabric. She walked to the oak dresser against the far wall, reached behind it, and grasped cold steel. Her father's shotgun.

She ran her hand along the stock's smooth grain, pushed the release lever, broke the barrel, and investigated the chamber. Empty. Satisfied, she placed it in the hallway then moved to her bedroom.

Basketball heroes and motivational sayings like "You miss all the shots you don't take" lined the walls she'd insisted on painting a light grey. She laid down on her bedspread's blue satin-smooth fabric and stared at the ceiling. Her favorite band Sleeping with Sirens' lead singer, Kellin Quinn, smiled down at her, making her feel young and foolish. This wasn't her life now. Never would be again.

She rolled over and stared at her television. Curious, she raised up and turned it on. White snow filled the flat screen.

"I knew it."

The government shut down the television stations. The National Guard will be here soon, she thought.

Invasion rumors circulated for weeks after FEMA blocked internet access. All communication would be gone. And soon. If she were going to reach anyone, now would be the time.

"I should've gone to California." Silent tears streamed down her cheeks. "What am I going to do? How the hell am I going to survive this?"

The old cliché, "Father knows best," popped into her head,

taunted her for not heeding her dad's admonition to go with them. He'd tried everything short of hogtying her into the bed of their truck.

She reached in her pocket and retrieved a broken cross necklace. She'd found it on the floor by the blood stain, the mark where her youth and innocence died. He'd ripped it from her neck as her shirt tore. Every painful thrust, every disgusting grunt he'd made, scarred her.

She hurled the necklace at the window. It hit the glass with a clank then fell. "Where were You?" she shouted.

Her core belief system in God shattered that night. The beliefs her parents worked hard to instill teetered on the edge of oblivion. Rage built, its numbing poison liquefying her veins. She could survive on it. It would scab over her gaping wounds, dull the pain, and the blinding reality that nothing would ever be the same. She felt ruined. In the same way hot, molten lava buried Pompeii, rage could bury her pain.

She wandered back into the living room where the ancient black wall phone caught her attention. On impulse, she picked up the receiver. The live line buzzed in her ear. Not even thirty seconds passed before an automated voice informed her if she wished to make a call, she should hang up and try again.

Did she?

Without a second thought, she dialed her uncle's number. When his answering machine chirped a request to leave a message at the beep, she punched the wall. Frustrated, she dropped the receiver back in its cradle and massaged her abused knuckles. What good would it do to leave a message? Her grandmother didn't have a landline. And what would she say anyway?

She unlocked the front door, went outside, and sat on the curb. Weeds poked through the sidewalk cracks. The wind carried the scent of a summer storm and lifted her hair off her sweaty back. Uneasiness curled her toes as she stared at the abandoned houses.

She knew nothing about being alone.

Not one thing.

Subsistence was a vocabulary word, an abstract thought, not her reality. She understood the definition, but the actual execution was difficult to grasp. What had she been thinking? She'd never traveled anywhere without her parents or her brother. She'd never lived anywhere but home.

She was terrified.

"What have you gotten me into, Uncle Tommy? What did I agree to?"

An engine's faint rumble cut the air.

A white Chevy pickup raced down the street and parked two houses down. Fall Out Boy pulsed through the radio speakers.

She squinted against the western sun. "Travis," she gasped.

Tears blurred her vision as she sprinted toward him. He stepped out the driver's side and she skidded to a stop, just short of launching herself into his arms.

He inhaled sharply as his eyes raked over her battered face. "Jesus. What happened, Lacy?"

She turned her head. "It's a long story."

A hell of a long story. One she didn't know if she could tell. It was too painful, too raw. Too dangerous. She knew she could never reveal the identity of her rapist, knew what he was capable of. Her stomach twisted into a painful knot.

Travis' deep brown eyes darkened. "Tell me."

She folded her arms. "Why are you here?" she asked instead. "I thought you moved to Texas with your parents."

He looked at his house. "My parents were shot trying to cross the border."

She winced. "I'm sorry, Trav. I thought the border was still open when you left. It's closed now?"

"Yeah. The borders are buttoned up tight. FEMA had the National Guard set up fast, but my dad wanted to try to cross anyway."

"How did it happen? Who fired on you?"

His face set in a grim line. "The Oklahoma National Guard. They are armed and willing to fire on anyone trying to leave the state. What about your parents? Did they leave in time?"

"I think so," she mumbled.

"Where did they decide to go?"

"California. My mom was born there. She received a letter that gave her and my family clearance through the closed states. That should get them there. But who knows."

"Why didn't you go with them?"

Her heart pinched. "My Uncle Tommy called."

His brows furrowed. "The great senator from Texas. What does he have to do with you staying behind?"

"He needed a family member to live on the farm as a bene-ficiary. It's in a Texas land trust. The National Guard shouldn't bother me or try to force me into a work camp since its techni-cally free land. Whether they'll follow that rule or not, I don't know," she said, her voice hard.

He raised a questioning eyebrow. "Why you?"

She sighed. "I was the only one willing to stay. There's bad blood between my father and Uncle Tommy. Besides, I grew up on those forty acres. It's like a second home to me."

"You should have gone with them, Lace."

She shrugged and deflected the conversation to him. "So, how did you escape?"

"I didn't try to cross the river. Thought it was a bad idea." He lowered his gaze. "Guess it was."

"I'm sorry, Trav. What are you going to do now?"

"Don't know. Evade the roundups if possible. Thought about hiding out here for a while. I'm good at disappearing into the woods." He gestured to the wooded area that stretched for miles behind their neighborhood.

She leveled him a challenging look. "You up for some hard farm work, city boy?"

"What did you have in mind?"

"I need protection. You need somewhere to live. I can give you asylum and you can avoid the work camps."

His eyes narrowed. "Protection from what?"

Anger and shame rose to the surface. She held her breath. Could she say it? Out loud? Slowly, she released her breath and whispered, "My rapist."

His strong arms wrapped around her and she sank into the familiar comfort of his embrace. When they were younger, their friendship had taken a romantic turn. It didn't last, but they'd remained friends.

He laid his cheek on her head. "Talk to me, Lacy."

5

L acy watched smoke from the burn barrels billow black and heavy, carrying the acrid scent of paper and garbage. She struggled to sort the plastic from the rubbish, but its distinct, signature scent polluted the air, revealing she'd missed some.

Heat waves snaked off the barrels, competing with the hot July day. The water hose lay uncoiled and water trickled between the barrels to stave off stray sparks that might start a grass fire or ignite the two brittle farmhouses. Since her grand-mother died, no one had maintained the farm and the signs were telling. Her father washed his hands of it because of the family fallout. Her horse remained the only reminder it had once been a working farm.

She turned and walked to the smaller farmhouse. Walking and breathing had become easier and the black eye and bruises were fading. The one thing that remained in full force and refused to yield was the ache in her heart. Too many questions with no answers plagued her mind, but the overriding one? Why? Why had he picked her? Even the silence surrounding her screamed the question.

She made her way through the kitchen and tiny living

room to the screened-in front porch then halted. The sensation to weep overtook her. Who saved plastic gallon milk cartons and stacked them thigh-high? She scrubbed her hands over her face and fought back tears. How many obstacles would she have to fight her way through?

Burning plastic was toxic. The fumes would choke any living thing within a ten-mile radius. She couldn't bag and throw them next to the non-existent curb. Waste management had never serviced the four corners area.

Tears broke free and burned her face. She waded through the jugs to the outer door and gave it a shove. It stuck. She rammed her shoulder against it and heard the wood crack. Dingy white paint chips sifted to the floor.

"What the hell?"

Furious, she kicked the milk cartons and wondered where she could throw them, then remembered the trash pit behind the shop.

She stomped through the living room and out the back door. She went out, rounded the house, and found a sapling blocking the front door.

As she looked at the innocent baby tree, the tension inside her erupted.

She let out a growl then launched herself at the tree. She kicked and rammed her shoulder into the eight-inch base. By the time she finished, her face dripped sweat and blood trickled down her scratched arms and palms from the rough bark.

She crumpled to the ground, lifted her head, and screamed.

She would never know why.

Never understand or unravel the Gordian knot.

Travis rounded the east end of the house and sprinted toward her.

"Damn it," she muttered, wishing she could melt into the ground. He must've heard her scream. She swiped her tears with the hem of her T-shirt.

He dropped to his knees.

"Don't touch me," she gasped and slapped his outstretched hand. "God, Travis, please. Just don't touch me."

"Are you hurt?"

"No," she whimpered.

He let out an exasperated breath. "Then what's the matter?"

She burst into tears. "The tree. It's in my way."

He looked around until his eyes focused on the poor, battered tree. Stripped leaves and branches lay in scattered chaos. "You know, there's an ax in that shed with all the junk in it."

She looked up. "Which shed? They all have junk in them."

Laughter erupted from his chest. "That's no lie. The one closest to the back door."

"The wash house?"

"Whatever. They're all tin sheds loaded with a bunch of crap."

She hoisted herself up. "My grandmother named most of them."

"Oh yeah?" he chuckled and pointed to another rusty shed beside the wash house. The roof had partially caved and the sun-bleached wooden door flapped to and fro in the breeze. "What'd she call that one?"

She wrinkled her nose. "That's the cat house. I need to burn it. It stinks."

He laughed again, then tipped her chin, and locked his gaze with hers. "What's going on, Lace?"

Her eyes darted to the ground. "I don't know."

"Yeah, you do. You need to talk about what happened. It will fester if you don't."

She shrugged and shifted away. "I'm angry, and I don't know what to do with it."

Pity clouded his eyes. "I'm so sorry, sweetheart."

She dug her Converse into the browning grass, watched

withered blades catch the breeze, and wished her pain could fly away with them.

What idiot said, "That which does not kill us makes us stronger?" she wondered because she'd like to sucker punch them in the throat. That ranked right up there with the other useless cliché "This too shall pass." This would never pass, and it sure as hell might kill her.

"What are you thinking?" Travis asked.

"About stupid clichés people say because they think they'll make you feel better."

He gave her a bemused smile. "Well, I'm all out of those. Let's go find the ax."

"Thanks, Trav. For caring, for being here. I know I'm not the only one hurting. I'm sorry about your mom and dad."

Sadness crept into his chocolate-brown eyes and she wished she could do something to ease it.

"You know, releasing your aggression is actually healthy," he commented as they walked to the wash house.

She gave a wry smile. "Are you volunteering to be my personal punching bag?"

He wrenched open the shed's weather-swollen door. "You gotta be kidding. You'd probably —"

The ground began to vibrate, and the thrumming sound of diesel engines sliced the air.

They looked around the shed to the west, but hills and scrub brush blocked their view.

"What is that?" He brought his hand up to shield his eyes and scanned the western horizon.

"I don't know." They needed a better view. "Come on." She jerked his arm and bolted forward.

She burst into the barn. Startled, her horse tossed his head and rapped her shoulder. She climbed to the loft, opened the door, then climbed the rope ladder to the roof.

Travis pulled himself up a few seconds later and they both

stood, wide-eyed, as a motorcade of armored security vehicles rumbled their direction.

"Sweet Jesus. They're here."

"Didn't think the Military Police would bother Shidler," he muttered. "We've got what, maybe two hundred people? Most of them already left."

A cold numbness settled in her stomach as she watched them stop at the front gate.

She turned to Travis. "We need to hide."

She flung herself into the loft and slid down the ladder. Her butt landed with a thud and pain wracked her tender ribcage. Ignoring it, she jumped up, grabbed Acer's halter, and led him outside. She slapped him on the flank, and he bolted across the pasture.

"Why are we hiding?"

She swiped hay off a trap door that opened to a root cellar. "Just come on."

They climbed down the rickety, wooden steps into pitch black. Debilitating darkness swallowed her, and she forced herself to take slow, deep breaths. The air was dank, ripe with rotting wood and damp earth, and stood stiflingly still.

"Do you have your lighter, Trav?" Her voice trembled.

"Yeah."

The sound of the flint igniting the fluid eased the itchy feeling crawling under her skin.

Dim light flickered off the cellar walls. Cobwebs and dirt coated the shelves. Old mason jars, blackened by mold, seed packets, and garden tools filled the drooping, moisture-drenched boards.

"Why are we down here? I thought we were safe on your uncle's property."

"I think it's better if they don't know we're here. Uncle Tommy said he'd be here within the month. I just hope no one catches us in the meantime."

Her rapist's warning rang in her head. If she didn't leave, he'd come back and kill her.

They sat in silence, listened for footsteps.

Travis cursed and dropped the lighter. "Damn thing got too hot."

Faint light filtered through the trap door, illuminating motes like faerie dust and one sliver of dirty floor. Yuck. She could feel the grime seep into her shorts.

Overhead, the military police searched the barn, their boots scuffling through the tack room then back out.

"No one here," one announced. "Let's roll."

"There's a horse in the far pasture," another said.

"Leave it. We have no way to transport it. We'll come back later. This is a human extraction mission. Stay on point."

Relief coursed through her when the voices faded. But what the hell? Human extraction?

She wondered how many people remained and what would happen to them. Rumors of the Oklahoma National Guard clearing every town and city in the state had circulated until the government shut down the media.

"How many people do you think are still in town?" she asked as they climbed up the ladder.

"The gas station has been closed for weeks and the city building is abandoned." Travis stretched his arms in the open air. "Depends on if they have somewhere to go. Most people don't."

"Yeah. Starve, or be hauled off like cattle." She turned toward town, hands on her hips. "What do you think the military is doing with all these people?"

He shrugged. "Some say they're taking them to gas chambers, like the Jews in World War II. Others say military bases have been turned into work camps. Forced labor to re-invent the economy. No one knows for sure. All we know is that no one comes back."

She turned and gave him a long look. "Your truck have gas in it?"

"Yeah," he said slowly.

"Let's go." She made a beeline for the white Chevy parked under the carport.

He ran behind her and grabbed her arm. "Hold on."

Face flushed, she jerked out of his grasp. "Don't *ever* grab me!"

"I'm sorry, Lace. I didn't think."

"Yeah, me neither." Travis wouldn't hurt her, she reminded herself.

He took a step back. His deep brown eyes radiated pity, and she turned away from it. God, she hated that. She didn't need him feeling sorry for her. It made her feel weak. Squaring her shoulders, she continued to the truck. She had no time for pity or to grieve over what she'd lost.

Travis followed. "What are you going to do?"

"We're gonna go take a look," she said.

"The hell you say," he yelled. "We just hid from those soldiers and now you wanna run straight to them?"

"Someone in town may need our help."

He tilted his head to the sky and muttered, "Help? She wants to help when we can't even help ourselves."

She left his one-sided conversation, opened the driver's side door, and looked under the mat. "Hey, Trav, where are your keys?"

"Oh no," he said, jogging over. "If we're going, I'm driving."

"Let's get moving."

"Women," he grumbled. He opened the passenger door and fished around the glove compartment and pulled out the key. "Can't reason with 'em." He gave the door a solid slam, rounded the hood, and nudged Lacy out of the way. He turned to face her as the engine turned over. "This is insane. You know that, right?"

"Can you please stop complaining and drive?" Apprehension gnawed her gut, but she settled back unwilling to acknowledge it.

He backed out of the drive. "Where are we going?"

She watched the familiar landscape drift by. "I don't want to go straight into town. There's an old oilfield road that runs parallel to the west end of town. We can park there."

"And do what?"

"We'll sneak down the alley on the edge of town and see what's going on."

Travis turned down the old dirt road and cut the engine. "This is a bad idea."

"Stay here then," she snapped as she got out.

He let out a growl and slammed the driver's door. "No way."

They squeezed through a rusted barbed-wire fence and hurried through the pasture. When they reached the alley, they turned south, searching. For what, she didn't know.

A swift breeze kicked dirt and trash into the air. Frowning, she raised her head. Leaves fell in clumps while thunder rolled like giant bowling balls in the distance.

She skidded to a stop. The wind carried a shrill scream from the street adjacent the alley.

An MP shouted, "Halt! Arms in the air!"

Travis caught her by the shoulder and forced her behind an old trashcan. Her foot bumped the container and a black cat jumped out, hissing at the intrusion.

A boy darted into the alley. His yellow hair stuck out every direction, swaying with the wind. As he passed, she grabbed his foot and his body hit the gravel. The smack knocked the wind out of him.

Travis helped the gasping boy to his feet. "Take it easy, buddy. Calm down."

"My mom and dad," he wheezed. "They took 'em."

Lacy pulled the hem of his black Ramones T-shirt and motioned him down. "Do you have any other family?"

"My brother, Ethan, and his wife, Hailey. We have to help them."

She looked at Travis then back to the boy. "Are you Matty Webb?" Her brother and Ethan had graduated high school together.

"Yeah. Come on," he urged. "They're hiding."

Travis rose with the boy. "I'll go." He turned to Lacy. "You stay here."

Trash cans rattled as the wind continued to drive down the temperature. The rain's clean scent rode the air. Large, blue-black thunderheads rolled in and blocked the sun.

Her gaze flitted up the alley at a loud squawking sound. "I'll be damned."

Amazed, she watched two russet-colored hens ruffle their feathers and air their grievances to the world. She shook her head. Just like two old ladies complaining about too many cocks in their hen house.

She glanced over her shoulder for Travis and the boy. The minutes ticked by. Hot, sticky sweat trickled down her back. Why hadn't they returned?

She turned and kept the chickens in sight. They stopped and pecked the gravel, their injuries forgotten for the moment.

She glanced back again, and relief rushed through her. Travis, the boy, and his family sprinted toward her. Her eyes widened as she watched an overgrown puppy lope along behind them.

"Let's go." Travis ushered her to her feet.

"Wait!" She pointed to the hens. "I want those."

He shook his head, confused. "You want me to catch two chickens? In the middle of all this"—he waved his hands—"mayhem?"

To strengthen his point, another gunshot split the air.

"Yes."

"Of course you do." He turned to the three who had stopped beside them.

Amusement lit Ethan's face. "I'll help."

"Whatever," Travis grunted. "You take the right and I'll go left." He turned to the boy. "Hey, kid, can you run around and get behind them?"

He bobbed his head up and down, grabbed the puppy's collar, and shoved it in Lacy's hand. "Hold him, will ya?"

"Sure," she muttered. The dog's intelligent brown eyes sized her up. She met his gaze. "Don't bark."

Travis lunged forward, arms outstretched. And fell flat on his face. The agile hen slipped out of reach.

Ethan captured the other and held it by its feet. It squawked at the cruel injustice.

Matty grabbed the crafty one by the wing. Dislodged feathers flew as he fought to hold it.

Travis dusted off his shirt and shot Lacy a lethal look. "Can we go now, Princess Mayhem?"

She waved her arm in a wide sweeping gesture. "By all means."

"You're lucky the MP moved to the other side of town with all the noise we've made." He stopped and leveled her a stern look. "Are you sure you know what you're doing? Taking in three more people?"

"We don't have a choice. Let's go."

They sprinted for the truck and she heard him grumble. "Oh, *now* she's ready to go."

When they reached the truck, she skidded to a stop, struck speechless. Two guys sat waiting in the short bed.

"No, no, no," she muttered. She recognized one, a former classmate. The other was a stranger.

"We were watching you," the stranger said. He eyed the complaining chickens with mild interest.

Travis pulled down the tailgate. "Thanks for not stealing my truck, Dylan."

Ethan, Matty, the chickens, and the dog piled into the truck bed. Hailey refused.

She's gonna be trouble, Lacy thought. What the hell am I going to do with all these people?

6

Lacy stood beside Travis' Chevy truck, arms crossed in defiance as their argument over a supply run threatened to boil over.

"I'm the boss."

He smothered the grin that flitted across his face and gave a frustrated sigh. "How could I forget? You remind me every day."

"Then I'm going with you."

"Lacy," he began again. "We need supplies and have little gas left. I don't know how far I'll have to go to get what we need. It could be dangerous."

His tone made her feel like a child too stupid to understand her ABC's. "Don't patronize me. I can help and you know it."

Her eyes drifted. Another hot, hazy August day. Heat waves rolled off the Highway 11 blacktop and dog-day cicadas sang mating songs in the mimosa trees. Could it get any hotter? The constant buzz grated her last nerve, and she felt the sudden urge to kick something.

She harnessed the adrenaline burst to batter against his fortified defense. "I just don't want to be left here."

A walking contradiction these days, she couldn't tolerate

the men's presence. But she hated being alone. Memories colliding with fear. Not a good mix.

Travis studied her intently.

"What?" she snapped.

"Don't you have some fences to mend?" he asked, cocking a brow.

"No," she huffed. "All done."

He rolled his eyes. "The guys will be back."

"They're hunting. And we both know they suck at it."

He burst into laughter. "True. But it's not like they'll be gone that long. Besides, you've got Castiel with you."

The Rottweiler turned his head, trotted over, and pushed his head under her hand.

She eyed him with disdain. "Why did Matty feel the need to give me this overgrown mongrel?"

"He's not a mongrel, are you boy?" He reached down, scratched the dog between the ears. "He's a long-haired Rottweiler."

She snorted. "Whatever. I don't need a dog."

"Yes, you do."

She caught him analyzing her again and wanted to smack the speculative look right off his face. She wasn't a damn bug under glass. "Whatever."

Shooing Castiel away, she pushed away wayward strands of hair and considered her options. Give up and stay or play her last card.

She caught his gaze and held it. "Travis don't leave me here. Not today."

The blistering wind lashed her hair, stinging her face. Irritated, she yanked it back. She braided it, dug a rubber band from her pocket, and wound it around the end.

She searched his face, tanned a deep brown. Before the world became politically correct, he would've been classified an Indian half-breed. High cheek bones and a ruler-straight nose attested to his Native American heritage.

He reached out, caressed her cheek with his thumb. "You wear me out."

Flinching, she stepped back. "Don't. Please."

"Yeah." He dropped his hand. "I'm sorry, Lace. If anything happened to you, I'd never forgive myself."

She lowered her eyes. "Nothing will happen."

"People are being hauled out right and left. You need to stay here. Where you're safe."

"It's not the Military Police I'm afraid of." Tears stung her eyelids.

His eyes widened in understanding. "That bastard won't touch you again, I promise."

"How can you promise that? You'll be gone and I'll be stuck here with nowhere to run, nowhere—" Her voice cracked. "He said he'd be back. It's been one month, today. Travis, please." Her chin quivered.

He swore and rubbed the back of his neck. "Okay."

She rounded the truck's hood and stopped to rest her forehead on the passenger window's hot glass. She hated feeling dependent on Travis—or anyone. Hated the violent act that shattered her heart and made her feel weak and helpless. Humpty Dumpty's vague image and the phrase "all the king's horses" swirled in her head. Would she ever be put back together again?

THE OLD PONCA CITY train station located downtown spilled over with men, women, and children of all ages, backgrounds, and ethnicity—a chaotic, horror-filled scene that reminded Lacy of the old black-and-white film, *Schindler's List*.

A wrenching scream pierced the air. A young husband, torn from his wife, struggled against two MP who dragged him to a boxcar. Without a care, they tossed him inside while their toddler clung to his mother's leg, his face buried from the violence.

The brutality made her stomach pitch. She couldn't believe the scene, even as it played before her like a drive-in movie.

Travis hid the truck behind an old grain elevator. Abandoned long ago, the silver monstrosity sported the name Robin Hood Flour in huge, faded red letters, and provided an excellent place to hide his truck.

Her skin pricked. "We gotta get out of here, Trav."

"I know."

"Get us out of here," she repeated.

Ignoring her, he continued to scan the crowd. Worry creased his brow. It looked as if he was searching for someone specific.

"Come on, Trav. Why did we come to the train station? This was supposed to be a supply run."

He muttered something unintelligible and inched his truck forward.

"I've got a bad feeling about this. We need to leave."

She waited, but he gave no response.

"We should've gone to Fairfax," she pushed. "Could've gotten what we needed there. I don't understand why we're in Ponca City."

"Lacy. Shut. Up," he ground through clenched teeth.

"Well shit, Trav," she snapped back. "You should've known the MP would be here."

Exasperated, he turned to face her. "I knew it would be like this. I tried to get you to stay. Remember?"

She threw her hands up. "What are we doing here?"

"Looking for someone."

Her brow creased. "Who?"

His shoulders tensed. "My grandparents."

Closing her eyes, she rubbed her temples. "Travis, you should've—"

"I know," he snapped. "I should've told you."

She surveyed the dismal scene. "How do you know they're even here?"

"I don't. Not for sure." His eyes tracked the crowd. "They sent me a text before the cell towers went down. Took me that long to scrounge up enough gas to get here. I'm still not sure if we'll make it back." He paused and pounded his fist against the steering wheel. "Damn it, Lacy, you should've stayed put."

She flinched and turned away, stared out the passenger window at an abandoned storage unit, and wondered if she would always be this frightened. Travis wouldn't hurt her, but his outburst rattled her.

"I'm sorry," he said quietly. "I'm sorry I scared you."

She shrugged off his light touch on her arm and inched closer to the door. "It's okay, Travis."

"Please look at me," he pleaded.

"I'm okay. Let it be."

"Please, Lace."

In that moment, she knew he still felt something more for her than just friendship. He'd stepped up and protected her, gave her strength and security. But could she return those feelings?

Something caught her attention. "Look!"

A woman fought an officer who tried to shove her into a boxcar. She grabbed her husband, but the officer shoved him down and zapped him with a stun baton. The man stiffened then went limp.

"They're killing him," she gasped.

His hands tightened on the steering wheel. "Holy hell."

The MP jerked the aging man to his feet. He shouted something to his wife before they tossed him into the boxcar with no more respect given a sack of potatoes. The older woman ran across the tracks and out of sight.

"We've got to help her." She lunged out the door.

"Lacy, no!" He let out a frustrated growl and revved the engine forward.

She didn't know how to help the woman, but it didn't stop her feet from rushing forward.

He pulled the truck beside her and shouted, "Get in."

"No." She stopped and put her hands on her knees, panting. "We've got to help her."

"We will. Just get in the damn truck before they spot you."

"Fine." She jumped in and searched the crowd. "Where'd she go? You see her?"

He drove around the dilapidated station. They spotted the woman huddled between two green dumpsters overflowing with trash. It reeked of human decay and the sight made her want to weep. How could the military, sworn to protect, follow orders in direct opposition to their creed?

"Get in," she urged. She pushed the door open and slid toward Travis.

Tears stained the woman's leathery cheeks. "Thank you. My husband," she choked, lowering her head in her hands. "They took him."

"We saw." At a loss, she patted her shoulder. No words could describe the inhumane way her husband had been treated.

She glanced at Travis. "We can't risk staying any longer."

"I know." He threw the truck in gear and sped away.

"I'm sorry we didn't find your grandparents." She placed a comforting hand on his knee.

The woman cleared her throat. "Where we headed?"

"Back to my family farm. You're more than welcome to come." She stuck her hand out. "I'm Lacy Monroe, and this is Travis Pappan."

Her eyes spilled over and she swiped at them. "I'm Catrin Wirtz. Just call me Cat. Nice to meet you kids and thank you for the offer." She fiddled with her faded blue hem. "My Ben. He would've wanted me to find a safe place."

"We still need to stop for supplies," Travis pointed out as he left the city streets and pulled onto Highway 60.

"Where are you going to try?"

He grunted. "Wherever the police aren't."

She crossed her arms and gave him a sidelong glance. As he punched the gas and the truck accelerated, nausea hit her hard. Her throat convulsed and she swallowed. "Oh God, Travis. Pull over. I'm gonna be sick."

"Crap. Just a sec."

He pulled into an empty warehouse and before the truck stopped, she climbed over Cat, jerked the door open, and tumbled out. Her stomach's entire contents ended up in a disgusting pool at her feet.

"Poor girl," Cat murmured. "Malnourished and pregnant. Not a good combination."

She turned to face the older woman. "What did you say?"

Cat looked confused then understanding dawned. "Oh, you didn't know?"

All the blood drained from her head and down to her toes.

"There are worse things than being pregnant, girl," she said and placed a firm hand on her shoulder. "Travis, help her back in the truck."

"How do you know she's pregnant?" he demanded.

"I'm a nurse. I see the signs and I've always had a sixth sense about these things."

She tried to swallow and looked at Travis. "Oh. My. God."

7

Jace scanned the Monroe farm from his vantage point in his father's ultralight aircraft and watched the early morning sun glisten off the plane's white wings. He looked down searching for Lacy and noticed the pastures had lost the luster of spring. August left them dry and thirsty, the grassland, a brown patchwork quilt from the sky.

Below, a rag-tag team armed with shovels struggled to rebuild the old pond dike. An impossible project without a backhoe. Shovels wouldn't cut it. Not easily anyway.

A Bob Cat sat idle back home in his pole barn. It would cut their project time in half and save the men back-breaking work, but Zach would never allow them to use it.

The men lifted their heads as the plane buzzed overhead. When he turned toward the barn structure, his eyes lit on a horse and rider and his heart flipped. Lacy's jet-black hair hung in a long braid and fish dangled from her saddle.

He grinned. She'd always outfished her brother. Hell, she'd outfished him a time or two.

A huge black dog trotted alongside her. Cautious and alert, the dog lifted his nose to the low-flying craft and barked. She followed the dog's gaze, lifted a hand, and shielded her eyes. She stared at the plane then turned her horse to the barn.

Relieved, he rubbed his hand over his forehead. She'd been on his mind since his best friend, AJ, informed him his little "headstrong" sister decided to stay on the farm alone. Satisfied, he banked the plane to head home. He glanced down once more, and his heart plummeted. Travis friggin' Pappan. What was *he* doing at the farm?

He watched as Travis helped her dismount, saw his hands linger too long on her lower back. His stomach dropped into a freefall that had nothing to do with the plane. Travis and Lacy had been an item in high school for a short time. They'd shared a prom together as well as being Shidler High's basketball king and queen their Junior year. He never thought he might encounter competition because in his mind, she was already his.

Stupid, given the fact beautiful didn't begin to describe her. Her round oval face held a pixie-like quality and possessed an alluring innocence that belied the smoldering fire banked in her eyes. Her rosy lips, full and supple, were perfect for kissing. He wondered if they were as soft as they appeared and would give his eyeteeth for just one taste of her. Her willowy body had filled out in all the right places, from mile-long legs to a slim waist and small perfectly formed breasts. But it was her crystalline green eyes that magnetized him, lured him in, and held him captive. His mom had told him eyes were a window to the soul. When he looked into her eyes, he saw a fiery will, intense determination, and an endless capacity to love.

Her brother, insanely overprotective, ran off any potential boyfriends during her high school career and he'd been all too happy to join that bandwagon. It had made waiting for her a little more bearable. Three years older, he'd held back, kept his feelings to himself, gave her time and space to grow. Because he wanted more than a high school romance. He wanted forever.

His brow furrowed as uncomfortable thoughts knotted his stomach. What if she was already in a relationship with Travis? That would explain his presence. His fingers drummed the control column.

Ill-at-ease, he turned the plane and headed home. His dad taught him to fly and he loved every second, even considered becoming a pilot. The light craft maneuvered with ease in his capable hands. Takeoff and landing always gave him a rush. He circled the Cooper spread and prepared to land. He decreased the rate of descent, reduced the thrust to zero, then touched down. The wheels hit the ground and glided across the pasture as smooth as butter on toast.

He cut the engine early to avoid detection. He didn't need another confrontation with his brother. The thought left a bitter taste in his mouth. Zero chance of that. Zach controlled the farm, the house, all assets, everything. And didn't care who murdered their parents.

Searching for clues delayed his move to the farm. His amateur investigation was a dismal failure. He'd never know who murdered his parents. Resting his forehead on the control column, grief washed over him, and the gory details pushed their way forward.

He'd left AJ at Shidler's only bar that night with a tipsy platinum blonde. He remembered because she had dangerous eye-poking torpedo breasts. Leroy's Bar was too crowded and cigarette smoke sucked oxygen from his lungs. Drinking had never been his scene. He didn't suffer the country affliction — work cattle, drink beer, chase girls — and refused to give up self-control to the drink, refused to become a certified alcoholic before his twenty-third birthday. He remembered asking AJ too many questions about Lacy. He hadn't had a valid excuse to see her in over a month, and his mind worked through several different plausible excuses to see her as he turned down the long, gravel drive. He parked by the barn and cut the engine.

The house sat dark, quiet. Odd, because his mother always left the kitchen light on when he went out. He stepped over the back-door's threshold, switched on the light and looked around. An eerie feeling settled over him. Too quiet, he'd thought, as he moved through the house turning on lights as he went. Still, an oppressive darkness he couldn't extinguish followed him.

He'd called to his mom and dad, positive they'd had no plans that evening. He entered their master bedroom, switched on the light.

And saw red.

Blood spatter covered the walls. The crimson stains, a stark contrast to their normal ivory color. Blood soaked the carpet. Iron and sulphur's acrid stench hung suspended in the air like a night demon. With a strangled sob, he knelt before his mother and cradled her head in his lap. A shotgun blast had ripped a hole in her chest. His father, shot in the back, slumped over his desk. And that's how Zach found him. Covered in his mother's blood.

He shook off the memory.

Time to go, make a clean break. He jumped from the cockpit, pushed the ultralight inside the hanger, and slid the metal door closed. He had to move fast. His father left a loose end he needed to tie up. He'd given him the task the day before he died.

He snuck into the yellow kitchen. It seemed dull now, lifeless. Like the yellow paint had faded and died with his mother. He stopped and looked at the sunflower clock hanging above the white distressed breakfast nook. "I miss you, Mom," he whispered, then hurried on.

He crept into his dad's office and pulled up the carpet under the desk. Underneath lay a floor safe. He'd known nothing about it until his dad revealed it and the content it held. Tucked in one corner stood a Mason jar filled with gold coins. His father's telegraph machine took up the remaining space. A special line was installed for the old contraption, a request made by Senator Monroe, his dad said.

He pulled it out, set it up, and typed a message to the senator.

Tap, tap, tap.

He shook his head and gave the old machine a dubious look. He didn't know what the dots and dashes symbolized and didn't want to. The government blocked all modern communication and forced his father and the senator to think outside the box. He held serious doubts concerning the machine's reliability, but he fulfilled his dad's last request, nonetheless. Thinking back, he wondered if his father knew his days were numbered.

The floorboards in the hallway outside creaked and his head shot up. Tiny needles pricked his scalp. He dismantled the equipment, shoved it into a backpack, then closed the safe and drew the carpet back. He left the gold, would come back for it if he got in a jam. Zach didn't know about the gold or the safe and he wanted to keep it that way. He flicked off the lights, opened the door, and ran smack into his brother's wide, sturdy chest. He stumbled back a step.

Zach smirked. "Well, well. What do we have here?"

He ducked his head, trying to ward off a confrontation. "I was just leaving, Zach. Get out of my way."

Zach sucked in a deep breath. "Hmm, I don't think so little brother." He flipped the light on and circled the room. "What were you doing in here?"

He scrambled for an answer but came up miserably short.

"Hmm. Well, maybe you can answer this. Why were you flying the ultralight this morning?"

Heat flushed his face. "Dad's plane, Dad's office. I have just as much of a right to be here as you do," he replied, folding his arms.

"What's in the backpack, Jace?" A nasty smile lit his face.

"Nothing."

He took a step forward. "Let me look."

"Go to hell, Zach," he said, and tried to push past his brother.

Zach's heavyweight stature outmatched him. By a lot. He knew he'd lose if it came to a fight.

Zach yanked the pack off his shoulder with enough force it knocked him against the wall.

"What the hell is this?" he asked as he unzipped the bag.

He stared at him in stony silence and tried not to squirm.

"Hmm. That important, huh?" He placed the machine on the desk, tapped the black keypad over and over. "I know what this is. It's a telegraph. Who are you communicating with?"

A National Geographic picture of a lion circling an injured antelope leapt into his mind. His brother made him feel hunted.

"I'll bet it's the high and mighty senator from Texas. Well, I'll just keep this for you." He grinned and spit tobacco juice on his boots. A little dribbled down his chin and he wiped it away with the back of his hand.

Jace rolled his eyes, disgusted. "Whatever, Zach. I've got to go." He attempted to cross the threshold, but his brother blocked his path.

He held out his hand, palm up. "The keys."

"The keys to what?"

"Your truck. You're not leaving here with it."

"It's my truck!" he exploded. "Bought and paid for by me. Hell will freeze before I hand over my keys to you."

"Then put on your skates, brother, because you're standing on a frozen lake of fire. Keys. Now."

"Not a chance."

His brother narrowed his eyes. "Hand them over, or Lacy will suffer the consequences."

Blood drained from his face, then rushed back. His body vibrated with anger.

"I told you once not to threaten her." His hands shook and he clenched them in tight fists. "Last warning."

Zach gave him a wolfish grin. "Or what?"

He shook his head, unable to wrap his mind around his brother's wacked thinking.

"Take the truck." He fished the keys out of his pocket, dropped them on the floor. "Just shut the hell up about Lacy. Forget whatever twisted idea you've got rolling around in your head. Because if you don't?" He stalked over, placed his face inches from Zach's. Outweighed and outmatched be damned. He was going to get his point across. "I. Will. Shut. You. Up."

He shoved past him, went to the barn, and saddled his horse. He grabbed a duffle hidden in the tack room, packed for the move, and hitched the handles over the saddle horn. He mounted his horse then bolted into the open field toward the Monroe farm.

8

L acy rode the farm's perimeter, letting her horse set his own pace. She reached down and patted his neck. The spirited gelding tended to throw his head, a bad habit her father never managed to break. Today, he was content to meander along the fence, munching the dead, crunchy grass underfoot. He raised his head and nickered.

She scrutinized the fence line for breaks then reined up when she noticed another stolen fencepost. She dismounted, walked over and inspected the dangling barbed wire, then looked around. Lingering paranoia drifted over her and her pulse quickened. She reached down, fingered the Bowie knife strapped to her waist, and whistled for her dog. He dropped a wild pursuit of a jackrabbit, trotted over and looked up, his bear-like face covered in grass burs.

"*Gute Hund.*"

Cat had taken one look at the pup and decided to train him in German. She insisted he would make a fierce watchdog. The woman, a sheer force of nature, managed both farmhouses from the moment she arrived. Lacy relinquished control of the day-to-day operations, grateful she didn't have to worry about feeding everyone. They'd starve on her cooking.

Cat also dealt with Hailey, a chore she avoided with gusto. Hailey had done nothing but complain from the moment she refused to sit in the back of the truck. Living with her was like being in an internment camp with the cast from Jersey Shore.

She mounted, turned her horse, and rode to the spring-fed ponds in the farm's far-east corner. The men worked hard to finish her great-grandfather's fish farm. Completed, it would provide a consistent food source. Pulling Travis or Ethan to fix fence angered her. Filthy thieves would get buckshot in their backsides if she caught them.

She halted at the main dike. "How's it going?"

Raul looked up and waved. "So far, so good."

Raul worked hard and knew something about every subject conceivable. To her surprise, he'd whipped out a design to reconstruct the pond in less than a day.

She studied him with open interest. His warm brown skin gleamed with sun and sweat. Black hair curled around his shirt collar and his shrewd brown eyes never missed a thing. They crinkled around the edges when he smiled and gave his otherwise impassive face a roguish charm. He offered no personal information when he'd shown up in the back of Travis' truck, but if she had to speculate, she'd place him in his late twenties. He oozed the typical machismo associated with Latino men.

A wide grin split his face. "Need something, Boss?"

He caught her staring and she felt heat rush up her neck, but she grinned back, not sorry in the least. "Nope. Just remember, the dike needs to be at least a foot above water level."

His eyes rolled and he gave a rich, throaty laugh. "Yeah. I am the one who told you that."

She laughed with him then clicked her tongue and Acer trotted a few feet up the dike where Travis worked knee-deep in mud. "Hey Trav, can I talk to you?"

He dropped the muck-covered shovel. Mud-caked Wranglers clung to his legs and rivulets of dirt streaked his face.

"Sure. I could use a break." He looked down and grimaced, then pulled a bright red bandana from his back pocket and wiped his sweaty face. "What's up?"

"Another fence post was stolen last night."

His brows dipped in concern. "Okay. I'll send Ethan over to fix it."

"We're running out of fencing supplies." She pinched the bridge of her nose. "Who's doing this?"

"Probably the MP trying to intimidate us. Raul's been working on new posts."

"You don't think it's..." She gave him a pointed stare.

"No. It's not him, Lace. Don't worry." He stepped over and gave Acer's nose a rub. "It'll be okay."

She turned Acer toward the barn. "Thanks, Travis."

His reassurance touched her, and she gave him a half-hearted smile as she trotted away even though she didn't believe him. Stolen posts weren't a big deal. They had no cattle to confine and her horse stayed in the corral by the barn.

To her, it was stolen security. The idea someone was lurking in the shadows like a thief unsettled her, caused anxiety to sink its poisoned claws into her back. It ripped any sense of safety away from her, however false.

She headed across the pasture and wondered if her life would ever be okay again, if she would ever be able to move past what happened. Her thoughts turned to the unborn child she carried, an incessant reminder of that night she couldn't ignore. She had no clue what to do with an infant. Could she stand the sight of it, knowing it was a product of the most violent, devastating night of her life? She had serious doubts.

Castiel darted past, a low growl rumbling from his chest.

She urged Acer into a gallop and followed the dog toward the front of the property. "What now?"

A lone rider reined in by the front gate and waited. Her dog reached him first and circled the stranger, fangs bared. She trotted up the gravel drive and, as she neared the rider, her hand reflexively covered her heart. She stopped a few feet away.

The rider shielded his eyes from the intense midday sun. "Little Lacy Monroe," he drawled.

She recognized the voice and squinted to focus on him. "Jace," she acknowledged.

She needed to keep the conversation short. Why he showed up, she couldn't fathom. Unless her brother asked him to check on her, in which case, he was too little, too late. She clenched her teeth and shoved unwanted memories away. It took all her strength to fend off the memories of that night. It invaded her mind with a frequency that would frustrate a priest.

Her dog continued to circle the horse's hooves. He leaned forward, stroked the mare's mane, then raised up.

A disarming smile graced his lips and a dimple formed in his right cheek. "Heard your family moved west to California."

Unease tightened her shoulders and she shifted. The smile caught her off-guard, unsettled her. "That's right. Did AJ call you?" The question sounded more like an accusation.

He cocked his head. "Yeah. He said you stayed behind but didn't say why."

Lacy tamped the urge to mock his little head gesture.

"How did your family get out of state?"

She pursed her lips. "My mom was born there. She got a letter of passage."

She wrapped the reins around the saddle horn and folded her arms. He needed to leave before she lost her temper. She stared in silence, then noticed a smile tug his lips.

Fan-freakin-tastic. He's amused.

She let out a huff.

He cleared his throat to cover a laugh and broke the silence. "Heard your uncle gave you asylum. How'd he do that?"

A dust devil whipped around them, lifting the braids off her back. Her horse threw his head and snorted dirt. "That's kind of hard to explain. Texas and California are seceded states."

Would he never leave? What the blue moon could he want? He seemed oblivious to her silence, immune to her apathy. She didn't need another complication. And right now, he looked like a giant sledgehammer waiting to knock her senseless.

"Free states?"

She shrugged. "I guess."

"What does the Monroe farm have to do with that?" he asked, confused. "It's not in Texas or California. It doesn't make sense."

"No, it doesn't."

Had her uncle given her the entire picture?

"Uncle Tommy placed the farm in a Texas land trust, so it's considered free. It's confusing." She paused. When he didn't speak, she asked, "So, Jace. What do you want?"

"Asylum."

She narrowed her eyes. "Why? Your family has money and enough clout with the government to be left alone."

He looked away. "My parents are dead."

"Oh." More death. She didn't know if she could stomach anymore grief. Too much surrounded her already. "I'm sorry. I hadn't heard."

"My older brother seized all property, assets. Everything. Not that they're worth anything now."

Castiel looked at him and growled, ears flattened, hair raised along his back.

"Better watch your step, Cooper. My dog doesn't like you."

He eyed the large animal, eyes wide. "Will he bite?"

"Castiel, *pass auf.*"

The dog moved into guard position, teeth bared, eyes locked on his prey.

"Impressive. Did you train him to do that?"

"A friend of mine did."

His eyes narrowed. "Travis?"

"No," she snorted. "How did you know he was here?"

He ignored her and asked another question. "What language were you speaking to him?"

"German."

His eyebrows rose. "I didn't know you knew how to speak German."

"I don't."

His mouth curved down and an uncomfortable silence fell between them. "How did you train him then?"

Irritated, she explained how she met Catrin. "Cat is German and can speak the language, so she offered to train him."

He continued to pepper questions at her. "Are you and Travis close?"

"What's with the Great Inquisition?" she snapped.

His questions gave her a headache.

He held up his hands. "I'm sorry. I just need somewhere to stay. Will you help me?"

She let out a huge sigh. "Follow me. You can stable your horse with mine."

He hesitated, eyes trained on the dog.

Her anxiety settled somewhat. The dog would keep him distanced from her. "Castiel, *fuss*."

The dog snarled then followed her to the barn.

Straw and manure's pungent odor greeted her as she opened the barn doors. She removed Acer's tack then stabled him. "You can stable your horse in the empty stall or set her to pasture. Your choice."

She hung the equipment in the tack room then returned with feed and a brush. His scrutiny as he watched her work irritated her.

She whirled around to face him. "Why are you here Jace? The truth."

He rocked back on his heels, cocked his head in consideration, then said, "You."

"Me?" She stilled. Her stomach fluttered in response to the intensity in his deep blue eyes and it made her…uneasy. "Did AJ put you up to this?"

"No, he didn't. I came because—" He met her gaze with a soft smile. "Little Lacy's all grown up, long black hair and deep green eyes."

Her muscles locked. Why would he say something like that? "Stay away from me, Cooper."

He arched a brow. "Why?"

Unwilling to give an answer, she turned to her horse and continued brushing. Tears burned the back of her eyelids, but she refused to give in to them. She sniffed and wiped her nose on her sleeve. She hated being afraid all the time. Her hands shook as she brushed out Acer's mane.

His feet shuffled forward, then faltered. "No answer?"

Her mind swirled. What did he want from her? "Just keep your distance, okay?"

"Don't know if I can do that," he said evenly.

The brushed dropped from her shaking hand. "Castiel!"

The dog bounded inside, snarling. She grabbed his collar and fumbled for her knife.

"Whoa. Wait a sec." He held up his hands. "Lacy, you know me. I'm AJ's best friend. I'm not going to *hurt* you."

"Look, I don't know why you're here for me, but I've got my own people here." Her voice tremored. "Steer clear of me. I mean it. I don't care if you were my brother's best friend. He's not here and I've got no reason to—" Trust you, she finished in silence.

The look he gave her pulled her up short. What was it? A look of pity? Sadness? She didn't want or need his sympathy.

"You want to get to me? You gotta go through my dog first," she threatened.

"What's happened to you, Lace?"

She froze. The question and the way he used her nickname pushed memories forward. They flashed through her mind like a home movie. They'd played street ball, camped and fished at the lake, spent countless hours in the family room watching Netflix and eating buckets of popcorn.

Her gaze rested on his dark-brown hair that fell on his brow and curled against his neck. His face emanated Greek God arrogance, softened only by unique cobalt eyes that sparkled with mischief and humor.

He picked up the brush, finished brushing Acer, then moved to his own mount and did the same. She watched him move with confidence as he brushed his horse, murmuring soft words with each wide stroke.

He looked up, caught her staring, and winked. Her lips parted and she blinked, sure her eyes were playing tricks on her. He did *not* just wink at her. Her stressed, PTSD brain had cracked, because he'd never flirted with her. Ever. She'd always been labeled AJ's little sister, tucked away in the friend zone.

He cleaned the brush and returned it to the tack room. He took his time and Lacy fidgeted with her braids. His presence made her nervous, edgy. She wasn't the girl he remembered. Never would be again.

"You can't stay here," she blurted when he walked back. "I changed my mind."

His eyebrows shot up. "Why?"

"Because." She blew out a frustrated breath. "Just because, that's why."

His sudden, vulnerable look made her tired. She scanned the rafters and wished an epiphany would drop on her head. She rolled her eyes at the thought. If anything dropped on her head, it would give her a concussion.

"I have nowhere else to go. Zach has taken everything. He thinks I—" He stopped short. Their eyes locked. Her stomach fluttered again; and she pressed a hand against it. What was wrong with her?

"For the love of God." The power his unique blue eyes held over her made her antsy. Strange. They never had that effect on her before. "Raul, Travis, and Dylan are sleeping in the loft. That'll have to do."

"Why isn't everyone bunking together in the two houses?"

She cast a cold smile. "What's the matter? Rich boy too good for a barn?"

He raked a hand through his hair. "No, that's not what I meant. I just thought—"

She cut him off. "Ethan, Hailey, and Matty are staying at the bigger farmhouse and Hailey is being one big pain in the ass. Cat and I are in the smaller house at the front. And I don't want to share a small shotgun shanty with a bunch of stinky guys."

He opened his mouth, but she held out a hand. "Stay away from me or I'll have Travis string you up and haul you out. I mean it."

Arrogance shot through his eyes and he crossed his arms. "He's welcome to try."

Soft laughter drifted behind her as she stalked out the door.

JACE LOOKED around the empty barn, a little lost. Where the hell was he supposed to sleep? He wandered the stalls then made his way up the loft's ladder. Jeans and plaid button-down work shirts hung on rusty nails tacked to the walls. Sunlight streamed through gaps in the tin roof, highlighting dancing dust motes. He dropped his backpack, scrubbed his face, then scowled, remembering Lacy's biting words. "Rich boy too good for a barn?"

He kicked a hay mound and wondered if he tripped into an alternate dimension. What the hell was the matter with her?

Mistrust had rolled off her in tangible waves. Her behavior made no sense. He wasn't a stranger for God's sake.

The barn door opened before he could finish the thought. He leaned over the railing and watched an older woman march in, hands on her hips. Her chestnut hair rested in a loose top knot and her tattered, blue dress had seen too many washings.

She peered up and smiled. "There you are. Come down and let me look at you."

Nonplussed, Jace climbed down. It occurred to him everyone probably obeyed this strange lady's commands.

As soon as his feet touched the ground, she stuck out her hand. "I'm Cat Wirtz."

He flashed a dimpled grin. "Jace Cooper."

One eyebrow arched over quicksilver grey eyes. "Ah, I see now."

He looked around. "See what?"

"Why Lacy's in a bad mood." Before he could respond, she continued. "You sure are handsome. Yep, easy on the eyes. That's what my Ben would say."

A laugh bubbled from his chest. He didn't know what to say. No one had ever accused him of being easy on the eyes, but the idea Lacy might think so intrigued him.

"Is Ben your husband?"

"Yes. The Military Police took him. He sacrificed himself so I could run." She swiped a stray tear and said, "Supper will be ready in about an hour. That should give you time to settle in here."

He reached out, placed a hand on her shoulder. "I'm sorry about your husband."

"Me too," she said softly and closed the barn door.

She reminded him of his mom. He missed her more and more every day. He clamped down the raw emotion clawing his throat. His life had changed, and his equilibrium struggled to keep balance. In a nanosecond, he went from wealthy rancher's son to sleeping in a barn loft. The thought depressed him.

He climbed back up, surveyed the loft area, and reality sank in. This was home. He scooped hay and formed a large mound against the wall and spread a horse blanket over it. He placed his backpack by the makeshift bed and laid down, testing it. Not bad. He threw an arm over his eyes, relaxed his body and his mind drifted.

"I do not mean to bother you, but…"

He jerked, then stumbled to his feet. Large brown hands steadied him. "Sorry," he mumbled. "Must have fallen asleep."

The man's brown eyes twinkled. "No problem. The boss' boss sent me to get you. It's time for supper."

His brows rose to his hairline. "The boss' boss?"

The man's face split into a wide grin. "Lacy is the boss, but Cat is her boss."

"I see."

"I am Raul by the way. I sleep here too." He gave Jace's back a good-natured slap and nodded to the door. "We better go."

Questions swirled about the stranger as they walked the short distance to Lacy's house. "So," Jace began. "Haven't seen you around here."

"No."

"Where you from?"

Raul's face hardened. "Nowhere of importance."

An argument on the front porch halted any other questions. Unaffected by the spat, Raul opened the screen door and walked around Lacy. Jace hesitated as her heated gaze turned on him.

Travis shot him a scathing look. "What's *he* doing here?"

She shrugged. "Cat invited him to supper. He's got to eat somewhere."

"No. What I mean is, why is he here? We've got enough to deal with. We don't need another mouth to feed."

She flung her hands up. "What was I supposed to do? He needed a place to stay. Besides, we'll work him hard enough."

"Yeah, right," Travis snorted. "Bet he never worked a day in his life."

Jace took a step forward. "Watch it." He saw Travis flex his right hand into a fist and flashed him a smug smile.

Travis swung on his heel then stopped. "This is a bad idea."

She followed Travis inside and he caught the words she mumbled under her breath. "Don't I know it."

9

The sun beat without mercy on Jace's head as he built new fence that stretched around the pond's east end. He couldn't understand why Lacy bothered. Seemed like a waste of time. He stopped, pulled off leather gloves and flexed his cramped fingers. Sweat poured from every pore on his body. He lifted his T-shirt and mopped his face. The heat had turned him into a human boiler.

The two-ton come-along cinched the top wire to the post. He dug cutters from his back pocket and snipped several lengths of straight wire. Sweat ran down his forehead and stung his eyes. Dropping the cutters, he pulled his sleeveless white T-shirt over his head and scrubbed his face and neck then tucked it into the back of his jeans.

His eyes searched the pasture and he spotted Lacy riding the property line. He wanted to help her, get close to her, but she avoided him. It was a Typhoid Mary kind of avoidance and it bugged the crap out of him. He hated to admit it, but it stung his pride. Women naturally gravitated his way, but not this one. She seemed immune to his charm.

He continued watching her and his heart flipped over. She was a sheer pleasure to look at. Her raven hair flowed long and loose with a slight wave. Her crystalline eyes, green as the grass by Salt Creek, held depth. She owned his heart, lock, stock, and barrel. Not that she took the time to notice. He sighed, ducked his head, and continued his work.

He looped a large piece of straight wire around the post and crimped it tight. The new posts looked good. Raul sacrificed long hours to complete them.

He'd been at the farm two weeks and Lacy made sure he worked every day. The physical labor chiseled his torso into fine form. Hard muscle formed over his chest and stomach. His arms' diameter increased, and he was pleased with the results. His father had made him work, but not like this. Their ranch hands had handled the grunt work.

He pounded the next post with extra force at the thought of his parents. He missed them, still grieved their death.

He looked down and growled. The post splintered down the middle.

"Damn it." Raul would rag doll his ass over that.

"Problems?"

Preoccupied, he'd lost sight of Lacy and she'd ridden up behind him. He looked at her and couldn't stop the grin from spreading across his face.

"Yeah, Raul's not going to be happy over that ruined post."

Her lips pulled into a secretive smile. "He's pretty picky."

He worked to bridle the instant irritation that rose and flushed the base of his neck. The implication she made was impossible to miss. Aggravated, he tugged the post out. "Like him much?"

Her eyes sparked. "Raul is incredibly smart."

"I'll bet." He picked up another post and thrust it into the empty posthole. "Is he even legal?"

Lacy snorted. "Of course he's legal. Racist much?"

"He could be deported anyway. The state's hauling all Mexicans back to Mexico. Even the ones born here."

He pulled the T-shirt from his jeans and scrubbed his face.

He looked up and caught her staring at his chest. He cocked a brow and watched a blush sweep her face. She averted her eyes, and his heart did a little dance. Not immune, he thought with satisfaction.

"That's a rumor. Besides, I can't lose Raul. He's the biggest asset I have."

"Using him for his mind?" he snapped, tossing the post digger to the next mark.

She smirked. "Sure am."

He walked to her and their eyes locked. She'd baited him on purpose. He'd never dealt with jealousy but recognized the emotion. Lacy with anyone else made him want to sucker punch the Pope.

He drew a deep breath. "So, just what is he to you?"

"He has an enormous knowledge base," she bragged. "He knows how to get things done."

"Well, I'm sorry you think he's your only asset."

She shifted. The barb stuck.

"Come on, I didn't mean it that way."

"Yeah, you did." He glanced away, realizing how little she knew him and what she had known, she'd forgotten. She needed to know him again, but somehow, he felt earning her trust would be difficult.

She sighed. "No, I didn't."

He took a step closer. "Just what did you mean, then?"

Before she could object, he reached up and grabbed her waist. He pulled her from the horse and drew her close. And knew exactly when her mouth caught up with her brain. He cut her protests by tipping her chin. "Forget it," he drawled.

She pushed him away, then mounted the impatient gelding. "Touch me again, Cooper, and you'll be eating your balls for breakfast."

He cocked his head and grinned.

She galloped away and left him standing in her dust. Well good, he thought and shoved his hands in his pockets. He watched until she disappeared. He had her off-kilter, which meant he was getting under her skin.

WHY DID he have that effect on her? And why, oh, why did she provoke him that way?

She urged Acer into a gallop, but the speed didn't relieve her anxiety. The wind whipped her face, scorched her cheeks, but not even the burn distracted her.

Sweet baby Jesus in a bar, the man pushed her buttons. He left her conflicted and angry. She didn't trust him, yet her heart dropped to her stomach like a meteor anytime she saw him. She chalked part of it up to fear. Men made her skin crawl, but she couldn't deny her physical attraction to him. She wasn't dead. Man, oh man, the boy was ripped.

Right now, stabbing her eyes out with an icepick seemed the only cure to erase the memory of the wolf-dragon tattoo on his back. She shook her head as she imagined many sleepless nights over that tattoo.

Confusion continued its tornadic swirl in her brain. He acted jealous over Raul. Why? It made no sense. He never paid her any attention before. In all the years she'd known him, never once had he acted interested in her. He couldn't be attracted to her.

She pulled up, dismounted, and handed the weather-cracked reins to Matty. Acer whinnied a greeting and shook his mane. Dust flew in his face and he sneezed. He grabbed the reins, gave a little tug, and led the horse toward the barn.

"Hey, stable boy," she said in the most cheerful voice she could muster.

The thirteen-year-old straightened. "I'm not a boy," he grumbled.

His bright yellow hair stood straight up, like he'd stuck his finger in an electrical socket. His buoyant personality reflected the same sentiment, but not today. An uncharacteristic frown covered his face.

She ruffled his hair. "Hey, I was kidding. I know you work hard."

He nodded without comment and moved Acer into his stall.

She followed, grabbed an old three-legged stool, and watched him give the horse a good rubdown. "What's eating you, kid?"

He shrugged and kept his nut-brown eyes focused on his work. "Ethan says I'm not supposed to complain."

She rocked the stool back, leaned against the wall, and chewed a piece of straw. "Well, I'm asking. You won't get in trouble with your brother. I promise."

He looked up and his chin quivered. "I can't stand living with Hailey. I hate living with her. She's mean. And I miss my mom."

She sighed and leaned forward, opting for diplomacy, but her mind screamed obscenities at the selfish girl. The stool's legs thudded on the compacted dirt floor. She had two options. One, she could do nothing. Meddling in family matters came at a cost. Or she could suggest he move into the barn with the guys. Neither option suited her.

"Well," she said, getting up. "I'll see what I can do. In the meantime, keep your chin up, and be as respectful as possible while ignoring her for the most part."

A smile tugged the corners of his mouth. "Yes, ma'am."

She gave him a conspiratorial grin and slapped dust from her jeans. "If anyone asks, I'll deny I ever said to ignore her. Yup, pleading the Fifth on that one, so keep your mouth shut."

He gave a snappy salute. "Yes, ma'am."

"For the love of God, kid. Stop calling me that. Call Cat ma'am, but not me. Got it? My name is Lacy so nix the ma'am crap." She shook a playful fist at him then turned and headed for the wash house.

She entered the dilapidated shed, let the old screen door

slam behind her. She covered her nose. The strong scent of must and mice droppings filled the air.

Two of her grandmother's wooden hand-cranked washers stood on the far south wall. Shelving painted a nauseous pea-green color covered the north wall, and she scanned them for items to make soap. A *Make Your Own Soap* book laid on top of an unopened lard bucket that hadn't seen daylight in decades. She pulled them off the shelf along with a lye bottle she hoped wouldn't blow up and deposited them on the concrete walk outside. Then she dragged out a scale, an old wooden table, and a pair of faded yellow gloves. She cringed as she stretched the crusty things over her hands.

She followed the directions and measured lye into a glass jar. She tried to concentrate but her mind kept straying to Jace, their little argument, and his tattoo. If lye fumes burned her eyes out, it still wouldn't erase the image of the intriguing wolf-dragon.

She picked up the lard and took it into the kitchen to heat. Making soap wasn't complicated, just time consuming, and she heaved a relieved sigh after pouring the completed mixture into plastic molds. She threw away the disgusting gloves, glad the soap could cure.

She came back out, a frown creasing her forehead and discovered Cat waiting for her. "Why did my grandmother have all this stuff? She never made soap in her life."

"Why are you so grouchy?"

"Don't ask."

Cat laid a sympathetic hand on her arm and chuckled. "That cute guy bothering you?"

She crossed her arms. "Why do you say that?"

"I have eyes. I see things you refuse to see. You'll have him and Travis fighting over you." She held up a hand to silence her denials. "Come and eat. You need your strength."

"I'm not hungry. This smell is getting to me."

"I'm sorry. I should've made the soap myself. I wasn't thinking."

She placed a hand over her abdomen. "You know, sometimes I can almost make it through the day without remembering I'm pregnant. Anyway, Hailey should've done it. It was her turn to do something."

"You've got to show more patience," Cat admonished. "Hailey is still getting her feet underneath her. She had quite a scare when the MP raided Shidler."

She rolled her eyes. "We all had a scare. Don't lecture me about hardships. Travis and I knew her from school. She's spoiled."

Cat raised her brows in disapproval.

"Well hell, just look at her," she huffed. "The woman hasn't lifted a finger since she got here."

"Time will tell. Now about supper. Travis caught a rabbit." She grimaced. "I did the best I could with it."

She smirked. "Well, at least it's not another pigeon."

Cat shivered in mock horror. "Dear God, what was that boy thinking?"

She turned and watched the sun dip behind the craggy terrain. "I do understand, Cat, and it terrifies me. Please keep Jace away from me."

Cat patted her shoulder. "Not all men are monsters."

Her chin quivered. She had serious doubts about that.

They walked into the house, each lost in their own thoughts. Cat didn't push her to eat and she was glad. Stress and lye fumes didn't mix. Her stomach pitched from the simmering rabbit stew. She plugged her nose, raced to the bathroom, and dry heaved. She got up, ran cold water on a washcloth, and wiped her forehead, then rinsed her mouth.

She swayed down the hall to her bedroom. Sweat formed on her upper lip and black spots blurred her vision. She leaned against the wall until the dizziness passed, then pulled a pair of knit shorts and a camisole from her dresser. Dead tired, she dropped onto the patchwork quilt.

Cat came and kissed her cheek. "Sweet sleep."

She gave a weak smile and rolled over. Under the window, Castiel turned three times and flopped down with a huge sigh. She fell into a fitful sleep, a wolf-dragon tattoo the last image she saw before darkness fell over her.

The nightmares started the same. She struggled to keep the knife in her grasp, but it slipped, dropping into inky darkness. The man killed her protector. Castiel was gone. She could hear the man, his harsh breath, his boots clicking on the wood floor. He moved closer and she froze. No more running. It ended here. His hands reached down and pulled her hair. "No, no, no!"

She jolted upright. Covered in sweat, her body quaked with fear and anger. She kicked the twisted comforter to the floor.

"Castiel," she called softly. The dog pawed her arm and whined. "Thank God."

She patted the bed. He jumped up and laid his head on her feet. She lay against her pillow wide awake, thinking about the man who raped and threatened her life. On impulse, she jumped up, got dressed, and grabbed her daddy's shotgun.

LACY CROUCHED behind the slim oak tree and cursed. A hoot owl screeched high above her.

"Whoa," she gasped. She exhaled and steadied her jittery nerves.

The moon, full and brilliant, cast enough light to check the shells in the twelve gauge. She clicked the safety off. The wraith who haunted her dreams sat at his desk, unaware. The stalker had become the stalked. The hunted had become the hunter. Unbelievable power shot through her system, swift and heady.

In a quick predatory move, she raised the gun and took aim. The laser's red dot marked his left temple. She had a clear shot. Beads of sweat formed on her forehead and trickled into her eyes. Or were they tears?

"Just shoot the bastard," she muttered.

She lowered the weapon, swiped at the tears, and aimed again. Her heart thundered as she concentrated on her prey.

Her attacker rose and closed the window. She watched as he sat back down. His arm grazed a stack of papers and they fluttered to the floor. He bent to retrieve them, and when he righted himself, she had the laser back on target. Yet something inside her wavered.

She gritted her teeth. "Don't be a coward."

And then, an image formed, took shape in her mind, and she lowered the weapon. There was no way she could bring herself to kill him.

10

L acy rose early the next morning, bleary-eyed and feeling the inexplicable need to shout at someone. The last time she felt this jittery, a high school classmate dared her to drink four tall-boy Monsters. Not a good day.

Her hands fisted and she swallowed a scream. Her rapist sitting at his desk, unscathed and unpunished, made her sick.

She turned to the full-length mirror, braided her hair, then rummaged in her dresser.

"Ugh," she groaned. "Cat! Where's my T-shirt!"

Cat appeared, lips pressed firmly together. "Why are you yelling?"

"Have you seen my black Hurley shirt?"

"It's still in the dirty laundry basket." Cat held a hand up. "I know what you're going to say, and I will go down and ask Hailey again if she'll do the laundry."

She scowled, grabbed another shirt, and slipped it over her head. "Fine. Just see that she does it. Because if I have to talk to her, it won't be pretty."

Cat placed a hand on her shoulder. "Where are you going? You need to eat something."

"I'm going to the barn." She kissed her cheek and stepped around her. "I'll eat later."

A soft southern wind cooled her face and soothed her nerves as she walked the gravel drive. The barn doors creaked open and sent madcap mice scurrying in the hay.

She climbed the roof to make some minor repairs. The sunrise, streaked a brilliant pink and orange, saturated the sky. She exhaled, steadied herself, and pushed away the night.

Travis had hauled tin sheets up the day before. After they argued about it. He didn't think she should exert herself in her condition. She scowled. He called her a stubborn mule and stomped away. Her dad always called childish displays that involved stomping feet "the stiff-legged stomp."

She grabbed the tool belt beside the stacked tin sheets and looped it around her waist. Her jean shorts sagged in pitiful defiance. She'd lost an unhealthy amount of weight. Her mind circled to what Travis called 'her condition' and the unwanted baby. She couldn't accept it, was in full-blown denial. But the baby would come despite her feelings about it. Then what? The thought nagged her subconscious like an irritating rash.

She turned her attention to the roof. Rust holes dappled the tin in a swirl of connect-the-dot patterns. She picked up a tin sheet, nailed it over a rusty hole and repeated the process until the roof resembled a rusty orange and silver patchwork quilt.

She gathered scattered nails then stood and scanned the horizon. The day promised heat. It had to be eighty degrees already. Lost in thought, she didn't hear Jace pull himself onto the roof.

"What are you doing up here?" he asked, his morning voice raspy and low.

Startled, she yelped, lost her footing, and stumbled backward. "Jesus H. Christ," she gasped, righting herself.

"Easy, love. I didn't mean to scare you, but I about lost it when I saw you up here."

His concern needled her. "Go away, Jace. I can take care of myself."

"Oh yeah?" His lips tugged into a smile.

"I fixed the roof."

"Why?"

"Why?" she sputtered. "It needed to be fixed, that's why."

He cocked a brow. "Why didn't you ask me to fix the roof?"

Was he mocking her or just trying to annoy her?

"It never crossed my mind."

"What am I gonna have to do to cross your mind?" he asked then reached over and folded her hand in his.

A tingling sensation rippled up her arm. Confused, she jerked away. "What are you doing?"

"Come on," he said and motioned to the rope ladder. "Let's talk."

Uneasiness settled on her shoulders as she followed him into the loft. "Talk about what?"

He closed the distance between them, and her chest tightened. Why had she followed him?

He stopped inches from her, and her heart beat double time. She stood rooted to the spot. His eyes smoldered and for a moment she thought he would kiss her. Instead, he rocked back on his heels and placed both hands in his back pockets.

Locked in his gaze, the rolling sensations puzzled her. She never dreamed she'd feel anything for a man except fear. She shuffled back until she felt the barn wall's rough wood behind her.

His jaw hardened. "You're afraid of me. Why?"

"I'm not," she breathed out, forcing herself to look at him.

"Yeah, you are. I told you the truth about why I'm here. What you've done with this place is amazing. I'd like to help, but you won't let me near you, and I don't understand why."

"Why do you care so much?" she whispered. "Why? You've never been interested in me before."

He squinted his eyes. "You sure about that?"

She blinked, dumbfounded.

"Think back to when things were different. No military threats, no food shortage, no FEMA takeover. Think back." He paused and gave her a wink. "You'll find me there."

She watched him leave with mixed emotions. Confusion, longing, fear all tumbled through her like clothes in an over-loaded dryer. What in the blue moon just happened? She dropped into the hay, laid her head back, and closed her eyes. What did he mean *think back?* She racked her brain for clues. A family camping trip flashed through her memory. What was it about that trip to Falls Creek? She drew a deep breath and concentrated.

Her family had driven to the Arbuckle Mountains over fall break her freshman year to camp and Jace had tagged along. She remembered the tree's vibrant red and pale gold leaves and the Kay Starr Trail. It had been her favorite place to explore and watch wildlife. AJ and Jace had gone fishing. She'd seen them coming up the trail, their poles slung in a careless manner over their shoulders.

They rounded a corner and Jace waved. "Hey, you. Where you going?"

"I was just headed down to the river to look for arrowheads."

AJ shook his head. "No, you're not. The river's flowing too fast."

She hadn't argued but hadn't listened either. Continuing down the trail, she veered left at a small clearing. The descent to the riverbank was steeper than she'd anticipated. Large, jutting rocks littered the embankment. A stone had become dislodged under her tennis shoe and to her shock, she'd fallen. Her head slammed into a large rock at the river's edge. The current had grabbed her body and dragged her down into the violent undertow. She'd fought her way to the surface but couldn't reach the bank. A large boulder jutted out of the water and she'd grabbed it, frightened out of her mind.

Before she could scream for help, she'd heard Jace's soothing voice. "Hold on, Lacy. Don't move."

He waded in, the violent current flowing between his legs. He stumbled forward, then planted his feet against the undertow and stretched out his hands.

"You're going to have to let go and grab my hand."

She squeezed her eyes shut. "I can't."

"Lace."

She opened her eyes and searched his face.

"Let go of the rock, love. I've got you. I won't let you fall."

As soon as she let go, his strong hands grabbed hers and hauled her into the safety of his arms. She'd clung to his neck and sobbed.

"I've got you," he'd whispered over and over as he carried her up the trail.

She opened her eyes, the memory faded.

How ironic. One man saved her, another ruined her. What was she supposed to do? Fear and intrigue played tug-of-war with her heart. She had to admit, Jace's interest fascinated her. It also scared the crap out of her. She had no idea if she could hurdle the obstacles blocking her heart.

The barn door crashed open. "Ethan!"

Lacy rolled over and buried her face in her arms. "God, not now."

Hailey Webb's strident voice made her want to stuff acid-laced cotton balls in her ears.

"Ethan!"

"He's not here," she called down. She rose, brushed hay from her jeans, and descended the ladder.

"Well, I need him. That stupid toilet is clogged again, and I need him to fix it. I just can't live like this."

Her blood pressure skyrocketed. "No one's making you

stay here. Why don't you go back to town and take your chances there?"

Hailey flipped long, blonde hair over her slender shoulder. "You don't have to get nasty with me, Lacy."

"Apparently I do. I don't have time to baby you. This is a working farm. Everyone's got to do their job, or this place you hate"—she waved her hands in the air—"doesn't work. There's a plunger next to the toilet in your bathroom. Use it."

She sniffed. "I don't plunge toilets."

Lacy took a step forward, eyes narrowed. "Then maybe you can do the laundry on Wednesdays and gather the eggs every morning like Cat's been asking you." She stalked to the barn door. "If you don't, I'll take you to town myself."

"You can't threaten me, Lacy Monroe."

"I can actually," she threw over her shoulder. "My farm. My rules."

As she walked through the barn door, the loud rumble of military vehicles sliced through the air.

Hailey rushed out. "They're coming!"

She caught Hailey's arm and jerked her to a stop. "Calm down."

"What are we going to do? They'll take all of us!"

She worked to temper her voice. "Look, I know you're scared, but screaming at the top of your lungs isn't going to help. Go hide in the barn cellar. Raul will be down shortly."

Panic-stricken tears streamed down her pale face. Her hands trembled as she wiped her cheeks and nodded her head. "Okay."

She gave her a little push toward the barn, then swung around and jogged up the drive.

Cat walked off the front porch to join her. "What do you think they want?"

She studied the military vehicles moving their direction. Trepidation filled her voice. "I have no idea, but I think we're about to find out."

11

Jace twisted his favorite baseball cap around to shield his neck from the blistering sun. Repairing fence sucked. A hornet-filled elevator would be more pleasant than the job he was doing now. He leaned against the pillar of sandstone rocks that made up the anchor post, grabbed the water bottle sitting on its edge, and took a long drink. Fall could not come soon enough. They'd suffered too many days in triple-digit heat. Even the grasshoppers, unchecked by yearly pesticide, had no spring in their hop. Everything seemed to melt in the overbearing heat like the Wicked Witch of the West.

He chucked the empty bottle toward his tethered horse, pulled on his leather gloves, and began rolling up old, rusted barbed wire along the fence line. He looped it over a fencepost and looked at the come-along strung taut between two snapped wires. The break looked deliberate, as if someone took cutters and snipped it. But why would someone cut the fence?

There wasn't a length of barbed wire long enough to cover the distance, so he cut a shorter length then cranked the come-along. He looped the cut length between the broken ends, twisting it to secure the break. The fix would hold for a while, but they'd have to abandon the fence sooner or later.

His horse tossed her head and whinnied. Nearby, crows lifted from the browning grass, cawing a warning. He turned his head at the low rumble of military vehicles. Fumes, sharp and gritty, billowed over the hill.

A knot formed in his gut. Why would the MP come here? His mind darted to his brother. Could he have sent them? Zach wielded enough power to commandeer the MP and have him thrown in a military prison. Cursing, he swung himself into his saddle and galloped to the front gate.

He tugged the reins and watched Bryan Rash strut up the drive. An impressive line of green, armored vehicles blocked the gate. His face settled in a grim line. Bryan Rash, a high school classmate, was a reputed hot head. Built like an NFL linebacker, he always exercised brute force to back up his mouth.

Lacy and Cat marched down the steps. Shoulders squared, Lacy held herself with dignified defiance. A grin settled on his face. Watching her reminded him of a Miniature Pincer his grandmother once owned. The dog fought with the attitude of a Doberman.

He dismounted, threw the reins over the saddle, and stood behind them.

"Lacy," Bryan greeted stiffly.

"Rash."

Bryan removed his sunglasses and looked around. "You've really cleaned up the place."

"Yeah. I'm sure we'll get yard of the month. What do you want?"

"I have orders to seize any property of value in your uncle's building."

Lacy fisted her hand, then released it. "Does my uncle know about this?"

"He doesn't have to. You may be able to live here. For

now," he emphasized. "But all property can still be seized under FEMA."

"That's a load of BS, but it doesn't matter. I don't have a key."

Bryan puffed his chest and took an intimidating step forward. "You're telling me that no one's set foot in that building?"

"My uncle owns this property and everything on it, you moron, and he's in Texas."

Bryan turned to the officer next to him. "Get a bolt cutter, Private."

"Yes, sir," the man saluted and strode to the nearest vehicle.

Jace sidled up beside Lacy, grasped her hand, and gave it a reassuring squeeze. A zip like an electric shock passed between them. She inhaled sharply but didn't pull away.

"Well, well." Bryan turned his attention to Jace. "I heard this is where the traitor landed."

Zach must've sent them. The Government had no use for old machinery, or anything else in the dilapidated building. It was an excuse, and a flimsy one at that. They wanted him.

"I didn't betray anyone, Bryan."

The private returned. "Sir?"

"Where are the cutters?" Bryan snapped.

"We don't have any with us, sir."

Jace raised an eyebrow. "I thought you were trained to be prepared."

Bryan's face mottled red. "I'll be back. For the contents in that building. And you."

"Get out of here!" Cat stepped up before Lacy could react. "All of you. Go."

She turned, wrapped protective arms around Lacy's shoulders, and whispered something in her ear.

She answered with a diminutive head shake. She glanced at him and in that split second, he saw her torn look—the raw, naked emotion of someone broken—before she shuttered it.

Bryan signaled to leave then turned to Lacy. "I'll be back."

"Yeah, okay, Terminator."

He narrowed his eyes. "Careful. You have no idea who you're dealing with."

Cat spun Lacy around and led her to the house before she could jab more insults. The girl had a sharp tongue and knew how to use it. Her wordy punches hit as hard as a mean right hook.

On impulse, Jace followed. "Wait a sec."

Lacy stopped on the porch and gave him a quizzical look.

Cat squeezed her shoulder. "I'll be in the house if you need me."

He bounded up the steps into the screened-in front porch. Lacy seated herself on the old wooden swing and pushed back and forth with her toes.

He sat down beside her. "You alright?"

She shifted away but smiled. "Yeah, I'm okay."

He wanted to touch her, to feel the strong electric current pass between them again. He sensed her struggle, could see it in her eyes. Something changed her and it troubled him.

"Why are you staring at me?"

He cocked his head. "You really wanna know?"

"Maybe not."

Chuckling, he changed the subject. He wouldn't push too hard. Instinct told him she wasn't ready yet. "You have a key, don't you?"

Her shoulders lifted in a careless shrug. "Of course, I do."

"So, what's in the building?"

"My motorcycle, gasoline, kerosene, an ancient welding unit, fishing supplies, my grandpa's old Chevy Nova." She toyed with the swing's chain, fingering each loop.

He pushed the swing with his foot. "Bryan will make good on his threat. He'll be back. Do you have somewhere to hide the stuff you want to keep?"

"I have a few ideas, but it will take some time to move it all."

He twisted to face her. "What did Cat ask you after Bryan threatened you?"

He'd seen the tense exchange. Something was wrong. He sensed it.

"Nothing." She looked away and her jet-black hair fell in a silky curtain, hiding her face.

With a turn of her head, she shut him out. A rush of frustration pushed him to his feet. "I'm not buying it."

"You don't have to. It was nothing."

He reached down, tipped her chin, and pinned her with a hard stare. "Yeah, it was."

With slow, deliberate movements, she got up and planted her hands on his shoulders. Staring into his eyes, she broke into an impertinent grin and said, "Forget it."

How he could love her and want to strangle her at the same time was beyond his comprehension. "I'm going to find out."

Challenge lit her eyes. "What did Bryan mean when he called you a traitor?"

Well, damn. Her quick-witted tit-for-tat backed him in a corner. He couldn't answer her question, not yet anyway. He didn't want her to know Zach suspected him of murder. It hurt too much.

Her lips twitched. "Okay then. Good talk."

She turned and left him standing, mouth agape. He snapped it shut and stomped down the steps.

His vagrant horse wandered to graze in the yard. Green patches of Bermuda grass struggled to survive the heat. The horse pulled on the hopeful sprouting blades, doing its best to exterminate the lawn.

"Crazy woman," he muttered as he led his horse to the barn. "She's driving me nuts."

He shut the stall's half door, folded his arms, and leaned against it. Her aloof attitude baffled him. Never once had he considered she might not want him, never thought he'd have to chase her.

Raul laughed behind him. "It looks like you are the crazy one. Talking to a horse."

Jace swung around. "Where were you hiding?"

"In the root cellar."

"Why? You not legal?"

"Legal enough," Raul said, unruffled by the comment. "Lacy showed me where to hide if the MP ever showed. Look, I know you have a little thing for Lacy."

His jaw ticked. "It's not little."

Raul held up his hands and took two steps back. "Hey, it's fine by me. She's my boss. That's it."

"That's it, huh?"

Raul smirked. "*Si.* Sorry she's giving you such a hard time, though."

"Let me ask you something," he began.

Raul waved him off. "I can't answer your questions."

"Someone has to tell me what happened to her." Irritated, he kicked the stall door. His horse flipped her ears back and stomped a front hoof into the hay.

"It is not my place to tell."

"But something did happen," he pushed.

"Yes. But that is her story. Don't go around asking questions," he warned. "Ask her."

"She won't talk to me," he said fiercely.

"Don't rush her, she'll talk when she's ready." He paused and studied Jace. "You should know this by now."

"Sorry about the legal comment."

Raul grinned and he couldn't help returning the smile.

"It's okay, I get it."

He walked outside and stared at Lacy's house. How could he ever get her to trust him? And what had destroyed her ability to trust?

L acy drug a hand through her tangled morning hair and sat on the back porch steps. How many complaints would she listen to before the gods considered it enough?

Travis kicked a dirt clod off the concrete path. "We need to get those chickens out of the barn. They're dirty, not to mention they wake us up at the butt-crack of dawn."

She tapped her bare foot in tandem with her pounding brain. Frequent migraines added to her depression. Bryan Rash's visit bothered her. Something about it gnawed at her, had kept her awake the entire night.

"Lacy." Travis snapped his fingers. "Are you listening?"

She jumped, then shrugged her shoulders. "Sorry, Trav."

"Well?"

She studied his expectant face and for the life of her, couldn't remember what he was grousing about. She had the attention span of a gnat today.

"Well, what?" She crossed her arms around her midsection. Nausea twisted her gut into a tight knot. The morning sickness should've been over by now.

Travis' brows furrowed. "The chickens?"

She slumped over, cradled her head in her hands. "Good God, Travis. Build a coop. You don't need my permission for every little thing."

He let out a sigh and sat down beside her. "What's wrong?"

"Not a blessed thing." She rubbed two fingers along the bridge of her nose. "Rash flaunted his power yesterday. I don't care what my uncle says. The government can do whatever they want."

"True."

She turned to face him. "I'm worried. What if the man who attacked me sent them?"

He scooted closer and wrapped a supporting arm around her. "I don't know if he sent them or not, but you're not alone in this, Lace."

His arm across her shoulders held a familiar warmth. Years of friendship outweighed her fear of men. She gave him a side-long glance. As she studied him, an idea occurred to her. "Hey, would you do something for me?"

"That depends on what it is."

Her idea quickly took root. She stood and paced back and forth. "Teach me karate. Just some defensive moves."

"No. Don't ask me to do that."

"Why not?"

"Because the workouts are tough. It's not a sport you can just pick up and learn over a weekend."

His gaze shift to her belly. The baby. That's what was bothering him.

"Please, Travis." She hated to beg. "You're a black belt. Just teach me the basics."

He rose and shoved his hands in his pockets. "What about the baby?"

She gave him a helpless stare. "What about it?"

"I can't," he said scrubbing his hands over his face. "I'm sorry, but it's too dangerous and you need to be careful."

Tears welled and pooled at the bottom of her eyelids. "I

can't do this, Travis. It's too much. All of this. The farm. The rape. The pregnancy. Everyone here. It's too overwhelming. Please." She paused, feeling helpless. "Please, help me."

He cursed under his breath. "I'm sorry Lace. I care too much about you to risk your health."

He refused her. She backed away. A sob rose from her chest and she let it out in a short laugh. She flung her arms wide and said, "Welcome to my asylum." Tears raced down her cheeks. "Take from me what you will."

She turned her back on Travis and ran. She had to get away. She felt herself breaking apart and had no idea how to hold herself together.

TWILIGHT FELL over the farm like a thief. Jace guided his horse home, grateful to be finished with the day's work. He dismounted, unhooked the string of fish from his saddle horn, and reached for the barn door, but stopped short. Angry voices filtered through the door's wide crack. He pressed his ear against it, straining to catch a fragment of the conversation. Not hearing enough, he slipped inside.

"Jace needs to leave her alone," Travis shouted. "You know what she's been through."

He halted. Adrenaline shot through his system. He dropped the fish on a wooden bench, moved past the empty horse stalls, then stopped at the tack room.

"That's not your call," Raul said, his tone unflappable.

Jace flung the door open. It crashed against the wall, rattling tack hanging on crumbling pegboard. "You got a problem with me, Travis?"

Travis wheeled around, his hands balled into fists. "You need to leave Lacy alone, man. You're upsetting her."

"Why? Has she said something to you?"

Doubt crept into his chest like a nasty cold. Had he done

something to upset her? Despite his efforts to get closer, she remained distant, unreachable.

"That's not the point. You're no good for her and she's dealing with enough as it is."

"None of your business, brother," Raul reminded him.

Jace looked from Travis to Raul, who had remained cool throughout the tense exchange. Apparently, they knew more about what Lacy needed than he did.

He resisted the urge to bare his teeth. "Did she say something or not?"

"You have no idea what's happened here. What she's been through. What she's still going through." Travis pinned him with a heated glare. "She doesn't need you rutting around her back door."

Jace shoved him against the wall. Bridles, bits, and curry combs clanked against the rough wooden wall and fell. "That is *not* what I'm doing."

Raul stepped up and pushed them apart, using his body as a buffer. "That's enough."

Travis backed away, nostrils flared. "She can't handle all this drama."

"I'm not trying to start drama. I just—" He heard the loud creak of the barn door and halted.

The men stood silent as Lacy walked into the tack room, her horse's bridle slung over her shoulder. Tack littered the floor and tension hung thick in the air. She looked at the scattered tack then at the men. Her back stiffened and the fire burning in her eyes turned them a brilliant emerald.

"What's going on?" she demanded.

"Nothing," Travis said, then slapped Raul on the back. "Come on. Let's get a poker game going so I can beat you. Again."

Raul snorted. "I am just learning the game. Soon I will be beating you."

Travis moved toward the door. "Yeah right. Keep dreaming."

Lacy sidestepped and blocked him. "Not so fast. What happened here?"

Jace stepped up. "It's my fault."

She moved from the doorway. Travis and Raul made a quick exit, bantering back and forth about who would beat whom at Texas hold-em.

Jace walked toward her with slow, deliberate steps, studying her face. "I'm sorry."

Her gaze fell to the bridle dangling in her hands. She picked at a strand of frayed leather. "What was going on here? Were you fighting with Travis?"

"Honestly?" He slipped the bridle from her hands and hung it up.

She leaned against a wooden table. Scraps of old leather and tools scattered its surface. "Well, yeah."

His steady gaze fell on her face. He hated the weary tone in her voice, hated the thought he may be the cause of it.

He let out a heavy sigh. "You. We were fighting over you."

Her face contorted in disbelief. "Why?"

"Travis doesn't like me being here. He thinks I'm upsetting you." He searched her face. "Am I?"

She scooted onto the table and swung her legs back and forth. "I don't know. I don't understand this hang-up you suddenly have with me. It's complicating my already compli-cated life."

"It's not sudden. And it's not a hang-up." The intensity in his voice surprised him. He worked to level the emotions rising in his chest. The girl didn't get it. With patience he didn't know he possessed, he continued. "Your mom asked me to wait."

Her head jerked up, eyes widening. "My mom? What are you talking about?"

He took her hand and gave a tug. "Come with me."

"Where?"

He dropped her hand and stuffed his hands in his back pockets. "Lacy, do you want me to leave the farm?"

She fiddled with the ends of her braids. "No." She gave him a puzzled look. "I have no idea why, but no."

Before she could protest, he grabbed her by the waist and plucked her off the table. He set her down and stepped back, careful not to crowd her. "Let's take a walk."

"Look. I don't mean to be difficult, but today," she paused, and a bright sheen covered her eyes. "Today really sucked for me."

"Yeah," he sighed. "I'm getting that."

He reached out, took her hand, and laced their fingers together. The electricity he felt the day before zipped up his arm with enough force it almost knocked him to his knees. "Please, Lace."

He never begged for anything, never had to, but he needed this girl like he needed oxygen. He felt her arm relax. It wasn't much, but he'd take the gesture as a yes.

Outside, twilight had given way to a full moon. Quail called out, "Bob White," and the scurry of something nocturnal rustled through the tall Johnson grass. They walked toward the unfinished ponds and settled against a wide mimosa tree. The cicadas still buzzed above their heads and a cool breeze swept across the pasture, bringing with it the sweet scent of bluestem.

He broke the heavy silence. "Your mom's a smart lady."

She gazed at the moon and its ethereal light illuminated the green in her eyes, giving them a feline effect. "Oh yeah? How's that?"

"One day, we were out in the street playing basketball. You were a freshman that year and AJ was giving you pointers." She looked at him, and he smiled. "You were determined to make the starting lineup."

She released a short laugh. "Yeah. Didn't make it though."

"Hey, you were the sixth man. A great position for a freshman. And as I remember, the following year you got your starting position."

She stared in amazement. "You remember all that?"

"I was at all of your games," he said, and watched the shifting emotions cross her face.

"With AJ," she clarified.

"Not because of AJ," he corrected. "Although he doesn't know that."

She flipped a braid over her shoulder. "What does all this have to do with my mom?"

"She was watching us through the window that day and something I did caught her attention."

"What did you do?"

He chuckled. "You burned AJ with a move. After you'd made your bucket, I picked you up and swung you around in the air."

"But you did that—" She stopped and shook her head, confused.

"All the time," he finished. "Your mom talked to me that day. She said I was too old for you. She asked me to let you grow up. And if I still felt the same way after you graduated, then I could ask you out."

"Wow." She let out a short, nervous laugh.

He gave her hand a gentle squeeze. "Now you know. This isn't just a little hang-up."

She turned to look at him. "I don't know what to do with all this."

He caught her gaze. "I know." To ease the tension he said, "I miss hamburgers. Big juicy ones with pickles and ketchup."

"You're crazy."

"Come on. What do you miss? There's got to be something you'd do just about anything for."

When she didn't answer, he gave her shoulder a little nudge.

"A Coke. Some days I think I'd kill for a Coke." She gave

him a dubious look. "This is a stupid conversation. It doesn't do any good to wish for something you can't have."

"Ah, but now I know what you'd kill for," he said in a playful tone. "You know what else?"

"What?"

He crossed his arms behind his head. "I know Snickers is your favorite candy bar."

Her jaw dropped. "And how would you know that?"

A smile tugged his lips. "You always had empty wrappers all over your bedroom floor."

"Did you and AJ snoop in my room?"

"Of course not," he denied with a grin and laughed at her horrified expression.

She sobered. "I really don't understand this, Jace."

He picked up her hand, tangled his fingers with hers. "I'll wait. You're worth the wait, Lace."

The look on her face pierced his heart.

"You don't know what you're getting yourself into and that's not fair to you." She rose and shook off his hand.

"Talk to me, trust me," he implored. "Just spend time with me."

He didn't understand the heartbreak that stormed into her eyes. She shook her head, turned away, and left him sitting under the mimosa tree.

13

"Pain."

Lacy opened her eyes, her bedroom awash in pre-dawn light. She rose and tried to focus on the blurry object at her footboard. Was that a man?

He didn't speak, yet his voice rang crystal clear in her head. Electricity crackled the air and little hairs on her neck stood up.

"Look down, Lacy."

Bright red blood ran down her abdomen. Dark circles pooled around her thighs. She tried to scream, but he clamped her mouth shut with a simple magician's hand wave. His lips curled into a cruel smile.

"You can't escape me," he taunted. "I'm coming for you."

Lacy's eyes flew open and her body shot up, ramrod straight. Her heart thrashed against her chest. "It was a dream," she whispered. "It wasn't real."

But the dream felt real. A sharp spasm sliced through her belly, and she doubled over in pain. She jerked the covers back. No blood stained the sheets. But the pain remained.

She shuddered and laid back on her pillow until her heartrate returned to normal. She glanced at the shotgun propped in the corner. If it came down to it, if he came back for her, could she kill him? She didn't know. She sat up and grasped her head between her hands, rocking back and forth.

"Get a grip," she breathed. "Don't lose it."

Needing an escape, she got up, threw on her sleeveless button-down hanging on the bedpost, then grabbed her worn Silver work jeans off the floor. She smacked the jeans against her bare thighs to shake out the wrinkles. Shouldn't dump them on the floor if you're worried about wrinkles. Her mother's voice floated from her subconscious like a well-executed ambush, and her knees threatened to buckle as a wave of grief rolled over her. She sat on the white wooden chair in the corner, tugged on her boots, and swallowed down tears.

She walked the gravel drive to the barn, twisted her hair into one braid then dug in her back pocket for a rubber band. The rubber, stretched thin, didn't have much spring. Looking down, she twisted the band around the end of her braid and ran smack into something solid. Not quite solid, her brain corrected. Her rear-end hit the ground and she let out a sharp yelp.

Annoyed, she wiped her dusty hands on her shirt, then glanced up. Cobalt eyes looked down, sparking with curiosity. Her gaze traveled to his chest and her heart skipped. No shirt. Again.

"The gods hate me," she muttered under her breath. At this rate, her heart would give out by the day's end.

A barn swallow hopped beside her, a thick piece of straw clamped in its beak. Frustrated, she swatted at it. The startled bird dropped the straw, fluttered up, and perched on the open barn door.

Jace burst into laughter, then offered her a hand. "That was kinda mean."

"What the hell, Cooper?" She scowled at his outstretched hand. Another spasm stole her breath. Gasping, she fell back on her elbows.

He crouched down. "You okay? You're white as a sheet."

"That tends to happen to people who get their feet knocked out from under them."

She got up, rubbed her temples, certain the sudden ringing in her ears could wake the dead. What it couldn't do? Stop her from staring at Jace.

He moved with a cat's prowess, nimbly springing to his feet. Sweat trickled down a well-defined six pack and jeans sat low on narrow hips. His broad shoulders, tanned a deep brown, intimated strength. She swallowed hard and forced her eyes to his face, her throat suddenly dry as the Sahara.

He flashed a dimpled grin, and she felt her face flush. "Don't you own a shirt?"

He walked to the barn door. "Sure do," he said over his shoulder. He stopped and leaned against it, a smile covering his face.

She walked over, eyes narrowed. "Then wear it," she snapped.

His smile grew. "Yes ma'am." He flipped his worn blue Shidler Tiger's ball cap around his head.

"You're so conceited."

"You're the one staring."

God, the man was insufferable. She stalked around him into the barn, smacked the tack room door open, and dragged Acer's saddle to his stall. She stopped, caught her breath, and sensed him behind her.

Her reaction confused her, caught her off-guard, and tears built in her eyes. If she could get away, she could manage her emotions, steady herself again.

"You're annoying me, Jace," she said without turning around. "I've got stuff to do. So, shoo." She flicked her wrist in the air.

He placed a gentle hand on her shoulder and turned her around. His eyes searched hers in concern. "What's wrong?"

She lifted her eyes to the rafters. Barn swallows fussed over their nests. She watched a few wayward strands of hay float to the ground in lazy spirals. "Nothing I can't handle." She forced the lie out, clenching her teeth.

Without a word, he opened the stall door and moved Acer out. Any protests she might've had died as she watched him. She could see every corded muscle ripple as he saddled the horse. He buckled the bridle, then handed her the reins.

"Thank you."

She led Acer outside and threw the reins over the saddle horn. Jace stepped behind her and touched her arm before she got a foot into the stirrup.

"Spend time with me," he murmured against the back of her neck.

His soft words bathed her in warmth. She turned her head slightly. "I gotta go," she whispered.

She couldn't deal with this confusion. Every time they crossed paths, he chipped her defenses, and she couldn't afford to let him in.

He stepped around to face her. "Why are you running from me?"

"Damn it, Cooper. You don't know what you're getting yourself into."

He took her face between his hands, his face serious. "I don't care."

She bit the inside of her cheek. Uncertainty clouded her brain. He looked as if his whole world hinged on her. His soft words, spoken with conviction, started a fissure around her icy heart.

She shook her head, couldn't believe her answer. "Okay, fine."

Pleasure flashed across his face as he backed away. "Okay. I'll get my horse."

"Hey, Jace," she called, swinging herself into the saddle.

He turned at the barn door. "Yeah?"

Heat flood her cheeks and she hated herself for it. "Please put on a shirt."

His mouth twitched. "Whatever you want," he said and disappeared into the barn.

Her shoulders sagged. What the blue moon did she just agree to? If he knew the truth, he'd turn tail and run. She groaned and turned Acer to the house Ethan, Hailey, and Matty occupied.

She reined in at the back door and noticed a crack in the cinderblock foundation wide enough a skunk could crawl through.

"Travis, you in there?" she hollered.

He came out a second later, a dish towel thrown over his shoulder. "Hey, what's up?"

She noticed it and her lips mashed into a thin line. "What are you doing?"

He shrugged. "It's my turn to cook breakfast."

A geyser erupted inside her. "What the hell? Hailey is supposed to do that." She held up a hand. "Never mind. I'll deal with her later. Tell everyone to chill today. I need a break."

His eyes lit. "Okay. What are you gonna do?"

"Get lost, I hope." A sarcastic bite tainted her words. She started for the barn, but he stopped her.

He walked over and touched her leg, a frown on his face. "Wait. Are you okay?"

She picked at the rein's fraying leather and lied. "I'm fine, Trav. Just trying to deal with stuff, ya know?"

"You sure?" He glanced at the barn and his frown deepened.

She followed his gaze. Jace waited, horse saddled and ready. From a distance, she saw him stiffen as he stared back at Travis. Cheese and friggin' rice. This could get ugly.

A GUST of wind blew over Jace, splattering him with dust and fine pebbles. Nearby, the old shop building's rusted steel walls groaned in protest. He scanned the western horizon but saw no threatening thunderheads that might ruin their day, then turned his attention to Lacy.

Travis touched her leg, and a rush of jealousy burned his veins. She leaned down, said something, then moved Acer into a canter toward the barn. Toward him. His shoulders relaxed and hope flared in his chest. He wanted this girl. Heart. Soul. All of her.

"Ready?" he asked.

Her eyes raked over him. He lifted a brow then chuckled at the blush racing up her neck.

"Thanks for putting on a shirt," she muttered.

He looked at his black muscle tee and smirked. Sleeveless, with the sides ripped to the hem, it hardly qualified as a shirt. "You're welcome."

Her eyes narrowed. "You're enjoying this, aren't you?"

He shouldn't goad her if he wanted her trust, so he tried his best to look contrite. "Where you want to go?"

She turned Acer north, her face thoughtful. "You know the old oilfield town, Big Bertha?"

He tugged his horse's reins. "Of course, I do."

The vast expanse of prairie land north of Highway 11 had been his playground. Cooper Ranch stretched north and west almost to the Kansas border. The government claimed the land when the president declared martial law. He pushed the painful thought down, tucked it away. His parent's death was still too raw to think about.

"Old man Lyman had a small stretch of pasture just north of Big Bertha. I remember a huge pond with a wooden pier."

He rubbed his chin. "I remember. That's a thirty-minute ride from here. You sure you want to ride out that far?"

He sidled his horse next to hers. A sudden pallor washed

her face of color. He leaned over, rubbed his forefinger across her cheek. "You okay?"

She drew a deep breath, let it out slowly. "Yeah. I'm fine. You think the MP will be out that way?"

He worried about running into his brother but then dismissed the idea. Zach's interest lay in finance, not the land. He wouldn't venture far from the house.

"Nah. Let's go."

The ride passed in silence. Wind continued to gust from the west, kicking dead grass and dirt into the air.

"This wind might blow in a storm," he commented, breaking the silence.

She snickered. "We really gonna talk about the weather?"

He raised an eyebrow. "Okay then, you want to tell me what's causing you pain?"

The question was loaded, and he knew she could answer several ways. Knew she hid more than physical pain. But he'd settle for any answer she gave.

She stopped. He reined in beside her and waited.

"Leave it alone. Please."

Her desperate words tied him in knots. She'd been hurt. He saw it in her eyes, on her face. A fierce protectiveness rose inside him. "I want to help you."

She nudged Acer forward. "You want to help me? Then distract me."

"Okay." He could do that. He'd do whatever she wanted.

The pond, set in a small cove of trees, glistened in the distance. The late September sun still held summer's strength and sweat trickled down his back. They skirted the pond to its far side where the wind whipped the tops of the tall cypress trees. They tethered their horses, then walked to the dock, weathered a light grey, which stretched over the murky pond.

He took a tentative step, testing the strength of the dry-rotted boards. It creaked and groaned as he bounced on the balls of his feet.

He turned to Lacy. "Seems okay."

She nodded, edged her way to the end, and sat. He followed and they stripped their boots and socks, rolled up their jeans, and dangled their feet in the dark water.

He gave her a sidelong glance, watched her measured breathing, and knew she was in pain. He ran a hand through his lengthening hair. She asked for a distraction, so...

He grinned, got up, and sauntered to the dock's opposite end. She turned and watched, curious. He winked, watched the blush creep up her neck, then took off his T-shirt. Her mouth dropped open and he burst into laughter.

The girl could deny it, but her eyes told the truth. She liked what she saw and that pleased him. Gave him hope. Before she could protest, he let out a loud whoop, ran, and launched himself into a forward summersault off the dock.

He landed feet first in the tepid water. As he plunged to the bottom, water filled his nostrils. When he broke the surface, he shook water out of his hair. He swam to the dock's edge and tugged her leg. She looked down and laughed.

"Victory!" he shouted. "And the crowd goes wild." He waved his arms in a football stadium frenzy.

She snorted. "Victory? Your landing was a bit off. I'll give you a..." She paused pretending to think, then held up an imaginary card. "Nine point two."

"Nine point two? You gotta be kidding," he grumbled. "Nine point two." He paused and cocked his head. "I was talking about getting you to laugh though, so I think I deserve a ten."

She looked down at him and he caught her eyes twinkling. Desire surged and spread through him like a shot of warm whiskey. "Come on," he coaxed. "Get in."

She shook her head. "Uh, no. I know the bottom is slimy and there's snapping turtles and water moccasins just waiting to scare the crap out of me."

"Well, the bottom is slimy," he admitted. "But what if I hold you up so your feet don't touch? And I'll protect you from snakes and turtles."

He searched his mind for something to coax her. A song sprang to mind, and he threw his arms wide and started to sing in a clear, baritone voice the lyrics to "Just Say Yes."

Beating water drums to the rhythm, he continued belting lyrics, bobbing his head up and down.

Her laughter rang, clear and pure, like silver bells at Christmas, and his heart turned over. He'd sing every day just to hear her laugh.

"I love Snow Patrol," she said. "And you have a great voice."

"Thanks." Turning his back to her, he said, "Climb on."

Her hands slipped around his neck, tentative and unsure. Her palms, rough with callouses, scraped against his throat. He swallowed hard and patted her hands. Her trust. It was a heady thing. He dragged her off the dock and swam to the center of the pond.

"What's your favorite song by Snow Patrol?" he asked.

His body bobbed like a human buoy and the wind rippled the water in soft waves, accentuating the strong scent of fish and moss.

Her warm breath tickled his neck. "Dark Roman Wine," she said, then added, "I'm a sucker for Irish bands."

He nodded, thinking of his mother's fascination with the band U2.

Her grip tightened and her legs wrapped around his waist. She leaned in and rested her chin on his shoulder. His body's reaction was instant, and he sucked in a sharp breath. Her body, warm against his back, sent fire through his veins. The girl was killing him, and she didn't have a clue.

"Can I ask you something?" she asked quietly.

He looked over his shoulder. "Anything."

"This tattoo on your back." She ran a finger down his spine.

He shivered. "Yeah?"

"Why do you have it? I mean, what made you get a wolf-dragon tattoo? It's unique."

"Do you want the short answer or the long one?"

She trailed her finger back up his spine. "Just tell me what was on your mind. Did you design it?"

"Yeah, I did," he said, his voice husky. Her fingers kept tracking his spine and he found concentration difficult. "I've always been fascinated with dragons. The symbolism behind the myth. I love everything about them. But the dragon needs temperance. With great power comes arrogance, conceit, and a thirst for even more power." He chuckled and glanced at her. "Just about everything you've accused me of."

Her hand stilled. "Jace, I—"

"It's okay," he reassured her, giving her leg a squeeze. "Don't feel bad."

"Go on," she urged.

He continued to tread water. "Well, the dragon holds immense possibility while the wolf relies on his instincts to guide him. Combined, the dragon sees all the possibilities before him, but the wolf chooses based on instinct. His heart guides him. It's a balance. The dragon embodies primordial power. The wolf checks it with his ability to relate to others. The wolf takes on everything the dragon is—his protection, loyalty, fearlessness, and strength—and enhances it, makes it stronger. The two combined incorporate everything I want to be. The tattoo is a reminder. Especially when I'm having a bad day."

She laughed. "Or when someone accuses you of being conceited?"

"Pretty much," he admitted. "Do you like it?"

"I do. You said you designed it. Does that mean you drew this?"

"Yeah. I knew what I wanted."

"Wow." She sounded impressed. "I had no idea you could draw. You're talented."

He grinned. "Girl, you have no idea just how talented I am."

"And the dragon rises."

Laughter burst from his chest. "Touché."

A red-eared slider swam their direction. "Look." He pointed at the turtle's nose jutting out of the water.

Her grip around his neck tightened. "Let's go back."

"He won't hurt you," he said, laughing, but swam back anyway. He helped her out then hoisted himself on the dock beside her.

He retrieved his shirt and offered it to her. "Dry off with this."

She took the shirt and mopped her face. "Pond water is so gross, but that was fun." She gave him a demure smile. "Thanks. I needed that."

He spent the rest of the day making her laugh. Being her distraction. But as the afternoon waned, so did her spirits. She shifted from cheerful to pensive.

The temperature dropped as the western sun burned to the ground. "I guess we'd better get back."

She sighed. "Yup. Duty calls."

They untied their horses and started back. When Highway 11 stretched before them like a winding, black snake, he trotted up beside her and grinned. "I saw the girl I used to know today."

They crossed the highway onto Monroe land then she turned and faced him, eyes full of pain and regret. "That girl is gone, Jace. She doesn't exist anymore. If that's who you're looking for then give up because you're wasting your time."

She gave Acer a nudge and galloped away.

Frustrated, he urged his horse forward. She wasn't going to run. Not this time.

He raced beside her and grabbed her reins. Eight hooves

skidded on dirt and loose gravel and halted in a dusty cloud
between the two farmhouses. His horse whinnied, tossing her
head.

She jerked her reins out of his hands. "That was a stupid
thing to do," she shouted. "I could've been thrown!"

Chest heaving, he jumped off his horse. His boots thudded
on the gravel. He stomped around Acer, trying to check his
frustration. The girl was scared, and he didn't want to
demolish the progress he made today. He reached up and
plucked her out of the saddle.

"Stop running from me, girl."

He studied her and saw her demeanor shift from anger to
fear. "I'm not going to hurt you. If you'd crawl out of your pain
long enough, you'd see that."

She flung her hands up, eyes glistening. "You don't think
I'm trying? I'm drowning trying to save everyone else, but
who's gonna save me?" She bit her lower lip and looked away.

He drew her into his arms and to his surprise, she didn't
fight him. He rested his chin on her head and whispered,
"Hold on to me. I've got you."

II

FIRE

Time is the fire in which we burn – Gene Roddenberry

14

L acy paced a circle in her room, counting each revolution as she went. She stopped and rubbed the tension between her eyes.

"I can't do it. It's not possible."

Cat crossed her arms and leaned against the doorframe, her lips pressed into a fine line. "You have to tell him."

How could she explain her pregnancy to Jace? He'd ask questions, want to know every detail. He'd want to know who was responsible. And he couldn't find out. Ever.

When the dizziness hit, she sat on the bed, then laid back, and propped her feet against the wall. Head dangling off the edge, she counted backward from ten until the panic attack eased and her breathing steadied. She studied the upside-down view of the outdated calendar. Even Alice in Wonderland would be confused if dropped down into this rabbit hole where nothing made sense.

She raised up. "I have my reasons."

Cat sat beside her. "That may be, but he'll find out regardless. You can't hide a pregnancy. And you look terrible. You need rest or you may end up losing the baby."

The abdominal pain continued. She hadn't mentioned the

blood on her underwear and in her urine. She pushed off the bed and ran an unsteady hand through her messy hair. She dropped in front of her great-grandmother's full-length antique mirror. A pale face with wide green eyes, hollowed by stress, stared back at her. She didn't recognize the stranger's face and it depressed her.

If only she'd moved to California. If she'd been smarter, faster, maybe she could've outwitted the bastard who'd done this. She stopped those thoughts in their tracks. She could lose herself in the what-ifs. They were dangerous and a waste of time.

"I do look bad," she admitted.

Cat rose and placed a cool hand on her forehead. "You haven't been able to keep anything down the last couple of days. I wish I had something to give you for the nausea."

She leaned into Cat for support, grateful for the quirky woman who'd come into her life. "Don't make me do this. Not today."

"Honey, he's going to notice. I'm surprised he hasn't already."

She grabbed Cat's slender, work-worn hand. "If he comes by, just tell him I'm sick. Make him go away."

Cat looked down, grey eyes sympathetic. "You know that won't work."

She mulled over the older woman's words knowing they were true yet wishing they weren't. She looked to the tiled ceiling, dirty and yellowed with age. Why did he push himself into her life?

The sharp knock on the back door gave her a start and Cat squeezed her shoulder before walking away. "Speak of the devil and he shall appear," she quipped.

"You could always tell him I left and joined a convent," she hollered at her retreating figure.

She heard Cat's light, tinkling laugh, then the creak of the back door. "Well, hello there, Jace. Lacy's in her room."

She picked herself up and trudged back to bed. With a huge sigh, she fell against her pillow. Booted footsteps landed in the doorway, but she didn't look up. Arm over her eyes, she wished he'd disappear. She peeked out and found him staring at her. She groaned and sat up.

"What do you want, Jace?"

He walked over and sat beside her. "Let's take a walk."

She fidgeted with her T-shirt. She needed to snuff out any hope he had before things became too complicated. "You need to leave."

"Why? I thought we had fun yesterday."

His confused eyes stabbed her heart, but the longer she led him on, the worse he'd hurt in the end. "We did."

He took both hands and ran them through his hair. "I feel like I'm on a friggin' seesaw with you." He paused. "What was yesterday, then?"

She studied her nails. She couldn't look him in the face and lie. "I told you. Yesterday was a distraction. I needed a diversion, and you were it."

He tipped her chin and locked his eyes on hers. "I don't believe you."

She jerked back. "I don't give a damn what you believe. You're on a seesaw huh? Well, my life's a never-ending roller-coaster from hell."

"Talk to me!" He pinned her with a hard look. "I'm not giving up."

She scooted back and leaned against the headboard. A sharp pain rippled through her and she muffled a gasp. "You probably should."

He studied her face and the frustration on his face, in his voice, softened into concern. "You looked too pale yesterday. What's wrong?"

"I feel off," she muttered. That much she could admit. The *why* got stuck in her throat and refused to budge.

He inched closer, placed a gentle hand on her forehead. "You sick?"

She shifted away and groaned. "Why are you still here?"

His hand slid from her forehead to her neck, his touch soft, seductive. He fingered a lock of her hair. "I like your hair down," he commented, his voice low and raspy.

Disconcerting warmth stole over her as he rubbed her hair between his thumb and forefinger, making her toes tingle.

She slapped his hand away. "Oh my God! What does my hair have to do with anything? You've got the patience of a saint, you know that? It's annoying."

He shoved off the bed and walked to the doorway. "You're pushing me away because you're scared."

He walked out, and her breath hitched. "I'm glad you're finally getting the message." She was. In theory. But her heart's painful twist said otherwise.

She heard him shuffle around the living room. To her surprise, he returned with an old Reader's Digest copy of *The Adventures of Huckleberry Finn*. He'd searched her grandmother's dusty book collection.

He held the book up the same way a child displayed a winning trophy. "I'll read to you. This was one of my favorites."

She stared, wide-eyed and speechless. He pulled a white wooden chair from the corner and sat, bringing with it a vivid memory of her father. Her dad always read to her when she was sick. He'd come home from work, sit by her bed, and read classics like *Catcher in the Rye*, or *Slaughterhouse-Five* until dinnertime. She hadn't read Mark Twain in years. The memory made her smile.

He cleared his throat and began to read. She remained silent, closed her eyes, and gave herself over to the sound of his voice, let it wash over her. Memories drifted as she floated into the dream-like state of being half-asleep where time was no longer linear, but relative.

He stopped reading, leaned forward, and pressed a tender kiss against her forehead. She smelled the scent of leather and saddle soap, and something uniquely him. A warm blanket of contentment wrapped around her heart and she felt safe for the first time since her parents left.

She lifted heavy eyelids and smiled. "Thank you."

"Welcome." He grinned. "I have some work to do, but I'll be back later."

She started to rise, but he placed a firm hand on her shoulder. "No need to get up. Everything's taken care of."

The door clicked behind him. She didn't move again until a painful explosion rocked its way through her.

She swung shaky legs off the bed. Her body teetered forward, and she grabbed the footboard for support. "Oh God."

She cried out as another pain shot through her abdomen. A surge of blood, thick and warm, flowed down her legs.

Cat flung the door open. "What's wrong?"

"Pain," she gasped. "And blood."

Cat grabbed her around the waist and guided her to the bathroom. "In the tub," she ordered. "I'll heat some water on the stove. I'll be right back."

She peeled off her blood-soaked jeans, threw them in the corner, then dragged herself into the big claw-foot tub. She turned the faucet, let the cold water wash over her legs, and watched the red liquid drain out. Fear inside her spread like frost on a windowpane.

The pregnancy was terminating. The little life-force inside her taking its leave like an unwanted houseguest. Tears dripped from her eyes. Agonizing shame mingled with overwhelming relief flooded through her.

Cat returned, steam rising from a large, blue-speckled stockpot. "Oh, honey," she soothed. Crimson-stained water swirled around her bare legs. "Watch out." She plugged the drain and poured in the hot water.

"The pain, Cat," she whimpered.

"Breathe," she instructed. "Don't hold your breath. You're having contractions. Work with the pain. Try not to fight it. I'll be right back with more hot water."

She trained her eyes on the ceiling's water-stained tile and began to count them. When a contraction hit, she squeezed her eyes shut, sucked in a deep breath. Another harsh contraction quickly followed. With a death grip on the tub's sides, she raised up and let out a raw scream.

Cat returned with more hot water. "Poor baby," she murmured, stroking her sweat-soaked hair. "It won't be long."

Neither she nor Cat heard the back door slam.

"Hello?" Jace called through the kitchen doorway. "Lace? Are you okay?"

"Oh God," she said on a sob. "Cat, please don't let him in here. Please."

The older woman's eyes filled with pity. "I'll do what I can," she said and shut the bathroom door.

She heard muffled voices draw near.

"I heard her scream from outside. What's going on?" Jace demanded.

She looked down. Water and blood soaked her shirt and clung to her sides. Panicked, she spotted a towel, raised up, and grabbed it from the towel bar then draped it over her thighs. It floated across her legs, absorbing the sulfuric-smelling water. If he insisted coming inside, she wanted her body covered, wanted to keep some dignity intact. She choked on a sob at the thought.

Another debilitating contraction hit. She bent over and bit her bottom lip until she tasted blood.

"Jace, stop!" Cat commanded.

The doorknob rattled. "Why?"

She heard the impatient response, then he opened the door. He crossed to the tub, saw the stained crimson water, and swore. "Jesus, Lacy."

She gasped as another hard contraction hit. "Get out. Just go. Please."

He knelt, arms crossed over the tub's side. "I'm not leaving."

His forceful words surprised her. "Why?"

She muffled a scream as pain sliced through her lower spinal cord. Her forehead dripped sweat into the water, corrupted by tissue and blood.

"I warned you," she panted. She looked into his eyes, full of hurt and confusion, and her heart plummeted. "I don't want to hurt you."

His jaw ticked. "Stop trying to spare my feelings and talk to me." He paused, gentled his frustrated tone. "What is this?"

She turned her head away, resigned. "I'm miscarrying," she whispered.

She squeezed her eyes shut. His silence unnerved her. She'd expected an explosion, a Vesuvius eruption, but not his reticence.

He placed a gentle hand against her cheek, turned her to face him. "Open your eyes and look at me," he said, voice firm.

She lifted her eyes to his and he continued, "You did warn me. I said I didn't care. And I don't. But you have to tell me what happened."

"Jace, I can't." She stopped, inhaled, and tried to breathe through the pain.

Cat strode in holding a small glass tumbler filled with amber liquid. She put it in Lacy's hand. "Drink this."

She smelled the liquid and grimaced. "Do I have to?"

Jace turned to Cat. "What is it?"

"Whiskey." She stopped short at the V etched between his eyes. "Oh, don't give me that look. She needs something for the pain. It's all I've got."

Lacy stared into the glass. Tears fell into the alcohol. She lifted it and drank, then bent her head. Silent sobs shook her body.

She wanted her mother, wanted to be somewhere else, anywhere but here. Why did this happen? Her brain circled around on itself trying to find the answer.

Cat's comforting hand stroked her back. "You need to relax. It shouldn't be long."

One last wracking spasm shredded her belly. She raised up, knuckles white against the tub's sides, and screamed. With one last push, something gushed out, bringing intense relief. Her whole body went lax, arms falling into the tainted water.

She registered Cat running clean water and washing the blood from her body, then the woman's faint voice asking Jace to carry her. She wanted to protest but couldn't gather the strength. He lifted her and carried her to her bedroom. Warm, muggy air hit her bare skin and she realized she was naked from the waist down. Exposed. Too spent to be mortified, she turned her head into his chest and wept.

Jace pressed his lips against her ear. "Hold on to me. I've got you."

THE DARKENED sky marked the beginning of the day's last act. Night fell, a death shroud over the farm, dropping the curtain on a day Jace wished he could forget. Lacy's front porch swing squeaked and melded with the night-time sounds. His ears rang with the cacophony until it morphed into white noise, a backdrop for the questions beating a war drum inside him.

What happened to her? Who touched her? The last question stung like viper venom because the answer would hurt either way. The thought of Lacy with anyone else, wanting anyone else, wrecked him. But he refused to accept the jarring possibility the intimate act wasn't her choice.

He watched Travis stroll up the walk and wondered if he and Lacy had been intimate. They had been an item their junior year in high school. He'd just started his sophomore year at the University of Central Oklahoma when AJ gave him the news. Too busy playing varsity baseball, he hadn't visited home as much as he wanted. That had been a miserable year.

Travis stepped up and pulled open the screen door.

He cleared his throat. "Evening."

Startled, Travis' hand froze on the door's rusty knob. "Hey," he said turning around. "Didn't see you there."

He stood, shoved his hands in his back pockets, and rocked back on his heels. Punching him would accomplish nothing. Except satisfy his anger. He needed a target and the younger man's forehead sported a bull's eye he wanted to obliterate.

He moved around to block the front door. "What do you want, Travis?"

"Look, man," he said defensively, "I just want to check on her."

"Why? Did you have something to do with this?" He inched toward him, watching his reaction.

"What do you mean?"

"I think you know exactly what I mean."

Travis took a step back, his face glowing bright red. "I would never do anything to hurt Lacy. I care about her too, man. And I never touched her. Ever."

He stepped forward, closing the gap between them. "That better be the case. If I find out differently, you will regret it."

Travis leaned into him, anger gushing out like water over a spillway, wild and reckless. "Don't threaten me, Jace."

One eyebrow rose. "I just did."

The younger man stepped into his space and shoved him against the door. "I knew you'd be trouble. You're no good for her. You'll hurt her."

Jace shoved him back toward the screen door. "I'm not gonna hurt her."

Travis raised his right arm, his hand curled into a fist. "You show up here acting like you own rights to her. You don't."

He widened his stance. "Do you? Are you dating her?"

His words hit the mark and Travis swung.

He dodged the right hook and plowed into him. The old wood cracked and splintered as they fell through the screen door and tumbled down the steps.

Jace jumped on him and plowed his fist into his face. "I'm not going to hurt her," he shouted. "I lo —"

Before he could finish the thought, cold water blasted his face. He raised his hands, blocking the spray. Cat brandished the water hose, her face lethal. She drenched them until they begged her to stop.

She dropped the hose. "Travis, go to the barn. Change your clothes and do something about that bloody nose."

"Yes, ma'am." He dragged himself up, wiped blood on his soaked shirt, and limped away.

She jabbed a finger at Jace. "You. In the house. Now."

Dripping head to toe, he turned and walked into the house. He stood in the living room, water puddling at his feet, feeling like a scolded child.

She marched into the room, nostrils flaring. "Well, that made about as much sense as an elephant walking a tightrope."

He let out a strangled cough. "Yes, ma'am."

"Don't try to get back on my good side."

"I understand you're upset," he began.

"Upset?" she interrupted. "Try again. What in the name of Sam were you thinking?"

Fire snapped in her grey eyes. She wanted to clobber him. He knew the look. His mother's eyes could light fire to an ice cap whenever he crossed a line.

Not waiting for an answer, she continued. "You started that fight, didn't you?"

"Well, not exactly," he stammered.

She held up a hand. "Travis didn't have anything to do with what happened to Lacy and you know it. I'll admit, sometimes he has no more sense than a snake in a snowstorm, but he cares about her. He protected her. Kept her safe." Her voice softened. "He loves her."

The statement vexed him. Selfishly, he wished he'd protected her. He should be overwhelmed with gratitude. But he'd have to be stone-cold dead in his grave not to be jealous over Cat's last comment.

She pointed toward Lacy's bedroom. "That girl in there has been through it. No doubt about it. But she's got a will of steel. She thinks she's broken."

"I want to help her. I—" He almost added he loved her but stopped short. Lacy should hear it first.

She snorted. "And you think starting a fight is helping?"

"No, ma'am." Now he was the senseless snake in a snow-storm. Stupid snake.

"Go get a towel. You're tracking up my floor."

He hurried to the bathroom, removed the waterlogged T-shirt clinging to his sides, and draped it over the tub. He grabbed a towel and ran it through his hair, then slung it over his shoulder, returned, and wiped the floor.

Cat waited, a bottle of Jack Daniels Old Number 7 in hand. She watched him swipe the towel over the puddle.

Satisfied, she leaned back on the couch and sighed. She pointed to the wooden rocker. "Pull that over here and sit."

He pushed the rocker next to her and she handed him a glass. She poured them both two fingers of whiskey.

She tipped the diamond cut glass and downed the entire contents. "You're not stupid," she said and poured herself another.

"Thanks," He sipped the liquor and frowned, then thunked the glass on the coffee table. "Never liked the stuff."

"Drink it anyway." Another order that brooked no argument.

He sighed and shot the remaining liquid. Fire burned a path down his esophagus, setting it ablaze.

She set her empty glass down. "I know you have questions.

I hate to interfere in Lacy's personal life, but at this point it's not fair to keep you in the dark. So, ask me your questions."

"What happened to her?"

She picked up the bottle, filled her glass to the rim. "You have to know what happened to her, Jace. Or at least have a guess. Like I said, you're not stupid." She looked at him, her face somber. "Take a good look at her. How she acts around men."

He shook his head. "No."

The image of Lacy being violated hurt too much. He wouldn't let himself think the word rape. Agitated, he got up and paced the floor.

Cat sighed. "She was raped two days after she moved here."

He wished she hadn't said it. But some things couldn't be unheard, just like some things couldn't be undone. His heart knew the truth. It lurked in his subconscious. Her skittish behavior, the melancholy attitude, the wall around her heart. It made sense. And it devastated him.

"She'll have to tell you the rest. She has her reasons for not telling you, though she won't tell me what they are. And I don't know all the details either."

He slumped back in the chair, lowered his head.

"You need to know," Cat continued. "You're changing her for the better."

He looked up, confused. "I don't understand."

"She never considered the possibility of love after what happened. She told me she couldn't stand the thought of a man touching her."

He winced and wondered how she tolerated the men surrounding her.

She grinned, eyes twinkling. "Then you came along. Infuriating her. Challenging her. Testing her." She reached over, picked up her glass, and finished her whiskey. "Bossing her. Don't stop. Don't treat her any differently."

Grateful, he stood and pulled her up in a hug. "Thank you."

She patted his back. "She feels something for you, though she refuses to admit it."

He leaned back and smiled. "I know."

She clucked her tongue. "My, my, aren't you arrogant? But with those dimples? I guess you have the right."

He chuckled and sat back into the rocker. When he looked up, Cat's grin stretched a mile wide.

"What?" he asked.

"So that's the tattoo."

He cocked his head. "What do you mean?"

"Well, Lacy's mentioned a particular tattoo. A wolf-dragon."

His ears perked. "Really? What did she say?"

She started to laugh like she'd just heard a joke from one of Jeff Dunham's puppets. "Now that would be telling."

15

J ace studied the barn door's hinge and frowned. He'd readjusted it three times and the dang thing still hung off-center. He flung the screwdriver down and cursed.

Raul led Lacy's horse out of the barn. "You're not getting anything done."

He turned and scratched Acer between the ears. "Nope, I'm not."

Raul unhooked the lead rope and let the horse wander. "Thinking about Lacy?"

"Yeah." He picked up the screwdriver, coated in dust. He couldn't erase her image. The pain, the blood, and the loss. "Cat let Travis see her," he added, frowning.

He raised a brow. "And this makes you jealous?"

"Of course it does." He kicked the door with his boot. "They have a history."

The rumble of ASVs filled the air as they made their way down the southern oilfield road. The military powers initiated a daily patrol around the farm's perimeter. The drab machine's giant tires kicked up white gravel dust, coating everything a dirty, lifeless grey. Cat complained every time dust stuck to the wet laundry hanging on the line.

"Go." Raul waved him away. "Check on her, do something for her. You're no use here."

"Do what?" He turned his back on the ASVs and walked inside the barn.

A white enamel washbowl and pitcher sat in the corner. He crossed over, glanced in the grimy mirror, and grimaced at the growth along his jawline. Tossing the bowl's dirty contents on the ground, he poured fresh water, scrubbed his face, then grabbed the towel hanging next to the mirror.

Raul watched, his face impassive. "Make her dinner or something."

"Dinner," he repeated, placing the towel back on the peg.

He hated feeling helpless. It nettled him. How could he help her? He knew she suffered from nightmares. What else did she suffer?

"How is dinner gonna help?"

"That is true. You would poison her, no doubt." A slight smile flitted across his face. "Maybe you should just pick her some flowers. They don't catch on fire like your fish do."

Jace gave up a laugh. "You're right. Blackened fish jerky wouldn't be helpful."

"The bonfire is set for tonight." Raul watched him with thoughtful eyes. "Lacy might like that."

"She might," he said flatly.

He needed to release his resentment toward Travis, but Cat's words tormented him. Travis loved her and he couldn't help the jealousy that rose when they were together.

"If you love her, put her feelings above your own," Raul said.

Jace let out a long-suffering sigh and wondered if Raul was clairvoyant. "You're right. I know you're right."

"Go. I'll fix that."

"Thanks, brother," he said.

He set off to find Cat. She'd know what to do.

After searching the farmhouses, he found her in the wash house, hands on her hips.

"I know I saw another bottle in here somewhere." She searched the ground around the shelf, clearing pop cans and trash as she went.

He leaned in the doorway and grinned. "Lose something?"

She looked up, pressed a hand against her heart. "You scared me." She smoothed her hair back, tucking a wayward strand behind her ear.

"I need your help, Cat." He stepped inside, skirting around old tin cans scattered on the compacted dirt floor.

She bent and retrieved a bleach bottle. "Ah-ha. I knew it was here," she said then hurried out. "Whew, fresh air. Okay, now you've got my attention. What do you need?"

He gave a schoolboy shrug under Cat's keen observation. "I want to do something nice for Lacy. Raul suggested I cook for her, but I don't think offering her burnt fish qualifies as nice."

A grin lit her face. "I think I've got something. Wait here."

She walked away then returned with a wine bottle. "Supper is ready so there's no need for you to cook. This," she said, shoving the bottle in his hands, "will be a nice gesture."

"Cat, I don't think alcohol—"

"Bah. Don't give me a prohibition speech. I always figured if the government considered a person an adult at eighteen, they should be allowed to drink. She's beyond eighteen and an adult in ways many people never reach."

Relenting, he held up his free hand. "Okay."

"Good boy." She patted his shoulder, stepped around him then added, "There are candles in the cabinet above the stove."

He strode to the back porch, wondering why girls made such a fuss over candles. He crossed into the empty kitchen and set the wine next to the bottle opener.

"Lace?" he called. He moved through her empty bedroom

to the bathroom door and knocked. "You in there?" He cracked the door open and peered inside.

"Get out, Jace," she shouted, sinking low in the tub.

The towel draped over the edge disappeared. She peeked over the side long enough to throw a soap bar at him. It smacked the door with a thud, then dropped to the floor. "What do you want?"

He cocked his head. What did he want? He wanted to lift her out of the water and show her, but he cut the thought short. "Come into the kitchen when you're finished."

"Why?"

Her obstinate tone needled him. At times, the girl maddened him beyond reason. "Do you have to make every single thing difficult?"

Her head popped up. "I don't make every single thing—" She stopped when he crossed his arms and lifted a brow. "Cat was right about you."

He scratched his head and grinned. "What?"

She slid into the water, vanishing again. "You are arrogant."

"I can live with that."

"Oh, I'm sure you can." She paused, peeked at him again. A smug smile spread across her face. "Dictator," she mocked, exaggerating the word dick.

He shot her an exasperated glance on his way out. "Don't push me, girl."

The candles were lit when she emerged, dressed and subdued. He wondered at the abrupt mood change. "You okay?"

"Yeah, just sad." She shrugged then added, "And ashamed."

He walked over and took her hand. Leading her to the table, he pulled her chair out.

Bewilderment crossed her face as she sat. "Thank you."

Her eyes widened when he crouched before her and asked,

"Ashamed? What have you got to be ashamed of?" He reached out, fingered her hair. "You couldn't have prevented the miscarriage. It wasn't your fault."

She lowered her eyes. "What do you know about my shame?"

"Nothing," he replied softly. "Not a damn thing."

He knew nothing about the rape, but thought he understood why she felt shame. Like racing fire fueled by the wind, anger swept over him. It had the potential to level him. He needed answers.

He stood, pulled her up, and wrapped his arms around her. He rubbed her stiffened back until she relaxed.

He tipped her chin. "Why are you ashamed?"

She closed her eyes. "Because," she paused. Tears ran down her cheeks. "I'm relieved. God, I'm so relieved. And that's a terrible thing to feel about losing a baby."

He rested his forehead on hers. At a loss, he said the only thing he could. "I'm so sorry, Lace."

He wiped her tears with his thumbs then guided her back into the chair.

"The candles are nice." She gave him a questioning stare. "You did this for me?"

"Ah, Lacy," he sighed and pulled his chair next to hers. He wanted to give her more. As cliché as it sounded, he'd lasso the moon if she asked.

He poured wine in chipped teacups. Years had faded the cup's painted yellow flowers, left them drab and wilted. He'd scoured the cabinets for Cat's glass tumblers, or anything resembling a wine glass. All he found were mismatched coffee mugs and plastic cups from the local Gas-N-Sip.

He gave her a lopsided grin. "Teacups were all I could find."

"It's fine." She motioned to the wine. "Where'd you get that?"

"Where do you think?"

He couldn't help the sarcasm. He didn't approve, no matter how practical Cat's diatribe sounded. He'd seen firsthand his grandmother's alcohol addiction, a treacherous road he had no intention of following.

She tasted the Moscato and a small smile formed around her lips. "It's good."

"You're beautiful when you do that."

She always gave an honest smile and it always reached her eyes, the part of her that fascinated him most. He never met another woman whose eye shade changed with every mood. Now, they were a thoughtful forest green.

She raised her eyes to his. "Do what?"

He almost laughed. The girl was guileless. "Smile," he said and gave her a wink. Heat climbed into her cheeks, flushing them rosy red. "And when you blush? You're stunning."

Dropping her head, she twisted a lock of hair around her index finger.

He served her Cat's fried rabbit and grits. In terms of their relationship, she needed to catch up and he just gave her a good nudge.

They ate in silence until he said, "Raul said they set up a bonfire at the ponds for tonight."

Her fork stopped mid-air. "Really?"

"Yeah," he said, his tone casual. "You wanna go?"

She put her fork down then drained her wine cup. "Jace, is this a date?"

He gave her a smile, slow and full. She was catching on. "Yeah. I think so."

She nodded. "Okay. Let's go. It will be nice to see everyone."

He wondered if everyone consisted of Travis, then forced himself to curb his jealousy.

They finished dinner and washed the dishes together in an easy way, the slight tension from his attentive comments gone for the moment.

You'd better grab a jacket," he said as they walked to the door. "It's gonna get cold tonight."

She turned to face him, arms crossed. "Do you have to boss me? About everything?"

"Pretty much."

"You do know I already have a father."

The comment gave him pause. He didn't want her to look at him as a father figure, didn't think of his bossing quite like that.

He sauntered to the back door. "Okay," he conceded, but couldn't resist one last jab. "Freeze if you want."

Her unladylike response made him laugh all the way down the steps and he knew she'd leave her jacket on the hook by the door.

16

J ace and Lacy walked the pasture as the sun dipped below the western horizon. Dusk settled over the landscape, dusting the sky a hazy purple. Jace saw the bonfire blaze shoot sparks above the pond's tree line, highlighting the sound of laughter drifting over the evening breeze. Matty's boyish giggle rose over the others and his mouth tipped into an easy smile.

"I've loved the smell of campfires since I was a boy."

The deep rich campfire smoke evoked strong memories of his father. Silly campfire songs they'd sung filtered through his mind. He remembered building a tent using canvas and a rope and how his dad taught him to build a fire that would last through the night. He'd taught him to survive.

Lacy's hand on his arm stopped him. "What is it?"

The flashbacks vanished and he turned to her, confused. "What is what?"

She shook her head. "Never mind. There was just a minute when you looked"—she shrugged—"I don't know, sad I guess."

"I was thinking about my dad." A sad smile flickered across his face. "I miss him."

She looped her arm through his, leaned her head against him. "I'm sorry, Jace."

He lifted his head and watched the stars struggle to shine in the half-light. He felt his father's presence guiding him still and was grateful. "Thank you, love."

They started walking again. A gusty north wind kicked up and a shiver rolled through her slight frame.

A few yards from the fire, she stopped and motioned to the new dike. "The pond is looking good."

"Yes, it is," he agreed. "Raul finished overhauling the pump. We should be able to start filling from the spring soon."

The natural spring provided water to both farmhouses and would fill the pond they repaired despite the hot summer.

"Did Travis finish the fish traps for the creek? We need to start stocking the pond after it's filled."

"Yeah," he said, a begrudging note in his voice. "He got them done."

Travis worked hard, he'd give him that.

"You don't like him much, do you?"

He could deny it. Wanted to, even. But why be dishonest? "No, not really."

"Why?"

Her baffled look bothered him. She couldn't be that oblivious to the younger man's feelings. "Are you kidding?"

Her brows furrowed. "No."

He looked to the sky and laughed. "Oh, Lacy."

She jerked her arm away. "What are you saying?"

"He likes you."

He refused to say love. Cat's opinion about Travis could be wrong, though he doubted it. He saw how Travis behaved around her. He felt something for her that went beyond friendship, but he didn't know how deep those feelings ran.

Her lips dipped into a frown. "So, you don't like him because he likes me. Is that it?"

"Yeah," he admitted. "I'd say that's it."

She started walking again. "Travis is a good guy, Jace. You really need to—"

Hot with nerves, he stepped in front of her. "No, I don't."

Jealousy was a hell of a thing to fight when he had no idea where he stood. The girl was a maze of emotions and her circumstances, a labyrinth he couldn't fathom.

He took her hand, drew her close, then rested his forehead on hers. They stilled, her breath faltered as an electric current passed between them.

"Breathe," he reminded her gently.

He wrapped an arm around her waist, then lifted his head. He searched her face and read hesitation. He lifted a hand, brushed his knuckles over her cheek. The girl needed another nudge. He needed to tread with care and not push her too hard, too fast. But he couldn't help what tumbled out of his mouth next.

His grip tightened. "I'm not sharing you with Travis, sweetheart."

She stiffened and her emerald eyes glittered diamond hard. "You can't say that to me. I'm not a piece of property you can own, you conceited jerk."

He laughed, then stunned her silent by laying his head on her neck. Strawberries and honey, sweet and addictive, flooded his senses.

"Stop running from me, girl."

He felt her rapid heartbeat against his chest as he held her close. God knew he didn't want to release her. But when she remained silent, he dropped his hands and took a step back. Knowing when to advance and when to retreat was like the art of fencing. He'd made a move, now he needed to fall back, let her adjust.

He grasped her hand, laced his fingers through hers. "Come on. Let's go."

He led her to an old horse blanket by the fire Raul spread out for everyone to sit on. The fire sizzled and popped, its flames licking the dry wood and emitting a comfortable heat against the damp September air. He hoped the sparks cast into the darkened sky wouldn't draw the MP's attention. They continued their daily patrol but hadn't paid another visit. Yet.

He sat beside Lacy, stared into the flames, and let his thoughts shatter into a million fragments. They became elusive shadows he couldn't catch. He leaned back on his elbows, closed his eyes, and enjoyed the drowsy, narcotic feeling.

Castiel ambled over, worked his way between them in his clumsy, doggish way, and rested his head on Jace's thigh.

"Hey." Lacy gave his shoulder a nudge. "What's up with you and my dog?"

A lazy smile tipped his lips. "You remember what you said don't you?" He kept his eyes closed, the fire's warmth soaking into his boots.

"About?"

"You said if I wanted to get to you, I'd have to go through your dog." He sat up and gave her a wink. "Mission accomplished."

She looked at the dog and scowled. "How'd you do it?"

"I took him hunting." He ruffled Castiel's ears, murmured German words of praise. "He loves to sniff out rabbits."

Her eyes narrowed. "I know you had help."

One side of his mouth tipped up. "Probably."

Cat came and sat beside them with an old burlap sack. She pulled out a bottle of Bacardi, unscrewed the cap and took a long, hard pull. "That's good," she murmured, then shoved it between Lacy's legs. "Pass it around."

Jace frowned. "Cat, where are you getting all this alcohol?"

Already, he could smell the distilled spirit's distinct odor, its unpleasant aroma mixing with the musky campfire smoke. He watched Lacy place the tip under her nose, grimace, then pass the bottle to Travis who took a long swig.

Cat harrumphed and crossed her arms. "Like I'd tell you. You'd pour all my rum into the fire." Her grey eyes caught the firelight and reminded him of liquid mercury, fascinating and dangerous.

"Simmer down, Captain Sparrow," he half-joked. He didn't want to vex her. She had a sharp tongue and quick wit, and he had no desire to be on the receiving end of it.

"Ben and I owned a bar once," Cat said, her voice wistful.

"That explains a lot," he muttered.

She reached over Lacy and swatted his knee and gave him a playful smile. "Back in '89, we were living off the Florida coast in Destin. Where the weather's fine and the water's clear blue."

"Why'd you leave?" Lacy asked.

"Ben was born and raised in Ponca City. His mother got sick, so we moved back in '99 to take care of her. Stayed put after that." She sniffled. "I sure do miss that man."

She leaned against Cat in a comforting gesture. "I'm sorry."

Cat took another long pull from the rum and passed it to Ethan. "Me too, girl, me too."

Stories rose and drifted into the night sky along with the smoke. Jace hated to admit it, but the alcohol had a relaxing effect and the communion bound them together. It created a sense of community he'd never felt before.

Curious, he watched Matty rise and disappear into the darkened pasture. He returned carrying a guitar case.

He sat it beside Lacy, cheeks flushed with excitement. "Travis said you play the guitar."

She gave Matty a long look. "It's been a long time since I've played. This was my grandpa's. Where'd you find it?"

He ran a nervous hand over his mouth. "In one of the bedrooms. I hope you don't care."

"I don't," she murmured.

She unlatched the torn black case and ran her hand across the Gibson's burnished wood. The fermented smell of old wood and time caught the breeze. She lifted the guitar, running her fingers along the neck, testing the strength of the strings.

"Can you tune it?" Raul asked.

"I think so." She gave it a test strum, then began plucking strings and twisting knobs.

Matty sat beside Jace. "What song you gonna play?" he asked.

"My grandpa taught me how to play." She leaned over Jace and winked at the boy. "So don't expect much."

She took a deep breath, bent over the guitar, and began picking the strings. "This song is called "Catie Rae" and it's the first song I ever learned to play."

Jace gave her his full attention as she picked the strings and sang. Her raven hair fell in a waterfall obscuring her face. The vibrato in her voice resounded, sweet and pure, and his brows rose in pleasant surprise. He'd never heard her sing. What else didn't he know about her? The question intrigued him.

On the second verse, her eyes shifted, locked on his as she sang,

As their meaning filtered through, his growing ache for her deepened.

Her eyes returned to the guitar as she sang the last chorus. Relaxing after the first song, she played several more, made the group laugh with her quirky rendition of "Kumbaya." After she segued into "Fare Thee Well," she placed the guitar into its case.

The group shouted protests, but Lacy was adamant. "I'm done, guys."

"You have a beautiful voice." Hailey said in grudging admiration. She turned to her husband. "Ethan, I'm ready to go. All this smoke is making my eyes water."

Lacy rolled her eyes.

Jace chuckled. He didn't know how Ethan put up with her.

Cat stretched her legs in front of her and yawned. "Well, guys, we better call it a night." She rose and the group roused themselves and followed her, disappearing into the dark pasture.

Lacy caught Matty before he raced away. "Will you take this back for me?" she asked handing him the guitar.

"Sure," he agreed. "You want me to put it in your house?"

She reached out and tousled the boy's hair. "That's fine."

He mashed his hair in place, his face glowering. "Quit doin' that, will ya?" He trotted off before she could respond.

Jace threw two more logs on the fire and sat beside Lacy. "You cold?"

"A little."

He patted the blanket between his legs and shrugged out of his jacket. "Come sit here." When she hesitated, he said, "You'll be warmer."

She scooted over. He settled the jacket around her shoulders then wrapped his arms around her middle and pulled her back. He felt her hesitate, then lean into him, resting her head on his chest. The simple act of trust tightened his heart.

He leaned forward and rested his chin on her shoulder. "Warmer?"

She nodded. "Yeah."

He ran his fingers through her hair. "I've waited a long time for you. I remember the first day of your freshman year. I hadn't been over to your house all summer because my dad shipped my brother and me off to my grandparents."

She yawned. "Where's this going, Cooper?"

"When you walked in the auditorium the first day back, I was stunned."

Stunned didn't cover it. Her figure had developed over the summer, but it wasn't just her body twisting him in knots. Something else changed. A fierceness radiated from her vivid green eyes he'd never noticed before. His whole world tilted off its axis that day.

She turned around, her face a sea of confusion.

"I was a senior. It wasn't cool for senior guys to like little freshman girls." He grinned at her. "So, I watched you. And made sure no other guy got within fifty feet of you."

She jerked back. "Come again?"

He shrugged. "I couldn't help it. It was pretty easy, since your brother had been doing it anyway."

She arched a brow. "I can't decide if I'm mad, flattered, or creeped out."

His gave her a cocky grin. "Oh, I'd go with flattered. I broke up with Shannon Burns that day."

"Wow. The head cheerleader? Bet you caught crap from my brother. What'd he say?"

He looked at her upturned face and the sudden urge to kiss her was almost too hard to resist. He swallowed hard. She needed time and he'd give her that. "He didn't know why. Still doesn't."

She rested her head on his chest and they sat in silence, staring at the fire until it died to embers.

"Where were you three months ago?" she asked quietly.

His arms tightened around her waist. "Not where I should've been," he said, his voice thick. "I'm so sorry, love."

She turned around and took his face between her hands, eyes solemn. "Remember something for me, okay?"

He nodded. "Okay."

"I'll tell you what happened to me on one condition."

"Anything," he agreed.

"You need to remember, nothing, not one bit of this screwed up situation is your fault."

Her forceful words chilled him. Why would she say that?

He got up and offered his hand. "Let's go back to the house."

"Okay," she said, her face set in forced determination.

THE HOUSE LOOMED BEFORE THEM, pitch black and silent. The wind shifted and warm air collided with cold. Thunder rumbled in the distance, promising rain.

Jace walked up the back steps and hesitated. His hand hovered over the doorknob as flashbacks of another darkened house hit him. Lacy walked up, placed a hand on his back.

"What's wrong?"

"Nothing. Sorry if I startled you." He shook off the edgy feeling and opened the door.

Lacy whistled for Castiel, and the dog trotted inside. He started to follow, but she tugged on his T-shirt. "Wait."

She didn't let go until the dog came back, wagging his stubby tail.

"Do you always have him check the house first?"

She let out a shaky breath. "Yeah."

He took her hand and led her through the kitchen into her bedroom. She walked to the bed and laid down. He followed and propped himself beside her.

He took her hand, threaded their fingers together. "What happened, Lace?"

She trained her eyes on the ceiling. "My parents helped me move out here. My dad called Uncle Tommy to let him know I decided to stay. It was against their better judgment. But I'm nineteen, legal to do what I want, and stubborn to a fault." She turned and gave him a half-smile. "Those are my dad's words."

"And true."

"I thought I could live here in peace. I didn't know anyone knew I was here, or even cared. But"—she took a deep breath and forged on—"my second night here I heard a noise in the kitchen and went to investigate. A man broke in. He—" Her voice cracked.

"Jesus, Lacy."

"He raped me." She forced the words out on a shuddering breath. "Then warned me to move to California with my parents. Said he'd come back and kill me if I didn't."

She faced him and he glimpsed fierce defiance sparking in her eyes.

"I ignored him and found Travis. He protected me. Stayed with me in the house until Cat and the others came along."

Pressure built behind his eyes. He lowered his head and cursed. She knew her rapist.

"How did he know your parents moved to California? You know him, don't you?"

She turned her face toward the wall.

"Jesus, girl. You have to tell me who did this to you."

"Why? What can you do?" She stopped and dragged in a deep breath. "I can't tell you, Jace. There's nothing you can do. It's done."

"It's not done," he shouted and rose to pace the floor. Hands raised over his head, he let out a feral growl.

"I don't want you to do something stupid. Don't ruin your life because of me."

He stopped cold, turned, and faced her. "Don't you think you're worth it?"

She shook her head. "You don't get it," she said softly.

He searched her face. "What don't I get?"

She looked down, studied a speck of dirt on her shirt. "You've become important to me Jace, and I don't want to lose you."

He sat on the white wooden chair, dropped his hands between his knees. Her words nailed him straight through the heart. He knew she kept a tight rein on her emotions, so the confession had cost her. He watched her fidget with her hem and chuckled. When she looked up, he gave her a cocky grin.

"You really are conceited. Just because you look like that" —she waved her hands at him—"doesn't mean every girl you come in contact with is falling all over herself for your attention."

He leaned back and grabbed his chest. "You wound me, girl."

"With an ego as inflated as yours?" She cocked an eyebrow.

He rose and sat on the bed. Outside, the storm released its fury. Wind rattled the windowpanes and rain leaked through the old tin roof, creating a puddle on the floor.

"I wanna ask you something," he said after some thought.

She gave him a wary look. "Okay."

"I want to stay here with you." He wanted to protect her, guard her, make sure no one ever hurt her again. "Can I?"

"Why? Jace I—"

He cut her off. "Do you still not understand?"

When she didn't answer, he leaned in, his lips inches from hers. "I'm in love with you, girl."

17

Standing in the living room doorway, Lacy watched Jace struggle to wake, his hair sticking up in adorable boyish fashion. Her lips curved, and she allowed herself a moment to admire him unnoticed. His effortless GQ look defied logic. He'd been sleeping on her cracked leather couch for over a month and her reaction never faltered. Little fireflies fluttered in her stomach, their light igniting a fire that raced through her. The boy was sinfully beautiful, although she'd never admit it. His ego was inflated enough.

He looked up and gave her a sleepy smile. "Hey, beautiful. You okay?"

Her thoughts crashed and burned. "Yeah."

Nightmares often drove her out of bed. When they did, she'd pad to the couch and curl next to his side. He'd pull her close and chase away her mind's shadows and the monsters hiding there. He made her feel safe. Protected.

"It's getting colder," he commented as he slipped his arms into his flannel button-down.

Early arctic air blasted the farm with surprising force and the temperature plummeted, leaching away autumn's warmth. Thousands of rusty brown leaves carpeted the ground, and to

Cat's dismay, blew under the back door and covered the kitchen floor.

The pond was filled, but not stocked, and the premature winter-like temperatures hindered the men's progress. They didn't have the proper clothing to combat the creek's frigid water to trap fish, and she protested the few times they tried. After Matty slipped on a rock and came back wet head-to-toe, she put her foot down.

She sat beside Jace. "I know. I still can't believe it's this cold."

Raul knocked at the front door then walked in, straw tangled in his thick brown hair. "We need to get the freezers in the fish house stocked with something, boss."

Food was low, and the cold weather made fishing and hunting small game difficult. They needed bigger game to survive the winter months.

The fish house, named for the three catfish holding tanks, boasted three freezers, a meat locker, and all the equipment needed to process deer. She sent silent thanks to her grandfather for her butchering skills.

She frowned at Raul's holey jeans and paper-thin windbreaker. "Well, good morning to you too, star shine. Is that the warmest thing you have to wear?"

He looked down, puzzled. "Yeah. I've never lived this far north."

She filed the fact Raul considered Oklahoma "north" to think about later. She walked over and picked straw from his hair. "Move your stuff from the barn into the house. It's just gonna get colder."

He nodded, then gave her a pointed look. "Where will Travis go? And Dylan?"

Where would Travis go? She cast a furtive glance at Jace and found him studying her in thoughtful apprehension.

She scrubbed her hands over her face. "Tell Dylan to move his stuff into the big house. He can share Matty's room."

She thought about Travis. He'd helped her, protected her, taught her to release some of her rage. He was a good friend, and she didn't want him to feel left out or hurt. She also knew Jace and Travis together would be like throwing firecrackers in a furnace.

"Hells bells," she muttered. "Let Travis decide where he wants to stay."

She turned to Jace. His disappointed look gave her the impression she hadn't achieved neutrality. She should've given a definitive answer. But damn. No matter what her decision, someone would end up hurt. She hated this. Hated the responsibility.

Head in a vise grip, she rubbed her temples. "We need to raid some houses for winter clothes, blankets, food and medicine. Kaw City is closest. Think it can be done?"

"We have a little gas left. I think Travis' truck could make it there and back," Raul answered.

"Good. Can you and the guys do that tomorrow? I'll have Cat make a list."

Raul nodded and walked to the kitchen. "I've got bows and arrows ready. And two shotguns. You want us to go deer hunting?"

She glanced out the window. The snow-filled clouds worried her. "Yeah. Can you gather the others?"

"Sure. Be back in five," Raul said and left.

She sat beside Jace. Neither spoke for several minutes.

She sighed and broke the silence. "I don't want to hurt Travis. He's been a great friend to me, Jace. That was the only answer I could think of."

"I know."

She laid a hand on his knee. "What are you thinking?"

He leaned back, raking a hand through his hair. "Oh, nothing much. Just trying to figure out how to avoid punching him in the face if he decides to move in here."

"You don't have to worry about him, Jace."

He shook his head. "I'm not so sure."

She reached out and touched his hair, rubbing a lock between her thumb and forefinger. It was longer than she'd ever seen it. She wanted to reassure him but didn't know how. He'd gotten under her skin and burrowed deep. He'd barreled through every roadblock she'd thrown at him.

"Please don't worry."

But the inept words fell flat. Why couldn't she just say what she felt? That she didn't think of Travis in a romantic way, that she only wanted his friendship. She was falling for Jace and every passing day, she fell deeper. From the moment he sang "Just Say Yes" at Lyman's pond, her heart started falling.

He gave her a long, unreadable look then his eyes twinkled. He jumped up and pulled her with him. In an exaggerated move, he drew her close and dipped her in his arms, his handsome face spread in a dimpled grin.

"Darlin'," he drawled. "I know I'm all you think about. Admit it."

His sudden closeness stole her breath. "No," she managed, but her arms wrapped around his neck. Cheeks flushed, her body responded to the passion swirling in his cobalt eyes.

"No?" He traced a finger down her neck. "I can feel your pulse racing," he whispered in her ear as he lifted her back up.

She closed her eyes and tried to think. What were they talking about? She couldn't remember to save her life. His arms, his dimpled smile, the sexy rasp in his voice drove away all coherent thought.

"I'd keep you in my arms all day if I could," he said, his voice husky, "but I hear the others coming up the drive."

And just as quickly as he'd drawn her close, he let her go. She watched him leave, her brain fuddled. She released a self-deprecating laugh. Wow. The man hadn't even kissed her and already he had her twisted six ways from Sunday. She'd never been addle-minded about a guy before.

Her mind wandered to how his lips would feel on hers. His full lips looked soft and warm. Heat pooled in her stomach. Hmm. She'd think about that later.

Forcing her feet to move, she headed out the back door. She surveyed the men standing around the bottom step. She never dreamed she'd be responsible for the well-being of eight people.

Jace walked over and placed a gentle hand on the small of her back. "You okay?"

She nodded, then grabbed his hand when he turned to leave. "Don't go."

His face softened and he threaded his fingers with hers. "I'm right here. Hold onto me."

Her heart tripped, making it difficult to think. Again. She forced herself to focus. Hunting off property was a dangerous gamble. Everyone needed to be careful. The MP tightened their grip, patrolling at different times each day. She organized the men into two teams. Each team would take a horse to haul their kills.

"We don't want the MP to notice we've been off property," she cautioned. "Be careful. Don't use the shotguns if you don't have to. They may be close enough to hear the report."

"I'll set rabbit snares by the creek while we're out," Travis offered.

She nodded. "Thanks, Trav. That will help."

Ethan shifted his feet. "When are we leaving? We need to find our spots well before dusk. We're catching the end of rutting season, so they should still be on the move."

"That's up to ya'll. Please tell each other where you're going so there's no doubling up or accidents." She gave everyone a sharp look. "Please don't have an accident."

The men dispersed talking amongst themselves.

She turned to Jace. "I'll go with you and Raul."

He took a step back. "You're not going."

The finality in his tone set her teeth on edge. She crossed her arms. "You can't tell me what to do."

He cocked his head. "You ever been hunting?"

She hesitated. "No."

"Ever shot a bow and arrow?" When she didn't answer, he continued. "You really gonna shoot Bambi?"

She shot him a dark look. The man was insufferable and the one person who stood toe-to-toe with her. She hated losing but knew by his tone she'd already lost the argument. Why she allowed him to run roughshod over her was anyone's guess.

Still, she couldn't resist saying, "Do I have to remind you on a regular basis that I already have a father?"

He closed the distance between them, leaned in, his breath hot on her cheek. "We both know I'm not your father."

"Really?" Her eyes raked over his face. "You're sure bossy enough to be."

Before she could react, he bent his head and brushed his lips over hers, light and sweet. He lingered long enough to steal her breath, then lifted his head. Her body hummed for more.

"Okay," she admitted, breathless. "Not my father." She walked down the steps putting distance between them then turned to face him. "But you still can't tell me what to do."

Eyes on hers, he sauntered down the steps. His subtle movements reminded her of a prowling lion. When he took a step forward, she took one back until he'd backed her against the side of the wash house. He put his hands against the tin siding, one on each side of her face, caging her between his arms.

He lowered his head and kissed her again. This time she felt his impatience, his pent-up desire. Heat curled low in her stomach and she pressed her body against his. He slanted his mouth over hers and teased her mouth open with his tongue. Heat singed through her veins.

When he lifted his lips from hers, she'd all but forgotten

her name. His smile was soft as he tucked a wayward strand of hair behind her ear. "Stay here with Cat. Please. Off property is too dangerous."

"That's not fair, Jace."

"What isn't fair?"

"I've never been kissed like that," she admitted and dropped her hand. She looked away before her next words slipped out. "It makes me want to agree to anything you ask."

He placed a hand against her cheek. "Look at me, girl."

She rested her eyes on his.

"I'll never use my love against you like that. I'll use it for you, but never against you."

His words arrowed straight through her heart. He challenged her stubbornness. Stubbornness was an innate part of her and served her well. Until it didn't. It's how she secured what she wanted most—her basketball scholarship, graduating with honors, learning to barrel race. And it landed her in her current condition, bruised and beaten.

She looked at Jace and considered how badly she wanted to win this disagreement. She didn't want to lose the men's respect, didn't want to appear weak.

As if he read her thoughts, he said, "Let me shoulder some of the responsibility. Let me help."

"Okay," she relented. No defense on earth could combat the way he said the word *please.*

He tipped her chin. "Thank you for that," he said, then released her and turned to leave. "See you soon," he promised.

She watched him walk away. Maybe he knew her better than she thought.

18

L acy leaned against the kitchen's door jamb and watched Cat evaluate their small horde of medicine. A sense of foreboding settled on her shoulders.

Cat looked up. "You okay?"

"Yeah." She pushed off the jamb. "Just can't shake this weird feeling I've got."

"About?"

She thought about it. "I'm not sure. It's probably because this will be the first time since Jace moved in that I'll be alone."

The boy knew how to hover. Sometimes she needed room to breathe. But the lengthening shadows outside had an unsettling effect on her.

"You'll be fine," she assured with a wave. "The shotgun is loaded. Where's that dog?"

"Hunting with Jace," she answered, a little miffed. The dog seemed to prefer Jace's company to hers and it rankled.

Cat gathered the few medicine bottles and put them in a burlap sack with the Jack Daniel's bottle. She opened the cabinet above the stove and pulled down a honey jar.

"Are you sure Matty has the flu?"

"I'm sure, and we're running out of medicine." Cat looked

at her, worry evident in her eyes. "I can make him a cough syrup, but I don't have anything to bring his fever down."

"Travis and Raul are going to Kaw tomorrow. Make a list of medicine they should look for. Could you write down clothing sizes too?"

"Sure thing, honey." Cat gave her shoulder a reassuring pat as she walked out the back door.

Lacy moved through the living room into her bedroom, needing a distraction. She eyed her grandfather's guitar leaning against the dresser. She hadn't touched it since the bonfire.

Her grandfather pushed her to play, told her music spoke to the spirit and was a saving grace. She'd forgotten his words until Matty trotted up and set his guitar beside her. As she looked at it now, she wondered if his words held any truth.

She walked over, picked up the case, and set it on the bed. She unbuckled and opened the lid then pulled the guitar from its crushed velvet cocoon. He'd given her a guitar for her fifteenth birthday and asked what bands she listened to. This Wild Life topped her list of favorites at the time. The first song she played at the bonfire was the first song he'd taught her. Her grandfather bought the band's current album and the sheet music. He taught her chords, then began teaching her songs.

She started playing, softly strumming the strings. Time fell away as she sang. She poured her heart into the lyrics. They touched the elemental part of her that hurt the most.

The sun set. Stars twinkled brightly in a moonless sky. Still, she played on, lost in the rhythm, lost in thought.

She didn't hear the back door creak. When she paused, she heard the familiar click against the wood floor.

And time stopped.

Oh God.

He was back.

She'd never forget the sound of his footfall.

Her heart thudded against her chest. She laid the guitar

on the bed and forced out a long, slow breath. And pulled herself together. His hands would never touch her again. As if casting a spell, she summoned her rage, and it dispelled her fear.

She tiptoed to the shotgun in the corner. With clammy hands, she picked it up and aimed.

The intruder opened the door and found himself staring down the barrel of a twelve gauge.

"Well, well. Little kitty's got a gun," he mocked, clapping his hands in a slow staccato rap. "I'm impressed."

The man lunged for the barrel and missed. Off balance, he stumbled and landed on the white chair beside her bed. The old wood cracked and broke under his weight. Her heart thumped a mad cadence as she stepped around him. She stood in the doorway blocking his escape.

As he rose, she trained the laser on his chest and imagined a scatter shot straight through his heart. He kicked the chair's broken legs aside, his glacial blue eyes locked on hers. The corner of his mouth tipped in a venomous leer.

"You don't know how to use that," he taunted.

She kept the shotgun steady. "Oh really?"

The malevolent look in his eyes shook her to the core and a lightning bolt of fear shot through her veins.

He inched forward, closing the distance between them. "Where's my brother?"

"Why are you here?" she asked, working to control the tremor in her voice. She cleared her throat and tightened her grip, the cold metal slick under her palms.

"I heard my little brother came to shack up with my left-overs," he sneered.

She choked on a sob. "You're a sick bastard, Zach."

His eyes raked over her body as he stepped forward. "The MP will be coming for him."

His statement rattled her. Why would the MP want Jace? Then she remembered Bryan Rash's statement. He said he'd return for Jace. She asked him about it, but he refused to answer. A sick feeling settled in her stomach.

He raised a brow. "He hasn't told you what he's done? You have no idea what he's capable of."

"I know what you're capable of," she replied evenly.

He crept forward another inch. "I've taken what I wanted from you."

Images forced their way forward and instant tears clogged her throat. "Why? Why did you do it?"

He spat tobacco juice on the floor. "I told you I had a score to settle. With my brother. Never could stand that little shit getting anything before me. He wanted you. Badly. I made sure I had you first." He glanced back at the bed. "Maybe I'll fuck you again. Punishment for not leaving like I told you to. Or better yet, I think I'll just take you with me. You'll be my little sex toy."

Sex toy? White hot anger seared her brain and cauterized her emotions. She racked the shotgun. Her finger skimmed the trigger. On impulse, she aimed lower. Her index finger squeezed until metal met metal. Buckshot scattered inside his foot. Bits of flesh, bone and blood splattered the floor.

His face contorted in pain, disbelief. And rage. She racked the shotgun again. The shell she emptied in his foot clanked on the floor.

"Get out! Or I swear to God, I'll kill you!" She rammed the barrel into his ribcage. She wanted to pull the trigger again. Craved it.

She backed him out of the house at gunpoint and took pleasure in his pain. He hobbled to his car, a trail of his blood staining the earth.

He opened the driver's door then turned to her. "You *fucking* bitch."

He slammed the door, revved the engine, and peeled out. His tires swerved, spit dust and gravel as they fought for traction. She raised the gun and shot twice more. One obliterated his license tag, the other shattered the back windshield.

A wild shriek escaped her lips. "If you ever come back, I'll aim for your head, you son of a bitch!"

Red taillights faded.

The shotgun slipped.

Her knees buckled.

Gravel scraped her palms when they hit the ground. The shotgun skidded across the rocks.

Cat running up the drive swam through her vision. She skidded to a stop and dropped beside her. "Are you shot? Bleeding? Are you hurt? Talk to me!"

Her world spun in theatrical slow motion. Cat's questions echoed in her ears. Her teeth chattered and she wondered if someone dropped her in an ice-filled vat or was just shaking the bejesus out of her. Every part of her frosted over until she felt nothing.

Body hoisted upright, someone commanded her to walk. She didn't want to, didn't want to lose the numbness. Her body floated above the ground and into the kitchen, then was dropped into a chair. A disembodied voice yammered on and on. She wished it would stop.

The slap to her cheek stung and instant tears formed on her lower lashes. She felt a glass placed against her lips, heard the annoying voice demand she drink. She swallowed a mouthful and her eyes shot open. She gagged as her mouth and throat were razed to ash.

"Cat?" she rasped out.

"Finish it." Cat forced the glass with the clear, liquid fire back to her lips.

She shoved her insistent hand away. "What is it? It burns."

"Everclear."

She grimaced. "No. No more."

Cat pursed her lips. "What the hell happened down here? Who did this?"

She closed her eyes and said nothing. The Everclear burned a path to her stomach. She waited for the numbness that always came with alcohol, welcomed it.

Cat went into her room, came back with a Jack Daniels bottle, and poured it in another glass. "Drink this."

She shot the whiskey. "The bastard came back for me."

Cat swore. "You shoot him?"

"Yeah. In the foot. I wanted to kill him," she confessed, her words stilted and strange.

"Should've blown his ball sack off." Cat paced the small kitchen cursing in German.

She turned her head, gazed out the darkened window. No light. Only darkness. How sublime. Would light ever shine on her again? Or was it her fate to stumble in darkness for the rest of her life? If so, she wished her days short.

Cat refilled her glass and pushed it to her. "Your reason for keeping your mouth shut better be a good one. Jace will have a hell of a fit when he gets back."

"I know," she said miserably. "What am I gonna tell him?"

"The truth." Cat looked around, perplexed. "Where did you shoot him?"

"My bedroom."

"Christ, Lacy. That gun was loaded with double-aught nines." She went to investigate then came back. "Boy, you did a number on the floor. Bet that hole is the size of a half dollar. Most of his foot is still there." She cocked her head toward the window. "Take another shot, honey. I hear the guys. They're back."

She heard Jace enter and move to the kitchen. She closed her eyes, heard his footsteps fall in the doorway. The instant she opened her eyes and looked at him, the smile fixed on his face died.

Panicked, he turned to Cat. "What happened?"

Cat sighed motioned to the whiskey bottle. "Sit. And take a shot, Jace. You're gonna need it."

He ran a hand through his wind-blown hair and yanked a chair back. "What does that mean?"

"Talk to her. I've got to clean her bedroom." She pointed at him when he rose. "Don't follow me. Sit back down."

He tipped the whiskey bottle to his lips, pulled hard, then slammed it down.

Lacy jerked, then dropped her head to the tabletop's edge, and counted the boards in the floor. Think of something else. Count each interlocking tongue and groove. How many are in this room?

Cat came back, took one look at her, and scolded him. "I said talk to her, not scare her to death."

He threw his hands up. "She's in no condition to talk to me. Just look at her."

"I was down giving Matty a cough treatment." She placed a hand to her forehead. "I wasn't gone long. The SOB that raped her came back tonight. She hasn't given me any details except that she shot him in the foot." She shook her head. "*Scheisse!*"

Lacy continued to count, unable to look at him. He could never know about his brother. He could never know he raped her because of him. Zach's confession still shook her.

Cat continued to talk, but she couldn't focus. Tears slid down her nose and puddled on her jeans.

Jace downed another shot then pushed his chair back. The legs screeched on the floorboards. She covered her ears against the abrasive sound and began to rock back and forth.

He knelt beside her. "Lacy," he said softly. "Look at me, love."

She looked up and when their eyes locked, her heart broke apart and fell at his feet.

Unshed tears brightened his eyes. He picked her up and carried her to her room. "Hold onto me. I've got you."

JACE PULLED night pants from Lacy's dresser and crossed to the bed where she sat, cross legged, staring a hole through a spot on the wall. She hadn't spoken since he returned.

"Lacy," he said, his tone muted. "Can you put these on or do you need me to get Cat?"

She turned, her face blank. "What?"

He pointed to the soft heather grey pants beside her. Compassion filled his voice. "Can you change into those? Or do you need help?"

She stared at the pants. "I can manage," she mumbled.

He turned his back while she changed. When she finished, he turned, pulled down the bed covers, and motioned for her to lie down. He clicked the bedroom door shut, shrugged out of his shirt, and hung it on the bedpost. He flipped off the light, pulled down the covers next to her, and slid in.

She turned to face him. "Jace?"

"You little idiot," he said, brushing hair from her eyes. "Do you think I'm going to leave you alone after what happened? You'll end up on the couch with me anyway. And if it's all the same to you, I'd like to save my back a few scrapes."

Mollified, the lines between her brows relaxed. She closed her eyes. Her sooty lashes stood in stark contrast to her pale face. He brushed his knuckles against her cheek and tried to calm the storm building inside him.

He should've taken her hunting.

"I'm sorry," he whispered.

She opened her eyes. "None of this is your fault, Jace."

"Yes, it is. If I'd only listened."

"No," she cut him off. "He would've found a way to get to me."

He drew her into a tight embrace. "Girl," he said, his voice shaky. "I'm not letting you out of my sight again."

"I think I'm okay with that." She sighed, sank into his arms, and fell asleep.

Long after her breathing evened out, he lay awake thinking. He wanted to kill the bastard. He *would* kill him, thought of many inventive ways to torture him, to beat him bloody. He'd use his hands and strangle him until the man's life drained away. It had to be done. Only one problem plagued him and it wasn't a morality issue. He would have no problem strangling or putting a bullet through the man's skull.

Lacy refused to identify her rapist. That was his problem. However, she unknowingly made him easy to recognize. All he had to do? Find the man missing half his foot.

19

J ace drew Lacy close as the late November winds shook the old clapboard house. He nuzzled the back of her neck and drew in the sweet scent of strawberries and honey. Mornings like this were too few and far between.

A protective feeling washed over him and melded with heated desire curling low in his stomach. He must be a glutton for punishment, sleeping with her this way. It wasn't a wise decision. He peeked over, watched her chest rise and fall in slow rhythm.

He rolled onto his back and stared at the ceiling. A broken tile, brown and crumbling with age, looked ready to fall. It reminded him of something his grandfather said.

"Jace." His grandfather placed an age-spotted hand on his shoulder as they looked across an ocean of grassland prairie. Black cows dotted the land, moving in slow, rhythmic, motion, unhurried and unconcerned. "Always remember. Life is ninety percent maintenance."

At the time, sixteen and bored, he'd wondered what the old codger meant. Now, looking at the unkempt tile, he thought he understood.

Shaking the memory, his mind turned to Lacy's rapist. Who was he? Where could he find him? The thought festered in his subconscious like a splinter he couldn't dig out. At first, he considered a military policeman then remembered her rape occurred before they arrived. Few stayed in the Shidler or Kaw City area after the government's brutal takeover. Who did that leave? He eliminated Travis and the others on the farm. No answer made sense. The injured foot was the one single identifier. But where did he start? He sighed. Million-dollar questions with plug nickel answers.

"Jace?"

He turned his head. "Morning, beautiful. Did I wake you?" He shifted to his side, reached out, and drew her close.

Her sleepy green eyes held his. "What's wrong? You look upset."

He wouldn't push her for a name, but damned if he didn't want to.

He gave her a wink to lighten the mood. Her lashes fluttered and a flush stained her cheeks. And his heart lifted. "I hope you're always swept away by my charm and good looks every morning."

"Ugh," she grumbled. "Why do you do that?"

"Do what?"

"Get conceited. Will it help your failing ego if I admit I think you're beautiful?"

He snorted. "Excuse me? Men aren't beautiful."

She raised up, eyes laughing down on him. "You are."

"You think you're funny?" He rolled onto her, grazing his unshaven cheek over her face.

"Eww." She laughed and pushed his face away, then froze. Her eyes widened and he knew the second she felt his physical attraction to her. He shifted away, slipped out of bed. Self-conscious, he ran a hand through his morning hair. God, he hadn't meant for that to happen.

He grabbed his shirt. "You okay?"

She looked bewildered and shook her head. "How do you do it?"

A slight frown creased his forehead. "Do what?"

"Sleep in the same bed with me, but not," she faltered.

"But not?" he prompted, shrugging into his sleeves.

Brows furrowed, she bit her lower lip. He knew what she wanted to ask but enjoyed watching her wrestle for the right words.

"You know." She let out an exasperated huff. "*Sleep with me.*"

He cocked his head, considering. "It's not easy." He came back and sat beside her. "There's something more. What is it?"

She lowered her eyes. "I know why you're so careful with me."

"What do you know?"

"You think I'm damaged. You act like I'll shatter if you touch me."

She sniffled and it broke his heart. Damn it. Had he been too careful? He took his cues from her, afraid to push too far. He wouldn't risk losing her by rushing into something she wasn't ready for. He could wait, was prepared to wait as long as it took.

He tipped her chin. Tears magnified the blue ring around her green eyes. "Lacy, I am going slowly. This is new for both of us. The last thing I want to do is scare or hurt you. In any way. You've been hurt enough. I want you, but you need to know"—he paused and pinned her with a meaningful look—"I don't share. There will be no room for anyone else. No memories, no ghosts. Just me. Just you. So, you need to be sure you're ready for that."

His eyes searched hers for understanding. He wanted her, but he wanted her for keeps. If she wasn't ready, he'd wait because he wouldn't settle.

"Hey," he said. "I love you, girl."

She turned her head to the window. "You know," she said, "I think you just might."

———

Jace crouched low in a clump of tall Johnson grass, baked crunchy brown from the past summer's heat, his rifle trained on a ring-necked pheasant.

He spoke in quiet tones to the dog beside him. Castiel's muscles quivered in excited expectation.

Vibrant against winter's dull colors, the bird strutted across the pasture, unaware they hid in the grass. Eyes trained on the bird, Castiel suddenly leapt forward.

"Cass, *nein!*"

The startled pheasant burst into the sky.

Jace swore and took aim. The shell scattered, missing its target. He scowled at the dog trotting his direction.

"What's wrong with you?" he scolded. "Looks like we're going home with nothing,"

He hadn't planned on hunting, but after this morning, he figured Lacy needed time alone. Cat promised to stay nearby. He hurried across the pasture, then veered left onto a worn foot path. He was anxious to get home, but a set of animal tracks pulled him up short.

He bent down, traced the print cast in the dirt. A bobcat. He raised up and scanned the horizon. The cat wasn't a threat to a horse or human but might take a swipe at Lacy's chickens. He'd tell Cat to keep an eye out, just in case.

Cold wind hit his face, reminding him a storm brewed in the north. They would get snow tonight. He slung the rifle over his shoulder and pulled his black beanie over his ears.

He rounded the path into a clearing and saw it. A wild turkey stepped into the open field, its rich brown feathers blending into the tree line.

He dropped a knee to the ground and commanded the dog in a hushed voice. "Castiel, *halten.*"

The dog stopped. He raised the shotgun, took aim, and pulled the trigger. The bird fell to its side, feathers scattering the ground.

"Hell yeah!"

He ran over and lifted it by its feet, pleased by the heavy weight. He wouldn't return empty-handed after all.

He moved up the path, mouth watering over a turkey dinner. They'd been living off canned vegetables, venison and fish. Lacy reduced mealtimes to breakfast and supper. Food was scarce and they couldn't afford to eat like they used to.

He opened the gate to the Monroe pasture and called the dog. He rushed past, knocking the back of his knees as he barreled past. He shook his head watching the catastrophic black ball of fur race through the pasture then secured the gate.

The turkey's head bobbled to and fro as he walked up the concrete path.

Cat opened the back door when he reached the steps. "Oh my," she said, eyeing the bird. "Wonderful! A turkey."

Jace smiled. He'd grown to love the older woman, even when she spouted unintelligible metaphors. "I'm glad you're happy."

"I am. Can we keep it for Christmas?" She led him into the kitchen.

He deposited the bird in the sink.

"I've got the perfect wine to go with it," she added with a cheeky grin.

He shrugged out of his coat. "Cat, is it your single intention to make every inhabitant on the farm an alcoholic? 'Cause you're on your way."

"Oh, for crying out loud," she quipped. "Go eat supper. I'll take care of this guy."

Eyes raised, he walked over and slung his coat on a kitchen chair. Lacy sat at the table, staring absently into her teacup.

He moved behind her and gave her a hug. "I got a turkey."

She gave him a distracted nod.

The aroma of fresh bread filled the air. He didn't know how Cat made it and didn't care. It smelled decadent.

He removed his beanie, tossed it on the table, and watched Lacy stare into her cup as if it were a scrying pool. Alarm edged his mind. Their morning conversation must've freaked her out more than he realized.

"You not eating?"

A venison sandwich lay untouched on her plate. She looked over and gave him a wan smile. "I'm not hungry."

His brows tipped down. "What's wrong, sweetheart?"

"Nothing. I just…" She stopped, twisting her hands. "I don't know how to do this," she whispered.

"Do what?" he asked, fearing the answer. "You don't have to do—"

She rose, solemn eyes focused on his, and closed the space between them. Her hands circled his neck. She raised up and brushed her lips over his.

The soft kiss swept straight through him, lighting his blood on fire. Her fingers twined in his hair, and her lips, soft and sweet, feathered his again.

Hands on her hips, he pulled her against him, felt every curve of her body, and deepened the kiss. She gasped and a wave of lust rolled down his spine. She slipped a hand under his button-down and a tremor rolled over him. He broke the kiss, stared into her clear green eyes, brightened with desire, and gentled his grip.

"Lacy," he murmured and gripped her wrist. "Don't."

Her eyes lowered. "Why? I thought…"

He dropped his arms and stepped back. "Look at me."

She blew out a breath then locked her eyes on his.

"What do you want from me?" he asked softly.

Her eyes swelled. "I love you. God knows I didn't want to. I'm scared, Jace. But I love you. And I want you," she said, voice firm. "That's what I want. You."

He shook his head, trying to catch up. He knew she loved him but didn't expect her to admit it. Not yet anyway.

He hesitated. "Are you sure? Because I'll wait. You're worth the wait."

She reached up and caressed his cheek. "I'm sure."

He searched her face, flushed a sweet pink. Her lips were swollen from his kiss, her pupils dilated wide with desire. He saw no reservations, no fear. It was the most beautiful sight he'd ever seen.

"I play for keeps," he reminded her. She needed to know once he had her, he was never letting go.

She nodded. "I know."

"Okay, then." He gave her a tender smile, gathered her in his arms, and kissed her again, slowly, lingering over her sweet lips. Then taking her hands, he led her to their bedroom.

DARKNESS SHADOWED the room when Lacy woke and she wondered how long they'd slept. She slipped out of bed and shrugged her arms through Jace's button-down he'd tossed to the floor. She rubbed her nose into the soft sleeve. It smelled of leather and saddle soap. And Jace. Her body tingled as she relived the sweet memory of what they shared. It shocked her how much she still wanted him. She sighed and a soft smile curved her lips.

She padded to the window, drew back the faded blue gingham curtains. Dark snow-filled clouds hung low in the sky.

Jace stirred. "Hey, beautiful," he said, his raspy voice thick with sleep.

She turned around. "Hey."

He got up and wrapped his arms around her. "You okay?"

She ran a hand through his hair. "Yeah."

Her mind swirled, a kaleidoscope of thoughts, questions, and feelings. He'd been her first. She couldn't count the rape. Zach took her by force, without permission.

Jace had asked, then filled her mind and heart until she was lost in him. She never gave anyone control of her heart. Her mind and her will were always her own. Until now.

She hoped he knew what he'd gotten himself into, because her situation hadn't changed. If he ever found out about Zach...

"You look good in my shirt," he said, fragmenting her thoughts.

She laughed lightly. "Thanks."

"What are you thinking?" He dropped his head and kissed her neck.

She leaned back, admired the strength of his jaw, the planes of his masculine face. He'd been her first, but she wondered about him. Girls in high school loved him. He was justified in his confident swagger.

"I had a few questions," she started, wondering if she'd lost her mind. She shouldn't ask. Her mom's voice echoed in her ears about curious cats. "I was wondering..." She stopped, tongue-tied and self-conscious.

"You can ask me anything," he said. "What questions do you have, Lace?"

"Well, I'm not experienced. I mean, are you disappointed? I know you..." Taking a deep breath, she continued. "I know you must've had others. You don't have to tell me. I was just kind of curious."

He tensed, dropped his arms, and sat on the edge of the bed. "You're asking me about my past."

She turned to face him. "Well, yeah." She put her hands on her hot cheeks. She couldn't keep the blood from her face to save her life.

"What makes you think I have a past?" he asked, face serious.

"Because you're so…"

His candid look stopped her short.

He cocked an eyebrow and folded his arms. "I'm so…?"

"Well." She shrugged. "Good at it."

He chuckled. "You're inflating my ego you complain about." He patted the bed. "Come sit by me."

Conflicted, she walked over and sat beside him. She didn't know if she wanted to hear about his past conquests or flings or whatever they were called, and regretted asking.

"You don't have to tell me." She backpedaled, feeling like an idiot.

"Lacy." He leaned over, brushed his lips against her temple. "I told you when I fell in love with you. I was seventeen, but my heart was yours. I didn't betray those feelings by being with another girl."

"Well, that was"—she paused to collect her thoughts—"just about perfect."

She believed every word. Her brain, however, must've been morbidly curious, because she heard herself ask, "But, how is that even possible?"

Oh stu-friggin-pendous. Someone sew her lips to the carpet. Right now.

His eyes sparked bright blue. "What?"

His stifled laughter irritated her. "Well, you can't look like that"—she waved a hand at him—"and not have opportunities. I saw all the girls at school that followed you around with puppy dog eyes."

He shouted with laughter.

"Oh, shut up," she scowled.

He reached over, pulled a hand from her lap, and laced their fingers together. "None of those girls were you, were they?" He gave her a nudge. "I knew what I wanted. And," he emphasized, "there's no way in hell I was disappointed."

He slid to the headboard, tugged her with him, and drew her close. They snuggled under the covers and lay in contented silence, listening to the wind. A gust shook the house and she nestled deeper into him.

He broke the silence. "Hey, girl."

"Yeah?"

"I meant what I said."

"I know," she said softly. "I love you, Jace."

His arms tightened around her. "I love you too."

They fell asleep listening to the howling wind. The blue norther brought a bitter arctic wind and over two feet of snow. The power went out later in the night. It never came back on.

20

The catastrophic storm left the skies a brilliant, blinding blue. Lacy surveyed the snow's high drifts sculpted by the wind. Southern fences caught snow like fishing nets. Winters before, she would've noticed the chaotic beauty wreaked by the blue norther. The sun-sparkled snow looked like ocean waves in the ditches along Highway 11 and the earth looked crisp and clean, covered in virgin snow.

Today, she saw the high snow drift against the barn door and a cut electric wire lying underneath her bathroom window. She picked it up, studied the sliced black plastic and copper.

She turned to Jace. "It's been cut." She threw it down, disgusted. It couldn't be fixed.He drew in a deep breath. "I know. The main wire at the other house is cut too."

She slapped a palm to her forehead. "Why didn't you tell me?"

"I'm telling you now."

The man infuriated her. She couldn't recall one day since he arrived that they hadn't bickered about something.

He pointed to his broad shoulders. "I told you I want to help with the responsibilities around here." He walked over, lifted her by the waist until they were eye level. "Let me."

Desire darkened his cobalt eyes. He set her down, lowered his head, and took her mouth. As she melted into the kiss, he deepened it, nipped her lower lip. The boy drove her crazy, mind and body. She pressed herself against him wanting more.

He drew back, brushed a strand of hair from her forehead. "Let me help," he whispered.

"Okay. But you can't keep things from me. You just can't." Her voice still held an edge.

His eyes danced with mischief. "God, you're beautiful when you're irritated."

"Don't change the subject," she snapped. Their clashing wills created their conflicts, but sometimes he needled her for fun.

Ignoring her, he continued. "Your eyes turn this brilliant shade of green. They're gorgeous."

He grinned down at her engagingly.

"My eyes turn—what?" she sputtered, then pointed. "Stop. This is a big deal. And proof we're being sabotaged."

"You think someone here is responsible?"

"Do you have a better explanation?"

The wind burnished the snow glassy white. No tracks remained, no footprints by the person responsible. Her thoughts darted to Zach. Would he brave the storm to cut the wire? Despite his hate for her and Jace, she didn't think he did it. The person who cut the wires knew the power was knocked out. Only a certified electrician could cut a live wire. But why cut it when the odds of the electric coming back on were slim?

Cat walked up behind them, rubbing her hands together. "I'm going to miss that old electric stove." She gave a short laugh. "That's not something I thought I'd ever say. Dear Lord, its cold. Feels like ten below at least."

Jace tipped her chin with his gloved hand. "I'll go help dig out the barn," he said then leaned down and whispered in her ear. "We'll finish this later."

She watched him trudge through the snow and smiled at his lengthening hair curling around his black beanie.

"You've got it bad, girlie," Cat said, interrupting her thoughts. A keen interest glinted in her steel grey eyes.

"That's neither here nor there at the moment," she said, embarrassed. "What are we going to do for heat? How are we going to cook?"

"There's a fireplace in our living room."

"Which hasn't worked for years," she retorted.

"Raul can clean it, get it working again, I'm sure. I can cook out of the fireplace."

She blew in her hands and walked to the back door. "What about heat for the other house?"

Cat followed her up the steps into the kitchen. "We can all fit in this house."

She stopped in the doorway and turned. Trying to keep her voice level, she said, "No."

"Lacy," she began, "it's the practical thing to do."

"I can't."

She could feel the panic she worked hard to bury. It remained too close to the surface. Its claws dug into her back like fishhooks, reeling her back to that night. How could she explain men still made her nervous, edgy? Outside in the open air, she dealt with their presence. But she refused to be stuffed in the same house with five men and a boy.

"There has to be another solution."

Cat cast thoughtful eyes on her. "Are you still having nightmares?"

"They're not as bad. Jace helps. I know it doesn't make sense, but I just can't do it."

She bent down, braced her hands on her knees, and started counting backwards from one hundred. Counting diverted her mind, evened her breathing, and stilled the panic.

"Don't worry." Cat looped her arm in hers, pulled her up, and led her to the living room. "Sit." She pointed at the rocker and she took a seat on the couch. "We'll ask Raul if that monstrosity of a stove in the shop building can be moved into the other house."

She nodded. "Okay." As her mind quieted, another thought took over. "Cat, when was the last time you saw the MP patrol?"

"It's been a while."

She rose, walked to her grandmother's bookcase, and skimmed the titles, the spines creased and worn. "I have a feeling they'll come soon. They'll take whatever they can find in the shop building, but it's Jace they want."

"Why do you think that?" she asked. "What's he done?"

She turned back. "I don't know. But you heard Bryan the last time he was here. They want him."

Outside the window she saw Jace pushing a wheelbarrow full of firewood. He rounded the corner and disappeared. What had he done?

She swung her gaze to Cat. "When they come, you're gonna have to hide him."

"Like I could manage that." She pulled an old, crocheted afghan from the couch and draped it over her shoulders. "He's too stubborn. He won't hide."

"Make him."

"Right," she said in a derisive tone. "What do you want me to do? Wrestle him to the ground and sit on him?"

She gave her an amused look. "You could lock him in the wine cellar."

"*Nein!* Does he even know we have a wine cellar?"

"Nope." She raised an eyebrow. "He'll find your liquor stash."

Cat sighed. "Your great-grandfather was a brilliant man. He left a treasure trove down there."

"My great-grandfather was a raging alcoholic," she corrected. "Come on, Cat. You've got to. I won't let them take him."

"I'll do what I can." A worried look crossed her face. "I need to go check on Matty and make sure he's not out in this cold trying to work."

"How is he?"

Cat rose, still clutching the blanket. "He's not over the flu. And he's hard to keep down. Thinks he should be doing the work of a man."

"I'm sure he could if he were able."

"Well, he isn't able and he's going to listen to me," the older woman insisted.

Lacy snickered. "What are you gonna do, Cat? Wrestle him to the ground and sit on him?"

Her hands dropped to her hips. The blanket slipped to the floor with a soft swish. "Boy, what a smart mouth you have." Cat clucked her tongue but gave her an indulgent smile as she passed by. "I'll be back later."

"Hey," she blurted, stopping Cat. "I'm kind of mad at you, by the way."

She turned, a curious expression covering her face. "What for?"

Her eyes narrowed. "You taught Jace the German commands for Castiel, didn't you?"

"Well," she hedged. "You needed a little push in his direction. He was so cute, coming and asking me for help. I couldn't refuse him."

"Great," she muttered. "Just what his ego needs. Another fan girl."

Cat opened the back door and sailed out, tittering under her breath.

She shook her head and jerked the screen door open. "I'm still mad," she hollered at her retreating back.

Jace walked up the steps brushing saw dust from his jeans. "Why are you mad at Cat?"

She took a long look at his boyish grin and rolled her eyes in mock disgust.

"I'm not really mad," she admitted. Her lips formed a small smile. "But I know she taught you how to speak to my dog."

"Yeah, she did," he said. He sauntered up and snagged her by the waist. "Knew you'd figure that out. Took you long enough."

She bit her cheek to keep her smile at bay. "You need to work on your arrogance. It's off-putting sometimes."

He rubbed his cold cheek, rough with stubble, against hers. "You love me anyway," he whispered.

She leaned into him and sighed. "God knows why."

He tipped her chin and the lust in his eyes mirrored her own. "Oh, you know why."

She did.

Feigning aggravation, she pulled back. "Has anyone ever told you that you can be annoying as hell?"

A grin swept across his face. "Has anyone ever told you that you can be a pain in the ass?"

She smiled despite herself. "On numerous occasions."

LACY LUGGED the water-laden laundry Hailey had left with Cat to the clothesline in her grandmother's back yard. The plastic-coated wire drooped between two rusted T posts. The old wicker basket slipped and dropped to the snow-covered ground with a dull thud. She looked down, eyed the men's work shirts and jeans, and her nose scrunched in disgust. She picked up Jace's soggy blue button-down, watched the soapy water drip from the hem.

"Damn it, Hailey. What a mess."

She left the basket and walked the short distance to the wash house searching for a clothes wringer. Her great-grandmother kept everything under the sun. Being a Depression Era kid made her a hoarder by circumstance.

An old cast iron wringer sat in the far corner. The wooden

rollers, cracked and splintered along the edges, looked ready to fall off their cogs. She tried the hand crank but it refused to budge. It would need oil and a few knocks with a hammer to turn again.

Kicking cans from her path, she rolled the heavy machine outside, then lifted her head as the signature sound of ASVs filled the air.

Cat trounced out the back door. "Here they come."

"Where's Jace?"

She turned toward the shop building and saw him. His long strides ate the distance between them.

He stopped beside her, his face etched in concern. "We didn't get everything moved into the barn cellar."

"We got enough." She pressed a hand to her forehead. "They don't care about the junk in the building. They're here for you. If they stop this time, they'll try and take you."

"How do you know that?" he asked, eyes guarded.

Cat sidled beside Jace and slung her arm around his shoulder. "Have I ever showed you my stash, Jace?"

Bewildered, he gave her a blank stare. "What stash?"

Urging him forward, she propelled them both up the steps. "Come on, I'll show you."

He quickly sized up the situation and pointed a finger at her. "I'm not leaving Lacy. I don't care what Bryan said about me."

She turned and saw the grim look on his face as Cat shoved him through the door. "Crap," she muttered.

He could be high-handed and knew she'd answer for Cat stuffing him in the wine cellar.

The ASVs stopped, snow crunching under the big machines' tires. Bryan Rash opened the lead vehicle's door and hopped out.

Travis trotted up the drive and stopped beside her. "Where's Jace?"

Travis and Jace were at odds over her. The loss of Travis'

daily visits pained her. She knew her choice hurt Travis, and whenever she thought about it, her heart ached.

"Hiding," she answered, eyes never leaving Bryan.

"Why?"

"Just let me handle this. Is Raul in the barn cellar?"

"Yeah, with Ethan and Hailey. They left Matty and Dylan holed up in the back bedroom."

"Good enough," she said. With everyone sorted, her shoulders relaxed.

Bryan walked over, handling a pair of bolt cutters.

She hoped Cat had hidden Jace.

"What do you want, Rash?" she asked, giving him a bland look.

His eyes raked over her in open appraisal. "I told you I'd be back."

"Yeah, terminator style. You're missing the Ray Bans, though."

Bryan's chocolate eyes smoldered black. "Where's Jace?"

"Not here."

His stance widened. "Our sources say he's still on this property. Now, where is he?"

"If he was here, he'd be free. I granted him asylum. You can't touch him on this property." She lifted her chin. "What do you want with him anyway?"

He turned to his men standing in typical military formation. Their obedience without question baffled her. She never took orders without asking questions first. A particular character trait her dad tried, and failed, to expunge.

"Search the houses," he commanded, then swung back around. "We'll search the entire property."

"Search away," she motioned, sweeping her arms wide.

"We're also seizing everything in that building," he said, pointing to the steel-grey structure.

"Search and seize. Got it."

He shifted his feet. A mixture of irritation and confusion flashed across his face. "Just stay out of our way."

She watched as they searched the houses. One by one, the men filed out her back door empty-handed. She sighed in relief.

Puzzled, Bryan returned. "He's not in there."

"I don't make a habit of lying." The statement itself was true. In most cases, she never lied, having discovered early in life lying always created more trouble. Easier to face problems outright than try and side-step them. Today, she made an exception.

He stomped his way to the shop and snapped the lock. It fell into the snow, disappearing under its white, icy layers. Lacy and Travis followed and watched him struggle to open the sliding doors. He stepped inside and his face contorted in disbelief.

Old newspapers, milk cartons, oil cans, and trash lay scattered over the stained cement floor. A mig welder, cylinders with argon gas, an air compressor, and an old engine were still lined against the east wall. Everything else had been hidden in the barn cellar or the trash pit.

He spun on his heel, stalked back, and rammed a finger in her face. "Where is it?"

She clasped her hands together. "Where's what?"

"All the stuff!"

"No need to yell. What were you expecting to find? Were you looking for something specific?"

He leaned in, stuck his face inches from hers. "You're messing with the wrong people."

The stink of chewing tobacco wafted from his mouth. A flashback of Zach and his kiss hit her hard. Flinching, she stepped away, hands clenched.

He walked out and looked around, frustrated. His eyes landed on the fish house and dread pricked her scalp.

"Search this building," he commanded, striding toward it.

She followed, stumbling in the snow. "Bryan, there's nothing in there."

He turned. "Scared now?"

"Nothing in there but food," reported one of his men.

"Take it all."

She grabbed his arm. "You can't take it."

His brown eyes hardened. "We can and we will."

"But we'll starve. Please don't take it," she pleaded, hating to beg.

"Good. The sooner the better."

She lunged forward. She wanted to rip out his heart and feed it to the buzzards. Travis grabbed her arm and jerked. She stumbled backward into his chest. "Let me go!"

"Go ahead," Bryan taunted. "Assault an officer of the law. I'll arrest you."

She jerked her arm free but stayed put. She watched helplessly as the soldiers carried away all the deer meat and fish. "Please," she tried again.

"The sooner this place is shut down, the better."

The puzzle pieces locked in place. "I'm that big of a problem for the National Guard? Why do they care if I'm here?"

"You don't get it do you? It's not you, honey. It's your uncle, Senator Monroe, and the threat of the Independent State of Texas starting a civil war. We need everyone in a controlled environment as soon as possible."

Incensed, she swung around to face the semi-circle of military men. "How can you be so willfully blind?" she shouted at them. "Our land will run red with blood. Start thinking for yourselves! How can you stand against and murder your brothers? Have we learned nothing from our country's past? How many of us will die before you wake up? You've declared war on the people you swore an oath to protect. Why? Because a tyrant sits in the White House and dictates your every move? He's turned you into an unthinking war machine and you are crushing our nation under the heels of your indifference. If it's a war you want, it's a war you'll get. But remember this: There is no more 'of the people, for the people, by the people.' Take a good look around you. This is all that's left of freedom."

The men stood motionless, looking down at their snow-covered boots. Only one lifted his head and stared at her, a contemplative look in his eyes.

The shakes started in her stomach and spread outward until her whole body quaked. She drew in a deep breath.

"Quite a speech," Bryan sneered. "I could arrest you right now for treason."

She took a step forward into his personal space. "I'm on free land. Get out of here before I decide to shoot you for trespassing and stealing." She turned away without a backward glance.

She counted her steps, concentrated on steady even breaths as the snow crunched underneath her feet. Seventy-eight steps from the fish house to her back door. She entered the kitchen and moved toward the voices drifting from the living room.

"Great adversity brings out the best in us. Or the worst. Sometimes both," Cat said.

She stopped in the doorway. "What are you talking about?"

Jace walked over and drew her into his arms. "You," he said, kissing her forehead. "You were amazing, Lace. We heard everything you said."

She leaned into him. "They took all the food, Jace."

"We'll replace it," he soothed.

"How? There's over a foot of snow on the ground."

She hated this burden, hated her uncle for breaking his word. She wondered why forty acres in Osage County, Oklahoma mattered to the old man.

She sat in the rocker and pushed it back and forth with her toes. A fire crackled and popped in the fireplace. Raul cleaned it out, but still needed to make some repairs. She felt heat drift from the burning logs and stretched her legs closer.

"I need my uncle and I have no idea how to contact him."
She paused and closed her eyes. "I'm out of my depth."

Jace sat on the couch. "What's he planning, Lace? Do you
know?"

She raised her head, her eyes catching his. "I have no idea."

21

T he barn roof's rusty tin creaked under the weight of Jace's boots. The slanted roof's snow-covered surface was treacherous. He slipped and lost his footing. Heart pounding, he righted himself, then bent over and brushed off a place to sit. His breath frosted the air and he berated himself. Stupid to sit in below freezing temperatures to avoid a certain tiny, green-eyed, raven-haired girl.

The cold metal penetrated his Levi's and numbed his rear end. Thankful for his old faded Carhartt jacket, he zipped it to his chin. The sun had long since set and any warmth the day held vanished with its last rays. He shoved his hands deep into the pockets and shifted, trying to get comfortable.

He tugged his black beanie snugly over his ears then turned his body east. He scanned the horizon but saw no flickering headlights in the dense inky darkness. The vast prairie land offered no light, natural or synthetic. Commercial air pilots called Osage County "the black hole." An eerie name, but it fit.

The MP continued patrolling the area at least twice a day. Where they got the fuel to waste, he didn't know. Bryan Rash knew they needed to hunt off property to replace their food supply, so he increased patrols at different times each day. Jace watched them for a week to decipher a pattern, but so far none emerged.

He shifted again, agitated. They needed to hunt. Rabbit snares set by the old oil field pipes crossing along the pasture wouldn't sustain them and the canned goods wouldn't last another week. No one ventured outside the farm's perimeters to scavenge.

It was impossible to fight the National Guard. They squeezed their military fist, draining the life from the farm. Their dicey situation needed a solution. Fast. The burden was too much for Lacy. This was her uncle's clusterfuck. He needed to show up and deal with it. And the only way for that to happen was to go find him.

The tin cracked, breaking the silence, and he turned. Lacy walked toward him, her arms stretched out for balance. Snow chunks fell as she shuffled forward.

"Be careful," he grunted.

"Well, hello to you too."

He sighed and lowered his head. He'd been avoiding her. He knew it. She knew it. He couldn't help it.

Leaving the farm undetected surpassed his definition of difficult. But in no uncertain terms would he risk her safety. He was leaving. Without her. Telling her his plan would lead to an argument he wasn't sure he'd win. Her determination was intractable. It tore his heart out every time he thought of leaving her. So, he chose the coward's way and disengaged.

He felt the tin shift and bend as she lowered herself beside him. "Ugh, it's cold," she complained, shoving her hands in her coat pockets.

He grunted again, eyes never leaving the dark eastern horizon. She sat beside him in silence. He felt her penetrating gaze focused on the side of his face.

"Jace." She said his name with barely controlled patience. "What are you doing up here in zero-degree weather?"

He turned to face her. The clouds shifted and the anemic winter moon cast pale, silver rays that shimmered on her hair and formed a halo. Her green eyes shone from her upturned face. The stereotypical definition of beautiful didn't apply. He couldn't think of a word strong enough to describe her in that moment. She was ethereal, gorgeous, with a touch of feline femininity. And she was his.

She nudged his shoulder, interrupting his thoughts. "What's wrong with you? You've been acting weird all week."

"The MP are making it impossible to leave the farm to hunt," he replied tersely. "I'm trying to establish a pattern. If we know their pattern, we can hunt."

"Any one of the guys could be up here doing that." She rose to her feet. "Why are you avoiding me?"

The veiled hurt in her voice crushed him and he hated himself a little more. "I'm not avoiding you," he denied. She caught his gaze, and he looked down at his gloved hands.

"The hell you say," she muttered.

She turned and climbed down the ladder. The crunch of hardened snow under her boots drifted upward then faded. His heart wavered. He should go after her and make things right. He couldn't avoid her forever. And he needed her.

After wrestling with himself, he climbed down and trudged back. He slipped into their room and found her fast asleep. Slipping under the covers, he snuggled against her back, wrapped his arms around her and pulled her close. His aching heart eased as he held her. He was still leaving, but he wouldn't push her away again. She'd been hurt enough. She deserved better.

SLEEP'S hazy fog lingered as Jace stretched his arm out for Lacy. He wanted her soft curves nestled close. His arm stretched further but found nothing but empty air and cold sheets.

He sat up and tried to focus. Her clothes, usually draped on the bedpost, were missing. She hadn't mentioned any early morning plans. Then again, he hadn't given her a chance. He thought separating himself might ease the pain of leaving. He scrubbed his hands over his face. It was official. He was an idiot. Nothing would ease the pain of leaving her. Stupid to think he could try.

However, his decision to leave remained firm. He was going to Texas to find Thomas Monroe. But first, he'd find the man responsible for hurting Lacy. He didn't have a clue what he'd do when he found him.

No light shone under the bathroom door. He looked at the battery-operated clock. The ghoulish green numbers registered six o'clock. He sighed and rubbed his gritty eyes. He dragged himself out of bed and pulled his jeans over his long johns. The biting air made getting dressed an Olympic sport. The fireplace wasn't big enough to heat the entire farmhouse. Even if it could, he'd still close their bedroom door, unwilling to give up their privacy.

Frustration built in his chest, layer by layer. He blew out a short breath and went into the living room. Raul slept on the couch and kept the fire burning during the night. He stirred at the obtrusive footfall then threw his arm over his eyes and continued to snore.

Cat walked through with a basket of eggs and chuckled. "What's got you up at this hour? Your hair looks like a flamingo nested there all night."

"Cute," he muttered, combing his fingers through wayward strands. He yawned and stretched his arms above his head. "Have you seen Lacy?"

She stopped and turned in the kitchen doorway. "No. Is she not in bed?"

"Nope. Did she mention anything she needed to do today?"

Concern crept in and mixed with his frustration. The girl paid absolutely no attention to her own safety.

She shook her head. "*Nein.* She never tells me anything she thinks I'll disapprove of. If she's gone and I don't know about it, you better start looking. It can't be good."

He ground his molars. "Right."

She cocked a brow.

"What?"

"Sometimes I wonder if you know what you've gotten yourself into. Bite off more than you can chew with her, Bub?"

He grinned despite himself. "With that little bit of girl? Please."

She shouted with laughter. "You won't break her, if that's what you're thinking."

"I don't want to break her, Cat. I just want her consideration before she goes off and does —"

He wanted her consideration, yet he'd given her none. He'd withdrawn, thinking it would lessen the pain when he left, but hadn't considered how it would affect her or their relationship.

"Whatever the hell she decides to go and do," he finished in a weak voice.

Cat's shrewd eyes cut him. "She won't bend her will to yours if it doesn't suit her. If you want her to discuss things with you, she needs to know and trust that you'll listen to her, see her side of things before passing judgement." She held up a hand silencing his rebuttal. "Honey, I've seen you overpower her. She just relinquished her end of the fight because she came to your conclusion as well. She doesn't answer to just anyone. I get the feeling her brother was the only one in her family that could do anything with her."

He thought of AJ and how he managed his sister. AJ loved her without question or reserve, often going behind her back to protect her from hormone-addled teenage boys. He listened to her without reproof and always validated her arguments, even if he disagreed. In the end, he always got her to fall in line. He needed to take a page from his best friend's book.

"I'm surprised he didn't have more sway over her when they moved to California," she mused. "Seems he would've done more to get her to go with them."

"Yeah, I wish he would've. If he ever finds out what's been done to his little sister…"

Her eyes locked on his. "You worry about what he'll say when he finds out about *you* and his little sister?"

He shrugged and a smile tugged his lips. "A little," he admitted. "At the same time, I wonder why he couldn't see how I felt about her. Her mom sure did."

She walked over and patted his shoulder. "That's a mother's intuition. It has nothing to do with people seeing or not seeing what's in front of them."

"True enough."

Raul lowered his arm. "Why are you both up?" His voice, gravelly from sleep, held more curiosity than annoyance.

"Did you see Lacy leave this morning?" Jace asked.

He scrubbed his face and hoisted himself up. "Yeah. She left an hour ago."

His hands balled into fists. "She mention where she was going?"

Jace looked out the window. The dawning sun's crown peaked over the eastern horizon.

"No. I heard her talking to Travis yesterday about wanting to go home. Something about a picture she wanted to get."

She'd talked to Travis. Damn it. He had no one to blame but himself for shutting her out. He grabbed his coat and beanie and headed to the barn. She had an hour on him, and he'd have to ride fast to catch her.

22

Acer cantered down the old, abandoned oil field road, hooves crunching on hardened snow and gravel. The path, rutted out and mostly dirt, had once been well-traveled by oil field workers. Lacy's dad taught her to drive on this road in an old yellow VW Bug. It took her a while to get the hang of driving a four on the floor, but once she did, he couldn't keep her off the road.

She took a deep breath of the crisp, clean, early morning air. Although pre-dawn darkness enveloped her, she felt free. Her lungs expanded and her chest relaxed. The farm suffocated her. She needed time alone to think and reflect. She missed her brother, missed his unconditional love and support. Missed his friendship most of all. Talking to him was effortless and she needed to talk to him about Jace.

"Wish you were here, AJ," she whispered.

She felt lost. After the MP's last visit, Jace had been distant. Something weighed on his mind. He tried to hide it, but she saw it nonetheless and it made her nervous. He'd pushed his way into her life, made her care about him, love him. What the hell was he thinking, blowing her off last night?

The oil field road led straight to Sarge Creek Cove on Kaw

Lake. As dawn broke behind her, she caught sight of white caps rolling on the water and smelled the sharp odor of fish and sand. She urged Acer into a gallop. They raced along the shoreline and she reveled in the freedom. The wind whipped her hair into a banner behind her. Only when sand and shore gave way to cliffs and rocks did she turn back. She slowed Acer to a canter, leaned down, and gave his neck an appreciative pat.

"Good boy," she murmured.

He tossed his head and nickered. He enjoyed the run as much as she did.

She looked up, scanned her surroundings, and saw a rider galloping down the oil field road. She reached for the pistol tucked in the back of her jeans and set it in her lap. The black metal of the Sig glinted in the sun. She'd found it in her grandmother's dresser, locked and loaded.

She pulled Acer to a complete stop and waited. The rider reined in, flung himself out of the saddle, and barreled straight toward her. She raised the gun.

"What the hell, Lace!" Jace shouted, stomping through the sand.

Agitated, Acer snorted and sidestepped.

"Put the damn gun down," he demanded, then reached for Acer's bridle. "Easy boy," he soothed in a tempered voice.

She lowered the gun to her lap and shook her head. "I didn't need you to follow me, Jace."

He threw his hands up and released a feral growl. "Jesus H. Christ! You are the most frustrating person I've ever known." He maneuvered around her horse. "You really gonna shoot me?"

She smirked. "Only if I have to."

He cocked an eyebrow in challenge. "I could take that gun from you before you could pull the trigger."

Her eyes narrowed. "Bring it."

His whole demeanor oozed confident self-assurance. His

eyes, a dark and dangerous blue, locked on hers. Before she could react, he jerked her from the saddle, laid her out flat in the wet sand, and expertly slipped the gun from her hand. He tucked it in the back of his jeans. A wicked grin flitted across his face.

"Get. Off. Me," she ground out.

He rose, reached down, and pulled her to her feet. "For the love of God, Lace," he muttered. "Give it a rest."

She stared at him and suddenly it hit her. She wasn't just irritated for his recent reticence. She was pissed.

"Give it a rest?" she shouted. "You have no right to follow me or boss me when you've done nothing, *nothing* but shut me out." Anger she'd tamped down erupted. "You made me trust you!"

Unable to control the fury his silent betrayal provoked, she lunged forward, and shoved him backward into the wet sand. Tears streamed down her cheeks as she watched him rise to his knees.

Still angry, she bent down, scooped up a handful of wet sand, and lobbed it at his chest.

He brushed the sand off his coat and rose to his feet. "Knock it off."

She hurled another blob of sand and clay. It hit his cheek with a sound smack then dribbled down the side of his neck.

"I mean it, Lace."

Another ball of sand and grit hit him square in the balls.

In two strides he had her by the waist, threw her over his shoulder, and walked out into the water.

He wouldn't ...

She pounded her fists on his back as he trudged against the wind and waves. "Let me go, you conceited asshole!"

He turned to look at her. "You gonna play nice?"

"Fine," she agreed through pinched lips. "But this isn't over."

His grip tightened around her waist as he hauled them

back to shore. The moment his feet touched the shoreline, she wrestled out of his arms and stomped to her horse.

"You arrogant, bossy, overbearing, vain, cocky…" She sputtered around for more insults as she untied a saddle blanket. "Pushy, pompous, conceited, jerk!"

He grabbed the blanket and wrapped it around her shoulders. "You said that already. The conceited part anyway." He leaned down and rubbed his wet, sandy cheek across her face.

"Oh, gross." She grabbed a fistful of his flannel shirt and wiped her cheek.

"Lacy, what are you doing?"

His patience drained her anger. Crestfallen, her shoulders hunched into the blanket and unwanted tears sprang into her eyes. "I want to go home, Jace. I miss my brother," she choked out.

He pulled her close. "I know you do, sweetheart. Why didn't you tell me you wanted to go home? Did you think I'd try to stand in your way?"

A struggle waged inside her. She didn't want to hurt him, but he needed to realize he couldn't control her. Not completely. She drew back. "Jace, I don't need anyone telling me what I can and can't do. I'll do what I want regardless."

He stiffened. "You didn't give me a chance, didn't even mention it to me." He kicked sand under his feet. "It's dangerous for you to go off by yourself. The MP are gunning for you, your rapist is still out there somewhere. You can't ignore that. You can't pretend the threat doesn't exist."

She stared at him nonplussed. He'd gone out of his way to avoid her, yet there he stood wondering why she hadn't consulted him.

He shifted his weight and ran a hand through his wet hair. "I'm sorry, Lace. I…". He let out a frustrated sigh. "You drive me crazy, you know that?"

"Drive you crazy?" she parroted. "You literally, and I do mean literally, pushed your way into my life. And for what?"

She pointed at him. "I didn't ask for this relationship. So, tell me Jace. Enlighten me. After shoving your way into my heart, why have you decided to take yours back?"

Shock covered his face. "That's not what I'm doing!"

"Well, that's how it looks to me," she shot back. "I can't believe you had the nerve to ask why I didn't talk to you about going home or missing my brother."

"Do you know, every day when I wake up, I'm afraid to leave you? Afraid that bastard will come back for you and I won't be there to protect you." He cupped her face in his hands. "And God, girl, you have to know I love you."

Doubt clouded her thoughts. "Then why have you shut me out?"

He answered her question with a question. "Why won't you tell me who hurt you?"

He asked the impossible. They were at an impasse. So instead of giving him what he wanted, she gave him what she needed. She reached up, drew his face down, and kissed him. His arms wrapped around her waist, crushing her against him. She threaded her fingers into his hair. His lips moved down, dropped kisses along her jawline then moved to her neck.

He lifted his head, his darkened blue eyes solemn. "I'm so sorry, love."

"Yeah," she sighed. "Me too."

His brow creased. "There's just one more thing."

"What now?" she asked, rolling her eyes.

"When I'm being a jackass, don't run to Travis. Talk to Cat, okay?"

She gave him a mischievous grin. "But Travis always agrees with me. Cat doesn't."

He leaned back. "I told you already. I'm not sharing you with Travis."

"And I told you. He's just a friend."

"Yeah," he muttered. "Just make sure he knows he's in the friend zone."

Her arms tightened, drawing him close again.

"So, are you going home?"

Her eyes raised to his. She didn't need her childhood home. Not anymore. She needed him. She raised up, pressed her forehead to his and said, "I am home."

23

J ace traipsed through a small copse of dark green Juniper trees that bordered Salt Creek in search of a Christmas tree. The arctic cold lingered and snow clung like a stubborn child to the dull brown landscape. His horse trudged behind him in silent reluctance. Snow, brittle and dirty, crunched underfoot and the raw wind cut through his layers of clothes and burned his face.

He stopped, untied the ax from his saddle, and took a few practice swings. Its wooden handle, once a bright fire engine red, had faded a weathered brown, and the rusted blade was as dull as a butter knife.

The constant cloud cover combined with the unforgiving temperatures left everyone cranky and depressed. Decorating a Christmas tree might cheer everyone. Or have the opposite effect. It depended on how they chose to look at their circumstances. All he wanted was to make Lacy smile.

She still refused to tell him what he wanted to know. Realizing she didn't trust him enough to tell him hurt like hell. Her words at the lake stung. They stung because they were true. She hadn't asked for this relationship. He'd pursued her without relent, pushed until she surrendered.

He kicked the snow under his boots. His mom said the things you fought for the hardest were the things you'd treasure the most. He'd fought for Lacy, was still fighting, but at times he felt so inept. He didn't know what the hell he was doing. Balance between being equal partners versus overbearing her eluded him. She needed to be checked, he cared more about her wellbeing than being at the receiving end of her sharp tongue. He just wished he could find a more diplomatic way.

He slung the ax over his shoulders and continued his scrutinizing search through the trees. He spotted a small one, a bit Charlie Brown-ey, but thought it would do the trick. He chopped it down, fighting the blade's smooth edge until the tree fell. Anxious to beat the darkness, he tied it to his saddle and headed home.

Cat greeted him as he walked in the back door, then gasped when she saw the tree.

"Oh," she breathed. "A Christmas tree. You are a good man, Jace."

He scratched his head. "You think?" He dumped the tree by the old leather couch and brushed snow and pine needles from his clothes. "I didn't know if it would help everyone's mood or not."

He shrugged out of his coat and tossed it on the couch. The fire burned a bright and cheerful orange and he gravitated to its warmth.

"Of course, it will help. We need some holiday cheer. I think Lacy mentioned something about Christmas decorations in the attic. Be a dear and get them down for me."

"Sure thing." He rolled his eyes, rubbing his hands before the fire.

"We don't have much food to celebrate Christmas tomorrow. That lousy Bryan Rash stole my turkey." She brightened, "But we have a tree now. And we've got wine."

He unfolded the attic ladder in the living room's ceiling. It came down with a hard thud and flecks of grey insulation particles rained a nuclear fallout cloud over his head and shoulders.

Cat burst into laughter. "I wish I had a camera."

He bent over and shook the dust clinging to his hair. "Where's Lace?" he asked as he started up the ladder. Microbic dirt crawled up his nose and he sneezed.

He lifted himself into the small opening and bumped his head on the small attic's rafters. Crawling on the grime-coated crossbeams, he searched the boxes until he found one marked Xmas in faded red sharpie.

"She's visiting Matty," Cat hollered up the ladder.

He reappeared at the opening and lowered the box. "How's he doing?"

"Not good," she admitted. "The flu's turned into pneumonia. I wish I had my stethoscope so I could listen to his lungs. Not that we have any medicine that will help."

He swung his legs around and climbed down. "Do we need to make a run? We haven't gone through all the houses at Kaw. Maybe we could find some antibiotics."

She set the box by the tree. "That would be up to Lacy. I know she worries about the MP patrols."

The screen door slammed and Lacy peered around the corner. "What would be up to me?"

Cat turned. "Making a run to Kaw to find medicine for Matty."

"He needs something. We could use the extra food, too." She nodded in assent. "I'll ask Travis about going. He knows the town and where to look."

"I'll ask him," Jace interjected.

Her lips turned down. "I can do it."

"Lacy," he started, his tone firm. "I'll do it."

She shook her head. "Why do you have to be so overbearing?"

He walked over and buried his face in her neck. "I'm trying, Lace, but please, when it comes to Travis, just…" He lifted his head and sighed. "I have never wanted anyone as much as I want you. And Travis still acts like he has a claim on you. I don't like it."

"He does not. Even if he did feel that way, it's one-sided, so relax, okay?"

"Lace." He raked fingers through his gritty hair and swore. "Just remember you belong to me."

She reached up and circled his neck, curling her fingers into his hair. Pulse racing, he bent down and kissed her. Hands on her hips, he tugged her closer, deepened the kiss, craving more. He wanted to drive every thought from her head except him.

Cat cleared her throat. "Ahem."

With reluctance he raised up. "Sorry, Cat."

She feigned a swoon then walked to her bedroom. "Ah, young love."

"I got you something," he said to Lacy and pointed to the anemic tree. Her eyes lit and his heart swelled. Exactly the reaction he'd hoped for.

She clasped her hands together and brought them under her chin. "A Christmas tree for Christmas Eve."

"Yup. I already got the decorations out of the attic." He grimaced at the dirt still lingering in his hair.

"Let's bring Matty up to see it," she suggested.

He considered. "Let's gather everyone for a party. Cat will enjoy trying to get everyone drunk."

"Yes, she will." Laughing, she caught his gaze. Mischief lit the tiny gold flecks against the green in her eyes. "Are you going to invite Travis, or should I?"

He scrubbed his hands over his face and shook his head. "You're a witch, sometimes. You know that? That was just mean. I'll go invite everyone."

She swatted his arm. "Be nice. It's Christmas."

"I'll be nice," he grumbled, slamming the screen door on his way out.

He walked down the drive, watched the sun dip below the western horizon. "Good God, she's a handful."

Frozen gravel crunched underfoot. In his haste, he forgot his beanie and the nippy air bit his ears. In the distance, a coyote howled. As he neared the larger farmhouse, he heard Castiel's soulful echo. The dog spent his days and nights watching over Matty as though he knew the boy needed him.

He opened the back door and noticed a card table set up in the kitchen. Travis, Dylan, and Raul sat playing Texas Hold'em. The shop's huge cast iron stove sat on a red brick platform along the outer wall and warmed the room. Matty sat in a rocking chair, a ragged quilt bundled around his shrunken frame. Castiel's huge body covered his feet.

He walked over and ruffled the boy's hair. "Hey, kid, hanging in there?"

His dulled eyes looked up. "Yeah," he croaked. God, the kid sounded awful.

He turned to Raul and grinned at his large pile of red, blue, and green chips. He slapped his shoulder. "You winning?"

His brown eyes twinkled. "I have mastered the art of the bluff."

"Whatever, man," Travis complained and picked up the Jack Daniel's bottle on the table. He poured a healthy portion into a faded plastic Gas-N-Sip cup. "It's called beginner's luck."

Jace shifted his gaze to all three, careful to include Travis. "You want to come up to the house for a party? Lacy's decorating a tree."

"Can we bring the cards?" Raul asked. "I like this game."

Travis rolled his eyes and folded his cards. "Nah," he said, raising his cup. "I've got my own party right here."

Jace silently cursed him for being difficult. If Travis didn't show, Lacy would blame him. He swallowed his pride, a bitter pill that stuck in his throat, and tried his best to be civil. "It would mean a lot if you came."

Travis snorted and slammed his cup down. Chips rattled and the ace of spades fluttered to the floor. "Yeah, well, I'm not in a fighting mood Jace, and since you can't seem to keep your fists to yourself when I'm around, I think I'll pass."

He shifted his feet, shoved his hands in his pockets, and tried to still his agitation. "Steer clear of Lacy, and we'll have no problem."

Travis stood, knocking the folding chair to the floor. "You don't get to tell me what to do."

"When it comes to Lacy, I sure as hell do," he shot back. He took a deep breath, needed to back off.

"God, what she sees in you, I'll never know," Travis muttered.

He clenched his jaw. "Look, I know I'm not handling this well, but you need to be clear on one point. Lacy is with me. Respect that boundary, and we're good."

Travis swiped the whiskey off the table. "She may be with you. For now," he said and stalked toward the living room.

He rubbed the back of his neck. "Shit."

Raul shook his head. "You handled that well."

"Lacy's gonna be pissed." He cursed again. He wasn't the one at fault this time.

"I see a lot of groveling in your future," Raul smirked.

Jace turned toward the door. "I agree. Can you tell Ethan to bring his family up? Lacy wanted Matty to see the tree."

Raul nodded. "*Sí.*"

Jace trudged back down the driveway, cursing Travis with every step.

———

CAT WAITED at the door for the small group and ushered them into the living room. A fire blazed and Lacy popped corn in a cast iron kettle. Liquor and wine bottles sat on the kitchen counter. Jace shook his head. Cat would enjoy every minute of this party.

As he walked through the living room, Cat pulled him aside. "Lacy told me I have your highness's permission to get everyone drunk." She bowed, and her laugh tinkled with merriment like wind chimes blowing on a soft summer breeze.

"Permission has been granted," he said in like spirit. "I hereby dub you the *Slainte* Queen."

"Ah, but I'm not Irish," she returned with a grin.

He cocked his head. "But your royal eminence is. So, please start serving my lowly subjects. Everyone needs a little cheer."

She gave him a spontaneous hug. "I knew I liked you."

"Yeah, well…" he trailed off as Lacy caught his eye.

Cat looked between the two and chortled. "Someone's in trouble."

"Where's Travis?" Lacy asked over the light chatter.

He sauntered to the kitchen table where she dumped popcorn in a red melamine bowl. "He had a date," he said without inflection.

She placed the hot kettle on an old wooden trivet. "A date? What do you mean?"

He looked at the ceiling and sighed. "He didn't want to come."

"Why?" she asked, drawing out the word.

"Aw hell, Lace."

"What did you do?" she accused.

He rocked back on his heels. "Nothing exactly," he hedged. "At least nothing today."

"What did you do to Travis?"

He blew out a frustrated breath. "I kinda plowed my fist into his face a couple times."

"Jesus Christ, Jace," she muttered.

He shrugged. "He needed to know you're my girl. I just

drove home that fact with my fists." He grinned at her. "Don't worry. I think it's all out of my system now."

She rolled her eyes. "You're such a caveman."

His chest rumbled with laughter. "I've been called a lot of things, love. But never that."

She crossed her arms. "Well, there's a first time for everything."

Dylan and Raul banged through the back door with the folded-up card table and four chairs. He helped set the table in the living room then sat in a folding chair and shuffled the cards.

Several oil lamps sat around the room. Their light flickered and cast odd shadows along the wall. He used to play cards with his dad, had avoided the guys' card games because his father's memory was still too painful. But tonight, he'd play to remember him. The ache in his chest had dulled a bit, enough to realize his father would want him to be happy, to remember him in joy, not sadness and pain.

The room's atmosphere lifted, and everyone cheered as Raul raised the tree. It stood in all its glory in a rusted milk can filled with gravel and rocks. Whiskey sloshed over the rim of Cat's cup as she strung silver tinsel. Hailey rummaged through the box of decorations and started hanging red and silver glass balls.

Lacy and Matty sat by the fire stringing popcorn. The party's excitement brightened his waxen complexion. He ate more popcorn than he strung. He watched Lacy pop a kernel into her mouth, then throw one at Matty's face. He giggled and tossed one back at her open mouth. It hit her nose and bounced to the floor.

"Lacy, will you play your guitar?" Hailey asked over the nonsensical chatter.

Lacy's head shot up in surprise. "Um, okay. What would you like to hear?"

She paused, a silver bulb dangling midair. "Anything."

Jace raised a brow. He'd never seen Hailey so amiable. Maybe she'd accepted her new life. His grandfather used to say the only thing kicking against the pricks got you was bloody feet.

Lacy rose and went for her guitar then sat by the fire, legs crisscrossed. Her fingers picked the strings to Jeff Buckley's version of "Hallelujah."

The whole room stilled. He dropped the cards as her voice rang out strong and clear.

When she finished, the room was pin-drop silent. She looked at everyone and gave a self-conscious laugh. "Maybe I should've started with a different song."

"No," he said. "That was perfect. Play another."

Her passionate voice saturated the air and drizzled the room with honey, warm and sweet. Jace attended enough church services with his grandparents to recognize an anointed voice, one that demanded an emotional response. The next few songs were similar, exacting everyone's attention. After singing "Sound of Silence," she lowered her guitar and looked at everyone, uncomfortable in the spotlight.

"Play 'Grandma Got Ran Over by a Reindeer,'" he suggested.

The lighter song lifted the mood. They drank Cat's wine, sang Christmas songs, and ate popcorn laid out on the fireplace hearth. With uplifted spirits, the small group staggered out the door on Christmas Day.

"The party was a great success," Cat declared on a hiccup.

"It was," Lacy agreed. "And Matty looked better tonight."

Cat patted Lacy's head. "Sure, he did. I'm off to bed."

Jace knew the boy wasn't improving and Cat's downcast look confirmed it. His wheezing cough doubled him over several times during the evening. After stringing popcorn, he watched the party, head tilted against the rocking chair. He needed a doctor, a hospital, medicine.

He stoked the embers and threw on more logs then motioned for her. "Sit with me."

She sat on the floor against the couch. He slid behind her then pulled her against him. He rested his chin on her shoulder and stared at the flickering flames.

His chest ached and his grip around her waist tightened as the thought of leaving crossed his mind. He needed to leave soon. If he didn't, he'd lose his nerve. She wouldn't understand his reasons and odds were high she would view his disappearance as abandonment. He had no other choice but to play those odds and try to explain when he returned.

She leaned against his chest and his body flooded with warmth. "I have something for you," she said.

"Do you?" he quipped.

She laughed. "Okay, maybe I have two things for you."

"I'm intrigued," he murmured, grasping her chin.

He tipped it up and lowered his mouth over hers. He took his time, savoring every sound she made. When she turned and pressed against him, a lightning bolt of desire hit him hard. He gathered her hair away from her neck, tilted her head back. He pressed his lips against her throat, kissing his way to her collarbone.

"I'm crazy about you, girl," he whispered.

Lips parted, she opened her eyes, hazed a bright green.

"Say you're mine," he demanded. Call him possessive, he needed to hear it.

"I am," she breathed.

He cupped his hands around her face. "Say the words," he rasped.

Her hands, wrapped around his neck, drifted into his hair. "I'm yours, Jace."

She raised up and he grasped her hand. "Where are you going?"

A smiled tipped the corners of her lips. "I told you. I have something for you."

She went into their bedroom and returned holding an anti-quated silver pocket watch, tarnished with age. She held it out in the palm of her hand. "It belonged to my great-grandfather."

"Lacy," he said, stunned. The case's carving, intricate and ornate, depicted the Monroe crest. "It's beautiful, but I can't take this from you."

"It's mine to give and I want you to have it."

He opened it and studied the small picture inside the cover. A bright smile lit a delicate oval face, framed in long jet-black curls. Rosy cheeks and full lips centered on the camera, but it was her eyes, crystalline green and alluring, that drew him. They'd drawn him from the start.

"Um, that's the only picture I could find around here." She gave a self-conscious laugh. "My senior picture."

"It's perfect," he murmured, taking her hand. "You're stunning."

He didn't mention he had a framed five-by-seven copy he kept on his nightstand. Her mother had slipped it to him at her graduation party. She probably didn't remember he'd attended her party with AJ. The whole high school football team, bois-terous and begging for her attention, filled the rented Red Cross building. She'd been a water girl for the team her senior year, and wildly popular with the players. AJ attended all of the football games, a watchful eye trained on his sister. The guys' flirty gestures and wandering hands had him hollering from the stands, "Get your hands off my sister before I come down there and break them off," with regularity.

His eyes slipped to hers and he thought of the small white box tucked away in his duffle.

"I have something for you too. I was saving it for your birthday, but..." He let the words hang, unsure how to continue. What if he wasn't back for her birthday? He rose to his feet and retrieved the box.

He sat beside her and offered it to her.

She looked at it, then back at him. "What is it?"

"Open it and find out."

She lifted the lid. "Oh," she gasped. "Wow. It's gorgeous."

He picked up the ring. "May I?" he asked, gesturing to her left hand.

She nodded, eyes wide. He slipped the princess-cut diamond on her ring finger. The one-carat sparkling star, surrounded by tiny amethyst gems and set in a white gold band, fit her perfectly.

She stared, enchanted. "My birth stones." Her eyes locked with his. "When did you do this?"

For the first time he could remember, his cocky overconfidence failed him. He held her gaze and wondered if she'd believe the truth. After her high school graduation, he talked with his mom about Lacy and his intentions to pursue her. It was the first time he'd spoken of his feelings to anyone. His mother gave him the diamond, set in a 14k-white gold band. It was her grandmother's ring, a gift to celebrate her sixteenth birthday. Somehow, she understood his feelings and encouraged him to design a ring that suited Lacy.

"Um." He lifted his head and gave her a lopsided grin. "Well, I've had it a while." He stopped and searched her face. "Too arrogant?"

"No," she answered in a soft voice. "Not arrogant at all." She lifted her hand. The firelight caught the clear stone, setting it ablaze. "You've made me feel special, wanted. The ring is beautiful and more than I deserve. Thank you."

He leaned down, pressed his mouth to hers. "Just a reminder of who you belong to," he murmured against her lips. He nipped along her jawline and down her throat then lifted his head. "I'm serious, Lace. I'm going to marry you."

The green in her eyes turned dark emerald and sadness crept over her features. "We'll see." She turned away, staring at the fire. "Just remember who *you* belong to."

Now what in the hell did she mean by that?

24

J ace raised his head from a sound sleep to the quiet. The north wind's constant roar that thrust its way through the window's cracks had died and left a noiseless void in its wake. He slipped out of bed and crossed to the window. A southern wind meant an increase in temperature. Traveling would be easier and safer although no plan solidified in his mind.

He needed his truck and that presented a problem because Zach held his keys hostage. He cringed at the thought of confronting his brother, but Cooper Ranch would be his first stop.

The clock on the bedside table read five o'clock. He dressed, stuffed a few things in his duffle, then turned to Lacy. Her hair veiled her peaceful face. God, he loved her, would do anything for her, turn himself inside out just to see her smile. His chest broke as he burned her image into his heart.

A thought crossed his mind, and he unzipped his bag, drew out the blue button-down shirt she loved, and hung it on the bedpost. He tiptoed over, brushed the hair from her forehead, rubbing the silken strands between his thumb and forefinger. He lingered there, his thoughts adrift. He didn't know how long he'd be gone, or when he'd see her again. He hesitated. Could he leave her? His gaze turned to the bullet hole in the floor and his resolve firmed. He turned and walked out the door.

Head down, he didn't see Cat stoking the fire.

"Going somewhere?" He stopped in his tracks. She eyed the duffle and her brows rose.

"Yes."

"Break in the weather what you've been waiting on?"

"Yeah," he replied, surprised by the approval he read in her steel-grey eyes. "Safer that way in case I get stranded somewhere."

He shifted, anxious to leave before he changed his mind. He eyed Raul sleeping on the couch. His soft snores filled the room.

She walked into the kitchen and motioned him to follow. She gathered bread, the last few pieces of venison jerky, and wrapped them in a clean dish towel.

He accepted it grateful for her support. "Thank you, Cat."

"Wait here." He watched her move in swift strides through the doorway. She returned toting Lacy's shotgun. "Take it. There's a bag of shells in the barn. Double-aught nines. Jace, I know you're going to hunt that man down. I don't know what you plan to do with the slimy snake once you find him, but I cast my vote right now for you to kill him."

Her seriousness shocked him. He never expected her to understand his need for revenge, much less her approval. "Thank you. I'm riding Josie home to get my truck. Could you have Raul go get her? I don't want to turn her out to pasture."

"Sure, honey. We'll be fine here." She handed him the shotgun and he slung it over his shoulder.

Hand on the back doorknob, he stopped and turned around. "Cat?"

"What is it?"

"Watch over Lacy. Make sure she doesn't do anything stupid."

She nodded and he walked outside.

The ride home allowed him time to think. Lacy gave him no details and a nagging voice inside warned him he wouldn't like the truth. Watching her suffer from the trauma and struggle under the enormous weight of the farm, left him no alternative. He would find her rapist then go to Texas. Her uncle worked in Austin but kept a private residence in Gainesville. Thomas Monroe and his father talked on a regular basis over the years, political affairs drawing them together often.

His impatience intensified and bounced inside him like a kid in the backseat of a car. As dawn's first light chased away the darkness, the Cooper barn's red spire came into view. He nudged Josie into a gallop.

He stabled his horse, jogged to the back door, and let himself in. He hoped Zach was asleep, so he could get in and out undetected. He crept to his father's office, a stealthy thief on light feet.

Zach used the office, and he assumed his truck keys were in his dad's desk drawer. He eased the door open, noticed the light, and peered through the crack. His brother sat with his right foot propped up on the desk underneath two bed pillows. Blood soaked through the crude gauze bandage and a sickly-sweet odor filled the room.

He froze as his eyes took in the scene. Realization struck him with acute arrow piercing pain. The only identifier stared him in the face. Zach's foot, blown apart by the force of scattered double-aught nine lead shots.

"What happened to your foot?" he asked, stepping into the room.

His brother's head snapped up. "How'd you get in here?"

"Back door."

Zach raked a hand through his short, cropped hair. "Shit. Thought I had that locked."

He took a small step forward, his mind reeling with information it tried to reject. It couldn't be true. Jagged pain ricocheted a daggered boomerang through his heart.

"What happened?" he asked again, motioning to his foot.

"Hunting accident," he smirked.

He studied his brother. "Huh. Looks pretty bad. Didn't even know you hunted."

"I don't," he sneered, then leaned back in his chair and folded his hands behind his head.

"Zach," Jace started, his voice grave, "what have you done?"

He needed to hear him say it. Out loud.

A slow, wicked smile spread across Zach's face. "Well, *brother*, I guess you know what I've done."

A flood of emotions slammed into him—hurt, hate, disbelief, overwhelming grief. But the need for vengeance trumped them all. "Why? Why'd you do it?" he asked, desperate to understand. "God, Zach. You know how I feel about her."

Zach shifted. "Like I told Lacy, I never could stand you having anything I didn't have first."

He stared, dumbfounded, unable to respond. Zach had raped her because of *him*?

"Remember your first dog when you were seven? Your first horse when you were ten?" Zach burst into hate-filled laughter. "I've destroyed all your firsts."

His first dog, a feisty German shepherd he named Rebel, went missing a few days after his dad brought him home. His first horse, a registered sorrel quarter horse, mysteriously died in his stall two weeks after his grandfather brought him to the ranch.

Rage hazed his vision. He stood, hands balled into fists, jaw clenched so hard the muscles ached.

And Zach continued. His confession leaked out and filled the room like the toxic fumes of Birkenau.

"I wanted to kill Lacy. Planned on it. Then I thought it would be so much better to watch both of you suffer."

Shock numbed his mind. His brother was a psychopath. Unfeeling, uncaring. Not human at all. His eyes raked over Zach. "Did you kill Mom and Dad?"

Zach bristled. "*I* didn't."

The way he said *I* caught his attention. "Did you hire someone to do it?"

"I think you have other things to worry about, Jace," he deflected. "Like the fact I plan on paying our girl another visit. I've told all the guys in town about her. They're willing to barter for her. I told Lacy I'd thought about bringing her here to be my little sex toy. She's a really good fuck. But then, you know that, don't you?" A vicious gleam lit his pale blue eyes. "Or maybe not."

His hands clenched, unclenched, then clenched again. "She should've blown your head off when she had the chance."

"I knew she wouldn't. I think she likes me."

"Stop," Jace commanded in a low voice.

Zach's eyes held sick triumph. "I took something from her you'll never get."

He took a step forward. "Stop. I mean it, Zach. Last warning."

"I took her first too. She was a virgin," he gloated. "I wasn't expecting that. A bonus."

His control, held on a tight leash, snapped. He lunged across the desk and wrapped his hands around Zach's throat before he could blink. The chair slammed into the wall, jarring them both. Family pictures fell. His grip tightened. His brother's larynx crunched under his thumbs and his face turned a mottled purple.

"You're evil, Zach. You deserve to die!"

Image after image of Zach violating Lacy burst into his mind like a bright Polaroid flashbulb. Sharp snap shots, harsh and crude, filled his vision: Zach's hands running the length of her body and ripping her clothes, his fists ramming into her face, him slamming into her over and over and over.

Zach struggled to shove him off, but Jace's heightened adrenaline strength kept him pinned to the chair. A gurgle rose from his throat. His face held a mixture of surprise and panic. His arms flailed like a penned chicken trying to escape a fox.

Zach's movements became slower. The fact he was close to killing his brother dimly registered. Could he live with it? Then the crude, horrifying words about bartering Lacy for sex came rushing back and a new burst of rage barreled through him. He squeezed harder. No one would ever lay a hand on her again.

Zach's hands fell limp, his blank eyes stared at the ceiling. Jace sucked in a sob. He was gone. His brother was dead.

He jumped off the chair, a strangled cry escaped his lips. Turning his back, he rifled through his dad's desk drawers until he found his keys. He dropped to his knees, uncovered the safe, and retrieved the gold coins. This wasn't just a jam he'd landed in, but a full-on train wreck.

He sprinted for the barn, grabbed his duffle and shotgun from his saddle, then ran hell for leather to his truck. He tossed them into the cab and sped away.

He could never go back.

He could never undo it.

God, what had he done?

He turned off his gravel drive onto Highway 11. Back roads to the Oklahoma-Texas border were the best way to avoid the National Guard.

The night sky lightened to a depressing predawn grey. He stared straight ahead, his thoughts stuck in a mind-numbing loop. His brother raped Lacy because of him. It was his fault. He was responsible for her pain. How did he get over that? Another realization ran in a tight circle with the others. Zach hired someone to kill their parents.

25

Lacy stood in the center of the wash house, a trash bag full of tin cans at her feet. She glanced at the old AcuRite thermometer hanging for dear life by one rusty screw. She wiped the perspiration covering her brow. The glass tube's silver mercury line read sixty-five degrees. Odd weather for January. She shucked her coat and hung it on the open shed door. Two large plastic containers sat alongside the pea-green shelving. She bent over and opened the first one.

Why in the world did her grandmother need a five-gallon paint bucket full of clothes pins?

"Bah," she growled, frustrated.

The Great Depression left its mark on her father's grandparents and the farm contained the evidence. Nothing of value was thrown away. Ever. Which wasn't always a bad thing. The old clothes wringer she found, the ingredients to make soap, even the material scraps found in the linen closet kept everyone's clothes patched. The Charmin she found stacked floor to ceiling in the small shed beside the larger farmhouse made her smile. That was like finding the lost city of gold.

Hailey knocked on the doorframe and walked through.

"You need any help? Cat's sitting with Matty so I thought I'd come check."

Hailey never offered her services. She studied the young girl's round blue eyes. Her blonde hair, tucked into a blue paisley bandana, lacked its usual luster.

"Sure. Can you empty that trash bag over there in the trash pit?"

She looked out the door, uncertain. "Where's the trash pit?"

Lacy walked out and pointed. "By that big pile of dirt."

Shielding her eyes against the noonday sun, she observed a convoy of military vehicles accelerating over the eastern hill.

Hailey's panicked eyes searched hers. "What do we do?"

She grabbed the girl's hand. "Nothing. Stay with me."

Jace invaded her thoughts. He'd disappeared two days ago. No explanation. No goodbye. Just vanished like a specter, taking her heart with him. She'd trusted him, let her guard down. Then he abandoned her. She placed a hand against her aching chest. Falling apart was not an option. A breakdown would have a dangerous backlash. She'd never recover.

If the MP wanted him, they were a day late and a dollar short. No lying necessary this time.

She heard Raul whistle as he walked up the gravel drive. He came and stood next to her. "Think they'll stop this time?"

"I don't know, but you don't have time to make it to the barn. Go hide in the wine cellar." She tossed a glance at Hailey. "Take her too."

"Okay. Travis and Ethan are on their way." He stopped and gave her an odd look. "Dylan is missing. He's been *actuando extraño*."

Her brows scrunched together. "Huh?"

"Acting strange."

"You mean stranger than normal? I've known him since grade school. He's always been an oddball."

After she spoke, she stopped short. More than once she caught him watching her with a peculiar expression. Then the day Jace left, he made the eerie comment, "Who will protect you now?"

At the time, she brushed it off, but now a chill snaked down her spine.

The ASV's brakes ground together and stopped. Cat stepped off the porch as Travis and Ethan arrived.

"What do they want now? They've taken everything," Travis muttered.

"I can't imagine," Lacy mumbled.

They would search for Jace again. She thought of Zach and wondered if he sent them. Charges of assault with a deadly weapon could be made against her. She hated violence and her behavior the past few months shocked her. Extenuating circumstances forced her to become someone she didn't recognize, and it worried her.

Bryan Rash jumped out of the lead Humvee and sauntered to the front gate. He hopped over and stalked toward her.

"I'm getting sick of seeing you, Bryan. You just keep turning up like a bad"—she gave him a little smirk—"rash."

He drew up his military-issue pants with his thumbs. "Real funny," he retorted. "Where is he? We need to know where he went."

"Who?"

"Jace," he said impatiently. "He's wanted for murder."

She stiffened. Of all the scenario's concerning the MP's interest in him, she never considered murder. "What the hell are you talking about?"

Rash crossed his arms. "He was under investigation for the murder of his parents. Then yesterday, we found his brother, Zach, dead. Couldn't even defend himself."

"Why is that?" She forced the question through clenched jaws.

"Zach shot himself in the foot in a hunting accident. Almost blew off the entire thing. We believe there was an altercation and Jace strangled him to death."

Cat grabbed Lacy's hand and squeezed until she felt the bones grind together. "Easy, Cat," she whispered.

She steadied herself, pushed all thoughts of murder aside. "Well, he's not here. I told you that the last time you were here. I don't know where he went." She shook Cat's hand off and stepped forward, used the anger rising to the surface. "And since you've left us to starve, why don't you get the hell out of here!"

"Oh, we're just getting started, honey. Search the barn," he commanded his troop. His sardonic smile set her teeth on edge.

They followed the MP to the barn and watched them take the last of their supplies. Fish traps, horses' tack, saddles, even Raul's handmade bows and arrows, all went into a pile out front.

When they'd finished their search, Bryan turned and pinned her with a glare. "Burn it."

Horrified, they watched the soldiers douse the pile with gasoline then move into the barn.

She lunged forward. "My horse!"

Travis grabbed her and wrapped his arms around her waist. "Dylan has Acer and Jace's horse is by the ponds," he whispered. "Raul's in your cellar. We're okay."

The soldiers returned and nodded to Bryan. He stepped forward, lit a match, and threw it on the pile, then stalked to the barn and lit it as well.

She turned her face away. Burning the barn and the supplies they needed broke her last thread of hope. She turned and leaned her head on Travis' broad chest. "The barn, Trav."

"It's okay, Lace. We'll recover."

She turned back and watched the old barn burn. Greedy flames consumed the dry wood and hay and ran up the walls to the loft. The fire reached the rafters and devoured them like a pile of brittle matchsticks.

Heaving its last breath, the barn roof collapsed. Sparks showered toward the sky, then rained on dry prairie grass below. Ethan sprinted to the shop building, drug out a hose, and sprayed the dry grass and dirt until a wet ring encircled the barn.

Lacy stood, wide-eyed, and watched. The fire's heat singed her eyebrows, and the acrid scent stung her nostrils. Cat dragged her away, both choking on the large plumes of black smoke.

Nostrils flaring, she jerked out of Cat's grasp. She snarled and rushed at Bryan. Travis caught her arm and swung her around.

"Jesus, Lacy," Travis snapped. He lowered his head and looked in her eyes. "It's not worth it. The barn's gone. Nothing you can do. Let it go."

Bryan walked over and jerked her arm. "I'll take you apart one visit at a time."

Wrenching her arm free, she drew her fist back.

"Lacy, no," Cat commanded. Her sharp tone broke through and she lowered her fist a fraction.

"*Nein,*" she repeated. "You're letting him win this way."

She dropped her arm, her hand still flexing a tight fist. "When this is all over, I will personally see you punished for your crimes."

She spat at his feet and walked away.

She marched into the house and opened the cellar's trap door. "You can come up now."

Hailey's fearful face peeked out. "Are you sure they're gone?

Lacy flung the door all the way open. "They're leaving. Go check on Matty."

Raul walked out the front door, his nose stuck in the air like a hound dog. "What's burning?"

Lacy followed him outside. "The barn. It's gone."

"Gone? What do you mean, gone?"

She rolled her eyes. "I mean gone. Burned to the ground."

"Burned?" he parroted.

"Are you going to stand there repeating every damn word I say?" she snapped. "Bryan Rash ordered his men to burn the barn. Everything's gone."

Jace was gone. The barn was gone. Her horse was gone. Her family was gone. She felt a strong urge to quit, to give in to a world turned upside down. She turned her back on Raul, ran to her bedroom, and shut the door. She flung herself on her bed. Defenses down, she buckled under and wept.

Cat rapped with a light touch, then opened the door. Lacy lifted her head. Cat stared at her with pain and confusion. Then she remembered. Bryan's comment about Zach's foot revealed her secret. Cat figured it out.

She sighed. "Go get a bottle, and we'll talk."

She went into the living room and sat in the old rocker. Staring into the fire, she pushed her toes back and forth, back and forth, a calming repetitive rhythm she could count. The truth of Jace's actions filled the silence in her head. He left her. He killed his brother. He knew his brother raped her. Her ears thrummed like a jet engine screaming down a runway. Was this what it felt like to go insane?

Cat appeared with a bottle of Bacardi and lowered herself to the floor beside the rocker. Not bothering with glasses, she unscrewed the cap, tipped the bottle, and took a long drink. "Start talking, girl," she said, handing her the bottle.

Lacy tipped the bottle and took a swig of the clear liquid. She forced it down with a gag and swore. "He did exactly what I was afraid he'd do if he ever found out."

Cat scrutinized her. "And what was that, exactly?"

She lowered the bottle. It hit the floor with a loud *thunk*. "He killed the man that raped me. Zach raped me."

Cat looked away. "I'm sorry. Jace's brother raped you."

"Yeah."

"And you kept that information to yourself," she mused. "Why?"

Agitated, Lacy jumped up and paced the room. "What do you mean, why?"

"Well, we could've done something," Cat said, irritated.

Lacy's voice rose. "Like what? What could you have done? Kill him? Believe me, I tried to justify killing him. I tried twice and couldn't do it. Zach Cooper was evil, but he was the only family Jace had left." She stopped counting her steps and gave Cat a helpless look. "He took something from me I can never get back. Jace is guilty of murder now and they'll take him away from me. If he even comes back." She sank back into the rocker. "He may not want me after this."

She twirled Jace's ring, watched the diamond catch the firelight.

Sadness filled Cat's grey eyes. "He'll come back. I've never seen a man so over the moon for a girl before." She placed a hand on her knee. "How could you not tell me it was Jace's brother? I'm so sorry."

"What's done is done."

No rewind button existed. No faerie dust, no miracle to prevail upon to change her past. As her mother used to say when she felt the whole world unfair, "It is what it is."

She picked up the bottle, drank again then looked her in the eye. "I'm sorry for pushing Jace on you so hard. How'd you do it? Get past it?"

Lacy shrugged and tipped her head against the rocker's high-spindled back. "He's very persistent, in case you hadn't noticed. I'd forgotten how much attention he gave me when I was younger. He's loved me since high school. He never told me how he felt until he moved here."

Her thoughts turned bitter. Jace left without a goodbye, no indication of his intentions or if he'd return.

She gave a self-deprecating laugh. "Now he's gone. Didn't have the decency to say goodbye. I can't believe how easily he left. It makes me doubt everything."

She plucked the rum out of Cat's hands. They drank in

silence, listened to the house creak as they passed the bottle between them. The alcohol's effect coursed through her, numbed her mind like lidocaine and her heartache receded. Her toes tingled. She kicked off her boots and wriggled them up and down.

Cat broke the silence. "You're wrong about something."

"Of course, I am," she mumbled. "Enlighten me, Yoda."

"It wasn't easy for him to leave you, honey. It devastated him."

Her eyes narrowed. "How do you know?"

"I spoke to him as he was leaving," she admitted. "He looked miserable."

"Did he say anything else?" she asked, somewhat placated and selfishly satisfied he was unhappy.

"Well," she hesitated. "He told me to watch over you. Keep you safe and make sure you didn't do anything stupid."

Her feet slammed against the wood floor. Her socks softened the impact, and to her disappointment, muted the sound. "What the actual hell. Why he thinks I'm an idiot, I'll never know."

Cat pinned her with a stern look. "This is what I know. Travis loves you whether you want to admit it or not. He'd do anything for you. He has no sense where you're concerned and that's a problem. You lose your temper and have a tendency to do rash things as a result. Unlike Jace, Travis follows your lead. You have no one to check you."

"Oh my God," she fumed. "Jace can go to hell."

Cat's gaze softened. "Watch your words and remember you love him."

She lifted herself up, walked to her bedroom, and slammed the door. She sat on the bed's edge, hands between her knees. She hated the fact Jace left her. But Cat was right. She loved him and that wouldn't change.

III

THE STORM

*And fate whispers to the warrior, "You cannot withstand this storm,"
and the warrior whispers back, "I am the storm."*

26

The eastern sun warmed Jace's face as he drove through the early morning. He was running. Running from what he'd done. Running from himself. As if he could out-run the truth with every mile his tires ate. Mindless of his speed, he barreled south down Highway 18's black asphalt and shut down his mind. The small towns flew by, a blur through his windshield, mere flyspecks on the map. Once oilfield boomtowns, their downtown buildings now stood decrepit and unkempt.

With a few hundred in population, the military evacuated small-town citizens with little resistance. Untrained and dislo-cated citizen militias were no match for a well-organized National Guard. It was easier to think about the injustice meted out by a government takeover than his own sins. He rubbed a hand over his forehead and concentrated on keeping his truck between the white and yellow lines.

After forty miles of winding road and potholes, he slowed and turned west onto Highway 64. Better kept by the state, it connected the 412 Cimarron Turnpike to Interstate 35, which led straight to the Oklahoma-Texas border.

He eyed the gas gauge and swore. Almost empty. Still, he

pushed on.

The needle dipped below the red mark after he put thirty more miles behind him. Forced to stop, he pulled into a deserted Conoco filling station outside Perry, a larger town situated on the I-35 corridor. The front window lay broken, its fragments scattered over the concrete walk, evidence of vagrants desperate for food, water, and gas.

His boots crunched the glass as he walked through the open window. Disconcerting silence enveloped him. Under normal circumstances, he didn't mind the quiet, even enjoyed it at times. But this stillness held an eerie sadness his soul felt. It pulled him, tried to draw out his own sorrow. He hated it.

He took a deep breath, strode down the short aisles, and filled his pockets with anything edible. A lone box of barbeque-flavored Corn Nuts caught his attention and he burst into laughter. He could understand why no one wanted to eat the hard stone-like kernels. Beggars couldn't be choosers, his grandmother said, so he took the box and hopped over the attendant's counter to locate the fuel pump switch.

After a brief search through papers and plastic sacks, he found it, flipped it on, then grabbed a white plastic bag with 'THANK YOU' written in bold red letters. He stuffed it full of snack foods. Not much nutrition in Zingers or Cheetos, but empty carbs were better than no carbs. No water remained on the shelves or in the wall-to-wall refrigerators, but he found the last three twelve-packs of Coke in the back storage area. He balanced them in the crook of his arm then stepped out the window, careful not to snag his jeans on the jagged glass.

He dumped the food into the passenger seat, rounded the hood, unscrewed the gas cap, and started pumping gas. He wanted to reach the border before dark. He couldn't take I-35, because it was the military's main artery north to south across the state. It would add time and miles, but he would dip south on less-traveled backroads to Thackerville.

Urgency thrummed through him like the buzz of an electric

wire. The faster he found Thomas Monroe, the faster he could return to Lacy.

Lacy. He shoved her name away, unable to process the information overload yet. He knew he'd have to face it. The overwhelming, unbelievable fact that Zach raped her. Underneath the surface, his emotions rolled like a tumultuous river.

The handle clicked and the pump stopped. Jace removed the nozzle and set the handle back in its cradle. As he climbed into the driver's seat, three military Humvee's bounced by. Their off-road tires whined like a beehive on the asphalt. He ducked as they passed and realized daytime travel was too risky. He'd find a place to hide until dusk.

He remembered an abandoned farmhouse a mile back and decided to go look. He gunned the engine, whipped back onto the highway, and backtracked until he found a large two-story white house. Its dejected roof sagged over the wraparound porch where two green rockers sat. Shutters of the same green graced the front windows. He pulled onto a dirt path, bumped through a cattle guard, then drove around and parked behind the house.

He got out and approached the back door with caution. No sound or movement came from inside. MP invasion marks scarred the home's outer layer. Bullet holes pock-marked the siding and shattered the back kitchen window, a confirmation the farmhouse had been evacuated. A crow, oblivious to the rhythmic bang, bang, bang of the kitchen window's aluminum blinds, perched on the open sill. The baleful bird eyed him before it gathered itself and flew away.

The crow gave Jace an odd feeling, a warning to tread with care. He pressed his ear to the door. Hearing nothing, he turned the knob. The door creaked as he pushed it open. His foot crossed the threshold and his heart stuttered. Without warning, a rifle's cold, steel barrel skimmed his cheek.

"Hold it right there, partner," a gruff voice commanded.

In a slow gesture, he raised both hands in surrender. He

couldn't see the owner of the disembodied voice. His eyes shifted sideways and he caught a glimpse of an old man, his tattered overalls faded and torn at the knee. The man kept the rifle trained on his chest as he shuffled around to face him. A black and white checkered bucket hat sat askew on his white-haired head.

The old man's sharp brown eyes sized him up. "What business you got breaking into my house?"

"I'm sorry. I thought it was abandoned. I just need a place to rest for a while. I'll go." He turned a slow circle to exit.

"Didn't say ya had to go. Just wanted to make sure you weren't military. You understand?"

"I do."

The man flipped the rifle over his shoulder and studied Jace. "What's your name, boy?"

He lowered his arms. "Jace Cooper."

The man fired another question. "Where ya from, Jace Cooper?"

"Shidler, sir. It's east of—"

"I know where Shidler is. Used to fish in tournaments at the lake there."

They stood in uncomfortable silence. Jace shifted his feet and wondered if the man would let him stay or if he'd decide to shoot him. Looked like a tossup.

"My name's Walter," the old man finally said and stuck out his hand. "Walter Edwards. Call me Edwards. Everyone does."

Relieved, Jace sighed and shook the offered hand.

"Follow me. You can rest in here." He propped the rifle by the stove then opened a door located off the kitchen.

Jace followed the man inside. The small bedroom's slanted ceiling gave the room a claustrophobic air. A twin bed graced the wall opposite the door, its brass headboard and footboard tarnished a dirty brownish green. The navy blue and white wedding ring quilt spread over the mattress looked worn, but clean.

The bed springs creaked as he sat on the edge. "Thank you."

"I'll make some sandwiches while you rest. You look dog tired." Edwards eyed him with astute curiosity. "What's your story, anyway?"

Jace scrubbed his hands over his face. "It's long and one you probably won't want to hear. You may not want me here if you know the truth."

Edwards plucked a hand-rolled cigarette from behind his ear, pulled a lighter from his pocket, and lit the tip. He leaned against the doorjamb. "Well," he said blowing an impressive smoke ring toward the ceiling. "You don't look dangerous. Besides, I can hold my own pretty good. Try me."

Jace sized him up and figured he could hold his own in a fight. He took a deep breath then relayed the whole story.

"I left to find Lacy's rapist," he explained. "Then I was going to Texas to find her uncle." He paused. This part of the story clogged his throat. Saying it out loud made it real.

"Go on," Edwards urged taking another drag from his cigarette.

"I—" he faltered, but pushed the words out through gritted teeth. "I went back home to get my truck and found my brother at his desk. His foot had been shot."

Edwards scuffed over and sat down beside Jace. "Dear Lord. The man Lacy shot in the foot was your brother?" He shook his head and gave Jace a sad look. "Then what happened?"

Jace needed to say it, to admit what he'd done.

Bile rose in his throat. He swallowed it down and finished his confession. "I killed him. I strangled him with my bare hands." He stopped, his heart numb and cold.

He could still hear, still feel the crunch and pop of his brother's esophagus as he strangled him. He looked away and watched the dust motes illuminated by the sun's rays.

"You know what the really messed up part is? I don't regret it. I'd do it again if I had to. And that screws with my head."

Pity radiated from Edward's eyes. "I'm sorry, son."

Jace dropped his hands between his knees and looked at the tired wooden floor. Anguish and rage tugged at his heart by turn. Saying the words didn't relieve the pressure. It still felt like an elephant sat on his chest.

His mom told him, give things time. Time heals. The proverb might be true, but for him the mystery was learning how to live in the moment. He had no clue how to coexist with the fallout of Zach's actions. He loved Lacy but loving her came with pain. Bone-crushing pain. Then came the rage. His skin crawled with it. She'd warned him. He hadn't listened. He pushed too hard for the truth and the truth led him straight to his brother. And murder.

Silence blanketed the room. He tamped down the stormy thoughts, raised his head, and found Edwards's eyes on him as he pulled the last drag on his cigarette.

"Can't say I blame ya. I know it will take time for you to come to grips with what you've done. It's a terrible thing, takin' a life. But son, you got to remember to keep things in perspective."

He frowned. "What do you mean?"

Edwards rose, walked to the window, and flicked his cigarette butt outside. "Perspective can be a tricky thing. You seem to be a pretty black and white fella, but I'm telling ya, the world is full of every shade of grey in between."

"Murder is murder," he stated flatly. He picked ruthlessly at a small hole in his jeans.

"Let me ask you something. If this had happened to your girl before martial law took over would you've done the same thing? Or would you have turned your brother in?"

He considered the older man's words. "I would've turned him in."

"Alright. Now, would you agree we're at war?"

He cocked his head. The old man piqued his interest. "Okay, yeah."

"Then answer this," he continued. "When a soldier goes to war and kills, is that murder?"

"Of course not. He's doing his job."

Edwards stared, unblinking until his meaning sank in. Because the president invoked martial law, local law enforcement wasn't able to punish Zach, so Jace acted in their stead. The old man could drive home a point.

He nodded. "Okay. I'll consider that. Thanks."

The idea his actions served as a service to society instead of cold-blooded, first-degree murder gave him pause. But he'd acted out of anger, and because fury drove him, he couldn't acquit himself in such a cavalier way.

Edwards nodded, adjusted his hat, and left.

He lay back and threw his arm over his eyes. Lacy's senior picture floated through his mind. He focused on her eyes, begged them for absolution. He'd charged into her life like the commander of the damn light brigade, completely oblivious. No wonder she'd shunned him at first. All the things she'd said, the warnings she'd given, assaulted his conscience. He'd run roughshod over her until he got his way. Guilt and shame laced with fury rolled and crashed against his heart. How she managed to overcome Zach's brutal act, he couldn't imagine. He didn't know if he ever could.

The thought of them together conjured pain he couldn't exorcise. Zach touched her, violated her, beat her. He'd gotten her fucking pregnant. His brother ruined another first without even knowing. Bile rose and stung his throat. He jumped up, hung his head out the window and puked until dry heaves shook him. A piece of jagged glass scraped his arm as he slumped over the sill.

He wiped his mouth with the back of his hand and staggered to the bed. He needed rest. The odds of locating the senator were slight and crossing the Red River remained a problem. His troubled thoughts slowly scattered, and he drifted.

Edwards poked his head through the doorway. "Sun's goin' down. Thought you'd wanna know."

He rose, rubbed his bleary eyes. "Thanks. I didn't mean to sleep that long."

"Those military men bunk at the casino and they turn in early."

"Why are they here?" he wondered and covered a huge yawn with his forearm.

Still exhausted, he stumbled over his feet as he followed Edwards to the kitchen table. The old man laid out sandwiches and potato chips. The bread, cut in thick, jagged pieces looked homemade and the chips spilled out of a Lay's bag onto the wooden-planked table, stained a deep brown.

"Take a seat." The old man waved a hand at a square stool made from the same heavy wooden planks then shuffled over and sat across from Jace. "Military trains stop at the old depot. That's where they spend most of their time. Nothin' else here except the Ditch Witch plant and they stripped it clean long ago."

"How did you escape the work camps?" he asked, taking a large bite of sandwich. The roast beef melted in his mouth. After venison for months, the beef tasted exquisite.

"Fought those sons of bitches off with my rifle." He looked to the broken kitchen window. "My wife was standin' right there. She was doin' dishes when they started firin' their guns at the house. Hit her in the head. Clean shot between the eyes. They were aimin' for her." A tear rolled down his leathery cheeks and got lost in the white stubble that covered his jaw.

Shocked, the sandwich fell to the blue and white Corelle plate. "Why?"

"Power move to show their strength. And, they got no use for an old woman. I heard they were thinnin' the herd of old people. Easier to shoot on sight rather than ask for surrender.

Came in, grabbed my son. Tried to kill me, but I just kept shootin' my rifle."

"They come back?" he asked crunching a chip. He forgot how much he loved and missed salt.

"They know I'm here, but don't bother with me no more. I'm old and not a threat. They figure I'll just die here."

"I'm sorry," Jace said, saddened.

It explained the bullet holes scattered over the home's exterior. He wondered if Edwards would consider moving to the farm.

"You could move to the Monroe farm," he suggested, taking another bite from his sandwich. "Lacy wouldn't mind."

Edwards chuckled and lit another cigarette. "I appreciate the offer, son, but the old expression jumping from the frying pan into the fire comes to mind. I think I'm safer here."

"You're probably right," he conceded, grinning.

The old man ashed his cigarette in an old red and white Budweiser can. "Been thinking about you crossing the border."

"You got an idea?" he asked stuffing another chip in his mouth.

"Got a canoe in my barn. You're more than welcome to it. May get you across the river if you go at night. We can strap it down in the bed of your truck."

Jace thought a moment. "That's a good idea. Better than any I've come up with. Thank you." He shoved the last bit of bread and roast beef into his mouth then stood.

Edwards rose, pushed the stool under the table, and dropped his spent cigarette into the aluminum can. "Better get ya loaded up. Get there fast, but don't use headlights if ya can help it. Don't want those SOB's to spot ya."

Jace followed Edwards to the barn. The old man moved spritely despite his age and shoved open the sliding double doors. Jace stepped inside the dim, musty structure and let his eyes adjust. Painted the same green as the house shutters, the barn was twice as big as the Monroe's. Rows of empty stalls ran along the north end suggesting a profitable horse business. Stairs led to a large loft with a steel desk and a series of filing cabinets.

They stopped along the south wall where the canoe lay hull up. Jace nodded to the stalls. "Where's all your horses?"

Edwards pulled a toothpick from his front pocket and shoved it in his mouth. "Used to raise Quarter Horses. Retired a couple years back. I sure do miss it." Edwards flipped the wooden canoe right side up. "A friend of mine made this. Had a real gift in woodworking. I hope it brings ya luck."

They each picked up an end and loaded it into his truck's short bed. The end stuck out over the tailgate.

"Got any rope?"

The old man stepped back, breathing heavy. "Yeah." He walked over and rummaged through an old toolbox. He pulled out several yellow bungee cords. "This ought to do it."

Together they strapped the canoe to the truck bed. Edwards gave it a good push to make sure it was tight. "I'll go get the oars."

He came back with two wooden oars, threw them in the truck bed then turned to Jace. "You ready?"

Overwhelmed with gratitude, Jace stuck his hand out. "I think so, sir. Thank you for everything."

The man shook his hand and patted his back. "Think on what I told ya."

"I will, sir," he said and hopped into his truck. He started the engine then rolled down his window. "Wish you'd change your mind and move to the farm."

Edwards adjusted his hat and hooked his thumbs through his overall straps. "I'll think on it."

He watched as Edwards faded from view and wondered if he'd ever see him again. His thoughts turned to the road and the lengthening shadows. If all went as planned, he'd be in Texas tonight.

27

A vicious nightmare woke Lacy and she bolted upright, heart pounding in her ears. The moonlight shadows played hide-and-seek on the wall. She wanted Jace. Tears welled in her eyes. She missed his strong arms wrapped around her. But he knew the truth now and she wondered what he thought. Did he still love her? The answer remained out of reach. Only Jace could answer it.

Raul rapped on her door. "You okay, Lacy?" he whispered.

She sat up, raised her knees, and tucked the quilt under her chin. "You can come in."

Raul opened the door and padded to her bedside. The edge of the bed dipped as he sat. His brown eyes focused on hers in concern. "You were screaming. I thought those nightmares were gone."

"Me too. I'm sorry I woke you."

"I was already awake."

She rubbed her eyes and tried to shake the lingering nightmare. "Why were you awake?"

He scooted to the bed's end, rested his back against the footboard. "Travis came a half-hour ago for Cat. Matty's worse. Said he couldn't breathe."

"The medicine we found isn't helping. We need to do something." She tapped her feet together, thinking. If they could manage a raid on Shidler's pharmacy, they could get him more medicine.

"Cat is doing everything she can. Travis said he'd be back later to talk. We'll figure this out."

She sighed. "That's not our only problem."

His posture stiffened. "Dylan."

"Yeah. Where the hell is he? He stole my horse."

"Travis says he's back but wouldn't answer any questions. He just walked in and went to bed. *El pendejo*."

Lacy rested her head on her knees, shoulders shaking in silent laughter.

"What?"

She glanced up. The moon cast a dim shadow across his annoyed face. "It's just funny when you curse in Spanish."

He grunted and stood. "You sure you're okay?" His voice softened a fraction.

Her smile dropped. "I'm okay."

No need to say otherwise. He couldn't help her. He wasn't Jace and that was the only person her heart wanted.

"Thank you for checking on me," she added, grateful for his thoughtfulness.

Nodding, he walked out and closed the door.

Snuggling back into the quilt's warmth, she fought sleep, but her exhausted mind and body betrayed her, and she drifted.

LACY OPENED her eyes to movement outside her door. The early morning sun bounced cheerful rays across her bed and beckoned her to face the day.

Reluctantly, she rose from her warm cocoon. Her bare feet slapped against the cold wood floor as she moved into the bathroom. Jeans, a long-sleeved T-shirt, and Jace's button-down hung on the door's hook. She grabbed them, dressed like she was in a race, then splashed cold water on her face.

In the kitchen, Cat stood at the sink washing eggs. Her hands, bright red from the frigid tap water, scrubbed the brown shells without mercy.

Cat scanned her head-to-toe as she walked through the doorway. "Heard you had another nightmare. Raul and Travis were here earlier, but I told them not to wake you. They'll be back later."

Lacy leaned against the yellow Formica counter. "How's Matty?"

Cat turned off the water, dried her hands, then draped the flour sack towel over the sink. "Not good. His breathing is too labored. I'm giving him steam therapy treatments. I hope it breaks up the junk in his lungs. We're out of antibiotics, but he's already taken two rounds of Amoxicillin. Either the bacteria's resistant, or it's a viral infection."

She nudged Lacy over and moved to the pantry.

"What medicine would help him? We've got to do something."

Cat pulled out the last package of cornbread, along with a box of dried milk, then plunked them on the countertop. She banged around the cabinets until she found a mixing bowl.

Lacy placed a hand on her arm. "What's wrong?"

"I just don't know what we can do. Malnutrition and the lack of heat are the main reasons his body can't fight off the infection in his lungs. If his organs go too long without enough oxygen…" She swiped at tears with the back of her hand. "If we had a nebulizer and Albuterol, he might have a real chance at clearing his lungs."

An idea started to form, but she needed to talk to Raul and Travis. "I need Travis," she muttered under her breath.

Cat dumped the cornbread mix into the bowl, measured milk and water, then cracked an egg into it with enough force to shatter the brown shell. Picking out the pieces, she tossed them into a compost bucket under the sink and gave her a sour look. Lacy watched her whip the mixture into a frenzy then dump it into an old tin pie plate.

"What?"

Cat grunted. "I'm saving my breath." She pushed her out of the way and stalked into the living room, pie plate in hand. She picked up the poker, scattered the glowing embers in the fireplace, and formed a hole.

She followed and swallowed the biting remark that nested in her throat like an adder. Handing Cat the popcorn popper, she helped her lower the cornbread into the ashes to bake, then raised her hands and folded them on top of her head.

She drew a deep breath and counted backward from twenty. Counting was losing its effectiveness. Soon it wouldn't work to calm her, balance her out.

"I need Travis, Cat. I'm not sure why you think that's so bad," she said in a placating tone.

Cat pinned her with a hard look. "Like I've said before that boy loves you. Maybe not as hard as Jace does, but the devotion is written all over his face when he looks at you. You two dated for a whole year in high school." She flopped in the rocker and leaned her head back.

Lacy dropped to the floor beside her and drew her knees to her chest.

"You can't be that oblivious to his feelings." She reached down and placed a gentle hand on her head. "You're not cruel either, so don't give him checks your heart can't cash. You chose Jace. Remember that."

And there it was. A flush of blood burned her cheeks. "Jace isn't here, Cat!"

Without another word, she strode through the back door and let the screen slam on Cat's reply. She didn't want to hear anything else.

She needed answers. From Dylan. Stealing her horse

crossed the line. He couldn't stay on the farm if she couldn't trust him. And she didn't.

Icy wind blasted her face as she walked toward the larger farmhouse. It rattled the tree's skeletal branches and cut through Jace's button-down.

Swinging the door open, she tromped inside. Travis and Raul sat at the table around empty plates. The faint smell of coffee wafted in the air. Matty, bundled in several quilts, sat in a rocker by the giant iron stove.

She zeroed in on Dylan who walked in, coffee mug in hand. Their eyes locked and she took a step toward him, wishing she had something to hurl at him.

"Where were you, Dylan? You owe me an explanation."

He set his chipped coffee cup on the table with quiet confidence. "I don't owe you anything."

His arrogant demeanor unnerved her. She wanted to throttle him but turned to Travis and Raul instead. "We need to talk." Swinging around, she pointed at Dylan. "I'm not finished with you."

LACY, Travis, and Raul huddled around the kitchen table her great-grandmother bought used in the late fifties. Age cracked the green and white speckled Formica along the edges and created rough ridges prone to scraping wrists and the tender part of the forearm. She picked up her coffee cup and took a cautious sip of the hot liquid. Yuck. The coffee, made from grounds Cat insisted on drying and re-using at least three times, looked like tea, and tasted a bit sour. She put the cup down and pushed it away. Cat's "waste not, want not," axiom held some major flaws.

"We need to go tonight," she insisted.

Travis folded his arms on the table and gave her a pointed

look. "Why do we have to rush this? This isn't a game. We could get caught."

"If trying to ferret out a mole was our goal, I'd agree with you, but that's not the only thing at stake here. Matty needs medicine. Now. Raiding Shidler's pharmacy is the quickest way to get it."

Raul leaned back, placed his hands behind his head. The chair's green vinyl squeaked in protest. "I agree with Lacy. The medicine should be our priority. If we give Dylan enough information to hang himself, then that's a bonus."

Travis scowled at Raul. "And if we're caught? What then? You're not even going on this suicide mission."

"I'll go and you can stay." He turned to Lacy for confirmation. "Lacy?"

Travis' chocolate eyes flared with heat. "No," he interjected. "I'll go."

Lacy watched the exchange in tight-lipped pensive silence. "I need you to be sure, Trav. I know Dylan's your friend."

His face pinched. "We don't know he's guilty of anything except stealing a horse."

"Yes, we do," Raul said. "I found heavy-duty wire cutters and gloves under his clothes. He cut the electric to both houses."

Travis' blank stare out the window tugged at her heart. "Trav," she began, "we can't ignore the evidence."

Travis turned suspicious eyes on Raul. "It's not solid. He could've had the cutters for another reason."

Raul snorted and straightened in his chair, lips pressed in a fine line. He returned Travis' gaze without reserve. "Name one."

His brown eyes blackened. "What business did you have snooping around Dylan's things anyway? Did you go through all our stuff?"

"Yes. I did."

"Okay, guys." She thumped the table with her fist.

"Enough." She turned to Travis. "I think Dylan made a deal with the MP to get his girlfriend, Gracie, out of the Fort Sill work camp."

Travis' eyes widened in disbelief. "You're speculating!" he half shouted. "You can't possibly know that."

"No, not for sure. But it makes sense and like it or not, he *has* betrayed us. I'm sorry, Trav. I'll do what I think is best for everyone concerned."

He covered his face with his hands. "Whatever," he muttered.

"I'll deliver the details to Ethan and make sure Dylan is within earshot," Raul said, ignoring Travis' disapproving glare.

"Make sure Cat doesn't overhear." She scowled. "I'd rather not deal with her right now."

Raul smirked. "Got it." He rose from the table, took his cup to the kitchen sink, then walked out the back door.

When she heard the screen slam, she turned to Travis. "I'm sorry. You don't have to do this."

"Oh, but I do," he groaned, eyes tight with emotion.

She absorbed his tormented expression. He was worried, but she saw more as his eyes grazed over her face. Apprehension flooded her and Cat's warning about Travis loving her flashed through her mind.

"Why?" The question slipped out before she could check it. His near onyx eyes bored into hers and she knew without a doubt. Cat was right.

His gaze never faltered. "You know why." He shook his head. "You've got to know why. I love you, Lace and wished you'd picked me instead of Jace."

She leaned back in her seat. Thoughts formed, then blurred. She couldn't deal with his feelings, couldn't stand the thought of hurting him.

"Travis, I can't."

What else could she say? Jace owned her heart. Even if he

didn't want her anymore, she couldn't give her heart to someone else.

He reached over, took her hand in his, and raised it to his lips. "I know, but I'm not giving up."

The soft contact of his lips against her skin shocked her. A flush swept across her cheekbones. She jerked her hand back and stood. The sudden force toppled the chair to the floor. "Don't."

His dark eyes bore into hers, an unreadable expression on his face.

She rubbed the back of her hand against the coarse fabric of her jeans. She couldn't handle this and wished he hadn't said anything.

She turned to look out the window to hide her confusion. "Let's just get tonight over and done. The sooner we get a nebulizer and medicine for Matty the better. And, you need to reconcile the fact that Dylan will betray us tonight."

Jace pulled his black half-ton Chevy Silverado up to the last railroad crossing he could find outside the border town of Thackerville and cut the engine. The long steel red and white crossing bars stood upright, swaying with the north wind. The brutal gusts battered the truck with tiny grains of sand. They splattered the passenger window, coating it in a fine layer of red dust. The black and white no crossing X loomed over two red eyes that glared at him in baleful disapproval.

He reached over, pulled a Maglite from the glovebox, then opened the door and jumped down. "This is a bad move," he muttered.

The wind blasted the side of his face like a frigid hell-bent banshee. He flipped hair from his eyes, clicked the rubber button, and flashed the light down the track. He crouched on the balls of his feet, studied the red rusted bars, and cracked, wooden crossties with grim resolve.

Driving across the river on train tracks was the dumbest idea he'd come up with yet. But he couldn't find an access road to the river, and the dense trees and rocky terrain forfeited any chance of dragging the canoe to its bank.

To the southeast, the lights of the Oklahoma checkpoint station off I-35 illuminated the night. It rose then bounced off the thick nighttime cloud cover, a stark reminder to tread with care. He shook his head in disbelief as he strode back to his truck. Before he opened the door, he raised his head heavenward and uttered a short prayer to a God his mother had taught him to believe in.

"If you're up there, man, please help me get across the river without killing myself." He continued as if tending his last rites. "And Mom, if you can hear me, if you're listening…I'm sorry." His chest tightened and his breath quickened. The wind howled around him in grave judgement. "I'm sorry about Zach. I hope you can understand and forgive me."

He folded the driver's side-view mirror inward, then walked around and folded in the passenger mirror. The width of the bridge was an unknown, but his truck's sides would no doubt scrape along the trusses. No way in hell would he have considered this option without the safety the side trusses offered. At least with them he wouldn't feel as if he were driving across a tightrope. He shuddered and wondered how long the drop was from the bridge to the frigid water below.

He hopped back into the cab and turned over the ignition. The engine, still warm from the long three-hour drive, roared to life. He inched to the crossing then turned his wheel to the left. The tires set down between the rails with a thunk and a bang. He cringed and silently apologized to his truck for the maltreatment.

He crept forward, the tires bumping along the crossties in a staccato bum, bum, bum. He stopped after a short distance, rolled down his window, and clicked on the flashlight. The beam cast its light down the line a few feet. The absolute darkness swallowed the light in one greedy gulp. The rims of his left tires hugged the inside rail. The grind of metal on metal made the hair on the back of his neck stand on end. He'd have to rely on the rail as a guide because using headlights was not an option. If the MP patrolled out here, he was toast. Burnt-to-a-crisp toast.

He drove the rail, stopping and starting, for seven long miles until he reached the bridge. The scary part, the kind of *Halloween* terror that turned your hair white. His white-knuckled hands squeezed the steering wheel in a death grip. He rolled the window down. Frosty air blew in the cab, the heater no match for the ice-numbing cold. He locked his jaw against the tremors that shook his whole frame and drew in a deep breath.

"I can do this," he reassured himself. "No problem."

He waited a moment longer, flashed the light down the tracks one more time. The bridge's steel trusses rose in the dark, suspended in the air like a giant, rusted jungle gym. It was attached to nothing but circular concrete piers below, spaced twenty feet apart. He could hear the Red River's strong wind-driven waves crash below him, and the scent of wet sand and motor oil made his eyes water.

Forcing his right hand off the wheel, he shifted into drive. His foot released the brake pedal and the truck inched forward onto the bridge. The deck groaned against the truck's weight. He swallowed hard, kept the wheel tight against the left rail. With steely patience, he crept across the bridge. One harrowing quarter of a mile over rushing water. His passenger door squealed along the iron truss. Its black paint transferred onto the iron bars in solemn testament to his stupidity.

Then his right front tire hit a broken crosstie and sunk below the rail. His heart jumped into his throat. His rapid pulse spun his brain like a top making him light-headed. He drew in a breath, steadied himself. The truck was four-wheel drive. He should be able to ease his way out of the hole. The problem was clearing his back wheel. If the crossties in front or behind the broken one failed, he'd end up fish bait.

If he waited much longer, another tie would break under the weight of the truck. He held his breath and gingerly pressed on the gas. He felt his tire grip the edge of the wooden tie in front of him, then ease forward. The back tire dipped into the hole and he heard the wood crack and splinter behind him. He ground his molars together with enough force to obliterate them.

Again, he moved forward, felt the back tire grasp for purchase in the open air, then grip the tie in front of it. He pushed the gas a little more, then cleared the hole. He stopped a moment, wiped cold sweat from his eyes with the sleeve of his flannel shirt, and cursed.

When he reached the end of the trusses, he stopped and shook out his cramped hands. The air in his lungs came out in a massive swoosh.

He looked back at the formidable bridge. "I'm an idiot."

He still needed to get off the train tracks and onto a road. After that, he needed the Senator's home address. His father kept a rolodex in his office, but he hadn't retrieved it. Because of Zach.

Guilt slithered like a serpent, wrapping itself around his mind. Reason pushed against it, but not before it deposited black seeds of self-loathing and condemnation. Coming to terms with his actions and dealing with the fallout would take time. He just didn't know if he could endure the time it took.

He shifted forward in his seat and followed the rails in the same fashion as before, then turned off onto the first crossroad he found. By the end, the muscles in his jaw, locked from sheer grit, ached and his bones felt as if they'd been through a rock polisher. The road hit a dead end at the south end of Gainesville and merged onto I-35. Left with no other choice, he followed the interstate to the town's edge and stopped at the first gas station he spotted. He cut the engine and jumped out.

Although the station appeared abandoned, no broken glass littered the walk, and no visible signs of a break-in were present. He stepped to the door secured by a thick, silver chain with two padlocks. He examined the standard three-pin brass

Master lock, then let it drop. The chain clattered against the glass doors. Almost anyone could pick a three-pin lock with a bobby pin or paperclip.

He leaned forward, cupped both hands to the glass and peered inside. Low lights from the walk-in beer cave illuminated a small portion of the tiny store, but everything looked normal, operational. He took a step back and considered his options. He needed to refill his gas tank and find a phone book, but an edgy feeling gripped his shoulders. Actual stealing didn't set well. If the State of Texas still allowed their citizens to operate businesses, then that's what he'd be doing.

Before he could decide how to enter or if it was wise to commit B & E in Texas, two men grabbed him from behind. He turned his head to the right, glared at a man with a bad buzz cut and a jagged scar running from eye to chin. He gave him a solid head butt from the side. Stars exploded behind his eyelids and his ears rang like a gong. The man grunted a curse and blood dripped from his nose, but he never loosened his hold. He didn't see the man on the left who knocked him in the head with his gun.

Two solid hits to the head and his knees buckled. He felt the warm trickle of blood slide down his neck, then everything went black.

JACE SHIFTED ON THE HARD, concrete ledge and rotated his left shoulder ninety degrees to ease the pain. The six-by-eight-foot jail cell consisted of three cinderblock walls, a stainless-steel toilet, and a cement ledge that protruded from its back wall. Less than three feet across, it provided the incarcerated inmate a place to rest. Sort of.

Unable to find comfort, he sat up and stared out the iron bars. His throat ached with thirst and his head throbbed where the blow knocked him unconscious. He placed his head in his hands and attempted to suppress the rising fury. He ran a hand through his hair, stiff and crusty from the blood that still leaked from his left temple.

He'd asked for Thomas Monroe, demanded to know why they detained him in the

Cooke County jail. He shouted to be released until hoarse. No one listened. The two men took his wallet and driver's license, shoved him into the tiny cell, and walked away. He had no idea how much time passed, if they left him to starve, or if he'd ever see the sun again.

Footsteps sounded from the hallway and his head shot up. He jumped to his feet, grasped the cold metal bars, and shook hard. The loud clanking of steel on steel echoed against the thick walls.

"Hey! Let me out of here!"

A well-groomed man in his late fifties approached the cell. His grey moustache twitched, a slight smile formed around his lips. "So," he began. "You're Jake Cooper's boy." His eyes roamed over Jace in quick assessment.

"Why am I here?"

The man took a step back. "Do you know who I am?"

"Right now, I don't give a rat's ass who you are," he fumed. He rattled the bars again. "I want out. Now!"

"You'd better care who I am, young man. I'm the one who holds the keys to your cell." He fished brass keys from his neatly pressed pants and jangled them.

Jace drew a deep breath. He knew the man, he just didn't want to give him the satisfaction of admitting it. But he wanted out of the damned cell more. "I assume you are Senator Monroe. Lacy's uncle."

"That's right," he affirmed.

Jace paced the length of the cell. "Why am I here?" he asked again.

"I could ask you the same," he answered evenly.

He let out a low growl. "I'm here for Lacy. I came to find

you. Where have you been? She can't handle what you've placed on her shoulders."

Thomas cocked a brow. "I never told her to take on eight extra people. She did that herself. And from what I've heard, she's quite capable."

"I don't know who your informant is, but you have no idea what she's been through." Infuriated, he slammed his hand against the cell door. "Let me out of here so I can get back to her."

Thomas stepped forward, his eyes piercing and direct. "Did you kill your whole family, Jace?"

Stunned, he staggered back and sat on the makeshift bed. How the Senator knew about his family, he couldn't fathom. "I have no idea where you're getting your information," he began, "but I did not kill my parents."

"And Zach?"

Jace shook his head. "I had my reasons." The softly spoken words felt like a death warrant and he deserved nothing less.

The Senator's sharp eyes cut straight through him. "There's something I need from you."

He eyed the man warily. The man's authoritative tone made him want to bare his teeth. "What do you want?"

He regretted asking as soon as the man began to speak. His mind reeled over what the senator wanted him to do.

Thomas gave him a long, measured look. "I'll leave you to think about it," he said and turned to walk away.

"Wait." He rattled the bars. "Are you just gonna leave me in here?"

"Until you decide," he replied, then turned the corner out of Jace's view.

He slumped back against the cold, concrete wall. His thoughts centered on Lacy as they had been since he walked out her back door. She was the celestial body his world revolved around, his orbit irrevocably altered by her.

He wondered if she'd heard about Zach. They'd have a lot

to work through when he returned. Somehow, she found a way to love him despite Zach. Not that he gave her a choice.

He considered Thomas Monroe's proposition. Blackmail was a more befitting word to describe it. The man lacked scruples, and he knew the unscrupulous senator would go to great lengths to get what he wanted. Why he wanted him for the job he outlined mystified him, but he shrugged it off and contributed it to lack of manpower.

He rose and paced the small cell, let his fingers brush along the bars. Oh, for a tin cup, he thought without humor. It wasn't like the senator gave him a real choice. A month of basic training, Texas Militia style, or stay in the six-by-eight cell indefinitely.

He wouldn't kill again. That was an intractable stipulation on his part. Monroe's mild amusement at his "condition" infuriated him.

"God damn it!" he shouted and shook the bars until his arm sockets screamed. "Hey! I know you're listening. Get down here!"

He heard the squeak of rubber soles on the commercial tile, not the Senator's expensive hard-soled black and burgundy wing-tipped shoes. The militia man with the buzz cut, and to his gleeful amazement, broken nose, walked to his cell door.

"Yeah?"

His voice sounded like he'd swallowed glass and by his looks, Jace figured the man could break a bottle neck with his teeth, crunch the glass, and swallow it without batting an eye or breaking a sweat.

His lips pressed into a grim line. "Tell Monroe he has a deal."

29

Miracles didn't fall from the sky on command like Skittles from a rainbow, but as Lacy stood in the doorway of her dad's old room and watched Matty's chest rise and fall with ease, hope stirred within her. But hope was a dangerous thing. It could knock you for six in a heartbeat, and she needed to remember that. Hope built a false sense of security, knocked your defenses down, and left you vulnerable.

She stepped into the room and looked around. A B-52 Bomber poster hung on the north wall, the edges curled and yellowed with age. A balsam wood airplane dangled from the ceiling with fishing line. It created an optical illusion of the plane in flight. Her dad had been an all-American kid who'd dreamed of flying in the Air Force.

She tiptoed to a spindle-back wooden chair beside the small twin bed and sat. The seat snapped under her weight. Matty cracked an eye open and gave a lopsided grin.

"Hey." His voice sounded hoarse and gritty like he'd crossed a dry sandy desert. He no longer looked thirteen. The illness stole the youthful spark from his features and his eyes held a grave knowledge no kid his age should ever have.

She arched a cynical brow. "Lookin' good, kid."

The dense air in the tiny twelve-by-ten room pressed against her. It reeked of sickness. His blonde hair lay matted and sweat-soaked to his scalp. But a rosy tint replaced his cheek's pallor, and the blue had faded from his lips.

"Cat told me what ya did for me." His somber eyes searched hers. "Thank you for the medicine. I woulda died without it."

Her eyes flitted away, embarrassed. "No problem." She gave his shoulder an awkward pat. "I'm glad you're better."

She rose and left the room. He needed a bath to wash away the lingering sickness. His sheets and blanket needed a soak in hot water as well.

She walked through the rectangular living room to the kitchen where Hailey stood at the sink. Mismatched plates clattered and silverware clanked as she gathered them from the drying rack.

She turned, noticed Lacy in the doorway, and placed a hand to her chest. "You scared me," she said, laughing.

"Sorry."

She shoved off the doorjamb, walked over, and leaned against the chrome-rimmed counter, and gave her a speculative look. Hailey had changed. She no longer complained about chores, the food, or even laundry duty. "Can I ask you something?"

She paused over the silverware drawer and turned a wary face to her. "Sure, I guess."

She crossed her arms and tried to think of a nice way to ask her question. "I don't mean to come off like a jerk," she started.

Hailey cocked a brow. "But you will anyway?"

She lifted her shoulders and one corner of her mouth tipped up. "Probably."

Hailey returned the half-smile, placed a fork in the drawer, and shut it. The silverware rattled like spare change in a tin box. "Okay, shoot."

"You've changed. You seem…" She searched for the right word. "I don't know, more content. Or resigned might be a better word for it."

Lacy crossed to the empty kitchen sink and stared out the window. She understood resignation. The hopeless acceptance of things with no power to change them.

Hailey came and stood beside her. "When Matty got sick," she began, her voice thick with emotion. "I didn't think anything of it. Ethan worried, but I was too busy being miserable to notice how sick he really was." She lowered her head. "Ethan finally had enough of my attitude and gave me an ultimatum. Stay and learn to be happy. Or leave." She turned to face Lacy. "I'm not like you," she admitted. "I don't have your bulldog tenacity."

She scowled at the comparison. She wasn't a dog or a racehorse for that matter. According to Cat, she had the temperament of a thoroughbred. She crossed her arms and harrumphed.

She placed a companionable hand on her shoulder. "That was a compliment. I'm an only child. I'm spoiled. I know that. But I love Ethan more than I love my misery, so I'm trying my best."

She gave an encouraging smile. "Well, I've noticed, and I like the new you." She stopped, surprised the words rang true.

"Was there something you needed me to do?" She retreated to the kitchen table and sat. An old cross stitch kit lay in front of her. "I found this in the linen closet. Do you mind?"

She walked over and looked at a large butterfly stamped on a square piece of cloth stretched tight over a small embroidery hoop. "Not at all. Matty needs a bath and his sheets need to be changed. Can you do that?"

Hailey took a deep breath and nodded. "Sure."

She stepped out the back door. Heavy, dark blue-grey clouds hovered close to the ground. Nothing stirred. Squirrels hunkered in their holes. Birds roosted, their heads safely tucked under their wings. Like the animals, she could feel the coming storm. Her bones ached with it. It brewed overhead like a witches' cauldron and blasted gusts of unforgiving north wind in her face. She thought of Dylan. He'd be a fool to return, but she couldn't shake the nagging feeling he'd do exactly that. Uneasiness stirred in her chest. The weather wasn't the only storm on the horizon.

JACE SCRATCHED at the noise-canceling headphone's wide plastic band stretched over his head. He readjusted the black leather earpieces, then raised the military issue Glock 19 into firing position. His long hair, still tangled in the tight band's clutches, fought for freedom and the earpieces smashed his ears like angry steamrollers.

He let out a frustrated huff, rolled his shoulders, and aimed at the target ten yards out. Slowly, he squeezed the trigger, his body absorbing the kickback. Sulphur and metal's unpleasant sting rolled up his nostrils and he blew out a cleansing breath.

He placed the gun on the metal table beside him then yanked off the annoying headphones and flung them to the cement floor. They skidded and hit the wall with a loud, satisfying clank.

The tactical instructor assigned to train him walked in the bullet-proof glass-encased stall. Sergeant Michaels, a big man with broad shoulders and a loud mouth, gripped his shoulder with sausage-link fingers.

"Good work, Cooper," he said, giving his back a sound smack.

The sergeant's huge, projectile missile hand launched him forward. Jace stuck his hand out, saving himself a face-plant into the bullet-proof glass. He steadied himself then turned and faced the sergeant, a scowl on his face.

"I know how to shoot a damn gun." He slammed his palm

against the target retriever button and watched the target roll up the tracks.

He was tired. He was homesick. He missed Lacy so much it hurt. His skin tingled as if all his nerves converged into a time bomb waiting to explode.

He wanted a good fight, needed to burn off his anger. But using his instructor as a personal punching bag didn't seem to be a wise choice. The sergeant would pummel him into a bloody mess. For a moment, he considered it. Being knocked unconscious would give his mind and emotions a break.

Michaels gave him a hard look. "You're acting like a complete jack wagon."

Jace snorted. "What are you? Nine? What in God's name is a jack wagon?"

His instructor chuckled. "Not really sure. My ten-year-old son calls his little brother a jack wagon."

"Well, there ya go," he muttered.

"I assume it means you're acting like an ass."

"Yeah well, I just don't like being forced to learn something I already know."

"Look, I know you can shoot a stationary target with impressive accuracy. But can you shoot a moving target that's coming after you?"

Jace paused. He'd never been in combat and didn't know how he'd react in a real-time situation.

He scrubbed his hands over his face. "I don't know, man. I just want to go home."

His life had disaster written all over it. He'd undergone more changes in the past six months than his entire life. His brother's face flashed in his mind. He'd never pegged himself as a murderer, never thought he'd take another life. But here he was, training to take more lives. He told Senator Monroe he wouldn't kill again. He meant every word and meant to stick to it.

Michaels pulled the target from the retriever. His shot hit

dead center. "Okay, Cooper." He shoved Jace into the shooting range's breezeway. "Let's see what you can do against the Red Man."

"What's a Red Man?" he asked as they cleared the building and walked outside. He followed him down a narrow sidewalk and stared at the sergeant's wide backside. "Where are we going?"

He raised his hand, shielded his eyes from the pale January sun. Its anemic rays held no warmth. He shoved his hands deep in the pockets of his jeans and hunched forward. His thoughts returned to Lacy. She was always there, a haunting, background melody. Her birthday, February fourth, was a week away and he'd miss it. He was stuck. He saw no way out, and it stoked the fire burning in his gut.

"You seem primed for a good fight," he observed. "So, let's see what you can do in close quarter combat."

He followed the sergeant's brisk pace next door to a large warehouse. Michaels punched a code, opened the double-steel grey doors and motioned Jace inside. His eyes adjusted to the dim lighting. Military training equipment filled the interior. An impressive line of steel, grey gun safes lined the entire north wall, and a boxing ring sat in the center.

"James," the sergeant bellowed. He turned to Jace. "Corporal James will test your CQC skills. I have to warn you. He's tough. No one's beat him yet."

An office door clicked shut and heavy boots on concrete echoed through the warehouse. He looked toward the sound and his stomach churned. Oh, hell to the no. Buzz Cut from the jail made a bee line straight to them.

A peculiar smile lit his scarred, pock-marked face when their eyes met, and reminded him of a cat about to pounce. The man recognized him and by the glint in his eye, craved payback for his busted nose.

Buzz Cut rubbed his hands together. Anticipation gleamed in his brown, beady eyes. "Well, well. What do we have here?"

"Suit up," Michaels instructed. "Let's see what Cooper's got."

He smirked. "Looking forward to it."

He watched him walk away with a mixture of fear and anger. He turned to the sergeant. "What exactly am I supposed to do?"

"Come on," he motioned Jace toward a door.

They walked into a small, non-descript room. The floors were the same dull concrete that ran throughout the warehouse. Brown splotches stained the floor. Blood stains. His apprehension ratcheted up a few notches. Buzz Cut, built like a tank, would demolish him.

The sergeant dimmed the lights. "Okay, Cooper. Your mission is to subdue the Red Man." He tossed him a set of handcuffs. "If you can get these on Corporal James, I'll tell Senator Monroe you're good to go."

He caught the cuffs and stuffed them into his back pocket. Getting those circular metal bindings around Buzz Cut would be no small feat. He needed to fight smart, be quick, evade punches. Tire him out, then strike fast and strike hard. Use his size against him.

"Good luck," Michaels said, shaking his head. "You're going to need it." He exited the dimly lit room.

"Thanks. Great pep talk."

As his eyes adjusted to the semi-darkness, a loud siren started to wail, and bright lights began to flash. Bright bursts, short and intense. The strobe light affected his equilibrium and his stomach lurched. He closed his eyes, took a breath, and listened.

He heard the door's quiet click and caught the soft footfall behind him. The light's rhythm flashed behind his eyelids and the shrill siren screwed with his concentration. Blocking out the distractions, he followed Buzz Cut's footsteps. His skin crawled and he darted away before Buzz Cut could wrap him in a choke hold. He opened his eyes. A flash of light caught Buzz Cut's face.

"What's the matter?" he taunted. "Mama's boy scared?"

He froze.

Who said that?

Buzz Cut or...Zach?

He shook his head, desperate to clear it. Blinked his eyes. It didn't help. Buzz Cut morphed into his brother. He grabbed his head. This wasn't right. Couldn't be right.

He drew a sharp breath and backed up. "Zach?" he whispered in disbelief.

Zach's image sauntered toward him. He took another step back. The cocky swagger, the hauntingly familiar words, messed with his head. What he saw couldn't be real. But a maelstrom of hurt and rage flooded him. Red bloomed like a mushroom cloud behind his eyes and he exploded.

The time bomb detonated.

Without thinking, he lurched forward, a guttural roar erupting from his chest. His body weight hit Buzz Cut dead center, full force. Unprepared for the savage assault, the man stumbled backward.

Buzz Cut's suit's hard outer shell did little to deter him. He knocked the man down, pinned him against the cold concrete, and pummeled the face mask with relentless ferocity. Buzz Cut tried to knock him off his chest, but was no match for pure, unrelenting rage.

Wounded, animal-like cries pierced his ears. "Why? Why'd you do it?"

He kept punching the plastic mask until it crunched underneath his fists. His knuckles cracked, but the pain didn't register.

Buzz Cut's shouts broke through the haze. "Get him off me!"

Bright fluorescent lights flooded the room, and Sergeant Michael's burst inside. Disoriented, he lost his grip then felt his body jerk backward. He flew through the air, landing flat on his back. The force of the fall knocked the wind out of him. His mind clicked off. An icy numbness covered him smothering the raging fire. It fizzled out and he shivered. Goose bumps covered his whole body.

Michaels loomed over him, his brows pinched in anger and concern. "What the hell, Cooper? You had him. All you had to do was cuff him, not beat the ever-living shit outta him."

His lungs wheezed. He'd totally lost his shit. "Sorry," he mumbled.

He cradled his head between his hands. He couldn't explain it, wouldn't admit he saw his dead brother in the strobe lights. Defeat washed over him, a tidal wave of despair, over-whelming and destructive. He had to get out of Texas, back to Oklahoma. Back to Lacy.

He couldn't breathe here. His breaths came short and fast. He lowered his head between his knees, water leaked from his eyes. The pungent odor of blood from his knuckles made him nauseous. Bile rose in his throat, and he swallowed convulsively.

Michaels hunkered beside him. "Easy, Jace. Take long, slow breaths."

The sergeant helped him to his feet. He wavered, unsteady, then felt large hands wrap around his waist. "Let's go."

His feet shuffled across the cement floor, through the door, then across the warehouse. When they reached the outer door, the dizziness passed, and he stood on his own.

Michaels shook his head. "I'll tell Senator Monroe you're ready to go home. I've never seen anyone get the better of Corporal James." He opened the door and let out a gruff laugh. "You got a lot of rage, boy."

Yeah, he did. He'd need to deal with it. Later. He focused on Lacy and home. He was going home.

30

The couch's cracked leather gouged Lacy's neck as she leaned against it. A long, weary sigh escaped her lips. Had she been wrong about Dylan? She thought the need for revenge, to get even, would gnaw at him. Yet he hadn't showed. It was exhausting, waiting for an attack, and left her mind a disheveled mess. Travis insisted she had nothing to worry about. His loyalty to Dylan was admirable, albeit misplaced and a whole lot of naïve.

Raul strolled inside, shook snow from his bright orange beanie, and dumped wood beside the fireplace.

"It's really coming down." He bent down and removed his muddy boots. Cat would pitch a fit over the muddy tracks. "I've never seen it snow like this." He rubbed his hands together before the fire.

She smiled her acknowledgement. She'd seen the big, fat flakes. They coated her bedroom window in wet, packable snow, good for snowballs and snowmen.

The snow reminded her of her brother. She never had a chance when it snowed like this. AJ, always faster and stealthier at packing snow into hard, icy balls, pelted her with a maniac relentlessness. He tagged her face every time, then laughed like an evil Sith lord. She almost wished he'd appear and bombard her with dirty, pee-soaked snow. Almost.

The floor snapped under Raul's weight as he lowered himself into the old rocker. He wrapped himself in an old fleece blanket and settled into a semi-comfortable position.

He'd taken the rocker so she could sleep on the couch next to the fire's warmth. Cat had started sleeping at the bigger farmhouse. The giant steel stove provided more heat than the living room's small fireplace.

She stretched out and pulled her quilt to her chin. She thought about Raul, who he was and where he'd come from. Sometimes he seemed too good to be true. Her pessimistic suspicious side kept waiting for... What? Something nefarious. Her paranoia climbed with each passing day and it annoyed the hell out of her.

She shifted to her side. "Hey, Raul."

"Yeah?"

"Have you really never seen it snow?" She couldn't help her curiosity. Her mother would call it nosey and remind her Nosey-Rosies often ended up with more information than they bargained for.

He sighed. "Mexico City has not seen snow in over fifty years. I have been skiing in the mountains once, so I have seen snow, but not falling from the sky like my *Abuela* plucking feathers from a white chicken."

"So..." She processed the new information. "You weren't born in the States?"

"No. I was born in Mexico City. My name is Raul Manuel Nieto."

The statement, said with pride and a hint of arrogant superiority, startled her.

"So, why are you here?" she pressed. "Don't you want to go home? Get out of this country?"

"Enough questions," he snapped. "Go to sleep."

"Fine," she huffed and shifted to her back.

Clearly, he didn't want to discuss himself or his background. His last name niggled her memory. It rang a faint bell of a history lesson.

The sound of shattered glass broke the silence.

Lacy bolted upright.

Half-asleep, Raul stumbled forward.

Wind-driven snow whipped into the living room.

She bounded to her feet. "What the hell was that?"

Raul put a finger to his lips. "I'll light the oil lamp," he whispered and walked on stocking feet to the kitchen table.

Not waiting for him, she crossed to her bedroom to investigate the broken window and stepped inside.

A gloved hand reached out and clamped her mouth. Her heart launched out of her chest like a rocket.

The universe must've gleefully tagged her as a danger magnet because it pulled her into its magnetic field every time. She struggled against his tight grip.

"Don't move," the intruder hissed. He pulled her back and pressed a cold steel blade against her neck. Its sharpened edge cut the soft flesh below her chin. Anger and fear ripped through her.

"You're such a coward, Dylan," she goaded, unable to stop the stabbing words.

The sharp blade pinched deeper and drew blood. Fear and self-preservation took over and she stilled. Swallowed the sharp, stabby words cutting her vocal cords to shreds.

The lamplight shifted the shadows. Raul had lit the lamp.

"Lacy," he called softly.

Dylan tightened his hand across her mouth with bruising pressure. "Shh."

Raul stopped, then the unmistakable click of the .38 Sig's hammer broke the stillness.

The lamplight illuminated fluttering snowflakes as Raul stepped into the room. The flame flickered with each blast of cold air. The effect was ethereal, and she wondered if she was stuck in a nightmare. But the blood trickling down her neck, instantly cooled by the winter wind, drove home the sobering fact. This was real.

"Drop the knife." Raul's menacing voice sent a shiver through Dylan and his hold weakened, but not enough for her to escape the blade's razor-sharp edge.

"She fucked with the wrong person!" he screamed. Spittle flew onto her cheek. "Fucked my plans, fucked my life!" His chest heaved against her spine in an unnatural rhythm.

"No, all she tried to do was help you. You fucked her over. Don't make me kill you." He stepped forward. "Make no mistake. I'll drop you where you stand if you don't let her go."

It wasn't a threat. It was a promise and Dylan realized it. "Fine."

In one swift motion, he drew the knife away from her throat. As he shoved her forward the knife slashed her upper right arm, and she felt the sickening slice of flesh and muscle.

She grabbed her arm. Blood flowed, trickled through her fingers as she squeezed the wound to stay the blood. Her knees buckled and she dropped like a stone. The floor rocked underneath her like turbulent ocean waves, the roar of its surf sounded heavily in her ears.

With the gun's barrel still trained on Dylan, Raul stepped over, then bent down. He gave no indication he saw her bloodied arm, but his voice softened a fraction from its hard marble inflection.

"Get up."

"I can't," she whimpered. "My arm."

He jostled the lamp's handle to his wrist, gripped her uninjured arm, and hefted her up. The ocean roared in her ears. Bile burned its way up her throat.

"I'm gonna puke," she slurred, staggering sideways into Raul. The oil lamp tipped but the flame held.

He heaved a long-suffering sigh. "Stay here a minute," he

said, then flipped the gun's barrel at Dylan toward the door. "Move," he commanded and forced him into the kitchen.

Lacy staggered to the bathroom. Her bloodied hands slid down the sides of the cold, porcelain bowl. She hung her head over the opening then her stomach convulsed and heaved everything out. Vomit-laced water splashed and hit her nose. She heaved until nothing remained. She reached up, pushed the silver lever down, and flushed away the sickness.

As the shock waned, the wound throbbed. She stilled, struck with an acute awareness she wasn't alone. She stood, took a silent step forward, and cocked back her good arm.

"You okay?"

Raul's voice brought tears of relief. Then panic. "Where's Dylan? Did he get away?"

"No. I knocked him out."

"What? How?" She stepped forward, then stopped, and braced her hand against the wall. The ground still rocked like a flat-bottomed boat on a white-capped lake.

"I hit him on the head with the butt of the gun. I need something to tie him up with before he comes to."

He grasped her good arm, led her to the kitchen table, and sat her across from Dylan who stirred, letting out a low moan.

Raul raised the lamp over her arm and cursed. "Take off your shirt."

"Why?"

He set the lamp on the table. "Your arm is a mess." He glanced at Dylan. "And I need it."

She studied her arm in the low light. The sleeve of Jace's button-down gaped open from shoulder to elbow. Blood-soaked material clung to her shoulder. It pained her to see the ruined mess. She'd worn it, slept with it like a security blanket even though his scent had long since worn off.

She slid her good arm out of its sleeve then tugged the other side until it hung limp in her hands. She felt like a two-year-old relinquishing a pacifier.

"Here." She handed it over, uncomfortable. The flimsy white camisole she wore barely covered her and she folded her good arm across her chest.

He twisted the shirt tight then pulled Dylan's limp arms behind his back. He wrapped his wrists together then secured it in a strong knot.

"That should hold him." He moved to the kitchen, grabbed the flour sack towel from the dish rack. "I'll be right back," he threw over his shoulder as he walked out.

He returned, the towel packed with snow, and placed it on her wounded shoulder. She held it against the angry gash, let the cold seep in and numb the pain.

"Keep that on there no matter how uncomfortable it gets. Your arm will need stitches. The snow will numb the skin." He reached behind his back for the .38 Sig and set it in front of her. "If he moves, shoot him."

She swallowed the lump of fear gagging her. "Where are you going?"

"To get Cat. Your arm needs *atención*. Then we need to decide what to do about him." He motioned to Dylan.

She laid her forehead down, closed her eyes. "Okay," she mumbled.

She didn't want to think about Dylan. The snow melted and dribbled down her arm. The icy cold burned in uncomfortable contrast to her wound's biting pain.

An uneasy feeling scuttled down her spine and she raised her head. Dylan's eyes glinted like onyx stones and fastened themselves on her.

He sneered. "This is all your fault."

"Why do you think that?"

He shifted forward. "Because your boyfriend killed the man I was working for."

Her face flushed, anger-induced heat burned her scalp. "Zach. I should've known." She set the slushy ice pack next to the gun. "You knew he raped me and wanted me gone." She picked up the Sig and shifted the safety off.

Their gazes locked. "Yeah, I knew."

No guilt registered in his tone. She studied his face, twisted with hate, then looked closer, and saw hidden pain. She thought of Jace. What would he do in Dylan's place? If she was in a work camp? Her answer a couple of months ago might've been different. But he killed Zach. Now, she didn't know what Jace would do to save her.

She switched the safety into the off position. People who lived in glass houses shouldn't throw stones.

"Did it ever occur to you to ask us for help?"

"You? What power do you have? Look around you, Lacy. You're barely hanging on here. Your uncle, the great and powerful Oz of Texas, isn't here." He hung his head. "I just want her back."

Lacy tried another tack. "What would Gracie have to say about what you've done?"

His face mottled red. "I don't care. You don't get it. She's pregnant. I'll do anything to save them."

Bitter wind blew in the back door as Cat, Raul, and Travis rushed inside.

Raul picked up the flour sack towel. "I told you to keep this on your arm," he chastised.

She held up a hand, silencing any other comments, and focused on Dylan. "How did you know Jace killed Zach? And after Zach was dead, who did you feed information to?"

Travis hovered over Cat's shoulder as she inspected the wound. She pushed the gaping flesh together and clucked her tongue. "This is bad."

She raked an accusing gaze over Dylan. "How could you do this?" she demanded. Then back to Lacy, "Are you up to date on your tetanus shot?"

"I think so," she said through gritted teeth.

Travis moved and stood behind her chair, one hand on her good shoulder, the other stroking the length of her hair.

She looked up and gave him a half-smile.

He gave his head a slight shake then bent and kissed the top of her head. "What is it with you? If there's danger within a hundred-mile radius, it finds you."

Dylan's eyes, trained on the tabletop, answered Lacy. "I followed Jace the morning he left. I was on foot, so it took me a while to get to the ranch. He left in his truck before I got there. I saw his horse in the paddock, went inside the house, and found Zach. Dead. Looked like there was a struggle, but with Zach's foot blown to hell, it wasn't much of a fight."

Cat turned to Raul. "I need peroxide and there's an old bottle of Merthiolate in the pantry. Will you get it?"

She cringed. "Please don't use that."

Merthiolate, an old antiseptic used to cleanse wounds, burned like the lowest circle of hell. Her grandmother called it monkey blood and used it often enough to leave a lasting impression.

He came back with peroxide, the antiseptic, a box of gauze, and a roll of tape. Cat ripped into the gauze, doused the wound in peroxide, then dabbed at it with the gauze. She repeated the process until satisfied the gash was clean.

Cat handed her fresh gauze. "Hold that on your arm. Firmly. I'm going to go get my sewing box and some alcohol."

She wondered what kind of alcohol. Her abused arm felt like a bomb had exploded from the inside out and hoped the alcohol was the drinking kind. She needed something for the pain.

Dylan hadn't spoken since Cat started cleaning her arm. She looked over at his hunched shoulders. Defeat never looked pretty on anyone and compassion stirred her heart.

Raul picked up the gun, sat next to Lacy, his eyes trained on Dylan.

"After you found Zach, what did you do?" Lacy asked wanting to know the exact timeline.

He raised up. "I came back to the farm, took your horse

and rode into town, and reported it to Bryan Rash. He seemed more shocked that I gave him the information than in the murder itself. I told him about my deal with Zach. Zach had a direct line to the governor. He was supposed to get Gracie out of the work camps, so I asked him if he would help me like Zach, if I gave up information about what was going on here."

"Damn it, Dylan," Travis muttered.

"What did he say?" Raul asked. He gave Lacy an inscrutable look.

Dylan cocked his head. "It was weird, ya know? I thought he'd be glad to get the information. I thought Zach was giving him reports and I asked him about it. Bryan said Zach hadn't been giving him anything, said all his orders came from the governor, and that he didn't want any information or help from me. He seemed really annoyed and told me not to come back."

Lacy's brows rose to her hairline. Rash turning away information? Weird didn't cover what that was.

Raul held up his hand. "Wait. Then how did Rash know we looted the pharmacy?"

Dylan shrugged. "I went back and told him, hoping he'd change his mind. He didn't. He threw me out of the building."

Cat walked back with a jar of apple pie moonshine, her glass cut tumblers, and plunked them down. She produced a needle, dental floss, and tweezers. She removed the oil lamp's chimney, held the needle to the open flame to sterilize it, then shoved a glass at her.

"Drink up, girl. This is gonna hurt."

Travis reached down and placed her hand in his. "Squeeze my hand if you need to."

Lacy poured a glass, lifted it, and breathed in apple blossoms and cinnamon. Maybe it wouldn't taste so bad. She took the shot and choked. The clear liquid was stronger than it smelled. Fire burned a path through her veins.

Cat took her distracted moment to pour on a healthy dose of Merthiolate and she felt the harsh punch in her gut.

"Gah!" she screeched and slapped at Cat's hand.

"Well, that's done."

Her eyes smarted. "Why didn't you warn me?"

Cat's grey eyes twinkled. "It would've been worse if I had."

Through narrowed eyes, she watched her thread the needle then poured herself another drink. She shot it down and found it didn't burn as bad as the first. She poured again. "Get on with it then."

Cat began the tedious task of sewing the four-inch gash. Afterward, she had twenty-four stitches. Cat wrapped gauze and tape around the sutures.

"That should do it. You should wear a sling."

"I'm not wearing a sling, Cat."

Raul got up. "What do you want done with him?" he asked of Dylan.

She met Dylan's gaze, gave him a slight nod. "Untie him."

"What?" Raul and Cat said in unison. They gaped at her like she'd just announced she was an alien from the planet Mars. Travis stilled behind her.

"Have you lost your mind?" Cat's harsh words penetrated the alcohol's pleasant fog.

"No," she snapped. "He's out of options. For some unknown reason, Bryan's not going to help him get Gracie back. Let's see if we can."

"Oh my God," Raul muttered. "He just tried to kill you. And how can we help get his girlfriend out of Fort Sill?"

"I'm not sure we can," she said honestly. "But when my uncle comes, maybe he can."

Raul turned to Dylan. "I have another question. There's a green truck parked in the driveway. Who does it belong to?"

Guilt scuttled across his face. "I traded Jace's horse for it. Stole it, really. An old man saw me walking the horse along the highway in the snow. He stopped and asked if I needed help. I threw him out and drove away."

"You left an old man on the highway in the snow? In this

cold with nothing but a horse?" Raul asked in disgust. He turned to Lacy. "Are you sure about this? He's too unpredictable."

"Give us your word, Dylan, that you won't work against us or harm any of us again, and you can stay."

"I give you my word," he said, eyes solemn.

Raul shook his head, walked over to release him. "I will be watching you."

Travis walked around and hunched beside Lacy, eye level. "You want me to get Dylan settled in Matty's room?"

She turned toward him and leaned her forehead against his. "Thank you."

His hand tightened around hers. "For what?"

"For being here." She placed a kiss on his cheek.

A knock at the back door startled them.

"Who the hell could that be?" Cat grumbled as she walked over to answer.

An old man stood hunched at the door, his old brown coveralls covered in snow. "Name's Edwards." He stuck a black-gloved hand out to Cat. "Met Jace about a month ago, said I could come check ya'll out if I got lonesome."

Lacy jumped up, ran over, and pulled him inside. "You've seen Jace?"

He looked her up and down, brown eyes smiling. "You bet. And you must be his Lacy."

Silent tears streamed down her cheeks. The old man had called her "his Lacy."

31

J ace bounced on the Cadillac's sleek, black leather seat, leaned over, and eyed the odometer. "Jesus H. Christ," he muttered under his breath.

Senator Monroe's eyes narrowed, his lips pressed flat. "Stop bouncing."

The sharp command grinded Jace's gears. "Well, if you'd drive faster than forty miles an hour, or let me drive my own damn truck, I could handle this speed. Maybe. If I had my own music. But your Credence Clearwater Revival CD makes me want to stab my eardrums out." If he heard "Bad Moon Rising" one more time, he just might.

The senator's moustache twitched. "Your truck is in good hands."

Traveling with Barnum and Bailey's Circus would've been faster than Thomas Monroe's Texas Militia Convoy. They lumbered east toward the border town of Powderly, Texas. The long procession of trucks filled with supplies, munitions, soldiers, and other necessities labored down the obscure state highway. Then, they would shift north and cross the border where Monroe had intel the line lay unguarded by the Oklahoma Military Police.

"This gives us time to go over our plans for the governor," he added.

The senator's words pissed him off, so he focused out the window. He didn't want to talk about abducting the governor. The whole plan crossed his moral boundaries.

Early morning sunlight tried to break the window's dark-tinted barrier. The asphalt road littered with potholes cut through trees and hills. Today marked Lacy's twentieth birthday and at the rate they were going, he'd miss it. Trying to release excess energy, he shook the water bottle in his hands.

"Stop doing that," the older man snapped. "Think about the mission. You're confident you can abduct the governor? If not, you'll have no choice but to take him out."

He scrubbed a sweaty hand over his face. The senator's demand on him in his political game infuriated him. He hated feeling like a pawn in a giant chess game.

"If you have a chopper pilot, I'll deliver. But that's all I'm doing for you. If this blows sideways, I'm still out. My slate's clean. And I won't kill the governor. Period."

"You're out when I say you're out," he said evenly.

Jace shifted his body to look at him. "Why are you using me? You have a whole truckload of trained soldiers who'd do a better job."

Thomas twirled one side of his moustache. "Well, you have a vested interest where the others don't."

"Vested interest," he repeated. "Lacy."

"Lacy," he confirmed.

"What are you going to do if I refuse?" he challenged.

"I'll bury you so far under you'll never see my niece again let alone the light of day. And I'm willing to bet she'd do just about anything I asked to get you out of the prison I have in mind if you renege. Either way, I'll have someone I know that won't betray me for a better deal."

He was already buried so far under, a grave digger couldn't find him. The senator had no plans to release him. His skin pricked with anger. He'd use him over and over until he was killed or until the man got what he wanted.

He turned back toward the window, watched the landscape slip by. "I killed Zach because he raped your niece. But I did not kill my parents," he said in a quiet tone. "I'll pay for my sins, but I won't pay for that."

"I know you didn't kill your parents."

He laid his forehead against the glass. Of course, the all-knowing senator knew. "Who did?"

"What does it matter now?"

He closed his eyes a moment then turned to look at the man's rigid profile. "It matters. It will always matter. They were my parents," he choked out. "Did Zach kill them?"

"No, but he ordered it. Someone on the governor's payroll did it." Thomas turned his head and his voice carried compassion. "Your mom and dad were good people. Your dad was a good friend of mine. They didn't deserve to die."

"Well thank you for that," he snapped. "You know Zach would've kept harassing Lacy. He ordered my parents murder, yet you're punishing me because I took care of the problem."

"I realize it's a bit"—he focused his eyes on the road—"convoluted. But as I've said, vested interest. You are"—he stopped again, considered his words—"a means to an end."

"Figured," he muttered and turned back to the window.

"There's one more thing we need to discuss."

He banged his head against the backrest. "Of course, there is."

"The chopper pilot you requested has been incarcerated. You'll need to retrieve him."

He let out a long sigh. "Go on."

"When we get back, the MP will arrest you for Zach's murder. My pilot is being held in Shidler at their HQ. They'll take you there first."

He rubbed the back of his neck. "How can I bust him out if I'm in jail too?"

"Let me take care of that."

He had no idea what the senator had in mind, but knew he wanted the governor. He needed him for that job, so he let it go for the moment. He leaned back and tried to sleep, to clear his mind of everything Thomas Monroe wanted. He didn't utter another word until they pulled up to the Monroe farm.

"Lacy." He breathed her name on a relieved sigh.

The sun had begun its slow descent. The trip from Gainesville to Shidler took twice as long as it should've, and his nerves stretched wire tight. He opened the Cadillac's passenger door then leaned against it, arms folded. His eyes focused on the woman at the clothesline. She stared back at him, frozen to the spot. His eyes drank in her every feature. Long, raven hair hung in loose waves framing her oval face. He wanted to run to her, pull her close.

A wet towel hung limp in her hands, close to dropping in the dirt. He held himself back, watched her body stiffen, her eyes harden. Closing his eyes briefly, he reminded himself of the stubborn girl he'd fallen in love with. This confrontation wouldn't be easy, but then nothing with Lacy ever was. Except loving her.

Thomas exited the car, arms outstretched. "Lacy. It's good to see you."

She dropped the wet towel in the basket and walked into his embrace. "You too, Uncle Tommy. It's been a while."

"Too long," he said, kissing her cheek.

She ignored him completely. He'd been gone a little over a month, too long for his comfort, and he wondered what had happened in his absence.

Raul and Cat strode out the back door. Thomas turned to greet Raul. "Raul. I trust things are well here?"

Jace studied the scene. The senator knew Raul? Oh, hell no. He watched Lacy's reaction turn from shock to anger.

"Well enough," he answered in his usual mild manner.

"You two know each other?" she demanded. "How?"

Raul shifted from one foot to the other. The senator remained silent. "Yes. My father is helping Mr. Monroe with certain ..." he hesitated. At the Senator's nod, he continued. "Political matters. My father was the President of Mexico a few years ago and still has much clout. As a favor to your uncle, I came to the farm to watch over you as he knew he would be detained."

"Why am I not surprised?" she muttered.

Cat took the moment to step forward and introduce herself. "I'm glad to meet you, senator." Her words were surface sweet, but underneath he heard an accusation. "I'm Cat. Your niece was kind enough to take me in when I had no other place to go."

He closed the car door and walked over. "Excuse me, senator, but could I have a moment with Lacy?"

He kept his tone neutral and watched her reaction. She avoided his gaze, eyes still trained on Raul. He raked a hand through his hair.

Lacy folded her arms over her chest and graced him with a heated glare. "Got nothing to say to you," she said, then turned, and bolted for the shop building.

He ran and caught her at the gate. Grabbing her arm, he swung her around to face him.

"What?" she exploded.

He held his hands up. "Look, I know you're mad."

"Mad? Mad doesn't even begin to cover it."

He touched her hand. "Talk to me," he pleaded. She jerked back as if his touch burned her.

Her eyes narrowed. "What do you want to hear? You wanna know why I'm so pissed?" In a mocking gesture, she swung her arms wide. "Why I didn't fall at your feet the second I saw you?"

Ah, there it was. Her smart mouth. He needed to stay calm, but she knew how to push his buttons. Before he could respond, she surprised him by continuing.

"Want me to talk? Okay, I'll talk. You left me. Without a word. You. Just. Left." She lifted her arms then let them drop. "No 'See ya' or 'Hey, Lace, I'm gonna run down the road and kill my brother who happens to be your rapist even though you told me to leave it alone.' I had reasons for not telling you who raped me! You ruined everything! You left me, and I hate you for it!"

Her words sucker-punched him and he staggered back. The realization she would've taken the secret of his brother to her grave shattered him. If they were going to salvage the relationship they'd just begun, they'd need to be alone to do it. They didn't need an audience.

He stepped forward, grabbed her by the waist, and threw her over his shoulder. She shouted and punched his back as he walked. Her fist caught his kidney with a solid punch. He let out a grunt. Damn, the girl had moxie.

He smacked her butt. "Enough."

Ignoring her threats to end his life in a variety of slow and painful ways, he walked back to her uncle who stood in the drive, issuing orders to his men.

"I need the keys to my truck," he demanded.

The older man observed the situation with mild amusement. His grey moustache twitched. "For what?" he asked, fishing the keys from his pocket.

During the five weeks Jace had spent with the man, he learned he was a hard screw best left unturned. The senator would use whatever or whomever he chose with no regard to their wellbeing, as long as he got his way. He palliated his actions with 'the end justifies the means' theory and Jace had landed smack in the middle of his agenda. The senator owed him this.

"None of your business," he snapped and jerked the keys out of his hand.

"Remember the part you have to play, Jace." The man's eyes flickered a warning.

He ignored it, strode to his battered truck, and opened the passenger door. He dumped Lacy without ceremony on the seat. Before she could bolt, he buckled her seatbelt.

"Stay," he ordered. "If you run, I'll just chase you down."

She harrumphed and looked away. "I'm not a child."

"Then stop acting like one," he said harshly. He leveled his face with hers. "Don't push me, girl."

He slammed the door harder than he intended and stomped to the driver's side. He slid into the seat, started the engine, and maneuvered through the military jeeps and Humvees to the blacktop highway, then turned west toward Kaw City.

Silence lay like a weighted blanket between them. He pursed his lips together, unwilling to break it. Only when he turned right at the Washunga Bay sign did she speak.

"Where are we going?" she demanded. "I thought you were taking me home."

"Nope."

After a few miles, he made a left turn off the asphalt onto a narrow, red dirt road. A sign with faded red letters warning, "Trespassers will be shot on sight," tilted sideways. He stifled a laugh. A white porcelain claw-foot tub sat in the meadow with a wooden painted couple enjoying a bath. The next sign, held by a disfigured mannequin, said, "Beware! Wandering hordes of zombies ahead."

Lacy rolled her eyes. "You're taking me to old Amos Hitt's hunting cabin? He's nuts. What if he's there?"

"Then we'll go somewhere else."

Amos Hitt called the one-room structure that rolled into their view a cabin. A summer house described it better. Surrounded by trees, it sat off a small cliff littered with rusty-colored limestone boulders that dropped off into Kaw Lake. An outhouse, built like a small room and painted the same rustic brown as the cabin, stood a few feet away. A deserted rock quarry lay west beyond the trees.

He parked the car by the outhouse and got out, not looking

to see if she followed. Conflicting emotions warred inside him. Thoughts of his brother, Lacy, and the job Thomas Monroe blackmailed him into, all tumbled and thrashed together.

He walked onto the wraparound porch, flipped the welcome mat over, and found a key. He opened the door and stepped inside. Lacy gasped over his shoulder. The southern wall facing the lake was solid glass. Sun sparkled off the water's clear surface and bounced through the spotless panes, creating a riotous color prism on the natural hard wood floor.

He turned to her. "I'm sorry you're angry I left you," he said quietly. He started there. They could work through this. His feelings for her hadn't changed. Had hers? His stomach pitched at the thought.

Her face turned sour. "You're sorry I'm angry. You're not sorry you left, though. That's not much of an apology." She walked onto the porch.

He followed. "You're right. I'm not sorry I left, but I am sorry I hurt you *because* I left."

She flattened her hands together prayerfully and brought them to her face. "Jace. I had a chance to kill your brother. But I didn't. Did that ever occur to you? I found a way to deal with my pain without adding more damage to an already fucked up situation." She shook her head. "Why? Why'd you do it? He was the only family you had left."

"I did it for you! He never would've stopped coming for you. You can't imagine the vile things he said."

"If I'd wanted that, I would've done it myself." She raised her voice to match his. "You did this for you! You're the one who couldn't let it go, couldn't live with him between us."

Again, her words knocked the wind out of him. Left him breathless, without a word. He watched her pace down the wooden porch steps, then back.

Face-to-face with him, she continued. "I got news for you. Unless you find a way to deal with your guilt, Zach will always be between us. Haunting us. Ruining us. You're the one who said, 'no ghosts,' remember? I found a way to heal, Jace. You healed me." She stopped and looked away. "Then you left."

He shook his head, confused. He'd wrestled over a month with questions. Questions he feared because the answers might destroy him.

His eyes sought hers. "How could you?" The burden, the weight of those three words flowed from his mouth of their own accord seeking answers. "How could you sleep with us both?"

She gasped, and her eyes widened in shock. Her hand snaked out and struck him hard across the cheek. Dumbfounded, he reached up and felt the warmth where she slapped him.

"What is wrong with you? I didn't choose to have sex with you both. You're an asshole." She raised her head and shouted, "God! Zach raped me! Don't you get it? Not my choice. You were my choice, Jace. You."

His heart sank and he dropped to his knees. "No, Lacy. God, no. You misunderstood my question. What I meant was, how could I even be a choice for you after what he did? Because of me." He looked her in the eye. "This is all my fault. How can you even look at me?"

"This isn't your fault. It's Zach's fault. I…" She faltered. "This is too much," she whispered, backing away.

He sprang to his feet. "God, girl." He let out a frustrated breath and in two quick strides ate the ground between them. His eyes locked on hers. "This spring, when the wind and rain come and the flowers bloom, I'll want you. When summer's heat melts away spring and the cicada's sing in the mimosa trees, I'll want you. When summer bows to fall and the leaves turn red, I'll want you. And when fall gives way to winter's death and snow sweeps down the plains, I'll want you." He took a breath, leaned forward, and rested his forehead on hers. Her breath, so close, brushed his smarting cheek. "I'm here. And I don't just want you." He leaned in, covered her mouth with his. He heard her breathy sigh, felt her give in, melt into the kiss, and his heart exploded. He leaned back. "I need you, girl. Don't you know you're the air I breathe? I love you."

"Don't go away again. You can't leave me like that." She dropped her head onto his shoulder.

He stroked her hair. "I'll do my best, love."

She raised her head, brushed her lips against his neck. "You got me?"

His breath caught. That had become his promise to her. One he'd never break. "Yeah," he choked out. "Hold on to me. I won't let you fall."

32

Lacy lifted her uninjured arm, wrapped it around Jace's neck, and brushed her lips against his. He came back. He wanted her. Needed her. She felt the tapestry of her shredded heart weave back together. His strong arms around her waist tightened as he deepened the kiss. The heady punch of desire hit her center, her body flushed with heat until she thought she'd burn from the inside out. She'd missed him. Missed this. He backed her against the porch steps. Her fingers tightened around his neck, then twined through his hair. The heel of her Converse caught the bottom step's rough wood, but his arms held her steady.

He raised his head. "Told you I wouldn't let you fall." His eyes flickered with doubt. Something she'd never seen in them, and she didn't like it. He dropped his arms. "Lace," he started.

"My God." She cut him off. "What happened to the conceited, arrogant, bossy, beautiful guy I fell in love with?"

His face lit with amusement. "You forgot to say conceited twice."

She laughed and sat on the top step. Low-hanging clouds scudded across the sky, the wind driving them south. The sun's rays broke through and made the brown earth and dead grass roll in waves as if the ground itself were alive and moving.

"Yeah," she agreed. "You got that in spades." She steadied her gaze on his eyes, full of mirth, all traces of doubt gone. She shook her head in mock disgust. "How quickly Adonis returns."

He dropped down beside her. Laughter rumbled from his chest. "Adonis? You think I look like Adonis?"

"I think the Greek gods blessed you with their arrogance," she stated primly.

A self-satisfied grin rested on his face. He nudged her wounded shoulder. "You think I look like Adonis."

She gasped as pain shot down her arm. He'd jerked her stitched-up arm when he chased her down, but she'd been too angry to notice. Now blood, warm and sticky, seeped through the sleeve of her long-sleeved shirt.

The two-day-old stitches pinched and pulled her skin. She changed the bandages twice a day, but it still wept blood. She'd been too stubborn to wear the sling Cat made and already ripped out two stitches. She'd squawked like a wet hen at Lacy the entire time she repaired them.

His eyes zoned in on the blood stain. "You're bleeding." He scooted closer for a better look. His voice hardened. "Why are you bleeding?"

"It's nothing," she muttered.

Why did she have to deal with this now? She'd rather have his arms wrapped around her, his mouth on hers again.

"Lace," he pressed in a low, dangerous tone.

"It's just a scratch, Jace."

When she leaned over to kiss his neck, he pushed her back and leveled her with a heated look. "You know I'm going to see it."

Her face flushed. He had a point. She couldn't hide it from him. Reluctantly, she drew the shirt over her head. The white camisole underneath did little to shield her from the wind, and a shiver scuttled down her spine. She unwound the gauze and peeled back the bloody bandage.

He examined the injury. Anger darkened his face. "This is a knife wound," he said with slow incredulity. His eyes targeted hers. "How did this happen?"

She shrugged. "Long story." Dylan's knife at her throat was a frightening memory she didn't want to remember, no matter how it played out. She hugged her arms around her middle, then stood. "I'm freezing. Let's go inside."

She turned and opened the heavy, wooden-planked door, bypassed the small, handcrafted table and chairs in the corner, crossed to the bed and sat.

Jace closed the door then sat beside her, let his hands fall between his knees. "We've got time."

She fell back against the fluffy, feather pillows stacked against the headboard, and stared at the dark-stained rafters, a perfect place for a loft. She imagined a rugged set of stairs leading to a tidy little space with an extra bed and fragrant herbs hanging from its ceiling.

He lay back, wrapped his arms around her, and drew her against his strong chest. She felt his heartbeat against her back, soft and steady, and the hazy pull of desire returned. He rested his head against her shoulder, brushed a strand of hair from her forehead.

"Talk to me, girl."

She sighed in resignation. "Not long after you left, Bryan Rash and the MP came to the farm looking for you. He told us about Zach. When he couldn't find you, he burned the barn."

Censure leaked from her voice, she couldn't help it. She'd wanted to keep that detail to herself. But her dirty laundry had been aired to the world like a reality TV star. She hated the looks of pity, real or imagined, from Travis, Cat, and the others.

His arm tightened around her. "I'm so sorry. It's my fault." He stopped and frowned. "How did Rash find out about Zach so fast? And how'd he know I killed him?"

"Dylan was working for Zach. Stealing fence posts. Cutting electric wires. Giving him information."

His brow furrowed. "Why?"

She thought of Dylan's girlfriend, ripped away from family and home, pregnant with no hope of escape, and shuddered. "His girlfriend, Gracie, was captured and taken to Fort Sill. She's pregnant, Jace."

"Go on," he urged.

She told him about Matty's need for medicine, then pulled in a deep breath. "We came up with a plan to trap Dylan and get Matty's medicine at the same time."

His jaw ticked. "What did you do? And who is *we*?"

A mounted deer head hung on the wall and glared down at her with dark, glassy eyes. She focused on the stag's accusing gaze and tried to gauge how angry Jace would be when she told him what she'd done. "Travis and I broke into the pharmacy in town."

He stiffened, iron-board straight, his hand at her waist fisted. "Why did you take that risk? Jesus, Lacy. The MP would've shot first and asked questions later. Or hauled you to a work camp. Or thrown you in jail. What the hell were you thinking?"

She tamped down her rising irritation. "I was thinking" — she drew out the word — "I couldn't let Matty die. He couldn't breathe, Jace. He was dying, and I was scared."

"Travis doesn't have the good sense God gave him," he muttered. "Someone else should've taken the risk, not you. Is that how you got hurt?"

His anger was palpable, but she continued, determined to get everything in the open. "No. And of course it should've been me taking the risk. I'm responsible for everyone living on the farm."

He twirled a piece of her hair, let it fall to her shoulder. "I'm sorry I wasn't here. I promised I'd help share the burden. I hate the fact Travis stepped up and took my place." He gave her a long, measured look. "He loves you."

Denying the fact would've been pointless so she didn't try. Instead, she locked her eyes on his blue ones. They shined like sapphire brilliants she'd seen once in a jewelry store.

"Yes," she agreed, "he does."

His brows knit together. "Did he make a move on you?"

She reached out and rubbed the worry lines between his brows. "Yeah. He did."

He took her outstretched hand, pulled it to his chest. "Do you love him?"

She rested her forehead on his. "No. I belong to you. I love you."

He tugged her closer. "Thank God."

She swallowed hard. "Will you kiss me now?"

He cocked his head. "I still don't know who knifed you or how it happened."

She let out a groan. "Fine. When Dylan realized he'd been caught, he came back to the farm and attacked me."

"What!" His nostrils flared. "Where is he now?"

She ran a hand through his hair. "Calm down."

"I'm gonna beat the ever-loving shit outta him."

"Let me ask you something. If the shoe was on the other foot, if you had lost me to a work camp and knew I was pregnant with your child, what would you have done?"

He opened his mouth to speak then snapped it shut.

She understood the conflicting emotions he battled. "I forgave him."

He studied her, then light dawned across his features like a sun-swept wheat field. He stared at her in curiosity. "So, does that mean you forgive me too?"

A smile spread across her face. "I guess it does."

Night had fallen on the lake. She looked out the transparent wall at moonbeams bouncing off the water below and thought of glass houses.

"Will you kiss me now?"

He let out a slow sigh, dropped kisses along her jaw. "Without question," he murmured as his lips brushed hers.

THE EARLY MORNING sun burned away the fog that had floated like a night wraith shrouded in heavy, grey mist, across the lake. In his sleep, Jace had thrown an arm and one leg over Lacy's small frame as if he were afraid she'd disappear. She lay, half-awake under his warm body and the white goose down comforter.

She tried to slide out without waking him. Her bladder needed relief. But the muscles in his arm flexed, pinning her in place.

His eyes, hooded with sleep, met hers. "Where do you think you're going?"

She leaned in, kissed the dark stubble along his jawline. "I have to pee."

Reluctantly, he released her. "Hurry back."

She got up, picked his plain black T-shirt off the floor, and slipped it over her head. The hem dropped to her thighs and his masculine scent enveloped her. She thought of his ruined button-down she'd slept with and worn almost every day. God she'd missed him. She stood lost in thought until he spoke.

"Hmm," he murmured, his voice low and froggy from sleep. "You look damn fine in my T-shirt, girl." He sat up, the comforter fell to his waist and revealed his rock-hard chest. "What are you doing?" he wondered, amusement coloring his tone.

She looked up and he arched a brow. He'd caught her staring at his chest again. "I'm just..." she stammered, surprised at the sting of tears behind her eyelids. "I missed you," she managed, then escaped to the outhouse to relieve her bladder and organize her scrambled thoughts.

When she returned, he'd lit a fire. The small fireplace, built from stones mined out of the cliff, emitted a comfortable warmth. He stood by the hearth barefoot, his unbuttoned jeans hung low on his hips. She closed the door and stood, staring again at his beautiful male form.

He moved toward her in his slow easy saunter, grasped both her hands, and pulled her down on a red-checked flannel blanket spread before the open flame. Saltine crackers and homemade jelly sat on a chipped, blue stoneware plate.

He waved a hand. "This is all I could find to eat."

"This is great," she murmured. Her hair hung in wild abandon around her shoulders. She grabbed it and braided it down her back. "I haven't had jelly in ages." She lifted the jar to her nose, inhaled the sweet fragrance of sand plums and sugar. "My mom used to make sand plum jelly. It's my favorite."

"Yeah, mine too."

He handed her a butter knife. "Let's eat."

She smeared jelly on a stale cracker and covertly watched his changing expressions. "What's wrong?"

He rubbed the back of his neck. "I need to talk to you."

"Okay."

She dropped the cracker onto the plate, her stomach queasy. He sounded nervous. Mentally, she braced herself, afraid of what he was about to say.

He stared at the fire. "After Zach, I drove to Texas and crossed the border into Gainesville. I thought I could find out where your uncle was and convince him to come help us. The Texas Militia caught me at a gas station and threw me in jail. Long story short, your uncle came. He knew I'd killed Zach." He swore, then looked her in the eye. "I've been in military training for the past four weeks. He wants me to abduct the Oklahoma governor. Actually, it would've made him happier if I'd agreed to kill him."

Her breath hitched. She knew her uncle had political ambitions, but she never dreamed he'd go this far. "He's blackmailing you into helping him because you killed Zach? Why?"

He swiped a hand across his face. "Because I have a vested interest, he said."

She folded her legs underneath her and leaned toward him, rested her hands on his thighs. "What does that mean?"

He cupped her face. "You. You're my vested interest. He thinks I'll do anything to keep you safe." He leaned in and kissed her. "He's not wrong."

"No." The one syllable word meant as a command came out as a plea. "You can't leave me. I'll go with you. Or we can run. Let's just take off, get lost somewhere."

He shook his head. "We're in the middle of the country. Closed borders on every side. We wouldn't make it out. And he's not going to let you go with me."

"He has no say over me."

He drew her into his arms, settled them facing the fire, sand plums and saltines forgotten. She sat between his legs, his arms wrapped around her middle. He rested his chin on her shoulder. "No, he doesn't. Do I?"

She leaned her head back against his chest. "You do," she admitted. "Please don't leave me, Jace. You promised."

"I said I'd do my best. At this point I think we're safer together."

"We are."

"There's one more thing." When she didn't reply, he continued. "When we go back today, the MP are going to come and arrest me. You're going to have to let me go without a fight."

Her body tensed. "I'm supposed to just let them take you?"

"Your uncle has a plan. I'm sure he'll explain when we get back."

The defeat in his voice infuriated her. "How can we possibly trust him after what he's done to you?"

"We have no other choice."

33

"Maybe they're not coming."

Hope. Lacy hated the sound of it in her voice because she knew the situation was hopeless. Jace would be arrested today.

She sat at the kitchen table with Jace and her uncle. They'd driven back from the cabin that morning, both lost in their own thoughts. He'd reached over and grasped her hand, laced his fingers through hers. When they pulled in, they'd found a dozen military tents had sprung up in the pasture overnight, like ugly, brown mushrooms after a spring rain.

"They'll come." The vinyl chair squeaked as Thomas Monroe fished a lighter and cigarettes from his pants pocket. He shook one out, lit the tip, and inhaled. White wispy smoke filtered from the glowing tip to the ceiling. He flicked ashes on his empty breakfast plate, his mouth set in a grim line.

Travis appeared in the kitchen doorway then stalled. His lips flattened as he glared at Jace. "I heard you were back," he snapped. "Military's coming."

Jace lifted his chin and his voice hardened. "Yeah. I'm back."

She heard the warning, saw his possessive look as he

glanced at her. She reached over and placed her hand over his and squeezed.

He turned to the senator. "I'm ready."

Her grip tightened. "I'm not." Fear churned knots sitting like lumpy dough in her stomach.

"Lacy," her uncle cautioned. "Don't make a scene."

The command made her want to bare her teeth. She hated being under his thumb, hated how he was using Jace. She hated forced submission. "Why are you doing this? There's got to be another way."

"My presence is making the military nervous. I have to appear cooperative." He twisted his moustache and took another drag off his cigarette.

"So Jace is your peace offering. You don't need him to help your man escape. That's it, isn't it?" Her head pounded like a bomb exploded inside her skull.

He gave her a contemplative look. "You're shrewd. And mouthy. I don't like it."

The rough knock on the front door drilled another painful spike through her brain and she jerked as if a marionettist had pulled a string.

Thomas Monroe stood, dropped his cigarette, and crushed it with his heel. With an easy grace he walked to the door. "Gentlemen," he stepped back and waved them in. She expected to see Bryan Rash, but didn't recognize the man who stepped inside.

She stood. "Where's Rash?"

"He's been detained," the new MP informed her with a condescending smile.

The man strode to the kitchen where Jace sat, arms crossed. He scraped his chair back, stood, then pulled her into a bone crushing embrace.

"I love you, girl," he whispered in her ear.

His warm breath tickled her neck. His strong, muscular

arms around her waist sent shivers through her. "I love you too."

Her mind raced. She felt the panic attack's telling signs as dizziness overtook her. Her grip around his neck tightened. She tried to catch her breath but couldn't. Her chest felt too tight. She was losing him again. Her mind spun, blurring her vision, a merry-go-round whirling so fast she couldn't find a place to jump off.

He leaned back, searched her face. His rough, calloused hand rubbed up and down her back. "Breathe," he murmured. He released his hold and cupped her face. "Hey. Look at me."

She averted her eyes and shook her head. She couldn't.

"Look at me, girl," he said, his voice low and raspy. "I'll be okay." One corner of his mouth curved. "See you soon."

The MP, a squatty man with muscles that bulged under his shirt sleeves like he lifted weights to compensate his short stature, turned to Jace. "Let's get this over with." He cleared his throat and drew handcuffs from his military belt. "Jace Matthew Cooper, you are under arrest for the murder of Zach Hadley Cooper."

Silver steel glinted in the dappled sunlight streaming through the window as he shook them apart. Jace stood and the man jerked him around, bound his hands behind his back. The click, click, click of steel on steel as he tightened the cuffs around his wrists made her want to scream.

Her head swam with adrenaline and she balled her hands into fists as the man brushed by her with Jace in tow.

"Love you," he murmured as they passed.

She swung around, her fisted hands pressed against her temples. "Do something!" she shouted at her uncle.

The door slammed shut behind them. She ran to the window and watched as they shoved him into the back of a Humvee.

Travis walked over, put his arm around her shoulders. "I'm sorry, Lacy."

She shook off his arm, turned, and faced her uncle. "You need him. What's your plan to get him back?"

He sat on the couch, smoothed the wrinkles in his slacks. "I've got someone on the inside that will help him escape," he said, his expression unflappable.

She paced the living room floor, counted each step, trying to calm her racing heart. She stopped in front of him. "Was it so important to your reputation to have him arrested for murder?"

His brown eyes flattened as he studied her. "It was. I'll need you to go pick them up tonight."

"Where?" she asked warily.

"The dirt road by the high school. I assume you know where that is." His brow lifted in challenge as his eyes locked on hers. "You want him back, don't you?"

Unblinking, Lacy stared back. She didn't know this man at all. They shared the same blood, but he was a stranger, one who had no regard for family.

Her eyes widened with stunning clarity and she understood why her father refused to help him. She'd been a fool to stay behind. Her heart sank with homesickness for her family.

But if she'd left, followed her family to California, she would've lost so much more. Jace had shown her the unending depth of love. He gave her its strength and endurance. Its astonishing ability to forgive, and a joy in lovemaking so bright she had nothing to compare it to. It burned brighter than the sun.

She didn't trust her uncle but wanted Jace. She had no choice but to do as he asked.

"Yes," she answered evenly. "What do I have to do?"

He crossed to the window, fingered the paper-thin gingham curtains. "Guard change is at midnight. I have a man on the inside who will give Jace and my informant a key. They'll slip out the back door and meet you by the old high school." He paused then turned to face her. "If they don't show by twelve thirty, leave without them. One of my men will go with you."

She wouldn't leave without Jace, but she nodded her head in agreement. "There's just one thing, Uncle Tommy."

If the plan fell through, she needed someone she trusted with her. Not one of her uncle's militia men. How insistent could she be, how far could she push him to get what she wanted?

"I want to take Travis with me instead of your guy," she worded carefully. "I trust him. We work well together."

She looked at Travis, a warning in her eyes, and gave her head a slight shake. His stance widened in anger but his face shuttered.

"As you wish," he conceded.

"Well." She turned for the back door. "I'm going for a ride. Acer needs the exercise and I need time to think."

"You've not been dismissed." The statement, uttered with casual indifference, held definitive, unyielding authority underneath.

Face flushed, she spun around, all pretense of cooperation gone. "Let's get one thing straight, Uncle Tommy. You have no say over me. You are not my father and I am not one of your militia men."

He closed the distance between them. His open hand reached out and struck her across the cheek with enough force that she stumbled back. Her eyes smarted against the blow. Travis lunged forward, but she caught his arm and shook her head.

"I told you I don't like your smart mouth. Your father should've taught you better manners. You will respect me," he mandated.

She stared into his cold brown eyes, hid the shock and hurt behind calculated sarcasm. "Respect is earned." She enunciated each word. "*Sir.*"

With slow deliberation, she walked out the door. When her

feet hit the concrete path, she lurched into a run, but stopped short as Cat and Edwards walked out of the wash house, both cackling like two teenagers.

Edwards's black and white checked hat sat cockeyed on his head. His white hair poked out the sides like ruffled chicken feathers. He'd been at the farm two days and fit in like spokes in a bicycle tire. The instant friendship between Cat and Edwards intrigued her. They were fascinating to watch.

Despite the sting in her cheek, her face broke out in a wide grin. "What are you two doing?"

Travis walked up behind her, placed a hand on her shoulder. She turned and shot him a silent warning. He'd better keep his mouth shut. Cat would hit the roof if she found out her uncle struck her.

Edwards, still chuckling, held out seed packets. "We're sorting seeds for a garden."

"He brought seeds, a roto-tiller, gasoline," Cat added, delighted. She set a keen eye on Lacy. "Where are you going?"

She turned her smarting cheek away. "I'm gonna run Acer down to the creek." Looking back at Travis, she added, "I have no idea what he's doing."

Travis snorted, shoved his hands in his pockets, but kept silent.

Edwards glanced at a small group of militia men gathered around the cut electric wires by the bathroom window. "They're fixing the electric."

"At least my uncle is good for something," she muttered. "Hey," she addressed Edwards. "Did you have a chance to talk to Jace when we got back this morning?"

"Sure did," he beamed. "Glad I came. Thanks for havin' me."

"No problem." She turned away and trotted down the path before Cat got a better look at her face. She felt the under part of her eye swell and knew it would blacken. She couldn't avoid her forever, but she'd settle for right now.

When she reached the shop, Raul had Acer out leading him away from the building.

"I was just coming for him." She reached out and rubbed Acer's velvety nose. He stuck his lips out and whinnied, ears pricked in anticipation.

"Good," he grunted. "He was getting restless. He does not like his makeshift stall." He handed the reins over and touched her shoulder. "You have a minute?"

"Sure."

Sunlight burst between clabbered, white, low-hanging clouds and highlighted her cheek. Raul stepped closer. "What happened to your face?"

She reached up and fingered the blooming bruise. "My uncle hit me."

His eyes tightened in concern. "I am sorry. He is not to be trusted."

She cocked her head. "I thought you were working for him?"

"I am here as a favor to the senator for my father. My father is working with Senator Monroe but wanted me to keep tabs on him. He does not trust his word." He stopped and looked around, made sure no militia men were within earshot. "Do not trust him," he said, voice low.

"I don't," she said. "Can you help me up? I'll just ride bareback today."

He laced his fingers together. She stepped up and threw herself over Acer's back. "Thanks for the warning."

He nodded once. "Where are you going?"

Acer pranced forward, anxious to run. "To the creek. Travis and I have to bust Jace out of jail tonight and I need some space."

A perplexed look covered his face. "Jace has been arrested? Why?"

"Just a while ago. MP came and took him for Zach's murder."

"Need help?"

"No. But again, thanks."

She was as impatient as her horse. She needed time to think. What if Jace and her uncle's informant couldn't get out? What could she do? She wasn't a criminal mastermind, for fuck's sake.

As if reading her thoughts, Raul said, "I have something for you. For tonight. Come find me when you get back."

"What do you have that could possibly help me tonight?" Acer pawed the ground and tossed his head, irritated at the delay.

"Pipe bombs," he said, and walked back into the shop building.

Well, that would give her something to think about. She loosened the reins and Acer bolted forward. Maybe she'd become a criminal mastermind after all.

The passage of time moved differently in a jail cell. Time was its own master. It had its own will and when its servants sat on hard concrete surrounded by steel bars, time became a sloth and moved in sluggish seconds.

Jace heard the clock's second hand ticking behind the commander's desk. He couldn't see it, but in the heavy silence, he heard each second pass. The sound mocked him, dared him to count each sixty-second revolution. He wanted to smash it, stomp its inner gears into tiny unrecognizable bits. He rose from the concrete shelf and paced back and forth.

His cellmate leaned against the cinderblock wall. "Dude, you're gonna have to chill. We may be here a while."

Bracing the steel bars, he looked out from the one cell lock-up that hadn't been used since the town sheriff retired. Shidler's old City Building served as the MP's headquarters. Dirt and dust streaks from decades of moisture running ceiling to floor created a spider web graffiti against the dull white concrete blocks. Jace stared at it for hours, and out of its random patterns, picked out a giraffe, a demon, and Daffy Duck. His nose itched from mice droppings and mold that saturated every corner.

He rested his head against the cool bars and tried to even his erratic breathing. His heart thrummed against his ribcage. The midnight guard change happened over thirty minutes ago. He watched the men in the small building rotate outside. Only four men guarded the headquarters, two in and two out.

"What happened?" he wondered.

The man slipped his hands behind his head completely at ease. "Don't know. Could be simple miscommunication or bad timing. Either way, we've missed our ride."

He banged his foot against the bars with each secondhand tick. "What do we do now?"

"Nothing we can do but wait," his cellmate said, yawning.

He hated waiting. He'd never been a patient person. Lacy was a perfect example of his impatience. He should've taken more time with her. Courting was an old-fashioned notion, but his mother had filled his head as a young boy with its romantic concept. He'd taken her on long walks, cajoled her sweet, animated side out of her from time to time, read to her when she was sick. But it hadn't been enough.

He wanted to marry her. He'd told her so. Told her, he realized. He hadn't asked. Hadn't gotten down on one knee in the traditional way. He'd demanded. But there wasn't a preacher around to marry them anyway. A story his mom told him about her Scottish grandmother floated into his mind. She'd been handfast to her first husband before they'd come to America. The idea settled on his shoulders as if his mother had wrapped a mantle around him.

Before he could finish the thought, an explosion rattled the bars, rocking the earth under his feet. Plaster and ceiling tiles rained to the floor in dusty clouds.

His cell mate sprang up, scattering large, chalky clumps of plaster across the concrete floor. "The fuck was that?"

Jace stood stunned for several seconds, the blast ringing his ears like church bells. His frenetic thoughts raced to Lacy.

The girl was reckless. How had she managed an explosion like that?

The sergeant at the desk jumped to his feet, upending broken tile and debris. He swore and barked orders to the other officer and rushed outside, leaving the front door wide open. Cold air swept in. Dust devils swirled the fine, white plaster particles and dirt into little snowy tornadoes.

Before rushing outside, the officer opened their cell door. "Must be your cue, boys. Time to go," he said, then rushed out the door.

His cellmate shoved his shoulder, and Jace lurched out of the barred cell. "Let's go," he hissed and bolted for the back door.

The man fumbled with the knob's lock until it squeaked open. They crept around the building away from the flaming ASV and the four MP circled around it, then sprinted into the inky darkness.

What the hell caused an explosion like that, he wondered as they weaved through abandoned houses, stumbling over rocks and broken toys. His cellmate's foot landed in a gopher hole and he fell to his knees.

Jace hoisted him up by the arm. "You okay?"

"Yeah," he grunted, rotating his foot. He lowered his weight and hissed. "Let's keep moving."

They continued at a slower pace until they reached the alley at the end of town. Jace stopped and looked around. "Where are we going?"

"Our pick-up point." The man in front turned down the alley and charged toward the old high school.

A black Cadillac sat parked at the edge of a dirt road. When they edged closer to the highway, headlights flashed.

His cellmate whipped his head over his shoulder. "Lacy's not going to like seeing me," he gasped between breaths.

Jace laughed outright as they raced across the highway. "I know."

They leapt over the muddy culvert and raced to the car. He wrenched open the back door and dove into the floorboard.

The man flung himself on top and shouted, "Go!"

Jace grunted, pinned to the floor. "Get off me."

He lifted himself to the bench seat and sucked in a deep breath. The car lurched forward slamming him against the seat. The back tires grasped for purchase on the dirt and gravel. The open door banged shut as they spun out and gripped the blacktop.

Jace climbed off the floorboard onto the seat. The man next to him sat stock still, eyes wide.

Lacy, riding shotgun, turned and faced Bryan Rash, a gun trained on his head. "What. The. Hell?"

Bryan held up shaky hands. "I can explain."

"Listen to him, Lacy," Jace coaxed in a low tone.

She glared at Bryan. "Why should I listen to him? You know everything he's done!" she shouted. "I should shoot you right now." She cocked the hammer back.

Bryan swallowed hard, tried to clear his throat. "I'm working for your uncle, Lacy," he croaked.

"Yeah, I bet." She elbowed Travis at the wheel. "You believe this load of crap?"

Travis gave her a sidelong glance and shook his head. "Come on, Lace. Put the gun down."

"Fine." She released the hammer and placed it in her lap.

Travis turned left into the Monroe driveway and cut the engine. All four exited, then stood and stared at each other like statues at the Metropolitan Museum. Jace glared at Travis, his lips pulled back in a snarl, hands curled into fists. He felt a vein pop in his neck.

Travis lifted his head and smirked like a man who held no regard for his own safety. He didn't comprehend how close he was to becoming dog meat.

Lacy turned, braced her feet, and stared at Bryan. "Explain. And it better be good." She grasped her right elbow. Red dirt streaked from her jeans all the way up her shoulder.

Jace walked to her and noticed blood on her shirtsleeve blooming red where her stitches were.

He swore. "Damn it, girl. What have you done to yourself?"

She spared a glance at her shoulder and grimaced. "I think my stitches ripped open."

Livid, he turned on Travis standing by the car's hood. "How did this happen?"

Travis looked sick. "The blast threw us a couple feet."

"What?" Jace raked both hands through his hair. "You mean to tell me you let her get that close to—" He stopped, threw his hands up. "What caused a blast like that?"

"Raul built us some pipe bombs," Travis admitted.

"A pipe bomb," he repeated, voice deadly quiet. "You let her light a pipe bomb? You are an idiot."

"She didn't light it. I did," Travis shot back.

His jaw ground together hard enough to crack his molars. "Why didn't you make her stay in the car?"

"Have you ever tried to make her do anything?" Travis shouted then shoved past him and stood before Lacy. His hand reached out and cupped her face. "Why didn't you tell me you were hurt?"

Jace grabbed the back of his shirt and swung him around. "Don't touch her," he warned.

Travis shoved him back a step. "Don't tell me what to do. You left her man."

He clenched his fists, sweat pouring down his back. "That's none of your business."

"It became my business!" Travis shouted. "Who do you think protected her while you were gone?"

"You"—he shoved a finger in his face—"didn't do a very good job." He stepped closer. "Now I'm warning you. Stay away from her."

Bryan stepped between them, hands outstretched. "Come on, guys. Take it down a notch."

Travis backed away, arms raised. "Whatever, man. But this isn't over," he said, pointing at Jace.

He lunged forward, but Lacy grabbed his shoulder. "Let it go." She wrapped her good arm around his waist and looked at him, eyes dulled with pain. "Please."

Her words cleared the anger fogging his brain as he focused on her. She was hurt.

"Bryan, go get Cat. She's been staying at the other house."

Bryan gave a military salute and trotted down the gravel drive.

Jace scooped her up and carried her in the house. Her petite frame weighed next to nothing. The girl needed to eat better. He maneuvered her through the door and onto the couch. The long-sleeved, vintage Van Halen T-shirt she wore had ripped at the shoulder seam. To his knowledge, she'd never owned a Van Halen shirt and he wondered where she'd gotten it. He frowned. It sure as hell better not be Travis's shirt.

He knelt in front of her and tugged on the hem. "This is gonna have to come off."

She leaned her head back and groaned. "I don't want to move."

"I'm sorry, love," he murmured. His hands skirted around her and he lifted the material to her armpits. His hands skimmed the sides of her perfectly formed breasts. He sucked in a breath and concentrated on cleaning her arm.

"Lift up," he instructed.

He felt her breath hitch between his hands. He looked up. Hooded green eyes, bright with longing gazed back at him. He gave her a lazy smile and dropped kisses where the thin white material of her camisole dipped at her navel.

"Stupid girl," he gently admonished.

She ran a hand through his hair. He loved it when she touched him, it didn't matter where.

"Not stupid," she contradicted. "Insane, mad, crazy is more on the mark."

He raised himself eye level with her. "Stop being crazy. I can't stand it when you get hurt like this."

A slow smile spread across her face. "Can't help that." She twirled his hair around her finger. "Haven't you figured it out yet? We're all mad here."

He brushed his lips against hers, feather light. "You could've been killed. You understand that, right?"

She shifted and he lifted the shirt over her head then down the injured side of her arm. He dropped the bloodied garment to the floor. He should get up and clean her arm. It looked like she'd skidded down a cheese grater. Dirt and tiny stone particles were trapped in grated strips of flesh. Most of her stitches remained intact, but a few broke loose in the middle, seeping blood. The wound needed to be flushed with water to remove all the dirt and road grit.

He started to rise but she wrapped her legs around his waist. "I need to clean your arm. It looks awful."

Her arm tightened around his neck. "No, you don't." She pulled him closer. "Just kiss me. Don't think. Just hold on to me. Please."

The girl had to stop saying the word *please*. It broke him every time. He'd move a mountain one shovelful at a time if she asked. He wrapped his arms around her, stood, then swiveled them around and sat on the floor. They sat face to face, his back against the couch. He cupped both hands around her face and for the first time noted her blackened eye in the flickering firelight.

"Your eye is—"

She cut him off. "I'll tell you later."

Before he could protest, she pressed her lips to his. Lust barreled through him. Everything could wait. For a while.

35

J ace had to admit, the senator knew how to get things done. The electric was fixed—let there be friggin' light —and a new electric water heater was installed. He stood in the bathroom doorway and watched Cat work on Lacy's arm.

Cat clucked her tongue as she worked antibacterial soap into Lacy's ground flesh. She sat in a kitchen chair, arm draped over the tub's rim like a rag doll, eyes screwed shut in pain. Cat twisted the four-pronged metal faucet handles and filled a plastic Gas-N-Sip cup then poured the warm water over the bloodied soap.

Jace walked over to inspect. Her shoulder looked like ground hamburger meat, swollen and raw.

Lacy gasped. "God that hurts."

Cat clucked again. "You got no more sense than a frog in a hailstorm. This is going to leave a nasty scar. I can't even repair the stitches now." She craned her neck to look at Jace. "She's gonna be a handful, that's for sure and certain. You sure you're ready for all this?" She waved a hand at Lacy as if she were a blown-up lab experiment.

Water droplets splashed his cheek. He brushed them away

and grinned. "I always knew she would be."

"God knows what Raul was thinking, giving this one an explosive." Cat yanked a clean towel from the towel bar and patted the wound. "Did she really threaten to shoot Rash? He told me she pulled a gun on him in the car."

He snorted. "She did."

Lacy groaned in pain and raised her head. "I'm sitting right here. I can hear you, ya know."

They ignored her altogether.

Cat got up and retrieved a tube of triple antibiotic ointment from the toilet lid. She unscrewed the cap and smeared a large, greasy blob onto the wound. "Did Rash explain what the hell is going on? Because I'm confused."

He lowered the toilet lid and sat. "He says Monroe hired him as a mole."

He didn't feel the need to legitimize the claim by explaining the senator tried to hire him for the same job.

"Hand me that gauze and tape on the lid behind you, please," she said. "A mole, huh?"

He reached around, grabbed the gauze and tape, and handed them to her. "Yeah. We had time to talk while we were in jail. He says he had two different orders to follow. The governor's and Monroe's. Must've been hard," he mused. "He said if it weren't for Lacy staying one step ahead of him, it would've made his job a lot harder."

Cat wrapped her arm shoulder to elbow, mummy style. "How so?" she wondered. She ripped a piece of tape with her teeth and taped the end.

"He said she made it difficult for them to crush her," he said with a smile.

"Damn straight," Lacy muttered and rose to her feet.

Cat eyed them both then turned her attention to Jace. "She's going to need something for the pain and swelling."

He cocked a brow, stood, and folded his arms. If she mentioned alcohol, he'd throttle her. Lacy had been through more trauma in the last six months than anyone should be allowed. It worried him. She could slip into the bottom of a bottle and never recover.

"I've got some Percocet from the pharmacy raid," she began in a reasonable tone.

And that was worse. He cut her off. "No."

"Now Jace, one or two isn't going to hurt her," Cat argued.

Blood raced up his neck. "She can take ibuprofen."

"But —"

He flung his arms straight out, cutting her off. "No. I need her coherent tonight, for one thing. Percocet will knock her out and as a nurse you know how addictive those things are. She doesn't need it."

Lacy stomped her foot. "Stop arguing over a decision I can make myself." She turned to him. "You." She pointed a finger. "Why do I have to keep reminding you that I already have a father? If I want a damn Percocet, I'll take one."

He dropped his hands to his sides. "Fine. Do you want one?"

She eyed him. "Why do I need to be coherent?"

He rubbed the back of his neck. "Because we're leaving. Tonight."

Her eyes lit in understanding. "Okay." She turned to Cat. "Just give me ibuprofen."

Cat moved out of the bathroom toward the kitchen pantry, muttering the whole way about tempests in teapots.

They moved from the bathroom back to the couch and sat.

Lacy turned her body toward him, tucked one leg underneath her. "Are we going to get the governor? Like, right now?"

He took her hands, felt the tough callouses made from hard work. They should be soft and supple, not roughened by toil. This wasn't the kind of life he'd pictured for them. She deserved better than a life on the run, which is all he had to offer her now.

"Yeah," he said, then hesitated. "Lacy. After this job is finished, I can't come back. The MP will just come for me again." He pinned her with an intense stare. "I can't stay here. If you come with me..."

She gave his hands a gentle squeeze. "I'm coming."

His eyes searched hers for any hesitation. "Are you sure? Your uncle may not even let you go."

She touched her bruised eye. "He's got no say over me."

His eyes narrowed. "Did he hit you, Lacy? Is that what happened to your eye?"

She climbed onto his lap, rested her head on his shoulder. "Yeah, he hit me."

His whole body tensed and knew he had to get them both out from under the senator's thumb. He pursed his lips and blew out a frustrated breath.

"Why?" he asked. The reason didn't matter though. He'd struck her.

"I was mouthy." She buried her face into his neck, her whole body sagged into his. "I'm tired. I'm so tired of all this. I want my mom and dad." A sob caught in her throat. "I want my brother."

"Shh," he comforted. He guided her head onto his shoulder, and he stroked the length of her hair. "After this is finished, we'll go. Tonight. We can go find your family."

"But how?"

He didn't know, but they'd find a way. He'd find a way. For her. He continued to run his hand down her hair.

"We'll find a way," he murmured in her ear. "I promise."

The senator, Bryan Rash, and Raul appeared in the living room doorway.

"I hate to break this up," the senator began, "but you are on a time crunch." He gave Lacy a pointed look. "Go to your room."

She trembled, from fear or anger, he didn't know. Without

a word, she got up and went to her room. Her door shut with a resounding slam.

The senator's eyes followed her, then he returned his attention to Jace.

"I'm going to need you to do something else for me."

He gave an internal eye roll and sighed. He should've expected nothing less from the man.

"What is it?"

"Raul was going to return to Mexico with a payment for his father."

He cast a glance at Raul who stood in resolute silence, hands held at his sides like a tin soldier. He had the expression to match and he wondered how Raul shuttered his emotions with so much effectiveness. He'd need to practice that. It was like playing poker. The less your opponent knew about the hand you held, the better off you were in the game.

His eyes flicked back to the senator. "And?"

"I've decided to keep him here a bit longer. You will take the payment to Mexico City for me. I've loaded a small, black trunk in the Cadillac along with a brown manila envelope with all the necessary explanations."

"What about border patrol? Where am I supposed to cross?"

His mind detonated with questions. He rose from the couch and stood before the fire, drummed his hands on the old wooden mantle. Bryan gave him a sympathetic look as if to say, "Sorry, dude. I sure as hell wouldn't want to be in your shoes right now." The empathetic thought didn't help. Raul still stood in the same emotionless stance. No help there.

The senator handed him a white envelope. "Hand this to border patrol. Cross at Laredo. There's a map in the car."

His eyes narrowed on the envelope. No address, no salutation. Nothing on the front to give him any indication of its contents. It was sealed. Great. He felt just like the patsy in an old gangster film; the shmuck who took the fall. He was the fall guy. The promise he made to Lacy filtered through his thoughts. She wanted out of this mess too. The Gordian knot that held them captive kept getting more complicated, more elusive in its secrets.

"What about Lacy?" he asked.

The senator slipped his hand in his pockets. "What about her?"

"She's coming with me." He tried to sound resolute, but his voice cracked. He already knew the senator wouldn't let her go. She was his insurance. His leverage against him.

"You know why I can't allow that."

His hands balled into fists. "You blackened her eye. That changes things."

Raul's eyes darted to Jace, a warning clear in his tightened eyes.

The senator looked bemused. "Yes, well I am sorry about that."

He didn't look or sound sorry.

He turned and widened his stance. "I'm not leaving her."

The senator's eyebrows rose. He guessed the man wasn't used to his word being challenged or even questioned.

"She will remain here until you have completed your tasks." He waved a hand, dismissing him. "Now go." He turned and walked out with Raul trailing behind.

His shoulders sagged as he turned to Bryan. "Let me say goodbye to Lacy. I'll be right back."

"Hey." Bryan grabbed his arm. "I'll do my best to protect her while you're gone."

"Thanks, man," he said and went to Lacy's closed door.

He opened it and slipped inside, eyes adjusting to the darkness of the empty room.

Empty.

Where the hell was she? He noticed the tarp at the window flapping at the corner. He turned and exited the room, his steps hurried.

"Let's go." He rushed past and motioned Bryan to follow.

"How'd she take it?" Bryan asked as they jogged down the back porch steps.

"She wasn't there."

"What?" he hissed at his back.

"Just get in the car."

He had a feeling Lacy was hiding there. A furtive glance at the back seat revealed a blanket-covered lump in the floor-board. He slid into the driver's seat, turned the key left in the ignition. Bryan slammed his door as he peeled out of the gravel drive.

"Where is she?" Bryan asked, adjusting his seat belt.

"Back there." He jabbed a thumb toward the back and punched the gas pedal.

The senator would be furious when he realized his niece stowed away like a refugee in a cargo hold. He heard rustling behind him, then she poked her head over the back of the seat.

"Hey, guys."

A grin plastered his face. He should be afraid, but all he felt was relief. She was with him and that was all that mattered.

He cast a glance back at her. "You've complicated things."

Goose flesh pimpled his skin as she leaned forward and kissed his neck. "I don't care."

"You probably should," he warned.

Their actions would have consequence, he just didn't know what they would be. The senator had unfathomable connections. Would they still be able to cross the border into Mexico? Or would they be thrown in jail? Thoughts continued to churn as he turned the car onto Highway 18. He'd take backroads to Oklahoma City and the governor's mansion. He wanted this part done and over as soon as possible.

In and out.

No complications.

If only it were that simple.

36

L acy opened her eyes and shivered. A bump in the road jarred her awake. Darkness enveloped her like a dark, living shadow leaching her body's warmth. She'd sprawled out on the back seat, hidden under the blanket she'd ripped from her bed.

Pain and fatigue had hit her hard after her escape and her heavy eyelids demanded to be shuttered. The smooth, constant hum of the tires had a Zen master effect, lulling and hypnotic.

She sat up, tried to rub sleep from her eyes. Lifting her right hand to her face took concentrated effort. It felt as if an elephant had stomped on her shoulder and pulverized it.

She glanced out the tinted windows. A black eye and disheveled banshee hair bounced back at her. Fan-friggin-tastic. She looked like a zombie from *The Walking Dead*.

Jace, face pale and posture stiff as double starched sheets, had the wheel in a death grip. Bryan's head hung limp against the passenger door. A soft snore escaped his lips.

"Where are we?" she asked as she groped in her jean pocket for a rubber band.

Jace jolted, then looked in the rearview mirror and gave her a wan smile. "Just outside Arcadia."

They had dropped from Highway 18 onto the historical Route 66 that would dump them right outside of Edmond.

He made a sharp turn onto a gravel side road that led to one of the many camping spots on Arcadia Lake. Her body slid, bumping her shoulder into the back seat. The tires spit gravel as he tore down the road.

"Ow," she groaned, shifting herself back up. Gravel roads demanded respect, or they just might spin you like a top before upending you in a culvert.

He skidded to a stop and laid his head on the wheel.

She leaned over the seat, placed a hand on his sweat-soaked back. "What's wrong?"

He raised up. "I need a minute," he muttered and flung the driver's door open.

The night air, thick with cold, filtered into the car. Bryan turned his head but kept snoring.

She opened her door and followed him to a nearby patch of trees. He dropped his knees to the cold ground, rocking back and forth.

She knelt beside him. "It's okay, Jace," she murmured, leaning into his side. "We're going to be okay."

"I don't want to do this. I *can't* do this."

She scooted closer till their legs touched and wrapped an arm around his waist. He twisted around and lowered his head into her lap. She brushed bangs from his forehead, leaned down and kissed his temple. God, she loved him.

"Let's go get this done," she said softly. "We can do this."

He lifted his eyes, searched her face. "If it comes down to it, I won't kill the governor. I know that's what your uncle wants. He doesn't care if he's dead or alive as long as he's contained, and I have no idea what he'll do to him once he has him."

"You've got the tranquilizer gun and I've got the Sig. Intel says he's alone. His family isn't there. He's not expecting this. We've got the advantage, so let's go and get this done." She paused, looked at the sky, still heavy with darkness. "We need to hurry, though. Let's get this finished before daybreak."

"I don't want you to help me. I don't want you involved if this blows sideways." He raised up on his knees, face to face with her. "I'll do this on my own."

"I'm going with you," she insisted. "I can help. If there happens to be someone else there that we don't know about, you'll be outnumbered."

"Listen to me. I can't have you implicated in this."

"No, you listen." She blew out a frustrated breath. "It makes more sense for you to have backup. Bryan's gotta get the chopper ready, so he can't go with you. I'm it."

He jumped to his feet. "God damn it," he shouted. He threw his hands over his head and walked a few feet away.

She watched him struggle like a man wrestling a lion. Impossible to defeat. She rose to her feet. The wind blew cold air down her neck. She raised the hood on her sweatshirt, tied the strings below her chin. The silence stretched. Birds, restless for dawn, began rustling in their nests, reminding her time was running out.

"We don't have time to argue about this." She walked up behind him, wrapped her arms around his waist. The skin on her shoulder, already trying to scab, sent a pins-and-needles sensation through her shoulder to her fingertips.

"Why won't you listen?"

"Why won't you?" she fired back. "I think I know what I can and can't handle."

He spun around, a stormy look on his face. "Do you, though?"

She took a step back. "Look. You wanted me. Well, this is me. You've got to take it all, the whole package, not just the parts you think you can control."

A smirk lurked around his lips. "When have I ever been able to control you?"

"Very funny," she said, bouncing on the balls of her feet. "Let's just go."

He strode past her, his gait fueled by agitation. She followed him to the car. His hand paused on the door handle.

"Wait," he said and pivoted to face her. "There's something you don't know."

His face, hidden in darkness, revealed nothing, but his tone sounded heavy, like the sound of rolling thunder.

"What don't I know?"

Jace rested his forehead against the driver's side window. "After this job is finished, I have to deliver a payment to Raul's father." He stopped, raised his head, and looked at her. "In Mexico. Don't you get it? This is never going to end. There will always be something else he wants me to do."

She stood there, mute. She had no idea what Thomas Monroe's political agenda was. But whatever it was, they'd landed smack dab in the middle of it. Red rover, red rover, send Lacy and Jace right over. Trying to sift through her mixed emotions caused her head to ache. Would things be better after her uncle played out his hand? Or would they find themselves worse off under his political rule? She had no idea. She did know her uncle hedged his bets and was playing to win.

"Okay," she said, dragging out the word. "I want to talk about this, but right now let's *go*."

He gave a curt nod and they slid into the car. Whatever Jace thought about her impassive reaction, his face gave away nothing. He started the engine, turned around, and sped toward the governor's mansion.

THEY PULLED into an abandoned neighborhood off Culbertson Drive, close enough to the mansion to hike in, yet far enough away to avoid unwanted attention. They needed to be prepared if their intel was wrong which suggested the place had been cleared of MP. If they were still on location protecting the governor, they were screwed.

Lacy leaned over the seat. "Hand me that Sig."

Bryan reached over, checked the safety then handed it to her.

She resented his presence and still held his actions against him. She thought about the barn burned to the ground every time she looked at him. She let out a huff and exited the car. The grudge she carried would be difficult to dislodge.

Jace slung a backpack over his shoulder and closed the trunk. She felt his piercing gaze on her as she fitted the gun in the waistband of her jeans.

She placed her hands on her hips. "What?"

He looked ready to say something then shook his head, his face grim. "Nothing. Let's go."

They took off due north at a brisk pace. Blocks and blocks of deserted homes left the area desolate. It made her shudder. The trek led them straight to the mansion's tennis court on the southeast corner of the grounds where the governor's helicopter sat like a giant toy whirlybird. Bryan would stay and hijack the chopper for the flight back.

"Keep going straight," Bryan advised. "I'll have the chopper ready by the time you get back. This has to work, guys. Everything hinges on what you do in the next ten minutes."

"Got it," Jace said then turned to her, his face inscrutable. "Ready?"

She took a deep, steadying breath. "Ready," she said in her most convincing voice, but feared what the next few minutes would bring.

The three-story mansion, pitch black and silent, looked like all the other houses they'd passed: deserted, like a haunted house in a horror movie. It stretched to the sky like a wide yawn. Rumors about the mansion being haunted by former governor "Alfalfa Bill" Murray and fueled by Friends of the Mansion during its renovation, spread across the state and increased tours and revenue. *Total hogwash,* she remembered her father saying. Her mother retorted that Governor Murray had been eccentric enough to do just that.

They stopped at the Oklahoma-state-shaped swimming pool to catch their breath. She cast a glance at the covered pool and frowned. A bit ostentatious and over-the-top for a state that could've put those funds to better use. Too bourgeois in her opinion for a fly-over state who ranked as one of the highest poverty-stricken states in the country.

Jace dropped his backpack, fished out a pistol-gripped glass cutter, and shoved it into his back pocket. He then pulled out a queer-looking pistol. She squinted in the now semi-dark-ness to get a better view. The butt looked normal enough, but the elongated wood and steel barrel looked cartoonish, like one Stewie would shoot on *Family Guy.* She watched him load a tranquilizer dart into the chamber then check the safety. He shoved the gun in his waistband.

He scrubbed a hand across his chin then turned his worried gaze on her. "I have the alarm code," he said, his voice low. "I'll cut the glass next to the lock on the patio door. The governor's quarters are on the second floor. I'll go up and get him. You stay by the door."

"What?" she hissed. "No way. I'm coming with you."

He shot her a furious look. "You will stay by the door if I have to hogtie you there," he snapped. "Don't make this any harder for me than it already is."

"Fine."

She'd stay by the bloody door if that's what he wanted, but if she heard anything suspicious, all bets were off.

They crept to the door. He reached around for the glass cutter then made a crude square cut next to the doorknob. He tapped the cut glass until it broke free. It clattered to the stone floor. Quickly unlocking the door, they slid inside. He motioned for her to stay, then turned and followed the faint beeping noise of the alarm.

She heard the alarm fall silent. The code worked. She let out a breath she hadn't realized she'd been holding. So far, so good.

Her heart hammered in the oppressive silence like a jack-hammer pounding a hole through concrete. Jace should've made it upstairs by now. With any luck, the governor was asleep. Then Jace could shoot the tranquilizer dart without an altercation. The big problem was carrying the governor's dead weight across the grounds where Bryan waited.

She took a couple of steps away from the door and looked around. A soft light glowed down a hallway to her left. Trepidation filled her and adrenaline shot her veins with jittery energy. She crept forward, careful not to knock into anything. She followed the light and coffee's warm, inviting aroma down the hall.

She tiptoed farther, then heard the unmistakable sounds of a fistfight: a clatter of silverware hitting the floor, a grunt, then a curse. Her heart plummeted to her feet then bounced back up into her throat. The governor was awake, likely trying to enjoy his first cup of morning coffee. Why hadn't Jace shot him with the tranquilizer gun? Had the governor ambushed him?

She reached around her waist for the Sig, pulled it from her waistband then stepped forward. A clip from the movie *Knight and Day* flashed through her mind and she wondered if she looked as ridiculous as Cameron Diaz when she'd freaked out in the old warehouse and randomly shot at everything.

Before turning the corner into the kitchen, she flipped the safety off and cocked the Sig's hammer. Deep steady breaths, she counseled herself. She had to show confidence even if her whole body shook like rocks through a polisher. She shoved her uncertainty into a box and locked it up tight. She took another fortifying breath then eased around the corner.

The governor, a short pudgy man with balding salt and pepper hair, wielded a butcher knife and took wide swipes at Jace who sidestepped each strike. The tranquilizer gun had been knocked to the floor out of his reach. Blood ran down his chin from his nose, soaking his shirt collar. The governor took a hard hit to the left eye which had swollen shut. Their harsh breaths collided, each man concentrating on the other.

She took a bold step and entered the kitchen, gun outstretched and trained on the governor. "Stop," she commanded. Her voice held steady to her great relief.

Surprised, both men halted and turned to face her.

"What's the meaning of all this?" the governor demanded. His furious eyes shifted from her to Jace.

"Drop the knife, governor." She moved around the black granite island. "Don't be stupid. I will shoot you."

His face paled when she took another calculated step toward him. He dropped the knife, and she stepped over and kicked it away.

"Jace, get the tranq gun."

He spit blood, wiped his nose with the bottom of his shirt. "I told you to stay by the door."

She cocked a brow. "We really gonna argue about this now?"

He shook his head. "You drive me crazy," he muttered and stalked to the refrigerator, bent down, and picked up the gun.

Without hesitation, he aimed it at the governor's thigh and pulled the trigger. The medicine exited the dart and the governor dropped to his knees.

"I don't know who you are," the governor slurred as he plucked the dart out of his leg, "but you'll pay for this."

A sad look crossed his face. "I'm sorry, governor. I had no choice."

The governor fell face-first onto the cold tile floor.

He tossed the empty gun at her then hefted him over his shoulder, dead-man style. With a loud groan he raised up.

"Let's go," he puffed. "Quickly."

She wanted to assess the damage to his body, but knew he was right. They'd run out of time. The ten minutes Bryan gave them had long passed.

"Are you okay?"

He smirked. "Never better, sweetheart."

They ran through the house to the patio door, swung it open, and jogged to the tennis courts. The governor easily weighed over two hundred and fifty pounds, but he kept a steady, even pace the whole way.

True to his word, Bryan had the chopper ready. Its giant steel blades whirred, cutting through the cold dawn. The downward wind swirled the ground cover into a tornado of fallen leaves and grass. The sun peeked over the horizon and cast the earth in golden and rose hues.

Bryan rushed to meet them. "I was beginning to worry," he shouted over the noise. "It's late and that cat-sized tranquilizer will only last a couple hours on a man that big." He eyed Jace. "You okay, man?"

"Yeah," he grunted. "He was already up, so it took a little longer to get him. Not a bad fighter for a man his age."

They ran to the chopper's open door. He grunted and hefted the governor off his shoulder and onto the floorboard. He braced his hands on his knees to catch his breath.

Bryan hopped into the chopper, drug the governor further inside, rolled him on his stomach, and zip tied his hands behind his back.

He stuck his head out before shutting the door. "Good luck, ya'll." He grinned at them. "I'll catch you cats on the flip-flop." Then he slammed the door shut.

They stepped away from the chopper. Lacy lifted her eyes and watched as it took flight. They'd pulled it off. She couldn't believe it. Mixed emotions whirled within her like the chopper blades against the clear morning sky: confusion about handing over the governor and fear of leaving the country. But overriding it all was a profound sense of relief that this part of their journey was finished. And for the most part, they came out unscathed.

With tears in her eyes, she turned and launched herself into Jace's arms. "Are you okay?" Her eyes swept over his face. "You're bleeding."

"I'm okay, love. He got in one good punch. That's all. I promise."

She buried her head against his chest. They were together. That was all that mattered.

He nudged her forward. "Let's go. We've got a long road ahead of us."

L acy looked out the open car window and watched the sun fall against the wide, brilliant Texas sky. They studied the map her uncle left in the car and decided not to cross at Laredo. Too risky in case the senator ordered them detained because of Lacy's defection. Instead, Jace turned west at Fort Worth. They'd cross the border into Mexico at El Paso. Getting out of Texas seemed like a good plan, all things considered, and El Paso was the quickest way.

The wind whipping through the car window, warm and balmy. She felt the sun's burn on her mangled shoulder, and it soothed the constant ache.

She sighed and looked at Jace. With every mile, his mood became more and more pensive and brooding. She studied his profile. Anger marred his handsome features. Depressing silence hovered over them and grated her nerves.

She turned on the radio and John Fogerty's unique rasp blasted from the speakers. Jace cringed and switched it off.

"Don't like CCR?" she asked. Seriously, if he didn't lighten up, she might throttle him.

"Not after eight straight hours of it," he grunted, eyes never leaving the road.

A Switchfoot song played through her head and stuck there like an earworm. She began humming the tune under her breath. When she came to the chorus, she belted out the words to "Love Alone is Worth the Fight."

He turned to watch her with a half-smile. "That's a good song. I love hearing you sing."

"Thanks. You should try it."

He watched her with a shuttered expression. Although she'd gotten a couple of sentences out of him, it didn't look like he wanted to talk. Something ate at him, she could see it in his grim expression.

She put her hands to her cheeks. They felt too warm, so she unbuckled her seatbelt and took off the black hoodie.

She pulled on the bottom of her T-shirt to straighten it and cast a glance at her bandaged arm. Blood and yellow pus seeped through the gauze. She needed to change it.

"You know, singing would help your mood."

His hands tightened on the wheel and he gave his head a slight shake.

"How long have you been awake?"

"Over twenty-four hours I think." He blew out a breath. "Not really sure."

"You need sleep. And food."

His brows furrowed and he muttered something unintelligible.

"When we left the farm, I threw a backpack in the trunk and saw a cooler back there. Maybe there's food in it."

"Maybe."

"Jace," she said, frustrated. "What the hell is going on in that head of yours?"

As they entered the town of Odessa, he pulled into an empty Petrol station and cut the engine. He exited the car, went around to her side, and pulled her out. He leveled her a dark, pained look, backed her up against the car, and took her mouth with passion-laced fury.

She brought her hands to his chest and pushed him back. "You're angry."

"Yes," he shouted. "What are you doing with me, Lacy? What the hell are you doing with someone like me?"

She felt his wild heartbeat beneath her hands. "I know who you are, Jace," she said with quiet reassurance. "And I know what you're not. What you've done, what we've done, doesn't define us. Don't let it make you bitter."

He raked a hand through his hair. "How can you say that? How can you compartmentalize all I've done? What we just did?" He took a step away from her. "How can you justify it?"

She studied him in silent regard. "Have you ever heard of the phrase 'peace through strength'?"

"Yeah, that mantra's been around a while."

"If you believe in that, believe that peace is the ultimate goal, then that statement upholds what we're doing. You may not like it, but the end will justify the means."

He shifted uneasily. "That's what your uncle said in so many words. I'm not sure I believe that. Look how he's using us."

She stepped away, opened the car door, and pulled out her worn quilt. She spread it over the hood, laid down, and stared at the wide open Texas sky. Pale blue, it looked as if it stretched to infinity.

She let out a sigh and wished for wings. Wished she could fly above the earth and all their problems. Then she thought of Icarus who flew too close to the sun. Better to stay grounded and face your problems head on than crash and burn into the sea.

Giving in, he let out a long-suffering sigh and joined her. "Your indifferent attitude worries me. You accept me, the things I've done without question or any sign of empathy." He turned his head to face her. "I don't like what this is doing to you. Or to me."

"I'm not indifferent or disillusioned Jace," she began.

"What happened to me at the farm changed me. Made me a realist. At first, I thought I was a monster because of the things I did. Then I realized, it's not me. The circumstances left me no other choice but to do and act the way I did. I do have compassion. I listened to Dylan's story and realized we've all been placed in an impossible situation."

He reached over and laced his fingers through hers. "Your mind fascinates me. Just when I think I've figured you out, you go and throw a curve ball."

She gave him a bemused smile. "I'm not that complicated. And I can tell you who I am if you're interested." She gave his hand a small squeeze.

He cocked a brow. "Do tell."

"I'm a girl who's desperately in love with you. All the way, head over heels, never going to find my way out." She lifted their joined hands and pressed her lips against the back of his hand.

He reached over and drew her close. "This isn't the life I had in mind for us." He brushed his lips against hers. "A part of me will always resent that."

"We have to accept what is. We can't change it."

"I'm getting that," he muttered.

She watched his shifting emotions, watched some of the anger drain from his face. He lowered his head and kissed her, moved down her neck and back up again in a slow, seductive rhythm that left her breathless.

He lifted his head, shifted onto his elbow, and looked down at her, his face serious. "Marry me," he whispered.

Her breath hitched. "What?"

"You heard me. Marry me. Right now." He lifted her left hand and twirled the amethyst ring on her finger. "You already have the ring."

"But…" she started completely nonplussed.

"It's important to me. Please, Lace," he implored.

"Okay." She smiled up at him. "How?"

"We'll find a minister in Mexico," he suggested, "or if we can't find one, we could always be handfast."

"Handfast?" She raised her eyebrows.

"It's an old Scottish tradition. You weave a three-stranded cord together, then bind the left hands with it and say vows in front of witnesses."

She stared at him as an overwhelming tide of love swept over her. They faced a multitude of unknown variables, had no way of knowing what the immediate future held for them in Mexico. Yet their future together was what he was thinking about.

"That sounds," she began slowly, "kind of perfect."

"Yes," he shouted and jumped off the hood.

He took her hand, drew her off the hood, and kissed her. When his mouth opened over hers, she felt the familiar burn of desire spread through her.

With reluctance, he broke the kiss. "I love you, girl," he murmured. "But, we have to keep moving."

She walked around the hood, opened the driver's door, and popped the trunk. "Let's see if there's food in here first," she said over her shoulder.

She opened the trunk and stopped short. A black case filled most of the space. In her hurry, she hadn't noticed it the night before because it blended in with the interior's black carpet. A brown manila envelope rested on the top. Curious, she picked it up and opened the clasp. She pulled out several documents. A letter rested on top.

"Jace," she called.

"Yeah?"

"What's this?" she asked as he rounded the corner, holding it up for him to see.

"A letter to Raul's father, I assume," he said as he popped open the lid to the little blue cooler.

She glanced over and saw packaged sandwiches, chips, and water. Well, her uncle wasn't a complete bastard. He thought of food for them at least. Couldn't have the pawns starve to death, she thought without humor.

She turned her attention to the letter, scanned its contents. Her eyes widened. Icy fear snaked its way through her veins. "Oh my God."

Jace came and read the letter over her shoulder. They looked at each other in shock.

"We're delivering a payment to secure an army." The truth hit her hard. Her breath quickened. "My uncle is starting a civil war."

She looked up at him. Fear shadowed his eyes. "We don't have to do this," he said. "We don't. We can go find your parents."

She shook her head. "You know we can't do that. My uncle will find us and there will be hell to pay. He'd take you away from me. He's got a lot riding on this."

He placed his hand on her back. "Breathe."

She took slow deep breaths then shoved the documents back into the envelope and tossed it in the trunk. Her thoughts scattered like white feathery dandelion seeds in the wind. She couldn't grasp a single solitary thought.

She grasped the sides of her head. "I can't think."

His reassuring arms wrapped around her waist. "How about this," he started. "Let's deliver this to Raul's father. Then who's to say we can't just disappear? Mexico's a big country."

She turned in his arms to face him. "Run?"

"Yeah," he said. "Your uncle gave me some money for the trip. And I have some gold coins my dad left me. What do you say? Will you be my Bonnie?"

She laughed. "Bonnie and Clyde were never married," she pointed out. "And they were shot to death."

He pulled her closer. "Okay, bad example." His face turned serious. "But it's going to get ugly, Lace."

She thought of the farm and about all the friends they would leave behind. It felt like they were abandoning them.

Could she leave them behind, let them fend for themselves? Cat had become her second mother. Could they survive her uncle? She didn't know. What she did know? Jace would be taken from her if they returned, thrown in a military jail for the murder of his brother. And she refused to live without him, as selfish as it was. In reality, they had no other choice but to run.

"Okay," she said simply. "Let's run."

A NOTE FROM THE AUTHOR

Every 68 seconds an American is sexually assaulted and in eight times out of ten, the rapist is someone the victim knows. If you or someone you know has been sexually assaulted, there is help. There is hope. Call RAINN's National Sexual Assault Hotline 800.656.HOPE (4673) or visit their website, rainn.org, for more information.

ABOUT THE AUTHOR

Susy Smith has a bachelor's degree in English and is a language teacher for the Kanza Tribe. Her debut novel, *Asylum*, won the 2020 Writer Con contest in the novel category. She loves creating a home on paper for the characters in her head and dabbling in poetry. She lives in a small Oklahoma town with her husband, four grown children nearby, and two spoiled dog-children.

www.ingramcontent.com/pod-product-compliance
Lightning Source LLC
Chambersburg PA
CBHW030602180626
46816CB00005B/1645